IMPERCEPTIBLE

A Novel by

Alan D. Henson

© Copyright 2013

This is a work of fiction. Names, characters, places and incidents are either the product of the author's imagination or are used fictitiously. Any resemblance to actual persons, living or dead, locales, business establishments or events is entirely coincidental.

All rights reserved.
Copyright © 2013 by Alan D. Henson
ISBN-10: 0-9892940-3-X
ISBN-13: 978-0-9892940-3-4

This book may not be reproduced in whole or in part by any means, electronic or otherwise, without permission.
For information, contact:

Earth Shadow Publishing
4326 S. Scatterfield Rd. #283
Anderson, IN 46013

esmedia@earthshadowmedia.com

Printed in the UNITED STATES OF AMERICA

CONTENTS

Chapter 1: Summer Wheat —5
Chapter 2: White Light —12
Chapter 3: Unnoticed —25
Chapter 4: On Display —38
Chapter 5: Fugitive —52
Chapter 6: Crossing State Lines —68
Chapter 7: Clandestine Rendezvous —82
Chapter 8: Moving North —98
Chapter 9: So Close —109
Chapter 10: Surveillance —126
Chapter 11: Hiding In Plain Sight —140
Chapter 12: New Objective —156
Chapter 13: Reunion —166
Chapter 14: A Plan of Action —176
Chapter 15: On the Run Again —189
Chapter 16: Storming the Beach —201
Chapter 17: The Serpent in the Garden —213
Chapter 18: The Truth is Way Out There —227
Chapter 19: Trajectory —239
Chapter 20: Intruder —253
Chapter 21: Changes —263
Chapter 22: Vengeance —278
Chapter 23: Target Acquired —292
Chapter 24: Counter Espionage —306
Chapter 25: Turnover —319
Chapter 26: Penance —331
Chapter 27: Recompense —346
Chapter 28: Witness Protection —361

CHAPTER 1: SUMMER WHEAT

A hot, dry wind blew through the open window of the isolated farmhouse. Outside, the weathered windmill turned in the breeze creating a high-pitched rusty tone that was almost inaudible, except to dogs. Emily stood at the open window and looked out at the scenery. The wheat surrounding the farmhouse shimmered in the noonday sun and mimicked her flowing golden hair. The deep azure sky that was darker than the color of Emily's eyes was host to a wide selection of fluffy white clouds that seemed to glow from within. A distant gray tree line marked the horizon and green rolling hills were vibrant in the midday summer sun. The scene through the window looked like it had been painted by *Grant Wood*.

Emily was a young, petite girl about eighteen years old with a porcelain complexion. She wore a long, white gossamer off-the-shoulder gown. Her bare feet scarcely touched the weathered hardwood floor. The room was sparsely decorated with only a single wooden chair and an elegant canopy bed. As she stared out the window, tears began to fall from her eyes. They ran down her cheeks and fell almost to the floor before evaporating in midair. She was about to collapse into a complete state of despair when a silver SUV pulled into the long drive to the farm. It drove recklessly up the extensive gravel road until clouds of dust obscured the driver's vision. The vehicle slowed to a crawl while the dust settled, then proceeded at a cautious speed until it reached the front of the house. Emily watched the SUV as it sat idling in the rectangular lot. The occupants peered out through heavily tinted windows, as if trying to decide what to do.

Finally, the driver turned off the ignition and the heated engine "tinked" as it cooled. The occupants exited the vehicle almost in total unison. A stocky, middle-aged man in a yellow polo shirt was accompanied, presumably, by his wife and two boys. The younger of the boys looked to be about seven. The other one was considerable older...maybe seventeen or so. He had dark auburn hair that had a natural curl to it. He was a handsome boy about to grow into a handsome man. His square jawline could be the envy of Hollywood actors and comic book superheroes. He was tall, thin and looked nothing like his father. He looked around in wonder, while his younger brother ran around trying to release some pent up energy from the long car ride. The couple looked at the house approvingly, even though it needed a lot of work. The woman was attractive and wholesome looking. She wore a pastel summer dress and a large, white brimmed hat. Her red hair and fair complexion indicated she probably did not spend a lot of time in the sun for safety reasons. The man and woman seemed to be looking at the house to determine if it would suit their needs as a family.

Emily could see a FOR SALE sign near the road, waving in the breeze. She was taken aback by its appearance. She didn't want the house to be sold. She felt safe there...lonely, but safe. She didn't know what this new family might be like. What would happen if they discovered her? She watched them as they continued up the steps to the front door. They climbed the steps to the stylish wooden porch and felt instant relief from the midday summer sun. The wooden surface of the porch was painted with thick, light gray paint that just seemed to imply coolness. The paint on the posts was cracked and peeling. The younger of the two boys peeled away a few paint chips and crushed them in his hand. He was about to taste one when his mother cried out, "Jimmy!!! Put that down!" Jimmy defiantly crushed the chips to dust in his hand and let them drift away in the breeze.

"Do you think anybody lives here, David?" asked the woman.

"From the condition of the place, I really don't think so Sue," replied David.

"Do you think we could just go in?" asked Sue, peering through the detailed, beveled glass window of the front door.

"Maybe we should knock first," said David. "After all, we didn't make an appointment or anything."

"Hello!" he shouted. "Is anybody home?" He banged on the heavy wooden door so hard that it bounced against its frame, echoing his knocks.

"Don't break the door, David!" chided Sue.

"It's a huge house," replied David. "I need to be loud enough so someone can hear us. Besides, I don't think anyone lives here."

Emily drifted down the stairs and stood before the front door. David peered in, cupping his hands around his eyes to allow them to adjust to the dim light inside.

"I think we have waited long enough," he said. "...and I don't see anyone. I am going to try the door."

"I don't know..." replied Sue, but David was already turning the knob.

"It's unlocked," he said. "See...they want us to go in."

"That doesn't mean anything," she said. The large door swung inward, passing right through Emily. David boldly proceeded into the house, also passing through Emily. Sue looked into the door timidly.

"Maybe you should call out again," she said.

"I am telling you that nobody's here," David said. He began to look around the house like he already owned it. "Anyway, look at this place. Everything is covered with dust. I don't think anyone has lived here for months...maybe years. Sue became a little bolder when she saw the dust and the condition of the house. Then she started mentally jotting down ideas for it. Nathan, the older of the two boys, stood on the porch silently. He was captivated by what he saw. He had watched his step-father walk right through what must have been the most beautiful creature he had ever seen. He saw how sad she looked. He could tell she just wanted them to go away. Nathan wasn't sure if she was a ghost or an angel. It didn't matter. He simply could not stop looking at her.

Are you coming in, Nathan? his mother signed.

Can't you see her, mom? he signed back.

See who? she signed.

The girl in the doorway... I think she is an angel, signed Nathan.

I don't see anyone, Sue signed. *It is pretty hot outside. You should sit down.* Sue smiled compassionately, kissed him on the cheek and went on to explore the rest of the house. Nathan looked back at Emily, who was looking directly at him.

You think I look like an angel? she signed.

You know how to sign? he signed.

Well, obviously, she signed. *You can see me?*

Well, obviously, he signed. They both laughed, but neither uttered a sound.

I can smell you too, he signed. Emily gave him a quizzical look. *You smell like apples...and summer wheat. I like it.*

You are sweet to say so, signed Emily. She made the motion of brushing his cheek with her hand. He touched his face where her hand would have touched it had it been solid. Sue looked back down the hallway and saw Nathan apparently signing to himself.

"Nathan?" she said, forgetting herself. She walked back to him and signed, *Sweetheart, you really should sit down for a bit. I saw a porch swing out front. Maybe you would like to sit on that.*

Yes, mother, he signed back. He obediently went back outside to sit on the swing, but not before motioning to Emily that she should come with him. Emily drifted through the wall and was on the porch waiting for him when he came through the door. Jimmy was playing in the gravel that covered the lot at the front of the house. The sun had moved across the sky enough to create a ledge of shade at the edge of the lot and Jimmy was busy building the best gravel castle that he could. It looked more like a mound of gravel with a stick in the top, but he was proud of it. He had constructed a moat around it using a large rock to make the furrow. Jimmy imagined it full of alligators and sharks; neither of which was indigenous to Iowa. Nathan sat on the swing and hoped Emily would sit with him. She drifted inches above the porch in the hot summer breeze and declined.

How long have you been here? Nathan signed.

I don't remember, she signed back. *I don't even remember how I got here. I remember you though. Is that weird?*

I don't know what weird is anymore, he signed. *...but I remember you too.*

I want to find my mom and dad, Emily signed. *Do you think you could help me?*

I will do anything I can, signed Nathan. *Where do we start?*

That's just it, she signed. *I don't know where to start. Somehow, I think we start here; but I can't tell you why or where we should go from here.*

Won't they be looking for you? signed Nathan.

I am sure they would, she signed. *...but it wouldn't be safe.*

What do you mean? he signed.

I don't know, she signed. *Everything is so confusing. The last thing I can remember is someone shooting me with a gun. I was running, trying to get away. I couldn't hear the gun, but I felt a sharp burning pain in my back. Everything turned to white light...that's all I remember.*

Until you were here? asked Nathan. Emily nodded.

Do you think your parents might be...? Emily cut him off by placing her hand in a "stop" gesture in front of his face. *I am not even going to consider that,* she signed. As she was signing, she noticed a black SUV pull into the long drive and throw up more clouds of dust as it sped towards them. It slid to a halt in the lot and threw gravel up against the house. Some of it pelted Jimmy and he yelled and began to cry. David and Sue came out of the house to find out what was wrong. Four men in black fatigues got out of the SUV. They carried weapons in their hands and wore some kind of unusual wrap-around sunglasses. Without uttering a word, they leveled their weapons at each of the family members and fired. Nathan looked into Emily's eyes. They were the last thing he saw as he was engulfed in white light. She watched the light go out of his eyes as he slumped to the surface of the porch. Tears began to run down her cheeks and fall almost to the hem of her gown before dissipating. White light engulfed her and she felt herself dissipate as well.

CHAPTER 2: WHITE LIGHT

Emily was engulfed by darkness. She was a disembodied spirit floating in a void. There was no sound or feeling. A pinprick of light appeared in the vast emptiness. The light grew like the beam from a locomotive in a tunnel. Emily began to panic as it grew larger and larger. It surrounded her the way the darkness had. When she had been shot, the light that engulfed her had seemed to come from within. This light seemed to come to her, not from her. Once it had encompassed everything, the light narrowed into a horizontal slit with darkness above and below. The slit grew thicker and more intense. It hurt her optic nerve. She was relieved to feel any kind of sensation. The intensity of the light began to fade and Emily could see that it had a uniform pattern within its matrix. As her eyes began to adjust, the light seemed to be confined to a white metal rectangle. It flickered for a second, or so she thought. Then Emily realized that the flicker was caused by the fluttering of her own eyelids. A shadow moved into the rectangle of light and hovered over her. Then the shadow spoke.

"Welcome back," said Doctor Stuart. "People tend to react differently to tranquilizers. It is hard to get the dosage right sometimes."

What's going on? Emily signed. Then she realized it was a pointless exercise. To her surprise, the doctor responded.

"You have been unconscious for a while now," she said. "...and yes I can see you. I have to use these, but I think we will work things out." The doctor was wearing the same kind of wrap-around sunglasses Emily had seen the men in the black SUV wearing. Emily's mind was spinning and she could not be sure if what she had seen was a dream or a memory...or possibly a combination of the two. The doctor was tall, slender and attractive. She looked too young to be an actual doctor unless she was really intelligent. Emily thought she couldn't be older than twenty; but she found out later that Doctor Karon Stuart was actually forty-one.

"So...I bet you are hungry; is that right?" she asked. Emily nodded. "Well, your meal with be here shortly. I am afraid you are going to be on a liquid diet for a while. It works better with the tests we are going to be running. Why don't we do some association tests to begin with...just to make sure nothing got jostled loose in the ol' noggin. Do you know your name?" Emily responded by signing *Emily Troy*.

"That's right," said Doctor Stuart. "You get a gold star. Now...would you like to tell me your medical history or should I tell you what we know?" Emily tensed up. Some of her memory was coming back to her now and she did not trust where the inquiry was going. She signed, *Tell me what you know. I am still confused on a few things.* Doctor Stuart didn't believe Emily, but she thought it would be best to humor her for the time being.

"Very well," said the doctor. She settled into a chair next to the bed Emily rested on. Emily looked around the room. It looked like a surgical recovery room. There was a wide array of monitors and equipment that Emily did not recognize. The only door to the room had a square window with wire-reinforced glass. Embedded in the wall to the right of the door was a long, dark rectangular mirror. Emily had seen enough police dramas to suspect that it was a two-way mirror and that she was being observed. To the right of that was a toilet with only a waist-high screen to provide the illusion of privacy. Black orbs mounted to the ceiling dispelled that illusion. Emily was sure that they contained surveillance cameras.

"Here is what I am authorized to tell you," said Doctor Stuart. "You are eighteen years old, you cannot speak...and you are invisible."

How can you see me then? Emily signed.

"These glasses," said Doctor Stuart. "They detect a wide range of light and heat spectrums and combine them to make a pretty clear picture, but only in black and white...well, shades of green actually. So, knowing that you are invisible, why in the world would you learn sign language?"

Maybe you should answer some questions for me first, signed Emily. *First of all, where am I and why am I here?*

"Actually, I am not authorized to tell you either of those things," replied Doctor Stuart. There was smugness in her response that Emily didn't like. She didn't trust Doctor Stuart. "You know, we have other methods of getting answers from you."

Really? signed Emily. *Do truth agents work on people who use sign language?* Emily somehow managed to convey smugness of her own. Doctor Stuart's face flushed. She was not used to having her bluff called. A sharp double rap came from the mirror and Doctor Stuart closed her eyes, dropped her head and expelled a breath. Then she obediently excused herself and left the room. Emily put up a good front, but she was frightened. Her invisibility had always been her best defense. Perhaps she had relied too much on her "gift" and had grown complacent. She accurately suspected that the surveillance orbs contained the same technology as the sunglasses. An IV needle had been inserted into the back of her right hand and there were needle marks indicating that blood had been drawn from her at some point. The IV was not attached at the moment, but had probably been used to replace her electrolytes. Somehow, she just knew.

Emily could hear a muffled conversation going on behind the mirror. If the surveillance room was meant to be a secret, they were not doing a very good job of keeping it from her. After a few moments, Doctor Stuart returned. She composed herself outside of the door before going in. She put her sunglasses back on, touching one of the earpieces for a few seconds. Emily suspected she was adjusting some kind of setting. Doctor Stuart returned to the chair next to her, sitting much straighter than before. There was no bedside manner this time.

"I have been authorized to share some of what we know," she began. "I trust you will do the same when I am finished." Emily signed, *We shall see.* That did not seem to improve Doctor Stuart's mood. However, she continued.

"We know that you were born to Charles and Alma Troy eighteen years ago on September 21st. You were born without the ability to speak. Other than that, you seemed to be a perfectly normal child. The doctors determined the cause was a combination of physiological and neurological defects. The problem could correct itself, but it is unlikely." Emily frowned and looked away.

"I'm sorry if this seems harsh," added Doctor Stuart. "...but if you wanted me to sugarcoat it for you, maybe you should have volunteered some information on your own. Shall I continue?" Emily brushed her hand to the side.

"I will take that as a yes," the doctor said. "You have an advanced intellect, but due to your 'condition', you were homeschooled. Your mother taught you sign language so that you could communicate with her and your father more effectively. By the age of six, you were testing at a middle school level. Your mother began preparing your curriculum to advance you further intellectually. Had you continued, you would probably have gotten into college by the time you were twelve."

I DID get into college when I was twelve! signed Emily with purpose.

"I thought that might get a response from you," replied Doctor Stuart. "We have your transcripts from the online university. You seem to have an aptitude for science and mathematics. Very impressive. We know that sometime before getting into college, your physiological condition changed and you became...like you are. Could you tell me when that happened?"

You mean when people stopped being able to see me? she signed defiantly.

"Yes, when your ability to become transparent manifested; when did that happen?"

*It's not a f****** ability!* Emily signed, spelling out the expletive in her statement. *You can decide when to use an ability! This is a mutation; it's a curse.*

"Whatever you want to label it; when did it manifest?" asked Doctor Stuart.

I was about eight, signed Emily angrily. *When other girls' bodies change as they start towards puberty, mine made me invisible. It wasn't bad enough that I couldn't speak. Nature decided no one should see me either; and on top of that, my other feminine changes started early.*

"When was that?" asked Doctor Stuart. "How old were you when you got your first period?"

I was ten, signed Emily. *Isn't that early? Even if it wasn't, I didn't need it on top of everything else. What did I do to make nature so mad at me?*

"Ten is not that unusual," replied Doctor Stuart. "Granted...with your complications, I am sure it was much more difficult to deal with in the beginning."

Yes, she signed. *Difficult...I was terrified...and the only way I had to communicate with my mother about it was with notes. You have no idea.* She began to sign with purpose again. *Now it's your turn! What is all this? Where am I? Where are my parents and what is going on?*

"All I can tell you is that you are under the protection of the federal government," answered Doctor Stuart.

Why do I need protection? From who?

"Your condition has the potential for applications that might be useful to national security. It could also be a threat." Doctor Stuart held up her hand when Emily started to sign more questions. "Other factions would go to extreme lengths to obtain the opportunity to study you."

You mean like lock me up in a secret location and keep me a prisoner? Doctor Stuart was surprised how easily sarcasm was recognizable in sign language.

"Oh, they would study you by whatever means necessary," she said. "...and they would not be above taking the lives of your family to get you to cooperate with them. You are very fortunate that we got to you first."

Somehow... Emily was going to sign, *somehow I doubt that*, but she thought better of it and finished with *somehow, I would like to go home.*

"In time," said the doctor. "Right now we will need to test you quite a bit. There are also some exercises that we will need you to perform."

Are you going to try to use me as a spy? signed Emily.

"We considered that," said Doctor Stuart. "...but your inability to communicate would prove to be problematic. Instead, we are hoping to replicate the process in others. You may be here for some time."

...and I have no voice in the decision at all? Emily realized the irony in her question the moment she signed it. Doctor Stuart tried not to smile, but failed in the attempt.

"I'm sorry," she replied. "Some things are just more important than our individual rights. We will just have to see how things go."

You never did tell me where I am! signed Emily.

"You get some rest," said Doctor Stuart, ignoring the implied question. "We have a lot of tests to run tomorrow. Maybe you would like to watch some television." She motioned to a screen attached to a swing-arm mounted to the ceiling. "We are doing important work here. It would be best if you remember that." She rose quickly and exited the room. Emily almost made a hand gesture, but suppressed it with her other hand.

Emily made another examination of her surroundings. She was wearing a typical hospital gown and nothing else. It snapped in the back and there were wires running under it that connected to a heart monitor. It probably wasn't serving any other purpose except as a security measure. *Just one more way for "Big Brother" to keep an eye on me*, Emily thought. The television screen looked as though it would also serve as a computer monitor in some cases. The keyboard had been removed and it was probably not connected to any outside server. Even if it had been, it would probably have been heavily encrypted.

The wall sockets were closed off except for the ones that were in use. Those seemed to be equipped with locking mechanisms, so that the equipment plugged into them could not be disabled. On the opposite wall from the toilet was a stainless steel metal "bulge" about waist high that Emily could not identify. Above it was another suspicious mirror...only smaller and vertically rectangular. She considered exploring the room, but didn't want to have to keep closing the back of her gown. At home, or in town for that matter, she could have walked around naked if she had wanted to. Sometimes she had. No one could see her back then. She wore clothes mostly as a courtesy to her parents; and because she loved clothes. Now, it was like she was really naked for the first time. Not only was she electronically visible, but her captors were shielded like voyeuristic perverts. She wondered if they knew sign language. If so, she might have a few choice gestures for them. But she decided to take the higher path for now and assume the posture of a helpless victim.

Emily had almost decided that she could not wait any longer to use the toilet, when the door opened and a young man in a dark red jumpsuit came in carrying a tray. He was about twenty-five and medium height and build. The tray contained a dish of Jello, a bowl of chicken bouillon, a plastic cup of apple juice and a bottle of spring water. The young man wore the same type of glasses Doctor Stuart had worn and Emily wondered if it was possible that she was the victim of an alien abduction.

"Sorry this is so early, but you can't have anything after six p.m. Tests in the morning, you know." His voice was much lower than his appearance would have suggested. Emily found it amusing. Since she could not speak herself, she was a student of other people's voices. She thanked him in sign language and he absentmindedly signed back. *I can hear*, she signed and smiled. His face flushed and he almost signed an apology. Then he said, "I'm sorry. Habit I guess."

Really? Emily signed. *Why?*

"My parents were both hearing impaired," he responded. "I learned how to sign before I learned how to walk. They met at Gallaudet in D.C."

That is a college for hearing impaired, right? signed Emily.

"Wow!" said the young man. "Not everybody knows that."

I looked into a few colleges around the country for people with special needs, signed Emily. *What is your name?*

"Michael," said the young man. "That is all I am allowed to tell you. Come to think of it, I maybe should not have told you that."

I won't tell. Get it? Because I can't talk...that's what makes it funny, signed Emily, turning on the charm. Michael smiled and shook his head. "Cute."

I don't hear that a lot either...you know, because people can't see me. Are you getting any of these?

"So what do you do when you are not doing stand-up?" he asked. "See what I did there...'cause you're invisible and stuff?"

I think I should be offended...but I started it I suppose. I go to school...online. I am working towards my Master's Degree.

"Impressive," said Michael. He already knew about Emily's degree. Her dossier had been given to him during a security briefing; but he felt he needed to develop a rapport with her. Emily sensed that her charm was getting through to him, so she tried to test its boundaries.

Can you tell me where I am? she signed.

"I am afraid I can't do that," he replied. "That was part of the briefing."

Can you at least tell me what time it is?

"I don't suppose there is any harm in that," he said. "Besides, the television shows usually have a time stamp of some kind. It's 4:30...in the afternoon."

What day?

"Sorry... that's *need to know*, I'm afraid."

Really? You can't tell me the day of the week? Emily's expression was a mixture of anger and confusion.

"Sorry again," said Michael. "If it was up to me, I would tell you; but I don't make the rules."

I understand, signed Emily. *It's okay. In fact, you are the nicest person I have met since I have been here.* She cut a sharp glance at the mirror, hoping Doctor Stuart was standing behind it. Michael broke into a big grin and bowed his head in an appreciative nod.

"That's very kind," he said. "...but I happen to know exactly how many people you have met. I comprise fifty percent of them."

You got me, signed Emily. Michael suspected she blushed, but it was impossible to tell through the glasses. He touched his earpiece to adjust the settings.

I know this is a lot to ask, signed Emily. *...but could I take a look through those glasses? I would like to know what you all see.*

"I don't know," said Michael. "...but then again, I don't believe that contingency came up in the briefing. I guess it will be alright... or you just got my ass in a sling."

I would never do anything to cause a problem. Emily lied very effectively. Michael looked over his shoulder and handed his glasses to her. He was amazed to watch her disappear before his eyes. She put the glasses on. The only difference she saw was in the color of everything. The room was bathed in a green hue. Other than that, it was what she saw all of the time. The only thing that amazed her was that her own body looked just like Michael's. She expected them to be different somehow.

"I should probably have those back," said Michael.

Of course, signed Emily. She took hold of Michael's hand and placed the glasses in his palm. He felt a mild surge of endorphins when she touched him. *You were so nice to let me have them.*

"Well, there was no tap on the window, so everyone must be taking a break," he said.

Would you do me a favor? signed Emily. *I really need to go to the bathroom and I feel like there is nothing but "pervs" watching me.*

"What do you need me to do?" asked Michael quizzically.

Emily paused. *I need you to stand in front of me so the pervs can't watch me.*

"You mean, while you go to the bathroom?" asked Michael.

Yes. I hate to ask...but I really have to go, signed Emily.

"Well...okay," replied Michael.

I am going to sit down...you know, in the corner; and I would like you to stand in front of me.

"I am not sure I should," said Michael. "They are supposed to monitor your every move."

THIS is a move they do not need to monitor, signed Emily. *...and maybe I could wear the glasses again. You know, so you won't be tempted to peek.*

"I am not one of the pervs!" Michael said indignantly. Emily folded her arms in an adamant way.

"Okay," said Michael. "...but I am insulted." He broke into a grin, indicating that he was not. Emily got out of bed wearing Michael's glasses. He could not see her but felt her move past him. The sensation intrigued him. It felt like a supernatural experience. He took up his post as soon as he had ascertained she was seated. He stood facing her at first, but her hands gently grabbed him by the waist and turned him around. Michael realized that the scene must have looked creepy to her. He maintained his post like a gentleman until she was finished. When he heard the toilet flush and felt her move past him, he returned to her bedside. She held his hand softly and placed the glasses once more into his possession.

Michael donned his glasses again. He thought Emily was beautiful. He was afraid that his opinion of her and his connection with his parents' impairment might make him less objective about her and therefore, less disconnected. It was too late. He could not help but be impressed by her. She was incredible in his mind. There was no one on the planet who could compare with her. He looked back over his shoulder, hoping his admiration of Emily was not readily apparent.

Thank you, she signed. *You were so kind.*

"Think nothing of it," replied Michael. "You should finish your 'meal'...if that is what you want to call it. They will be running a lot of tests tomorrow. You will need your strength."

You are the best ever, signed Emily. *I am so glad to have met you.*

"And I you," said Michael. "I hope everything turns out well for you."

Emily knew what he meant.

I hope I didn't get you in trouble, she signed. *You have been great. I may have to wait until you are on duty each day to go to the bathroom.*

"Really, I am honored," said Michael in a mildly sarcastic way. "I am at your beck and call."

You are too kind, sir, signed Emily.

Michael bowed slightly and excused himself from her presence. He opened the door and checked the hall. He looked back and softly said, "T.G.I..." and left the room. Emily heard the door lock when it closed. *T.G.I...* she thought. *It's Friday!* The last day she remembered was a Wednesday. She had been unconscious for at least three days!

CHAPTER 3: UNNOTICED

Emily was born on September 21st to Charles and Alma Troy. Charles was tall and muscular; exactly what one would expect of someone who owned a farm. While he did do chores around the property, he didn't do farming. He left that to others who leased the fields from him. He was actually adept with computers.

Alma Troy was a librarian. Before meeting Charles, she had been the Director of the Research Department in Des Moines. She was petite, attractive and had short brown hair. Her large red-framed glasses made her look intelligent and a little nerdy. They were what attracted Charles to her when he first saw her.

They were so excited to have a daughter...especially Charles. He was so certain that he wanted a son right up until the moment Emily was born. The birth scared him for more than one reason. First, it was the first time he had ever been in a delivery room. He was afraid to move; worried that he would break something or do something wrong. He didn't feel qualified to be there. Secondly, Emily was born *breech* and that just didn't seem right to him. Thirdly, she was so purple. He thought babies should be pink, soft and wrapped in a blanket. Finally, it was her smell. He expected a newborn to smell like baby oil, baby powder or baby lotion. He did not expect one to smell like baby back ribs. He was sure the smell was from dried blood or fluids from the amniotic sac, but that was what it made him think of. On any other day, it might have made him sick; but Alma had been in labor for eleven hours and neither of them had eaten all day. Charles thought it was a strange way to connect to his new baby, but he called her his little *pork chop* from that day on.

Due to the difficult birth, Alma required some minor surgery to repair a tear to the birth canal. Charles spent the time getting to know his new daughter. She gripped Charles' finger as if to say, "You will never abandon me." Charles, being new to fatherhood thought, *I would step in front of a bus for you.* It frightened him a bit. Here was a new person that he helped to create who depended on him for her safety. The sense of responsibility was overwhelming. Looking into her sky-blue eyes however, gave him a deep sense of calm. Serenity washed over him and the two bonded instantly. When the surgical procedure was finished, a nurse came over to give Emily to her mother. Neither Charles nor Emily really wanted to let go. Alma didn't mind too much. She was glad they had developed such a strong bond so soon.

Emily was perfectly normal except for her inability to cry out. At first, the nurses just thought she was a quiet baby. She slept the usual amount, which was a lot. When given a heel-prick test, she did not cry out as the other babies had. She breathed heavily and made rapid sighs; tears rolled down the sides of Emily's face, but she never cried out. The doctor who delivered her examined her throat and then called in a specialist. They could not determine a reason for the condition. Emily's throat seemed normal for a newborn and, for all intents and purposes, should have allowed her to make noise. The doctor scheduled an appointment to see her at three months and told Charles and Alma to watch her very carefully. Unless things changed, Emily would not be able to alert them when something was wrong. Things did not change and more tests were performed on Emily when she was three months old.

It was determined that nothing was wrong with her hearing. Even her vocal cords seemed more or less functional. They did seem to have a sluggish and restricted movement, but they should have produced some sound. The family was sent to a specialist again, who suspected the cause might be neurological, psychological or possibly a combination of the two. He tried to comfort the parents with the standard compassionate statement that "she might grow out of it." He scheduled periodic appointments over the next three years. Each time, he was no closer to an answer. Emily simply wouldn't or couldn't speak. She functioned exceedingly well in every other aspect of development. Alma took sign language classes with her to teach her to communicate. Emily was a quicker study than her mother and Alma soon realized that she had a little genius on her hands. Once Emily mastered the alphabet, she started learning to read. By four years old, she was reading at a fourth grade level; by five, she had advanced to the level of a middle school student.

Alma had taken an extended leave from her job at the library to be with Emily full time. She homeschooled her, not because Emily couldn't speak; but because she was so advanced, she would not be able to relate to others in a special needs class. In most cases, they would be much older than her and there were no schools in the area that offered educational programs for exceptional children. Emily didn't mind. She loved being at home with her mother and couldn't wait for Charles to get home from work each day. She would sign to him and outline what her activities had been that day. He would try to slow her down, but she was too excited. Charles was the least accomplished sign language student of the three. Emily, being wise beyond her years, would place her hand over his mouth when he tried to speak to her. She insisted that he sign until he became proficient. That process was a little tough in the beginning, but soon he was signing almost at Alma's level. Neither of them could hold a candle to Emily, however.

Charles was a successful and much sought-after I.T. expert. He and Alma first met when he was contracted to help the library upgrade their computer system. When they met, it was love at first sight. Actually, it wasn't. Alma thought Charles was arrogant and condescending to everyone that did not understand computers the way he did. Even though Charles was attracted to her, he thought Alma was stuck in a bygone age of index card file drawers and the Dewey Decimal System. Fate designated that they work together on the project and they were soon learning the art of compromise. Being the consummate professional, Charles waited until the project was finished before asking Alma out. She, also being the consummate professional, would not have accepted had he done otherwise. Their first date was at a frozen yogurt shop. It was quiet, unassuming and informative. They both found out so much about each other as far as likes, dislikes, pet peeves and even movie preferences.

Their second date was at an actual drive-in theater. It was one of a handful that was still surviving in the age of video rentals and HBO. The drive-in no longer had speakers attached to posts. Instead, they were required to use the car's radio to hear the movie. After playing the radio for almost the entire first movie, Charles thought he should run the engine for a minute or two to keep the battery up. There was a moment of tension when it struggled to turn over, but it did start and the moment passed. Charles got to *second base* that night. He and Alma saw each other regularly for over a year after that before he popped the question. Being the romantic that he was, he asked her at the drive-in. She accepted, but with an odd reluctance. It was then she told him that she was pregnant. His first impulse was to ask if it was his; not because he didn't trust her, but because he was terribly insecure. He knew she would never cheat on him and he embraced her saying, "This is the best night ever!" The scene was played out with the movie's closing theme music playing over the radio. The movie was a romantic comedy, so the music was perfect. While they were waiting for the second feature, Charles started the car...or tried to. This time it didn't start. Fate, as they would come to discover, had a twisted sense of humor.

Charles and Alma were married in a church, technically. They were married in the pastor's office. It was a very simple ceremony that was only comprised of them and two witnesses. Alma was not interested in a large ceremony and instead, suggested they use the money to have an incredible reception and honeymoon. Charles was the one who was a little disappointed. He was looking forward to renting a tuxedo. They compromised by wearing formal wedding attire at the reception; so everyone was happy. Jesse Whitson gave the first toast after the best man. He was the one who had given Charles and Alma a jump-start the night their battery died at the drive-in. His vehicle stood out to Charles as he was going from row to row, trying to find someone with jumper cables. Jesse had driven his tow truck to the drive-in and was equipped for just about any automotive emergency. There was a lot of honking and laughing as he hooked up the cables to Charles' battery and applause when the car started. Charles tried to pay Jesse, but he wouldn't hear of it. "Just invite me to the wedding," he said. Charles wasn't sure if he was psychic or just joking, but he took down the number from the side of his truck and did the next best thing. He invited Jesse to the reception, which was better because there was alcohol.

Alma didn't want to drink because of her condition, so she and Charles prepared a prop to use. Using an empty *Dom Perignon* champagne bottle, they filled it with sparkling grape juice, replaced the cork and fashioned a foil wrapper around the neck. Only one person asked to have a sip of the very expensive *champagne*...Jesse Whitson. Alma couldn't refuse him after the kindness he had shown them and the heartfelt toast he had given. He took only a small sip, held it on his tongue for a moment and said, "I think I like the cheap stuff better." Alma slowly let out the breath she had been holding and she leaned over and lightly kissed him on the cheek. "Congratulations," he whispered, "...and on the baby too." He drifted off to dance with someone who may have been his wife while Alma watched him walk away. *How did he know?* she thought. She felt like there was a possibility that everyone knew. In reality, no one did. When Emily was born eight months later, no one suggested anything other than she was premature or advanced for her age. They said it meant that she was headed for great things. They could not have known just how right they had been.

Charles and Alma bought a huge farmhouse on the edge of town. It was old and elegant and surrounded by wheat fields. They planned to have a big family someday and the house seemed perfectly suited for that. It was close enough to town to be convenient, but remote enough to enjoy the quiet and privacy of the country. Emily seemed to embody the characteristic of the house. She was close, yet remote. There was a peacefulness and yet, a depressing sadness in her nature. Her hair was the color of the ripened wheat that surrounded the house and it waved in the summer breeze the same as the amber fields did. She liked to sit on the porch swing and feel the breeze caress her face. Her lips would barely part as she breathed through them. Alma thought she might be trying to hum. She thought it was adorable. Emily thought it was frustrating. There were so many things she wanted to do and so many things she could; but that didn't satisfy her.

It is the nature of some humans, possibly all humans, to want what they can never have. Emily wanted to be a cheerleader. She knew it probably would never happen. She could go through the movements and do the routines, but shouting was impossible. When she was eight, any hopes she might have had were dashed when her metabolism changed. It was fourteen hours before she noticed the change. It was fourteen hours and eleven minutes before Alma made a frantic phone call to Charles to tell him something terrible had happened.

"Tell me what's wrong!" Charles demanded over the phone.

"I can't tell you," Alma cried. "I have to show you! Just come home as quickly as you can." Then she added, "Be safe, please."

Charles was not safe, but he was lucky. There were two near misses and almost a speeding ticket that he was able to avoid. The almost speeding ticket was due to another motorist who sped past him that the police officer considered being a greater threat to society. Charles pulled into the long gravel driveway to the house and ignored the pelting the undercarriage was taking from the rocks flying up from the tires. He skidded to a stop in front of the house, throwing gravel up and ran in the front door.

"What's wrong?" he asked in a panicked tone. "Tell me!"

"It's Em...Emily!" stuttered Alma. "She's...gone."

"Gone?" yelled Charles. "Did you call the police? What happened?"

"That's not what I mean," said Alma. "She's still here...but she's gone."

"You're not making any sense!" yelled Charles. He was scared and he was coping by getting angry...one of his worst traits.

"It doesn't make sense," cried Alma. "She is right here...but I can't see her!" Charles stood silently with his mouth open slightly. He tried to determine if Alma was playing a sick joke or had gone insane. He worried it could be a combination of the two. He was about to unload a volley of angry words at her when he felt two arms grasp him around the waist. Looking down he saw nothing. His first instinct was to jerk away, but he could feel the arms trembling. Charles reached down and felt Emily's trembling shoulders. Her head was pressed against his side. He unclasped her arms, knelt down and held her. With his eyes closed, she felt no different than a thousand other times he had held her. He felt as if he was the one who might have gone insane. Alma joined him and embraced Emily from the back. The three remained there for a long time in a group embrace. To an outside observer, it would have looked like Emily and Charles were afraid to touch each other. No one would possibly have guessed that Emily was between them.

After each of them, including Emily, had calmed down, they sat on the floor to sort things out. Emily made signing gestures which neither of them could see. Alma could feel the movements in the air and stopped Emily from signing. She got up from the floor, got a pad and pen and gave them to Emily. The items seemed to slowly dissolve as Emily took them. Alma looked at Charles and Charles stared at the empty space where the tablet had been. They heard frantic scribbling and then Alma felt a tug on her sleeve. She grasped around until her hand made contact with the tablet. As she took it, the tablet seemed to form in her hands. On it were written the words *WHY ARE YOU SAYING YOU CAN'T SEE ME?* Alma almost wrote her response on the paper forgetting, in the heat of the moment, that Emily could hear.

"We really can't see you, sweetheart," she said, looking into where she hoped Emily's face was. "Can you see yourself?" There were more rapid movements in the air.

Finally, Emily took the tablet from Alma's hands and it vanished once again. There was more scribbling; then she placed it back in Alma's hands. On it under the first sentence was written *WHY ARE YOU BEING SO MEAN? THIS ISN'T FUNNY!!!* Tears formed in Alma's eyes as she read the message. She held her arms wide and then narrowed their field until she embraced Emily. Both of them were shaking and Emily knew at that point that it was not a joke. Alma held her close and stroked her unseen hair. Charles joined them and the three sat on the floor of the farmhouse trying to sort out the events that were unfolding. Charles and Alma conversed quietly and calmly to help Emily relax. Their first item for discussion was possible causes for Emily's condition. It reminded Alma a little of the conversation they had had in the doctor's office when discussing her inability to speak. This session was different however, because they had no frame of reference. To their knowledge, there had never been a case like this.

They talked quietly for an hour. Emily provided a small amount of input, but she was as much in the dark as they were. There were more questions on the tablet than answers and it mirrored what was on the minds of Charles and Alma. Evening found the three of them still sitting on the floor. The house grew dark and Alma heard Emily's stomach rumble. Her motherly instinct kicked in and she rose with a sense of duty.

"Emily needs to eat," she said. "I think we all do. Our blood sugars must surely have bottomed out."

"That could be part of a solution," said Charles with a positive tone in his voice. "It could be chemical in nature. Maybe it's just a phase."

"Like her other phase?" asked Alma pessimistically.

"I don't know," said Charles. "I am grasping at straws here."

"I'm sorry," said Alma. "I know you are just trying to help. I just feel so helpless. Are you sure we shouldn't call someone?"

"We discussed that," replied Charles. "Who could we possibly call?" They had discussed their options at length and weighed the pros and cons of every action. If they took Emily to a hospital, she would most likely be subjected to tests. That is, if they didn't get thrown out altogether for trying to play a prank. If word got out about Emily's condition, she would become the focus of a media circus, or worse yet, a government investigation. They suspected the government would want to do extensive research to determine if this was something they could use in a military application. That always seemed to be the case...at least in the movies. They considered having the family physician examine her, but they were pretty sure he would not be skilled in the field of study they would need. If they ran out of options, they would call him. For the moment, they adopted a *wait-and-see* attitude.

The realization struck them that, at some point, they were going to have to explain Emily's disappearance. The only solution they could come up with was that they would have to move. Both of them were skilled in fields that could provide them with employment anywhere if need be. They didn't want to leave the home they loved so much if they didn't have to, so moving was a last resort. They were hoping that Emily's invisibility was simply a phase. There would also be another branch of the government with which to deal. The IRS could prove to be a problem since they would still have to claim Emily on their taxes. Neither of them would even consider the thought of faking her death. At the time, they did not fully appreciate the irony of maintaining the identity of a person no one could see or hear.

Alma prepared a quick meal for the three of them. Several times, she and Charles forgot to eat because they watched Emily's food literally disappear from her plate. There was no disgusting display like in the movies about invisible people; it just seemed to dissolve into thin air. Her glass of milk would disappear and then reappear with diminished content. After the meal, they all sat quietly in the dimly-lit kitchen, pondering their future. Suddenly, Emily emitted an involuntary burp and the tension was broken for the first time that entire day.

Even though it was just a bit past seven in the evening, Alma took Emily upstairs and put her to bed. The stress of the day had worn them all out and she wanted a chance to talk to Charles alone. Some of the things they needed to talk about would probably scare Emily and Alma felt that her daughter didn't need anything else to be frightened about. Alma placed her in the large canopy bed and covered her with a comforter. Like the food on Emily's plate, the comforter seemed to dissolve at the places where it touched her body. It didn't look torn or damaged; the comforter just seemed to blend into the other bedclothes. Alma was reminded of a chameleon blending in with its background.

Charles was sitting quietly on the sofa when Alma rejoined him. He was holding the remote in his hand, but the television wasn't on. The large black flat screen reflected the two of them as they stared into its void. Finally, Charles pushed the power button. A moment later, a movie flashed on the screen. It was in black and white and seemed almost out of focus. One of the actors was bandaged as if he had been in a horrible accident. He was trying to consume a meal in spite of the bandages and got terribly angry when someone burst into the room without knocking. Charles realized the actor was Claude Raines and that the movie was *The Invisible Man*. Fate's twisted sense of humor was not going to let up, it seemed. He scanned the menu until he found a weather channel and pushed the buttons on the remote. He was still shaking and he hit the *four* twice before hitting the *nine*. A heavyset man in a dark gray suit was dancing with himself and speaking in Spanish. He was emceeing a Hispanic game show and Charles didn't understand anything he was saying except for the occasional English word interjected in a sentence. Charles pushed the buttons again and a colorful weather map appeared on the screen. Music played while a computer rendering of a storm front moved across the state. Charles didn't notice that the storm was headed their way. Alma put her head on his shoulder and took his hand in hers.

"What are we going to do?" she asked without expecting a real answer.

"We will do what we have always done," he responded. "We will cope."

"This is bigger than anything we have ever dealt with," said Alma.

"True," replied Charles. "…but things have a way of working out."

"But what if they take her away from us?"

"We are not going to let that happen…no matter what it takes." Charles held her hand to his lips and kissed her knuckles. "We will disappear if we have to."

"Was that supposed to be funny?" asked Alma.

"Not really," said Charles. "…but I guess it was…a little."

"Why couldn't we just have a normal child?" Alma was almost in tears.

"Because we got an exceptional child," said Charles. "She is and always has been a gift. We both know that and that is our strength. It will be our edge."

"I hope so," said Alma as she drifted off to sleep on his shoulder. The stress of the day had taken its toll on her too. Charles really wanted to go to sleep in his bed, but he didn't want to disturb her. He laid his head back on the couch, content to just rest his eyes.

He awoke to a loud clap of thunder. The house was dark and a pyrotechnic display of lightning was illuminating the front porch. The electricity was off and Charles thought of Emily being all alone in her room. Alma was still asleep on his shoulder and the front of his shirt was wet with a spot of drool. He gently moved her to the side and prepared to race up the stairs to comfort Emily. He was almost to the foot of the stairs when he hit an unseen object. It hit the floor with a thud as lightning flashed through the front door followed by a house-shaking thunderclap. For a second, Charles could see a faint outline of Emily and thought he might have dreamed the whole invisibility thing. He knelt down and picked her up. She was crying and trembling. He held her close and comforted her as well as he could. Alma was wakened by the thunder and joined them. Heavy raindrops pelted the windows and the porch swing pitched in the wind. Charles considered going out to secure it; but another bolt of lightning and Emily's shaking made him think better of it. The little family remained at the foot of the stairs while the storm raged on for another twenty-five minutes. When the lightning seemed less intense and the thunder more distant, they felt like they could relax a bit. Charles held Emily in one arm and caressed Alma with the other. He let out a long sigh, but jumped as the lights came back on. Charles lifted Emily and prepared to take her upstairs while Alma turned out the lights in the living room. Emily slept between them that night and would for many more nights to come.

CHAPTER 4: ON DISPLAY

Emily awoke to a bright glow shining in her face. It was the artificial glare of fluorescent lights. The rectangular light panel in the ceiling above her was controlled from somewhere other than in the room she was in. The grid in the light panel was comprised of a pattern of chrome-plated hexagons that were recessed about half an inch. The effect was that of a soft ambient light everywhere in the room except directly underneath the panel, which was where Emily's bed was located. The result was a glaring light that caused her to squint. There was a mechanical click of the door lock and Dr. Karon Stuart came in with a metal clipboard. The harsh light reflected off of her black sunglasses as she perused the list of tests that would be performed on Emily that morning.

"I trust you slept well," she said. Emily responded with sign language indicating that she had not. *It is difficult to sleep when you are up going to the bathroom every fifteen minutes*, she signed.

"Well, we have to be sure there are no *surprises* when we run our tests," Dr. Stuart said with a trace of a smirk. Emily didn't like her. She also hated being controlled. While her invisibility had its restrictions, it also gave her a considerable amount of latitude. She could come and go as she pleased and she could wear whatever she wanted; even if it meant wearing nothing at all. Since she had regain consciousness, she had been under constant scrutiny and had been fed practically nothing. Emily suspected her captors were trying to rid her body of toxins, so that they could fully understand her ability with as few variables in her chemistry as possible. If she became visible to them, then the answer would be in the toxins. That was an unlikely scenario, but they would be considering all possibilities.

Dr. Stuart looked around for a moment in an agitated state. She lightly touched the earpiece of her dark glasses and breathed a slight sigh of satisfaction. Emily suspected that the dark glasses were pretty finely tuned and that the settings had to be just right for Dr. Stuart to see her. She also determined that there must be tiny controls on the glasses to make spectrum adjustments. The doctor went about doing routine *doctor stuff* such as taking Emily's temperature, blood pressure and pulse. She wrote the results on a page attached to the metal clipboard she carried under one arm. Emily didn't like her. She didn't like being violated. Being unseen and unheard, while inconvenient and frustrating, also afforded her a sense of sanctuary and comfort. These people had taken that from her and Dr. Stuart was their representative. Emily wanted to see her parents…to know if they were alright. Not knowing was more frustrating than invisibility had ever been.

"Someone will be in soon to take you down for some tests," Dr. Stuart said curtly. "Don't give them any trouble. It would not go well for you if you did." Emily almost responded…with purpose; but she chose to once again take the higher road and simply remained expressionless. Dr. Stuart left the room and Emily subtly rubbed the needle mark from the blood extraction. She had no intention of showing weakness to *that woman*. Just seconds later, a tall man came in guiding a gurney to the side of her bed. He too was wearing dark glasses and wore red scrubs. He reminded Emily a little of Will Smith with his dark glasses and his friendly demeanor. He opened his arms with his palms up, inviting her to get on the gurney herself. Her rebellious nature came out and she pretended not to understand. The attendant must have been on a schedule because he pulled her sheets down, grabbed Emily by one ankle with one hand and under her arm with the other. With a swift movement, he moved her to the gurney as if she was weightless. Obviously, he had done it many times before. He strapped her wrists and ankles with padded leather restraints and covered her with a fresh sheet from under the gurney. As he positioned the gurney to face the door, the electronic lock clicked and the door opened as if by magic. Emily knew that someone somewhere in a control room had flipped a switch or pushed a button; but it was still unnerving.

As she moved swiftly down a brightly lit hallway, she stared up at the recessed ceiling lights as she passed under them. She hated not being in control. Emily could feel a mild panic attack welling up inside her, but she suppressed it. The hallway wasn't deserted, but the few people she passed seemed not to notice her. It occurred to her that they weren't wearing the special dark glasses and couldn't see her. From their perspective, the attendant was merely pushing an empty gurney to some random destination. Most of the rooms on either side of the hallway were secured with formidable-looking electronic locks and were closed. The door to one room on her right was ajar about six inches and she caught a glimpse inside. What she saw was the edge of a stainless steel table, a counter with gleaming surgical instruments on it and a wall comprised of square stainless steel doors. Emily had seen enough crime dramas on television to know what a morgue looked like. The momentary glimpse of the room sent a wicked chill throughout her entire body.

There was another electronic click and another door whooshed open. Emily was steered into a room with a large white device that she recognized as a CTG scanner. She had been placed in one by a hospital employee when she was younger. That was during the period when her parents and her family doctor were trying to determine the cause of her invisibility. The sight of the machine evoked bittersweet memories for her and a tear rolled down her cheek. She missed her parents and she was terribly worried that something awful had happened to them. Instead of lapsing into depression and self-pity, Emily was determined to remain focused and forced herself to memorize every aspect of the facility that she was exposed to. A tall stocky woman in dark electronic glasses came over and looked her in the eye. "Are we going to have trouble with you if I take off these restraints?" she asked. Emily simply shrugged and directed her gaze to the ceiling.

"We can always sedate you, if that is what you would prefer." There was more of a malicious threat in her voice than concern. Emily shrugged again and then shook her head in resignation. Her hands were literally tied and she had no choice but to give in to the woman's demands. Besides, she was not in the mood for any more needles if she could help it. The stocky woman wore a nametag, but most of the name was obscured by a device that Emily could only surmise was a radiation badge. It made her wonder what kind of research they were doing that such a precaution would be necessary. She helped remove Emily's restraints and the attendant helped move her to the CTG scanner. Once on the movable platform, she reached behind Emily's neck, untied her gown and unceremoniously pulled it off, leaving her naked and vulnerable on the table. "That's so the gown doesn't interfere with the tests," she said with a smirk. Emily knew that was a lie, but there was nothing she could do about it. The attendant pretended to be uninterested, but kept shooting glances her way when he thought no one was looking. Emily wasn't sure if the stocky woman just wanted to humiliate her or if she might be gay. She felt the vote could go either way, but she was angered by the liberties the woman had taken regardless.

Emily had been naked in front of people lots of times, except the people didn't know it. Since no one could see her, it had not been unusual for her to walk down the long gravel drive and check the mail completely nude. Sometimes, she would stand next to the mailbox and wait for the mailman to put the family's mail in the box. It felt liberating and a little naughty. She remembered thinking that it must be how people at a nudist resort feel. But this was different. These people could see her, after a fashion. Emily felt violated and exposed for one of the few times in her life. Her mind strayed to thoughts of vengeance; but that depressed her. She had no idea of how to seek vengeance on individuals working for a government agency.

The stocky woman (whose name was Evans) and the attendant (Maxwell) entered a control room and her voice came over a speaker giving Emily instructions to relax and keep perfectly still. Emily stiffened unconsciously, perhaps as a form of rebellion.

"I still have the sedative needle ready," said Evans over the speaker. "...and I WILL make it hurt." Emily forced herself to relax and the CTG scanner began to make a series of metallic clicks and hums as her body was incrementally drawn into it. Her mind began to drift and she thought about the first time she met Nathan. She was sixteen when his family pulled their silver SUV into the driveway of her family's farmhouse. He had been different somehow and it only took Emily a few moments to realize he was deaf. He and his mother signed back and forth as Emily had watched. She had been taught sign language at an early age to be able to communicate with her own parents. That was before she developed her chameleon-like condition. Nathan was cute and he had seemed shy. His deafness seemed to make him insecure; but in reality, he would have been insecure even if he had not been deaf. It was just his nature. Emily had gone downstairs to get a closer look when the family had approached the door. It was only then that Emily became convinced that Nathan could actually see her. She was glad she had been wearing clothes that day. She had been even gladder that she had brushed her hair. It would not have done to have made a bad first impression with the only person who could actually see her. To Emily's delight, Nathan's family and hers became close and they eventually shared the secret that Nathan already knew. Emily really didn't know why Nathan could see her when no one else could; but she didn't care. She finally had a boyfriend and not a moment too soon. Her teenage hormones had been raging, as had his. She was glad the government did not know his secret, or else they would be testing him too. At least, she hoped they didn't know.

"Okay. We're all done here," said Evans through the speaker. "You can get dressed now if you want; but it's not really necessary." Evans was still smirking through the glass of the control room. The attendant seemed disgusted with her behavior and averted his eyes in earnest. Emily put her gown back on, but felt like she was being forced to perform a reverse striptease. She even thought she could detect a small amount of saliva forming at the corner of Evans' mouth. She was yet one more person on her list of people to hate. Emily jumped up on the gurney without assistance and signed to Maxwell that she would behave...that he didn't have to restrain her. Maxwell looked at Evans for direction; but she gave him a stern look and motioned for him to fasten the restraints. He shrugged and gave Emily an apologetic look. Emily's expression told him that she understood and would not resist her bonds.

Her next stop was not only embarrassing, but physically invasive. Emily was placed on a padded examination table like any doctor might have in his office. It was covered with a sheet of gleaming white paper that rustled as she positioned herself on it. Once on the table, her arms were secured by restraints on both sides of the table and her ankles were bound with straps to adjustable stainless steel stirrups. An individual came in and looked at the table with a puzzled expression. Apparently, he had not been apprised of Emily's condition. He was in his mid to late fifties, had a severely protruding stomach that probably was a sign of some medical condition and had eyebrows that, while they did not meet, were really on intimate terms. They also had several wild hairs that stuck out like antennae searching for a signal. His hair was salt-and-pepper colored with considerably more salt than pepper. It looked like he had combed it with a buttered bran muffin. His brow protruded so much that it made his eyes squint all the time. He was not very tall and his girth made him look even shorter. He wore a lab coat that was way too long for him, completing the dwarfish effect.

"What do we have here?" he asked Maxwell. His voice reminded Emily of *Mr. Potter* in *It's a Wonderful Life*. Maxwell simply handed him a pair of special dark glasses. After a moment of fiddling with the adjustments he said, "Oh, I see. My, my. Interesting." Emily could see that his nametag was also obscured by a radiation device with only the letters S P E N visible. She inferred that his name was Spencer and was right, even though she didn't know it. He squatted on a three-legged stool and rolled over to the foot of the examination table. There, he donned a pair of purple rubber gloves, took one of Emily's feet in each hand and paused to examine her toes. She wasn't sure if he was just fascinated by her invisibility or if he had a foot fetish. Either way, it creeped her out. Just when she thought she could not be any more uncomfortable, he pushed back on the soles of her feet, bent her knees, placed her feet into the stirrups and spread her legs apart. She felt like a Thanksgiving turkey exposed to the world. Maxwell had every intention of turning away but he was, after all, human. After a moment, he composed himself and pretended to check his watch. Emily pretended not to notice his initial gawking. They were seeing something few people in the world had ever seen, but she felt as though she was being raped. The feeling became complete when Dr. Spencer produced a stainless steel speculum. It felt as though he had stored it in liquid nitrogen. Emily had never felt anything so cold and so much pain at one time. He was not in the least bit gentle and didn't seem to have a lot of experience on how to treat lady parts. In a way, he reminded Emily of a doctor who might have worked at a concentration camp...doing cruel experiments and extracting information. In this case, he was extracting body fluids and tissue samples. He also clipped her toenails and she hoped they were not for his personal enjoyment. Each of the samples were placed in vials or small plastic bags and labeled with a black permanent marker. When he was finished collecting samples, he leaned in between Emily's legs as if he was checking to see if he had left anything behind. Emily could feel his breath on her vagina and tried not to think about what he was doing down there. When he remembered he was not alone in the room, he looked over his shoulder and was met with Maxwell's scowl. He furrowed his already furrowed brow and cleared his throat. "I'm a doctor, dammit!" he huffed and left the room abruptly, suspiciously hunched over.

Maxwell walked over and closed Emily's legs and moved the stirrups to their passive position. Then he unbound her ankles and wrists. She composed herself as she sat on the side of the examination table. She felt herself bonding to Maxwell, but she resisted it. He was still in league with the enemy as far as she was concerned and she didn't want to let her guard down. After a few moments, she breathed a deep breath, got down off the examination table and jumped up on the waiting gurney without assistance.

Through the special dark glasses, Maxwell could see a stain left behind on the examination table paper. He was not totally familiar with what the color spectrums of the glasses meant, but he was pretty sure it was blood. He felt Dr. Spencer had been much too brutal with Emily and considered filing a report. He decided his complaint would just fall on deaf ears and might jeopardize his chance for advancement within the agency. Instead, he would deal with Dr. Spencer in his own way and in his own time…a covert way.

After more rooms and more tests (some invasive, some not), Emily was wheeled into a room that for some reason didn't seem as threatening as the others. The white walls and cold stainless steel were the same, but the mood of the room seemed more welcoming and more serene. Emily realized it was because the lighting was different. Instead of the harsh glare of the fluorescents that she was used to, there was a soft ambient glow coming from the fixtures. There was something different in the color of the light. Instead of it being an uncaring blue-white glare, it was soft pink in color…almost magenta. She began to feel relaxed. Maxwell unlatched the wrist restraints and showed Emily to a somewhat comfortable-looking chair. It was like an orthodontist's chair and was upholstered in a soft light blue vinyl. An attractive young woman with auburn hair and wearing special dark glasses appeared at the side of the reclined chair. Her nametag was again obscured by a radiation badge, but Emily could see the beginning of a name; A-N-G. She began to run through a list of names: *Angie, Angela, Angelica, Angelina*; in her mind, she settled for simply *Angie*. She was holding a suspicious-looking device that could only be described as a futurist Halloween mask. Two black opaque bulbous mounds rose up from where the eyeholes would be and a crimson plate in place of a nose was in the shape of a half-pyramid. Curved black strips extended back from the forehead piece, fitted with arrays of electrodes.

Extending from each side of the eye mounds was another strip with a crimson disk at the end. Emily shrank back as *Angie* tried to place it on her face.

"This isn't going to hurt," she said. "It's designed to stimulate and record your brainwave activ…" Maxwell cleared his throat deliberately and directed his eyes up to the security camera. Angie caught his meaning and picked up where her sentence was interrupted. "It's a painless procedure and might even be a bit relaxing. Don't worry." Emily relaxed a little and allowed the device to be placed on her face. The disks were fitted to her ears and the strips with the electrodes were pressed tightly, but not uncomfortably against her scalp. With the mask in place, Emily began to experience sensory deprivation to three of her senses. The temperature of the room had also been modified to closely match her skin temperature. The chair was also slightly heated for the same reason. Emily hardly noticed that restraints had been secured to her wrists and ankles once more. They too had temperature modifications. After a moment, she began to feel like she was drifting. A warm feeling of euphoria washed over her and she thought she began to see images in the blackness.

In her left ear, Emily could hear a light wind blowing…like a summer breeze. She thought she could feel the breeze on her forehead. Off in the distance, she could hear the soft screech of the rusty windmill on her farm. A horizontal slit of light appeared before her. It grew to form a tree line and she could see a bright light forming in the middle of it. The bright light became a sunrise on the horizon. It increased in intensity, almost to the point of being blinding. Emily stared at it, not worrying about any adverse effects. Somehow, she knew that her mind's eye couldn't be blinded; at least she hoped it couldn't. The sun rose to the noonday position and stopped. She was standing in the middle of a wheat field. She could feel the soft cultivated ground under her bare feet. She dug her toes into the soil and felt it turn to powder between them. It felt so real. She wondered if she had only been dreaming about the government research facility.

A cloud of dust rose up from the edge of the wheat field and a silver SUV pulled into the long gravel drive of the farm. It continued to throw up dust as it made its way to the farmhouse. Emily could hear the 'tinking' sound coming from the cooling engine. She could smell the mixture of dust and exhaust blending with the breeze coming off the wheat field. A tingle of excitement ran through her body. She knew the SUV. It was Nathan and his family.

She had first met Nathan three years ago when his family came to the farmhouse. Nathan's mother, Sue Saunders, was a photographer for *Rural Homes* magazine and wanted to use the house in a layout she was working on. When they had first approached the house, Nathan thought he was seeing an angel or a ghost when he had seen Emily. She had been equally amazed that he could. His family had thought he was playing or was having some kind of episode. Sue was given permission to photograph the house to her heart's content. Alma Troy was proud of her home and had been delighted to share it with the world. Charles Troy worried that the public exposure would lead to exposing Emily's secret to the world.

The images before Emily's eyes continued to reflect modified memories from her past. She could not tell if the smells she was experiencing were generated by her own mind, or if they were being triggered by the apparatus covering her nose. The image of Nathan relaxed her, but it could also have been the ambient atmosphere of the room and the specially designed chair. Angie collected readings on an electronic pad she was holding and transmitted them to unseen individuals who would interpret them, collate them and send them to other unseen individuals for analysis. The government is nothing if not full of redundancies. Emily settled into the comfort of the chair without realizing she was doing so. To her, she was standing on the gravel drive in front of Nathan. She was nearly weightless, so the gravel did not seem to press into the soles of her feet. It was like being on the moon perhaps. Nathan was looking into her eyes with his usual expression of amazement. They spoke through sign language. Nathan had been trained in it because he was deaf. Emily had learned it because she was mute...before she became invisible. She had to reacquaint herself with it when she met Nathan. Why he could see her when no one else could remained a mystery and it remained their secret. It was a precaution she was glad they had taken, or else the government would be running tests on him and have him confined to a secret facility as well.

Nathan had told her that her image amazed him more than he could express. To him, she was solid, but he could still see through her. The color of her skin and hair seemed normal, but it was as if she was made of water or a transparent gel. Nathan loved it. Sometimes he would poke her arm with his finger, expecting it to go through. Instead, he would feel how solid she was and he loved how the tip of his finger would turn transparent when he touched her. Being a healthy young male, he could not help but wonder what kind of other reactions he could get if other body parts were to come into contact. He was a gentleman however, so he kept those thoughts to himself. Nathan became an expert at signing covertly so he did not look like a lunatic; but Emily's parents suspected something was up. They did not interfere though because, from what they could tell, Emily was happy and that was all that mattered to them.

Emily stood before Nathan for a long time. The scene in her mind changed from noonday to night. The sky was a thick, midnight blue drape. It was ripped down the middle exposing billions of stars and galaxies in the Milky Way. She wasn't sure if the luminosity of the celestial scene was a recorded memory, or if it was embellished by her imagination. It didn't matter. She took in its brilliance and it took her breath away. The starlight twinkled in Nathan's eyes and Emily could read his thoughts. In her mind, she could hear what his voice would sound like. It was the voice she gave him when she read the signs he was making. It was a soft, lilting voice; not deep or harsh. It was gentle and comforting. It made her feel safe and...normal. For a moment, she thought she might have mouthed his name and was worried that the attendants might be able to read lips. Her fears were allayed when she tried to press her lips tightly together and felt that they already were. In her mind, they conversed like any young couple might. Her own voice was sweet and caring as she carried on a sensory-deprived hallucinogenic conversation with Nathan. They talked about nothing special; events of the day, plans for the future. They spoke honest compliments of each other and reassurances about minor, almost insignificant flaws. As their eyes met, Emily could see starlight out of the corner of her mind's eye, shimmering off of her golden hair. The scene behind Nathan turned horizontal and they were lying in a huge brass bed. Starlight gleamed on the polished brass. Emily was lying next to him on and under midnight blue satin sheets. They were naked and about to consummate their relationship for the first time. Emily's lips parted and she breathed out a soft, moist breath against Nathan's chest. He moved in to kiss her and Emily felt the mask apparatus being pulled from her face.

"Okay," said Angie. "I think we have all the results we need for the time being. Maxwell will take you back to your room and I hope your experiences have not been too unpleasant." Emily thought Angie sounded like a flight attendant. She had even managed to sound sincere. Maxwell helped her back onto the gurney and secured her restraints once more. He shook his head, trying to clear his mind of the overwhelming compassion he was feeling for her. It wasn't like him to be so concerned over a test subject. He was trained to suppress those kinds of feelings. It never occurred to him that the same sphere of influence that rendered Emily invisible to almost everyone also impelled compassion in some, even fierce loyalty. The longer Maxwell remained in her presence, the stronger the influence was becoming; even to the point of becoming irrevocable. He tried to shake it, but the urge to help her was too strong. Once back in her room, she sat on the side of her bed. He gave her a knowing look and she seemed to understand. It was as if she could read his mind the way she had read Nathan's in her hallucination. Emily tried not showing any emotion, but she knew that a change was coming soon and she needed to be prepared for it. Maxwell spoke in a guarded code to her as he prepared to leave.

"That's it for today," he said. "You can do what you like until *lights out*. Have a good *night*." The inflection on certain words told her the *when*. She would have to wait to find out the *how*. Emily went ahead with her daily routine and evening ablutions. The normal lights out came at nine, as usual. The *how* came at three forty-seven in the morning.

CHAPTER 5: FUGITIVE

Emily thought she had misread Maxwell's signals. She had drifted off to sleep in a mild state of depression. There was only the slightest of clicks at three forty-seven in the morning that caused her to awaken. The only difference in her room from the usual darkness she had experienced was that the green diodes on the surveillance cameras were not lit up. A slightly louder click at the door brought her to full alert. The silhouette of Maxwell appeared in the open door. Everything behind him was dark, but not as dark as her room. He was a black shape in a dark gray frame. He moved to the side of her bed and whispered in her ear softly.

"I know this is going to sound bad but I need your gown." Maxwell's concern for her modesty was touching. "There are tracking devices in them. You'll also need these until you get outside. Then, discard them and move to the west gate. You will understand when you get outside. From there, DO NOT go through the gate. There is a manhole cover near the gate. Normally, it is locked. Right now, it isn't. Go down the manhole and head south. There is lighting down there so you shouldn't get lost. Go about two hundred yards until you come to a ladder. Take it to the surface. From there, you are on your own, I am afraid. I don't want to know where you are going. That way, they can't find out from me." Emily leaned up and kissed him on the cheek. He was still wearing his special dark glasses. She removed her gown and felt a momentary flush of modesty. It subsided when she reminded herself that there was nothing she had that Maxwell had not already seen.

The items he had given her were her own set of special dark glasses. They were adjusted to the night vision setting and the hallway was bathed in an eerie green light when she donned them. She looked down at the other item Maxwell had given her. It was a pass to open the outer security doors. It belonged to Dr. Spencer. His first name was *Abner.* His middle name was *Samuel.* His initials were *A.S.S.* Emily thought that was fitting. She also thought it would be fitting if he was blamed for her escape. That was probably what Maxwell had in mind. There was a chill in the hallway as she made her way to the stairwell. Somehow, she knew she needed to go up. Two floors up, she met two men in coveralls coming down the stairs carrying futuristic tool boxes. Emily backed against the wall and froze. They looked directly at her and she was sure that she was caught. She began to make up a story in her head about how Dr. Spencer had set her free so it would match Maxwell's story. She didn't need to. The two men continued on past her, down to the next level. They were complaining about the frequent power outages and saying that if the company was going to keep using such high-powered equipment, they needed to upgrade their wiring. Their special dark glasses must not have been tuned to a frequency that detected Emily.

She continued up until she saw light through one of the vertical narrow windows in the stairwell doors. Emily estimated she had gone up five flights and didn't dare go higher in fear of overshooting the ground floor. Her heart stopped when she saw that someone was standing in front of the door. She was trying to decide her next action when he seemed to sense she was there, turned around and opened the door. It was Michael, her other attendant. "Emily?" he said softly. He looked behind him and then donned his special dark glasses. "I thought you might be along. I have something for you." Emily hoped it might be clothes. Running around naked in a government facility was a bit unnerving. But it wasn't clothes.

"This is some high-tech equipment here," Michael said. He sounded almost proud of it. "It's a voice generator. We, I mean, *they* use it when they want to impersonate someone. It can be tuned to sound like almost anybody. I *borrowed* it to make phone calls to my friends. They thought I was Christopher Walken. I thought you might use it to find your family without being traced. Don't use it for too long though. This one is an early experimental model and the battery gets hot when you use it too long. Just stick it to your throat and it does the rest. There are tiny adjustments on the sides that fine-tune it to the voice you want. I don't know if it will work with your condition, but it is worth a shot. Good luck, Emily. There are six more doors to get out. Make sure no one is on the other side when you open them. No one up here has the security clearance to have the setting on their glasses to see you. So, you should be fine. Be careful and be safe."

Michael disappeared down the hall just as a security patrol was making its rounds. When the hallway was clear, Emily exited the stairwell and headed for the first security door. No one was on the other side, so she slid the card into the slot next to it and the door opened easily. *Five more to go,* she thought. She remembered something about American soldiers raiding enemy fortresses at four in the morning because it was the optimum fatigue time for guards. The halls were empty and it was possible that those who were supposed to be vigilant were drifting off about this time. She made it through two more doors before she saw anyone. Even then, it was a guy in a white shirt and black pants getting coffee from a vending machine. The machine seemed to take forever to vend the coffee. When it did, it neglected to provide a cup. This caused the man in the white shirt to utter a few expletives that echoed in the dim hallway. He searched his pockets for more change and was about to insert it into the slot when he had a mild epiphany. He reached up into the cavity of the coffee machine and retrieved the cup that had lodged there. He placed the cup in the necessary position to catch the stream of coffee that was about the cascade down and then put his money in the slot. A cup came down this time, effectively knocking the first cup out of place and causing both cups to land on the floor. The man in the white shirt looked as though he was about to experience an aneurism and cursed the machine to eternal damnation. Emily was worried that she was going to be missed and that they would begin searching for her. She considered taking a chance and going through the door even with someone present. At that moment, a security officer rounded the corner in a bit of a rush. She froze, expecting that the search for her was on.

"Is there a problem here?" he asked the man in the white shirt. "I heard a commotion and I thought someone was being attacked."

"I am about to attack this coffee machine," he yelled. "Two cups, no coffee…and at a buck fifty a pop. I am out three bucks!"

"I think you need to calm down," said the security detail.

"Calm down? I need coffee! I don't have any more change!" The man in the white shirt seemed to be shaking.

"The machine takes bills," the security detail replied calmly.

"I….didn't notice that," said the man in the white shirt rather sheepishly. The security officer reached up to a rack of small envelopes on the front of the vending machine. "Fill this out and you will get your refund in a couple of weeks," he said. "...or whenever Congress gets around to approving the budget." The security detail smiled and walked away through the door Emily wanted to go through. The man in the white shirt opened his wallet and found that he only had a twenty-dollar bill. "DAMMIT!!!" he cried and stormed off to his office.

Emily wasted no time going through the remainder of the security doors. The last one had a security officer at a desk next to a metal detector. Emily walked through the detector and it made a weak, crackling beep. She suspected it was because of the voice generator in her hand. The security detail stirred a little but was apparently asleep. She swiped the card of Dr. Spencer in the locking mechanism next to the door and a security code prompt came up on a black screen in bright green letters. Emily began to panic. They had not given her a security code. They probably didn't know it. She was sure they had started to look for her. She was about to give herself up when she noticed the numbers 4-2-7-7 written on the back of the card in blue ballpoint ink. Deciding that there was nothing to lose, she entered the numbers on the keypad and the door swung open silently. Emily was grateful for her stroke of luck, but a little worried about the state of National Security. Once outside, she prepared to discard the glasses and security card in a dumpster when she noticed the security detail from the coffee machine behind it. He was smoking a cigarette. Again, Emily had to wait...this time, a long agonizing seven minutes. Finally, he ditched the butt in the dumpster, put a stick of gum in his mouth and went back inside. A plain white sign outside the building was painted with stenciled letters indicating that the WEST GATE was to the right. She looked back at the unassuming building she had just left. High on the wall near the corner was painted BLDG 19A. She didn't know why, but she thought that might be important somehow.

Emily took a deep breath before crossing the several rows of vacant numbered parking spaces. She had been naked outside before, but she was a stranger in a strange land and everything was foreign. She knew there were security monitors and she wasn't sure what they might pick up. Her parents had taken pictures of her with several types of cameras, trying to capture her image. The result was disappointing. She appeared as little more than a blurry shape in the pictures. The condition that caused her invisibility made her react to the background the way a chameleon does in its own environment. She hoped the security cameras did not have any advanced settings as she sprinted across the concrete towards the gate. The manhole cover was not right next to the gate as had been suggested. It was actually some forty feet from the gate on the left. Emily thought a manhole cover should have been easy to find, but it was concealed by some shrubs and she crept right past it the first time. It wasn't until a patrol unit drove by and she instinctively ducked down into the shrubs that she found it completely by accident.

To say that the manhole cover was unlocked was a passive term for what Emily encountered. The large metal disk looked as though it had been manufactured by a company that made bank vaults. The steel surface had overlapping circular patterns made by tool and die machines. Three small cylinders protruded about an inch above the surface of the disk. Each had a futuristic key slot in the center of it. Emily suspected that the cylinders popped up when the key was turned. In the center of the cylinders was the head of a large hex bolt. Next to the cover lay a crude-looking iron socket wrench that matched the size of the hex bolt. She figured Maxwell must have left it there earlier. She fitted the socket to the bolt and turned it counterclockwise. After three complete rotations, something in the metal disk clicked. The entire cover rose about two inches, revealing a handhold below the lip. Emily placed her delicate fingers in the handhold and lifted it as easily as opening a squeeze ketchup bottle lid. She had been worried that it would be too heavy for her, having read somewhere that manhole covers could weigh a hundred pounds.

The open hole was dark and a damp musty smell rose from it. Emily wondered if she should have kept the special dark glasses and considered going back for them. As her eyes became accustomed to the darkness, she could see that there was light below. It was very dim, but it was enough to see by. A metal ladder was attached to the right side of the manhole. Emily climbed down the ladder, reached up for the metal handle on the bottom of the cover and pulled it closed just as the patrol unit drove by a second time. Her bare feet slipped off the damp rung of the metal ladder and she hung by one arm from the underside of the cover. She felt it close completely as she heard tumblers lock into position. There was no going back now. Emily scrambled to get her feet back on the metal ladder and wrapped her arm around a rung. When she felt confident that she was secure, she forced herself to let go of the handle. The voice generator was still gripped tightly in her left hand and she wished she had pockets. She thought about putting it on, but she didn't want to risk making a noise accidentally. Her silence was to her advantage right now and she didn't want to give that up.

The metal ladder only extended to the bottom of the hole. From there, rectangular slots were built into the tiled walls like at the deep end of swimming pools. She paused before sticking her toes into the first damp opening, hoping something wasn't living in there. It was almost as bad as she suspected. Moss or something was growing in it, but no living creatures as far as she could tell. She quickly descended before she could find out about the others and then crouched on the floor of a barely lit tunnel about four feet high. It didn't look tall enough to be a maintenance tunnel, but Emily had no real knowledge of those things. It seemed like a regular sewer tunnel except it had a narrow raised walkway down the center. An extremely shallow stream of water ran down either side of the walk and it was headed south. A layer of semi-opaque grime coated the recessed lights making their purpose almost nonexistent. Emily tried to clean one off, but stopped when the effort seemed futile. Besides, the stuff on her hand felt icky. She began her crouched walk down the dimly lit tunnel, keeping watch for any sign of a ladder. After what she estimated to be about a hundred yards, her back began to ache and she stopped to keep from pulling a muscle. A bundle of pipes and cables ran along the top of the tunnel and dripping water echoed in the distance. Once the pain in her back subsided, Emily continued on. The sound of dripping water grew louder and a little more intense. She was sure she had gone the second hundred yards, but there was no sign of a ladder. She wondered if she had missed it in the near darkness and paused to reconsider. In the shadows, something skittered across her foot and she jumped. She let out a silent shriek as she tried to imagine what it was before deciding she would rather not know. Having renewed resolve to find the ladder, she continued her crouched walk down the tunnel at a quicker pace. She thought she had missed it and was about to retrace her steps when she noticed a dark circle in the direct center of the low ceiling. The pipes and cables veered around it.

    It was a hole leading upward and looked like it might have been added later than the original tunnel. Emily was confused. She was supposed to look for a ladder. *This couldn't be it, could it?* she thought to herself. She stood up in the hole and stretched her back. Feeling around the sides, she felt a metal ladder. She felt around the bottom of the ladder. The supports on both sides felt rough, as if they had rusted and broken off. Maybe the ladder had extended down farther at one point. In any case, Emily was ready to exit the tunnel. Water was dripping profusely around the tunnel and it was echoing to the point of being torturous to her eardrums. Since she was going to have to hoist herself up, she was going to need both arms to do it. She placed the voice generator on her throat and it stayed there through the miracle of the government's secret technology. It hummed mildly before going silent. She grabbed a rung second from the bottom and tried to pull herself up, but her hands slipped free because of the condensation on the ladder; she fell back on the cold concrete walkway. She uttered a simple "ouch!" which came out in a metallic robot voice like a sideband radio transmission. The sound both surprised and amused her. She began to chuckle in the robot voice. That amused her more and she began to laugh at her own laughter. The interaction with her new sounds went on for several minutes before the novelty and humor wore off. Emily composed herself and attempted the ladder again. This time she gripped tighter and pulled herself up until she could wedge her knee against the inside of the hole. When she obtained the next rung, she positioned her other knee in a way that allowed her to reach up two more rungs. Once she was sure she had a solid grip, she placed her foot on the bottom rung and pushed up until she was near enough to the top to feel the metal disk that covered the hole. She pushed on it and wondered if it was locked down. It didn't budge. So Emily climbed higher on the ladder and put her shoulder against it. She uttered a grunt and it struck her as funny. She sounded like a robot chipmunk. That made her laugh again and she had to wait for the humor to run its course before continuing.

Placing her shoulder against the metal disk again, Emily exerted all of her effort and it began to give. She raised it half an inch and a sheet of water washed in and drenched her. She slipped from her perch again and was only saved from falling by her arm wrapped around the top rung of the ladder. She cursed out loud for the first time in her life and she no longer saw the humor in the sounds she was making.

She was cold, naked, hurting and drenched with water. Nothing was that funny. Emily braced for the shock of cold water against her skin and forced the metal plate disk up and to the side. Another sheet of water spilled down her right side. In addition, huge water droplets splashed on her shoulders and Emily realized it had begun to rain while she was navigating the tunnel. She climbed out of the manhole feeling like a drowned rat exiting a flooded chamber. It was nearly sunrise, but there would be no sun this morning by the looks of it. She stepped into the wet grass surrounding the manhole and looked around. A small rectangular sign told her where she was: WPAFB SOUTH GATE – Authorized Vehicles Only. The drive to where the gate must have been did not look well used and the road it came off of looked like little more than an access road. The only thing Emily knew was that she was in Ohio and that she was near Dayton. She wondered how many people on the base knew of the existence of BLDG 19A. It was far removed from the other parts of the base and it had been suggested that the crashed UFO from Roswell was housed somewhere near here. She had thought the rumors were just made up to sell books. Now she was not so sure.

    She started down the road heading west. She knew that Dayton was somewhere in that direction and it seemed the most likely choice. Something made her turn around. The other side of the sign she had read was blank. That meant traffic did not come from the direction she was heading. That meant she was headed for a dead end. She turned around and headed the other way. It was a little more pleasant walking in that direction anyway. The rain had been pelting her in the face. At least this way, it was pelting her in the back. The drops stung against her bare butt and she wrapped her arms around herself to try to stay warm. It wasn't helping. But, as Maxwell had said, she was on her own now.

It felt as though she had walked for ten miles before she came to any sign of civilization. Actually, it had only been two. Ahead of her was what looked to be an abandoned garage. It didn't offer much hope of clothing, but if she could get in, at least she would be out of the rain. She approached cautiously just in case it wasn't completely abandoned. The large wooden garage door was secured with a rusty padlock. The side door was rotting and looked like it hadn't been used in quite some time. The doorframe gave in easily to a little pressure and the door creaked open on rusty hinges. Emily closed it behind her so as not to arouse suspicion should anyone pass down the nearly unused road. Inside, it was remarkably dry for such a rundown structure. In the back corner were seven or eight unmarked fifty-five gallon oil drums. Shelves lined the back wall and contained canisters and a few wooden boxes from bygone days, manufactured by bygone companies. A workbench stretched along the wall behind the side door. Rusty tools laid in the last place someone had placed them. A metal lamp with a wing-nut adjustment at the elbow hovered above the bench. Emily tried turning it on, but she already knew there would be no electricity. *Probably better*, she thought. *No point in drawing attention to the window.*

Emily had hoped for a pair of coveralls or something she could wear; but there was nothing. The garage smelled like old oil and grime. It was dry, but unpleasant. She really didn't want to stay any longer than she had to. Her stomach growled and it reminded her that she had not had anything to eat the day before because of those blasted tests. She was about to leave when she noticed something that had been in front of her the entire time...curtains. The curtain rod above the single window over the workbench supported two cotton fabric curtains that also smelled like old oil. Emily pulled down the rod, dislodging one of the supports from the wall. She removed the curtains from the rod and looked around for something she could use for a drawstring. Under the workbench she found a spool of coated wire. It was better than nothing. A rusty pair of tin snips needed persuading before they would work, but soon she had the wire cut to the length she needed to make a skirt and hooded shawl from the curtains. She threaded the wire through the hem at the top of one and tied it around her waist. It was just big enough to go around her with a daring slit along the side up to the top of her hip. The other curtain draped around her shoulders with enough fabric left over to form a hood. The ensemble didn't cover her completely, but it was better than nothing. Emily began to shiver a little as she warmed up and she had to force herself to go back out into the rain in spite of her new apparel.

No sooner had she closed the side door behind her and cinched the makeshift hood around her chin than a military vehicle drove past with an aspect of urgency. Emily suspected her absence had been discovered and that they might be looking for her. However, they were not wearing the special dark glasses so she relaxed a little and continued down the road. She was glad that no one could see her in her window treatment. If they could, she would have said, "I saw it in the window and I just HAD to have it." She would have said it in her robot chipmunk voice and it would have been hilarious. It was more hilarious when *Carol Burnett* said it, but Emily would have made it work. She smiled as she continued down the road in the rain. Soon she came to a main road that still looked pretty secluded. It ran northeast and southwest. She walked along the left side so she could see any oncoming traffic, but there wasn't much. The occasional vehicle that did pass her seemed to intentionally throw water up on her; even though she knew that wasn't possible. If anyone had seen a nearly topless girl wearing curtains for clothes, they surely would have stopped; at very least, they would have slowed down.

Emily continued on the road forever until it turned into a genuine highway. She finally came to a travel center. Semis pulled in and out of the busy truck stop throwing up sheets of water as they did. She was getting tired of being drenched and was beginning to take it personally. She stepped into the travel center and was immediately met with a rush of cold air. The air conditioning was on in spite of the cold rain outside. A large burly man headed towards her with a cup of coffee and brushed her as he headed out the door. He looked back curiously to see what he had hit, shrugged it off and went on. Emily waited, trying to acclimate to the temperature. Then she moved to the circular racks of shirts near the restrooms. She felt guilty for what she was about to do, but she couldn't go around naked or wearing curtains while searching for her parents. She searched the tags until she found a sweatshirt in her size. It was emblazoned with an OHIO STATE logo. Next she found a pair of sweatpants that matched the top. It didn't have to; but even invisible, Emily had a sense of fashion. There were socks of all kinds and tennis shoes of every size. It was perfect. She took an extra sweatshirt with her to the restroom with which to dry off. She could have dressed right there, but she didn't want people watching clothes disappear before their eyes. Once in a restroom stall, she dried off and regretted not stealing a comb or a brush. *Next time*, she thought. Emily pulled the cushioned-sole socks onto her bare feet and felt comfortable for the first time in days. Lacing up the shoes, she felt human again. She opened the door and stepped out. Behind her, the sensor on the toilet triggered and the toilet flushed. She worried about what kind of light spectrum it registered that it would react to her. Then she relaxed when she realized it had probably reacted to the movement of the door.

Now that her clothing needs were met, she moved on to the more pressing need for sustenance. The restaurant attached to the travel center had the most delightful aromas coming from it and Emily's mouth began to water. She wasn't sure how she was going to get something off the menu. The problem solved itself when she saw that the restaurant had a lunch buffet. She made her selections from it and went to a back booth with fried chicken, dinner rolls and a baked potato that fortunately was not too hot to handle. She ate quickly, but not so quickly that she would make herself sick. She grabbed a glass of milk off a table as she passed. The waitress took the blame for its absence, saying that she must have forgotten it…and that she would forget her head if it wasn't attached.

Having been dressed and well fed, Emily pondered her next move. She had to find her parents, but if they had not been captured, they would surely be in hiding. She might be able to contact Nathan. As far as she knew, the government was not aware of their relationship. Even if they were, they would probably not consider a deaf boy could have any way of communicating with an invisible girl who couldn't speak. She needed to get to a computer bank at a library, so she needed to find a library. The best way to find one was with a phone. She was going to have to steal one from somebody…at least for a few minutes. A business man was in a long line at the checkout talking on his cell phone. When he finished his call, he placed the phone in the pocket of his sport coat. Emily thought it might be an easy task to remove it without his knowledge. She almost had her hand in his pocket when the phone rang and he answered. That made her nervous and she dropped back to reconsider. A little boy stood next to a bin of toys looking around nervously. Emily knew what he had in mind. He was about to put a toy racecar into his pocket, hoping no one would notice. Emily touched an adjustment on the side of the voice generator and leaned down to speak into his ear. The voice that came out was a slightly feminine *Christopher Walken*.

"You know....," she said. When she heard what she sounded like, she couldn't help but go with it. "You know...little boy... They have...security cameras...here...in the stor-ah. You...are going to be caught...and sent...to juvey." Emily thought it was a pretty good *Christopher Walken*. The little boy thought he was busted. He whipped around and saw no one. He slipped the racecar back into the bin anyway and left the store in a hurry. Emily felt a sense of pride and renewed courage. She swiftly removed the phone from the businessman's pocket, ignoring the irony that she was stealing.

Fate proved to be kind to Emily or it felt it owed her one. The East Branch of the Dayton Public Library was less than two miles away. With her new shoes and warm clothes, she was there in no time. A flyer on the front desk announced upcoming events including self-defense courses and yoga classes. Emily took one and borrowed a marker from the desk. She also secured a small strip of tape. The bank of computers was visible through a large set of glass doors. She slipped through the doors and was fortunate enough to see someone getting up from a computer without logging off. She knew how to get around the log on procedure, but was glad not to have to. She wrote a note on the back of the events flyer and stuck the tape to it. Just as she did, she saw the lady that had gotten up from the computer coming back to log off. Emily stuck the note on the screen just as it came into her view. The note said OUT OF ORDER. "Wow. That was fast," the woman said. "I just left." The out of order sign was enough to make her feel secure and she left again. Emily typed in Nathan's email address and sent a cryptic message. SOMETIMES, I FEEL LIKE I DON'T EVEN EXIST she typed. An instant message popped up in the corner. It was Nathan.

E??? WHAT HAPPENED? WHERE ARE YOU?

I CAN'T TELL YOU RIGHT NOW. DO YOU KNOW WHERE M & D ARE?

NO...BUT M CONTACTED ME TO FIND OUT ABOUT YOU. SHE WILL CONTACT ME LATER. CAN I TELL HER YOU ARE OKAY?

YES. BUT USE A COMPUTER IN TOWN FROM NOW ON. I WILL TRY TO CONTACT YOU TOMORROW.

OKAY. BUT I AM WORRIED.

ME TOO. BUT WE WILL GET THROUGH THIS. THANKS FOR BEING SO SWEET. HUGZ.

HUGZ BACK.

They both signed off just as a guy that looked like he might be homeless prepared to sit on Emily's lap. She moved just in time and he started to read their messages. She held the power button down and the screen went black. The man cursed and moved to another computer. Emily relaxed a little, knowing that her mother was still free. She also was happy that Nathan seemed to be safe for the time being. She would send him another email later to set up a time they could message each other. At least she didn't feel so alone in the world. She headed back to the travel center. If she was going to travel, maybe a semi would be the way to do it.

CHAPTER 6: CROSSING STATE LINES

If Emily had been a normal visible girl, getting a ride somewhere would probably have been easier. She would have just flirted with a trucker or a businessman and he –or she– would have taken her where she wanted to go with few questions asked…for a *price* of course. Instead, her very existence raised too many questions to count, so she was reduced to stowing away. Semis with sleepers were too small to effectively conceal her for very long. Sooner or later she would come in contact with the driver. Riding in one of the trailers could prove dangerous. She could be bounced over the interior or crushed by its cargo in one way or another.

Getting a ride was not going to be as easy as it seemed. Not only did she need to find a mode of transport that was headed in the same direction she wanted to go, but she needed to find one that was accommodating for a long journey. Even motorhomes, which would be the ideal choice, were hard to come by. If they were going in the right direction, they usually had too many occupants to deal with. Emily waited around all afternoon without any luck. The sun went down and the long florescent lights flickered on, bathing the lot in an artificial but not unfriendly light. The weather was uncharacteristically warm for mid-October. Emily thought about taking her sweatshirt off, or at least stealing a t-shirt, but she felt she had cost the establishment too much money already and made a promise to herself to pay them back when she could. Then she slipped back into the restaurant to see what was on the dinner buffet. Wandering through the restaurant also gave her the opportunity to eavesdrop on the diners and find out where they were going. Eventually, she would like to go to Iowa because that was her home. That was where Nathan was. But *they* would be expecting that, so she needed a different game plan. *They* knew she was missing by now and had probably instituted an intensive search of the area. Emily imagined military roadblocks and black unmarked helicopters scanning the countryside. She had expected dark government vehicles to pull in and out of the travel center all day. The fact that none of those things had occurred puzzled her as she dined on the best chicken and noodles with mashed potatoes she had ever had. She sat in a corner booth near the back to avoid detection. Twice a busgirl had cleared her table while she was sitting there and she had to start over. Emily finished off a piece of apple/rhubarb pie just before the busgirl grabbed the plate and uttered an obscenity under her breath. The girl thought she was being played by her coworkers.

    Emily grabbed a bottle of water from a rack in the cooler and went outside to look for a likely prospect she had discovered in the restaurant. He was a retired gentleman who was going to visit his son in Wyoming. His wife had passed away recently after suffering a stroke. They had been married for forty-one years and he was devastated. It had been their plan to travel around the country in their RV. Now he was all alone except for his son, who was more than happy to take him in. The poor man, whose name was Murray, had poured his heart out to the waitress and had made Emily and the waitress cry. But a ride was a ride and she was determined to be onboard when he departed. The dangerous part was that the route would go directly through Iowa. But Emily felt that if she was to overshoot that destination and approach it from the other side of the country, it might throw *them* off.

While she was waiting for Murray to finish his meal and take care of a few incidentals, Emily watched the activity in the travel center lot. Two girls spent an abnormal amount of time standing around the lot doing nothing. Then a trucker or business man would approach one of them and they would disappear somewhere for a short time. The man would leave and the girl would resume her stance. The other one spent some time in the sleeper cab of a semi before exiting. Emily knew about *Lot Lizards*, truck stop prostitutes. But these girls looked like they were barely out of high school. Emily thought it made a statement about the state of the economy and of society as well. She shook her head and tried to be positive. Murray came out of the travel center after paying his fuel bill and headed for an enormous champagne-colored RV. It looked like something a rock star would travel in. She slipped in the side door after Murray and let it swing open, making him think that he hadn't latched it. He double-checked the latch as he closed it a second time and Emily settled in for what she expected to be a long journey.

Murray must have liked to drive at night because the traffic on the highway was lighter. Emily watched the road for a while, but the steady pulse of white lines had a hypnotic effect on her. She found herself searching for a place to rest for the night. The oncoming headlights created rhythmic light patterns on the wall of the RV and Murray had the satellite radio tuned to a Big Band Era station. *Rhapsody in Blue* played softly and Emily was asleep on the narrow RV sofa before the song concluded. She had been careful to remove the voice generator so as not to utter anything in her sleep; a problem she had never had to worry about before. She had placed it safely into the pocket of her sweatpants.

Emily longed to be back in Iowa with her family…and Nathan. Their lives had been peaceful in spite of her *condition*. That was how the family doctor had referred to her invisibility; *her condition*. Alma and Charles Troy struggled to make a decision about who to tell. The family doctor seemed like a logical choice, but they were not sure if he would have been bound by the law to report Emily's condition to someone. He was also their friend however, so they took the chance. The town of Cedar Pike was small and a rarity in that the town doctor still made house calls and townsfolk usually kept to themselves. Dr. David Cornell had graduated at the top of his class, but came back home to serve the little community in which he grew up. The area wasn't so rural that he got paid in chickens or anything, but he had been called on occasion to treat a farmer's prize heifer more than once. When he first encountered Emily's invisibility, he thought he was going to be treating her for some simple childhood disease or an allergic reaction. When Charles and Alma led him to her room, he thought it was some kind of joke. Alma guided him to feel Emily's arm, but his mind still refused to believe what his senses were telling him. Charles and Alma quietly explained their first encounter with their invisible daughter. Once his nerves settled and he accepted the situation, he became intrigued. Dr. Cornell went back to her room, spoke to her softly and experimented with the field or whatever she seemed to be generating. It was as if material objects seemed to bend to Emily's will somehow. Objects that were placed near her by others seemed to blend naturally into the background. She could pick up three dimensional objects and they would fade from existence almost instantly; but a sheet laid over her blended with the background, looking as if it had been tossed loosely on the bed.

    Dr. Cornell considered calling colleagues and others who were experts in their respective fields, but Alma and Charles were afraid someone would come and take Emily away. They had been very careful to conceal her condition without denying her existence. No one thought it unusual when they chose to homeschool her since everyone knew she was born without the ability to speak. Alma gave up her job as a librarian to devote her full attention to Emily; and she proved to be an excellent teacher. Emily was an exceptional student and progressed at a rate that was at least two years above her age group. Dr. Cornell honored the Troy's wishes and kept Emily's secret. He kept her vaccinations up to date and did a variety of tests to determine the cause of her invisibility. A minor breakthrough in her treatment came one day when he was drawing some blood for testing. Emily couldn't cry out when he missed the vein, but she made a noise like someone blowing through a hollow reed. It occurred to him that if she could make that kind of sound, an electrolarynx or *throat back* might allow Emily to communicate with him. She and her parents had learned sign language when she was younger, but that proved useless when she turned invisible.

    Emily ran the charge down on the throat back by the afternoon of the day she got it. She went around the house talking to everyone and everything...sounding like an invisible robot. She sang songs that sounded a little like *Stevie Nicks* singing *The Eensie Weensie Spider*. The throat back allowed her to guide the needle to exactly where it needed to be and greatly improved Dr. Cornell's study. He was both amazed and confused by her blood sample. It wasn't invisible, but it didn't look like any blood sample he had ever taken. It looked almost like tinted vapor at first. Then it seemed to solidify into a tinted gel. It stayed that way for at least twenty-four hours before turning into a completely normal blood sample. He tested it himself the best he could without sending it to a lab for analysis. He knew that the sample would raise too many questions, but it limited what he was able to find out. He also tested her saliva, perspiration and even her urine. Each of the samples looked normal, except for an element with which he was unfamiliar. When in a closed container, the element seemed inert; but when exposed to the air, it turned to vapor. Dr. Cornell determined it was something similar to a pheromone which clouded the perception of those around Emily, rendering her invisible. In addition, when it mixed with the chemistry of her skin, it seemed to give her the ability of a chameleon; causing her to blend with her background instantaneously. The applications were extraordinary. If the trait was somehow a recessive ability that was once part of a particular group of primates, it might explain why gigantopithecus, or *Bigfoot* as it is more commonly known, could stay undetected throughout the centuries. It could also explain why no samples had ever been recovered since the samples would have remained camouflaged for some time after they were left behind. Dr. Cornell was already writing a research paper in his head, even though he might never get to publish it. He was sure it would, at very least, get him a nomination for a Nobel Prize.

Dr. Cornell struggled with his conscience for a long time. Something on the news swayed his decision to keep Emily's secret. It wasn't directly related to her condition. It was a story about an embassy bombing and a military response. He wondered what the military would do with such an ability. The doctor wondered what would happen if it fell into the wrong hands. Then he wondered what would happen to Emily if *she* fell into the wrong hands. He imagined them, whoever they would be, testing her without any regard for her humanity. Dr. Cornell imagined them programming her to carry out covert assignments and assassinations if they were unable to duplicate her invisibility. He wasn't going to let that happen. He vowed to keep her safe and work to find a cure, or at least a method of controlling her condition. After all, he didn't graduate at the top of his class for nothing.

Brrrrruuuuuuudddddrrrrrappppppppp!!! Murray must have dozed off for a second because he ran over the *wakeup strip* at the edge of the road. He blinked widely and forced his eyes to stay open. Emily started as she awoke and for a moment thought she was safe at home in her bed. Her heart pounded wildly and she suddenly had to pee very badly. She was about to risk using the toilet in the RV when it shifted to the right, taking the ramp into a rest stop. Murray maneuvered the enormous RV into a long, angled parking place reserved for semis and oversized vehicles. He killed the engine, got out and closed the door behind him. Emily heard it click as he locked it from the outside. She decided to risk going out instead of using the RV's facilities. She had never been in one and wasn't quite sure how everything worked. She unlatched the door and stepped out in the cool predawn air. The eastern horizon was just beginning to glow pink and Emily realized that she had slept all night. She sprinted across the lot to the restrooms. The ladies' room was empty and Emily didn't have to worry about making noise. The sounds seemed hollow and amplified in the cavernous restroom and she wasn't used to the noises which came out of her body. The toilet flushed automatically, which unnerved her a little, but she thought the automatic faucet and soap dispenser were pretty cool. She washed her hands two more times just for fun.

In the lobby of the rest stop was a huge map of Illinois with an arrow indicating that she was just a few miles from St. Louis. Something didn't seem right and she checked a large United States map on the opposite wall. If Murray was headed to Wyoming, he was going the long way about it. They appeared to be headed through Missouri and not Iowa. It saddened her a little not to get to see her home state, but she thought it might be safer. After all, they wouldn't be looking for her in Missouri for any reason. Emily wanted to be cautious and this route was pretty safe. She returned to the

RV and found the door locked. Murray had started the propane generator and was most likely sleeping soundly. *Great*, she thought. *I guess I will just hang out here for a few hours like those ladies at the travel center.* She went back inside because the morning chill was a little intense. She looked at the maps again and leafed through a few brochures. Emily became familiar with Illinois' finest vineyards and several themed attractions. There was an AmTrak brochure with departure and arrival times for various destinations. She thought that was interesting and looked at it for quite a while. The sun came up but did not shine very bright. The weather was cold, overcast and threatened rain. Emily walked around the lot and looked at the scenery. She decided she might need to steal a winter coat if it got much colder. She panicked once when she couldn't find the RV and thought Murray might have left without her. But a semi carrying a load of hogs had pulled in next to the RV and had hidden it from her view. The hogs were making an unusual amount of noise and Emily hoped they might wake Murray. She waited next to the door just in case, holding her nose. Murray must have been sleeping like a rock because the hogs didn't disturb him. The driver was sleeping as well. The hogs didn't seem to be disturbing him either, but he was probably used to it…and the smell.

Emily went back to the rest stop lobby, determined to wait there until Murray showed some sign of waking up or the rig pulling the hog trailer left. She looked through a few more brochures and then curled up in a corner near a window. Cars came and went, semis pulled in as others left. The scene was busy and varied, yet monotonous. Emily drifted in and out of sleep with her forehead resting against her folded knees. She wasn't sure how long she had been asleep or if she had slept at all, when she heard a commotion in the lot. The hogs were squealing at a fevered pitch as bluish-black smoke poured out of the dual exhaust pipes on the semi. The gears ground slightly as it shifted into gear and pulled out of the rest stop. Emily could see that the RV had also been started because it too had exhaust coming out of its tailpipe. She ran across the lot, narrowly avoiding being run over by an SUV with a family of six inside. Murray had shifted the RV into gear by the time she got to it and the vehicle was moving forward slowly. She began to panic and looked around frantically for some way to make Murray stop. Emily grabbed the aluminum support of the retracted awning and shook it violently. The awning slipped out of its perch on one end and hung ever so slightly out of alignment. The brakes on the RV emitted a high-pitched squeal as they were applied and Murray exited the vehicle to see what had caused all the noise. Looking up at the awning he muttered, "How in the hell....?" and secured it back in place. He double-checked the fasteners to make sure it was not going to come loose again. Emily, in the meantime, had slipped quietly back into the RV and was sitting unobtrusively at the end of the couch she had slept on. Murray returned to the driver's seat and was about to put the RV into drive when he decided to check the road atlas again. She watched him trace his finger from St. Louis to Peoria and could tell that he had made a miscalculation. He then marked a route through Missouri and Nebraska to southern Wyoming, sighed and shifted into gear. On the dash was a perfectly good navigator, but Murray didn't use it. Emily wondered why.

    Murray didn't use it because it was a gift from his late wife; a gift that had caused an argument. At first, he tried to show appreciation for it, but he hated learning new things. It was a long time before he even got a cell phone. Etta, his late wife, didn't like the disappointment in his eyes and responded with uncharacteristic anger. Murray fired back and they went to bed angry for basically nothing. Sometime during that night, Etta gripped Murray's arm; her eyes filled with panic. He rushed her to the hospital where she slipped into a coma.

She died at 9:41 that morning. Murray blamed himself. He always would. He kept the navigator on the dash of the RV as a reminder to always be kind to those who are close to you, but he still refused to use it.

Emily watched the traffic and looked at the scenery through the large panoramic windshield of the RV. They crossed Missouri in a little over three hours and arrived in Kansas City in time for the afternoon rush hour. They were stalled in traffic and Murray was cursing a lot under his breath. He had hoped to avoid the southern route and avoid Kansas City. He looked at the navigator with contempt, picked up the atlas, traced his route again and then threw it over his shoulder. It hit Emily on the top of her head and she mouthed a silent *owww*! She picked up the atlas and gave Murray a contemptuous look as well. She looked at the page and at highways around Kansas City. There were a lot of options for travel and Kansas City was bound to have quite a few libraries. She decided that it might be time for her and Murray to part ways. She was going to miss him even though he never knew she was there. He was a sad man living a sad chapter in his life and she wished she could help. But Emily had her own chapter to live out and it was in a different direction than Murray's. She knew he would fuel up the next chance he got. His stomach had been growling and he would look for the first travel center he could find. Emily would pick up a change of clothes and maybe have a shower. She was feeling a little ripe.

Emily's hunch was on target and once traffic started to move, Murray took the first exit that looked promising. He pulled the enormous RV up to the gas pump and fueled up. He then pulled the rig into an RV parking space and went inside to the restaurant. Emily followed, but stayed behind in the travel center to look over the racks of clothes. It was a bit disappointing that the clothes all looked the same except for the name of the state. She wondered if she might get a ride to a strip mall where she could find more fashionable items. She grabbed a fresh sweatshirt, a new pair of sweat pants and this time, a zippered fleece hoodie. She also grabbed a fresh pair of socks and a package of boy's underwear. She wondered why the travel center did not accommodate girls. A voice came over the loud speaker saying *Number 14, your shower is ready.* That reminded her that she wanted to shower before trying to find a library. Emily was about to brave the door into the shower area when she noticed that the sweatpants she had stolen didn't have pockets. She went back and exchanged them for a pair that did. After all, it wasn't like she could carry a suitcase with her. She did, however, grab a laptop case that fit close enough to her body to remain invisible with her. Then she worked up her nerve and headed for the showers again.

Inside, there were six lime-green doors with numbers on them. Emily was relieved that the showers were so private. Two of the doors were open and had recently been occupied. Rumpled wet towels hung off of a wooden bench and wet soap with residual bubbles rested in the soap dish built into the wall. The sound of running water came from behind two more of the doors, indicating they were not vacant. The last door on the right actually looked inviting. Two fresh clean dark blue towels rested on the wooden bench with a new wrapped bar of soap on top of them. Emily prepared to occupy the shower herself when a large naked man came around the corner wearing only a pair of transparent plastic shower slippers.

He was not large in a sense that he was tall. He was more round and somewhat layered like the Michelin Man, but not as well built. Emily would have squealed if she had been able. She had never seen an actual naked man before in person. She wasn't sure she wanted to ever see another one. She tried to avert her eyes, but it was no use. The damage had been done. The pudgy man stepped into the shower and before he shut the door, Emily was treated to a long agonizing view of his backside. He had a hedge of back hair that ran all the way across his shoulders. Another smaller hedge ran across the base of his spine and his almost non-existent buttocks formed an inverted "T". Emily felt a little nauseous. She was slightly under the impression that men looked like the actors she had seen in the occasional R-rated movie. The door closed behind him and she felt the tension in her chest release. She breathed deeply and turned to check the other vacant shower. As she did, a second door opened. This time, a man came out who was tall, rugged-looking and very easy on the eyes. He was exactly what she needed to drive the other image from her mind. He also had the decency to wrap a towel around his waist before exiting the shower. His muscular chest was adorned with just the perfect amount of chest hair for Emily's taste. The man did not have six-pack abs, but he by no means had a beer gut. He was a healthy specimen and he redeemed the gender in Emily's eyes. As he walked around the corner into the next room, he slipped the towel off exposing his butt. Emily let out a silent squeal and felt a mild tingle run through her body.

    Getting back to business, she noticed that he had only used one of his towels. Emily quickly stepped inside the stall, undressed, hung her clothes on the hooks provided and started the shower. The hot water poured over her like a blessing from heaven. She even used the soap he left in the dish. Emily lost track of time as she enjoyed one of the few joys she had experienced in a while. She had to force herself to turn off the water. She dried off quickly, dressed in the clothes she had stolen and ditched the others in the dirty towel basket. Emily was almost out the door when she realized that she had left the voice generator in the pocket of the dirty sweatpants. She retrieved the device and put it into the laptop bag she was going to use as a carryall.

Murray was gone when she got out of the shower. She was sad to see him go and wished only the best for him and his new life in Wyoming. Emily stole a comb and a brush. She no longer had any moral conflict about taking things. She brushed her damp hair to keep it from tangling. A little girl looking through the DVD selection closed her eyes and wondered where the spray was coming from. Emily moved to a more deserted part of the travel center and finished brushing her hair. Then she made her way to the restaurant to see what was on the menu. It was a dinner buffet again with pretty much the same fare that was on the buffet in Dayton. She didn't care. She was starving. She constructed a beef Manhattan with green beans and a dinner roll on the side. A waitress taking drinks to a table was missing one soda when she got to her destination. Emily again found a secluded booth and finished her meal quickly. She grabbed an apple and a banana off the buffet before leaving and stuffed them into the laptop case. The case gave Emily an idea. If she could steal a laptop, she could contact Nathan from anyplace that had a Wi-Fi connection. That thought caused another moral conflict to emerge. She didn't like stealing from people. Businesses are insured and she intended to pay them back. Stealing from an individual just seemed wrong. Emily was about to give up on the idea when a salesman of some kind blew up at the girl behind the counter. He didn't get his receipt at the pump because it had run out of paper. The girl said she was more than happy to run a receipt for him but that just made him angrier. He said he didn't have time for that and he wanted her name to report her to the home office. She had done nothing wrong, but he had her in tears. Emily's moral conflict faded away and she went out to the lot to find his car.

It wasn't hard to figure out which one belonged to the salesman. Two suits in dry cleaning bags hung on a hook over the backseat window. There was also a box that looked as though it held brochures of some kind. Sure enough, there was a laptop bag on the floorboard of the backseat. Emily unzipped it, removed the laptop and power source and zipped it up again. He would probably be at his motel before he would ever know it was missing. *Serves him right*, she thought. Her only fear was that she might have somehow gotten the wrong car. Her fear faded as quickly as her moral conflict when the irate man stormed out of the travel center and headed directly for the car she had just raided. He drove off in a huff, squealed his tires and threw up gravel as he sped out of the lot. He was followed immediately by a state trooper who happened to be pulling in at the same time. It looked as though it was not going to be a good day for the angry salesman.

    Emily was fortunate that the laptop was not password protected. Her greatest difficulty would be finding a place with Wi-Fi where she could use it covertly. The travel center had Wi-Fi, so Emily decided to try it out. Behind the building were two dumpsters that concealed her perfectly. The internet signal was a little weak, but it worked well enough for instant messaging. However, Nathan was not online at this time, so she left him a cryptic email telling him to be at *that place* at *that time*. He would know what it meant. He would be logged on at the library the next day at three-thirty. Now her next step would be to determine the route she would take from Kansas City and what mode of transportation she would use. Emily decided to let fate help her out; she went back into the travel center and restaurant to eavesdrop on some other customers and see what destinations they had in mind.

CHAPTER 7: CLANDESTINE RENDEZVOUS

Nathan Saunders arrived at the library a little early. He took the precaution to look natural and not like he had an appointment. He was anxious for some contact with Emily. He hadn't seen her in some time and he was worried about her. Nathan wasn't sure how much she was going to be able to tell him or how much he could tell her about her parents. He didn't think the government would know if they knew each other, but he didn't want to take any chances. Nathan checked in his usual way…by sliding his library card to a librarian named Sheila with whom he was familiar. She signed to him that the bank of public computers was pretty well open, but he signed that he was not quite ready and wanted to look some things up first. What he was really doing was stalling until the appointed time he had agreed on with Emily.

Nathan had been surprised that his own family had not been the subject of an investigation. No men in black suits had come to the house with warrants. There were no interrogations in harshly lit, overly hot rooms. Nothing. That is not to say he was disappointed. He was relieved. And Nathan suspected his parents felt the same way. They had been friends with the Troys since he was seventeen. Their friendship with the family began almost immediately. The Troys were almost desperate for friends, especially Alma.

She had remained in a form of self-imposed seclusion for so long; she was willing to risk a little exposure to the outside world. It made Charles a bit nervous, but having friends seemed to relieve a lot of pent-up tension. Nathan had seen Emily on the first day and thought she was an angel. Light shimmered through her as if it were shining through crystal. She would have been beautiful to him even if she did not look so celestial. The connection between them was almost instantaneous and their mutual difficulties had blessed them with a level of wisdom beyond their years. They chose to keep their relationship a secret from their families. Nathan told his mother that he had been mistaken about seeing an angel. He signed to her that it was a trick of the light and he didn't see her anymore. A few months later, when the Troys confessed their secret about Emily, the Saunders thought it better to keep Nathan and his brother Jimmy out of that particular loop…Jimmy especially. His mouth had a mind of its own and he often spoke without thinking.

Nathan and Emily worked out a way of signing to each other without being noticed. Nathan would conceal his hands with a large book when he signed and he spelled out words that would require large gestures. Sometimes, Emily would pass him notes she had written and he would write notes back to her, pretending he was doing homework. Their system was foolproof and neither of the sets of parents caught on, or they shielded themselves in denial the way a lot of parents do. Sometimes Nathan would go for walks and Emily would join him. Their relationship progressed the way a normal teenage relationship usually progresses. He would sign to her *why not?* She would sign back *because I'm just not ready.* It didn't matter. In reality, he wanted to wait. He wanted their first time to be perfect and, to be totally honest, he wasn't quite sure what to do. His parents had never had *the talk* with him. *The talk* was awkward enough for parents. It was even more so when it had to be done with sign language. Emily's parents had the same dilemma and were also in denial that their little girl would even think of such things. They were in no hurry to burst the pristine bubble they had encased her in.

Emily helped Nathan with his math problems and he helped her with computer tech stuff. He was a bit of a hacker and was able to install an IP block on her computer so their conversations couldn't be traced. That way, their parents would not be able to view their notes to each other and they would be able to communicate freely. That was liberating for both of them. They felt normal for the first time in their lives. By the time both of them turned eighteen, they had a solid foundation for their relationship; and without sex. Sex would have ruined it as it does with a lot of relationships. Instead, they took time to enjoy the romance and learning about each other.

Nathan tried to look as casual as possible in the library, but he was bursting with anticipation for Emily's message. He looked though a selection of computer technical reference materials, but he was familiar with all of it. He could have written many of the books he looked through. He designed webpages for a few of the kids at school and even for a couple of the teachers. He had a natural talent for creating abstract, eye-catching design. Nathan liked to include subtle details that only the observant viewer would notice. Sometimes, he would create a backdoor link into the background so he could remotely access control of the site. He didn't want to do anything nefarious; he just liked knowing that he could if he wanted. Most of the time, he still had the passwords to the sites anyway. People trusted Nathan and he never blatantly betrayed that trust.

He moved on to the classic science fiction section while casually checking his watch. He loved the works of Jules Verne, but H. G. Wells was his favorite author. He ran his finger along the titles and stopped on one in particular; *The Invisible Man*. Nathan had read the book before he met Emily. He was not very old at the time and some of the words and phrases were difficult for him due to their Victorian English spellings and syntax. He got the gist of the story though. It was also tragic in its conclusion, as much of the literature of that time period was. Nathan did not want anything bad to happen to Emily. He wanted to protect her. He imagined her in the role of the protagonist in The Invisible Man, being hounded by police and townspeople; being betrayed by those she had trusted. Tears formed in the corners of his eyes and he wiped them while looking around to make sure no one had noticed. As he did, he noticed his watch. He was late. He went back to the information desk, trying not to look too anxious and gave Sheila his card and pointed to the bank of computers. She smiled, gave his card back and motioned him to an empty chair in front of a friendly screen with a friendly library logo serving as its wallpaper. Nathan sat down, tried to log in and ran into trouble right away. The computer did not recognize his log in keystrokes. He tried again. Nothing. He slowly and deliberately pressed the keys to log in one more time; fearing he would get locked out for too many failed attempts. He held his breath as he struck the last key. The screen went black.

There was a slight flicker and a WELCOME screen appeared asking Nathan to agree to the library's policies and restrictions. He selected the appropriate response and clicked ACCEPT. He quickly entered the information for his backup email address. The one he and Emily used…the one that no one but they knew about. There were six messages from someone named Kyle. Nathan opened the first one not sure what to expect.

Hey buddy. What's up? I know you haven't seen me in a while, so I just thought I would touch base with

you and maybe set up a meet. It would be great to see you again. E...mail me.

The text seemed strange to Nathan and at first he thought it might be a mistake. He did his computer magic and checked the IP address. He did not recognize it and it wasn't a different library. He was about to delete it when he noticed a couple of things that seemed out of place. The way the letters were separated in Email and the mention of *you haven't seen me in a while* and not *we haven't seen each other*. He felt comfortable that it was from Emily. Nathan opened the other emails and each had the same cryptic phrasing, but each seemed progressively more frantic. He responded right away.

Kyle! You are right! It seems like forever since I last saw you. What have you been up to? Yes, it would be great to see you again. We have got to get together. Just name the time and the place. N

An Instant Message box came up in the corner of the screen.

```
K: Finally!  Where have you been?
N: Sorry... I got hung up.  What's
   with the IP?
K: I got a new computer... from a
   guy.  Still getting used to it.
N: Okay.  When and where can we
   meet?
K: I was thinking we could go see
   a movie.
N: That would be great.  When?
```

```
K: I was thinking Wednesday,
about eight.
N: But that is two days away!
K: I know, but I need to make
some arrangements.
N: I understand.  I will just
meet you there then.
K: Do you know anything about…
```

Emily was going to delete the last line, but hit ENTER by mistake. Nathan caught her meaning and responded anyway.

```
N: Yes.  I know a little.  I will
tell you when I see you.
K: Okay.  I can't wait.  It will be
great.  Same time tomorrow.
N. Sure.  That will be fine.
```

"K" went offline. Nathan stared at the dialog box for a moment before clicking the X in the corner. He wanted to tell Emily to be careful. He wanted to tell her how much he missed her. But he knew they had to be careful. There was only a slight chance that the government might be monitoring their conversation, but an even less chance of being discovered with Emily using a fake male persona. Now he was going to have to wait two days to see her. It was going to be a long two days, but he would see her soon at *the movie.* He knew exactly where she meant; the abandoned drive-in at the edge of town. They used to meet there sometimes when they wanted to be alone. Nathan wasn't sure what kind of arrangements Emily needed to make, but he suspected it had to do with transportation and he didn't want to ask too many questions. Two days was a long time to wait, but Emily was worth it.

Nathan logged onto a couple of sites of interest to him, mostly gaming sites. He attempted access to a porn site that was blocked by the library. He only did that to throw off anyone that might try to investigate him. Then he deleted his browser history as another way of covering his tracks. His time was up on the computer anyway. Sheila would have let him continue well beyond the half hour limit, but Nathan didn't want to abuse the privilege. He waved at her and signed *thank you* as he left. He was excited but tried not to act like it. He forced himself to slow his pace and behave more casually. He headed home which would have been the normal thing to do. Today, however, he needed to discuss something with his parents; something that was long overdue.

Nathan really didn't expect his father to be home yet when he arrived. He wanted to talk to his mother first, alone. David was not Nathan's biological father and had grown to resent the attention the boy received from Sue. Nathan's father had died in Afghanistan before he and Sue could get married. He was scheduled to come home while Sue was still in her first trimester, but was delayed due to a rise in casualties and a drop in recruiting quotas. He was killed by a roadside bomb somewhere in the Kandahar province while scouting for insurgent strongholds. Sue nearly miscarried when she first got the notice. She had heard of casualties on the evening news and somehow in her heart, she knew Nathan's father was among them. But she continued to hope against hope that it was not true right up until she was notified in person by the commanding officer of the local National Guard. She kept the tri-folded American flag that had draped his casket on a bookshelf in the living room, along with his picture and several of his medals.

Nathan was proud of the father he had never known, but still admired David for stepping up and raising him as his own. At first, David was an excellent dad. He gave Nathan his last name, in spite of a mild protest by Sue. When he and Sue were notified that Nathan was deaf and probably would be for life, he took it all in stride. He learned sign language with Sue and helped teach it to Nathan when he was little. David was never as proficient at it as Sue was and the stress of learning it and maintaining a family wore on him over the years. When Jimmy came along, he basically lost interest in Nathan. Jimmy was healthy, unimpaired and shared David's DNA. Nathan became more of an annoyance to him. He didn't keep up with his sign language, but managed to retain enough to discipline Nathan and order him around. Each time he did, David would look over at the memorial on the bookshelf and grimace. Sue never said anything, but each time he did it, it strengthened her resolve to keep the items right where they were.

Where have you been? David signed in a manner that made it obvious that he was annoyed. He really didn't care; he just felt like giving Nathan trouble.

I was at the library, he signed back. *Is mom around? I need to talk to her about something.*

Talk? David signed back with a smirk.

You know what I mean, signed Nathan with a scowl. *Is she here?*

Are you giving me lip? David smirked again knowing he had just insulted Nathan. *You know I don't like that.* Nathan took the higher road and ignored the insult. *Sorry*, he signed. *Will you please tell me?* Sue walked into the living room at that moment and signed, *Tell you what, Nathan?* Nathan frowned because he had humbled to David for nothing. Also, he didn't really want to have this conversation with both of them at the same time. He averted his eyes to the bookshelf indicating he had something to discuss about his biological father. David threw up his hand and went back to reading his Kindle. He suspected Nathan had found some interesting bit of information about his father at the library and David didn't really want to hear about it. He hated having to compete with a dead man. David had swooped in like a hero to rescue Sue from a life of single motherhood and he did not feel properly appreciated. He resented Nathan and he resented his father. David even allowed his ego to convince him that Sue had trapped him into the marriage. It wasn't true, but no one would ever be able to convince David otherwise.

Sue motioned for Nathan to come into the kitchen and he followed her obediently; glad to be out of the atmosphere of judgment he felt in the living room. Once in the kitchen, he signed to her that he really didn't want to talk about his father. His mother gave him a questioning look. Nathan paused for a long time, checked to make sure David hadn't entered the room and then signed, *It's about Emily.*

Sue turned pale and swallowed hard. She wasn't sure how to respond. She tried to form the beginnings of several questions. Sue didn't think he really knew about Emily and when she and her family disappeared, she was glad he didn't.

What about Emily? she signed finally. Nathan paused again. *I could always see her*, he signed.

When you say "see her"... Sue used air quotes as she signed. Nathan answered her before she finished. *I mean I can see her. I always could. Remember? I thought she was an angel.*

I just thought you had a vivid imagination, she signed. *I am sorry we tried to keep her secret from you, but her parents thought it best...and given that they have all disappeared, I think they were right in doing so. Why are you bringing Emily up?*

Because she needs my help, Nathan signed. A tear rested on the lower lid of his left eye. *I think the government took her and she got away. She wants to find her parents. Do you know anything about what happened to them?* Sue looked around as if she expected government agents to burst through the door at any moment. *I think it is best if we just stay out of it, Nathan... for everybody's safety.*

I can't, signed Nathan. *She needs my help... and... I love her.* This time it was Sue's lower eyelid that had a tear resting upon it. Another joined it and they trailed down her cheek. She had always hoped that Nathan would find love. She knew that when he did, it would be complicated; she just never expected it to be THIS complicated. She hugged him and kissed him on the cheek.

I am afraid I don't know anything about Emily's parents, she signed after a long pause. *There were some people that were seen around town after they disappeared; people that no one recognized but who looked pretty normal. They asked a few questions, mostly about casual things. But they seemed pretty interested in the Troys and a couple spent a lot of time in Dr. Cornell's office. A couple of nights ago, his office was robbed. People said it was kids looking for drugs, but I suspect it was the strangers. I think they were gathering information on Emily.*

Do you think they found anything? signed Nathan.

I don't know. All I know is that after the break-in, no one saw them again. I wish I could be more help. Sue hugged him again. As she did, David came into the kitchen wondering what they could be talking about. He didn't want to hear any more about Nathan's father, but he didn't like being left out of the loop either. He felt that the more Sue built him up, the more inferior he would look in Nathan's eyes. Sue expected David to be coarse and angry, but he was congenial and in a good mood. His personality was a bit on the bipolar side; except Nathan thought David could probably control which side he wanted to be on. When it served his purpose, he could be the best guy ever. But most of the time, he spent on the other side...the dark side. With a knowing look, Sue let Nathan know they would conclude their conversation later. They didn't need to make any explanations to David. He thought he knew what they were talking about and was glad to be spared the details. Nathan signed to them that he was going back out. His mother signed for him to be extra careful. David smiled sardonically and just waved.

Nathan walked to the middle of Cedar Pike. The four-way stop on Main Street marked where the middle was. There were not a lot of shops on Main, but those that were there had been there for a long time. A major hardware chain had located near the highway, intent on driving the local mom & pop store out of business. They never expected the customer loyalty the rural town maintained. The huge store closed within a year despite its prime location and the mom & pop store endured. Bisecting Main Street near the four-way stop was a dual set of train tracks. They did not belong to a main line, but trains still stopped traffic on them once in a while. Occasionally, someone would not be paying attention to the flashing lights and warning bell. Sometimes, there was a near miss; sometimes there was a funeral.

Nathan veered from Main Street when he got to the tracks. He had been warned not to walk along the tracks because he could not hear a train coming, but today he threw caution to the wind. Well, mostly to the wind. He walked on a path beside the track. If a train came along, it might startle him if he didn't feel the vibration beforehand; but he was not foolish enough to walk in the middle of the tracks. He also knew what to look for with the signal lights. Green for instance, meant that the track was clear. That was great for the train, but not for someone on the track. A red signal would indicate to stop because the track was blocked up ahead. Nathan was not sure what different combinations meant, but he knew the important ones. After a quarter of a mile, another double set of tracks intersected the first one. Nathan looked a little like a first grader as he checked both ways twice for each track. Then he carefully stepped over the tracks, making sure to avoid the switches on the other track. He had seen movies in which someone had gotten their ankle trapped at just the wrong time and he wasn't going to let that happen to him. After another half mile, the two tracks parted ways and Nathan took the track to the left. It passed through a wooded area, cutting a precise swath between the trees. The branches of the larger trees formed a high canopy over the tracks and Nathan felt like he was in a tunnel. The feeling was unnerving and exhilarating at the same time. He hadn't noticed that his pace had quickened, so he slowed down to keep his calm.

    He stopped on the end of a tie for a moment and cleared his head. Beneath his feet, Nathan could feel a slight vibration through the wooden tie. He touched the steel rail and was sure he could feel electricity as the vibration traveled up his arm. He wondered if others could feel it or if he was especially tuned to it because of his deafness. Ahead, the track curved and disappeared in the woods. He looked behind him to see if he could see the light from a train. At first he thought it was just the reflection of the sun on the polished tracks, but then it began to grow more intense. As Nathan stood and stared at it, he became mesmerized by it like a bird caught in the gaze of a serpent. The intensity began to hurt his eyes. The light was so bright. The vibration grew stronger and Nathan liked the experience. It was the closest thing he had to hearing. The vibration turned to a rumble and the light took on the likeness of the sun. Its beams blocked everything else out. The rumble felt like an earthquake. The railroad tie he stood on began to shake. Nathan felt hot wind push against his face. Tiny specks of rock stung his check and he threw up his hand to block them. In doing so, the spell was broken and Nathan dropped to the side of the track just two and one-half seconds before the freight train bound for Cedar Rapids and points east rumbled past him. The engineer could be seen through the open window of the engine yelling what was probably every expletive in his vocabulary. He was shaking his fist and shaking his head. His last gesture was to extend his arm out the window and extend his middle finger.

    Nathan sat on the ground as tons and tons of freight train thundered past him. He couldn't imagine the noise it must be making. The markings on the freight cars were little more than blurs to him and the motion made him dizzy. He panned his vision in time with the movement of the cars and he could read a few of them. He noticed the elaborate graffiti on a few of the cars and wondered if the artist even considered applying his talent to something more lucrative than vandalism. Sometimes, he thought, people just do art for the sake of art. The rush of wind that had probably saved his life had been pushed ahead by the engine. As the last car passed, another gust of wind was carried in its wake. Nathan watched the last car pass and then stared at its flashing red light until it disappeared around the curve. As he sat there next to the tracks, he tried to avoid thinking about his near miss. He got to his feet and his knees did not want to support him. Nathan vetoed their protest and forced himself to begin walking. Around the curve, the canopy of branches overhead became denser, but it was somehow relaxing. He thought of what the engineer must have been thinking when he saw him. He must have been blowing the train whistle continuously while trying to apply the brake. He must have thought Nathan was on drugs. Nathan wished for a moment that he could have the opportunity to defend his actions.

Nathan's knees stopped their protesting and he used his new reserve of adrenalin to speed ahead. Soon he was out of the trees and harvested wheat fields stretched out on both sides of the track. In the distance, Nathan could see what was left of the weather-beaten outdoor movie screen and the roof of the abandoned concession stand. Nathan thought that checking out their meeting place ahead of time might be a good idea. Besides, he wanted to get away from David whenever he could. He remembered how David used to be and he loved *that* David. *That* David hadn't been around for some time. The landscape on each side of the track dropped a few feet and Nathan walked on the path beside it. Ahead was a row of eight windbreaker trees. Three of them were dead, but they all still towered majestically in the near-dusk light. They had probably been planted to protect the movie screen from the strong winds that swept across the fields.

Nathan left the path and crossed the harvested field to the drive-in. When he reached the windbreakers, he saw movement and dropped to one knee. He could see a car parked near the boarded-up concession stand and someone walking from it. The individual pulled open a plywood sheet that was serving as a door and disappeared inside. There was the old box office near the rusting frame of the old marquis. Its windows had been broken out long ago and the door hung on one hinge. A black SUV drove past it, throwing up dust as it went. It cut across the rows of speakerless speaker posts and bottomed out twice. It threw up dust and gravel as it skidded to a stop. The driver rushed inside the same door as the individual before. Nathan wasn't sure what to do. He knew it had to do with Emily and he was certain that, somehow in spite of his precautions, they had intercepted her messages to him. He began to breathe rapidly and was working himself into a panic. He couldn't think. He needed to calm down. He put his hand in his mouth and bit down on the space between his thumb and index finger. He was sure he had drawn blood, but he had only succeeded in making a decent impression of his bite pattern. His breathing steadied and he began to think more rationally.

Nathan knew he needed to warn Emily, but he also needed to know what they knew. They HAD to be government. If they were just ravers or vandals, they would not be in identical SUVs. The shadows of the windbreakers stretched across the drive-in lot and across the roof of the concession stand. It would be dark soon. Nathan thought that might give him an opportunity to find something out. Even though he couldn't hear, he could still read lips. It was only a matter of obtaining a line of sight but remaining undetected.

He rounded the fence row around the border of the drive-in. His intention was to approach from a blind side, if there was one. Whoever was inside would probably be expecting someone to come from the main drive. Nathan thought that might work to his advantage. He managed his way around to the framework of the screen. The rusty playground equipment stood like a monument to some kind of apocalypse. The wooden seesaw had rotted and broken into a chevron shape. Rusty chains hung from the swings and the slide looked as though just sitting on it would be a reason to get a tetanus shot. The last orange glow disappeared from the western horizon and darkness covered the lot. Nathan hoped he was moving silently as he carefully made his way to the snack bar. A dull yellow glow escaped from the edges of the plywood nailed to the windows. He was within twenty feet of the snack bar when a pale glow illuminated one of the SUVs. A black silhouette emerged from the plywood door and walked towards the front of the snack bar. Nathan froze…sure that he had been detected. The silhouette stopped for a moment, then opened another plywood sheet and disappeared behind it. Nathan could barely make out the faded stenciled letters on the side of the building: MEN.

Nathan moved to the only window that was not completely nailed shut. It was one of two small openings in the projector room. A small square of plywood hung askew on a single nail. He moved like a shadow to the opening and slowly peeked inside. A row of folding cots were lined along one wall. A man was handing out Styrofoam containers from a diner near the highway. He was saying something, but he had food in his mouth and Nathan couldn't make it out. Two others were sitting in folding chairs. One of them was bound with zip-ties. The other mouthed the words, "Maybe we should feed him first." Then he lit a cigarette in spite of several state laws and fire codes forbidding it. In the glow of the lighter, Nathan could make out the face of the prisoner. It was Charles Troy!

CHAPTER 8: MOVING NORTH

Emily liked Dr. Cornell. He seemed more like a family member than the family doctor. He went out of his way to keep the family healthy…even if it meant running tests that were not covered by their insurance. He was always sensitive to Emily's suffering and sincerely felt bad when he had to hurt her. He tried not to be too invasive, but the nature of her condition required it sometimes. He took detailed notes and filled countless college-ruled notebooks with his handwritten observations. He said he was going to transfer them to his hard drive, but Emily suspected he never did. After more than a decade of study, he was no closer to finding a cure for her condition than when he ran his first test. Dr. Cornell managed to determine the cause of her condition, but it was locked into Emily's DNA. He was unable to replicate it due to his limited resources; modifying it required a controlled environment that was nearly devoid of any moisture in the air. Even then, she appeared as little more than a shadow or a reflection of light. Those tests left her dehydrated and weak, so he put them on hold.

However, Dr. Cornell never gave up. Several times he returned to "square one" to see if he had missed anything. He thought that he might be looking too closely at the problem and should start over from scratch. He hired a young doctor who had just finished her residency at the county hospital to take care of much of his workload so he could devote more time to Emily. Her name was Bethany Hertz. Dr. Hertz was an unfortunate name for a physician, but she made up for it with an upbeat, compassionate bedside manner. Dr. Cornell never let her in on Emily's secret and she never asked any uncomfortable questions. She seemed content to be part of a real practice…even if it was in a small town like Cedar Pike. She liked the people and the relaxed atmosphere. Dr. Cornell was left free to pursue his study of Emily's condition; that is, until he disappeared.

* * * * * *

"It's doing it again mom!" said Paige.

"Doing what again?" asked Ellen.

"It says someone is using the Wi-Fi on our phone."

"Probably a glitch," said Ellen. "We are on the highway. Anyway, if someone is using it, they won't use it for very long. The signal isn't THAT strong." Paige shrugged and went back to playing Candy Crush.

Emily sat at the kitchen table of the dimly lit fifth-wheel trailer as it was being pulled down the highway by a dark blue Silverado. The trailer was a little cramped when the pullouts were retracted, but she didn't mind. She was surprised when the laptop before her glowed as it detected a Wi-Fi signal. Emily thought she would have to wait until the next travel center before she would be able to contact Nathan.

She had overheard Ellen and her daughter discussing their new life in Des Moines while at the travel center in Kansas City. She was able to discern that budget cuts necessitated the need to move and that the divorce from Paige's dad had been messy and hateful. Emily had felt a warm glow of appreciation for her own parents while at the same time, feeling pity and compassion for the two troubled people in the next booth. From their conversation she learned that Ellen had won custody of Paige (who was nine), as well as the truck and the fifth-wheel in the divorce. They would begin a new life in Des Moines and the trailer would give them a place to live. The house the family had shared was upside down with a second mortgage and they agreed to let the bank take it. Ellen's now ex-husband reluctantly agreed to pay off the balance not covered by the foreclosure.

The trailer wheels ran over a large chunk of tire left on the road by a blowout from an 18-wheeler. The laptop left the surface of the table and came back down with a clump sound. The screen instantly went black and Emily froze. Nathan had not yet contacted her and she didn't want to lose the only link between them. She examined the damage and discovered that the bump had dislodged the laptop battery. She quickly reinserted it and waited for the system to boot up. While she was waiting, she raided the refrigerator. The contents were meager and Emily didn't want to impose too much on the mother and daughter in the truck ahead. She decided on a cold hotdog and a slice of bread that had gone beyond its freshness date. She sat back down at the computer and connected to the Wi-Fi signal again. She checked the covert email she had created to talk to Nathan. There were no new emails except for some spam that promised amazing results for curing erectile dysfunction. Emily suspected that had something to do with "Kyle's" browser history.

She began to worry about Nathan. He was always so punctual and organized. He considered it a personal defeat to be the least bit late. The very least he would have done was send an email of some kind. The battery life on the laptop showed it was down to 28%. Emily had tried plugging into the power source, but there was no power to the trailer unless the generator was started; and that would raise suspicions. The refrigerator ran on a propane source when the power was off. Emily leaned over a counter to look out a window and try to determine her location. It seemed like she had been on the road for a long time since breakfast, but the mile markers indicated that they were not yet near the Iowa border. She sighed and sat back down. She knew it would probably be a long time before she could find electricity for the power source and she thought she should probably save what power she had left until a time when Nathan would most likely be online. Emily was about to shut down when she noticed a small one in parentheses in her email tab. She opened her email and was so excited to see Nathan's fake name in the column that she clicked on the wrong line and opened the erectile dysfunction email. She mentally cursed not having deleted it and tried again. Nathan's words were in all capital letters and looked like something out of a spy novel: LOCATION COMPROMISED. DO NOT ATTEMPT CONTACT YET. WILL SEND ALTERNATE LOCATION WHEN I AM SURE IT IS SAFE.

An electrical shock went through Emily. The message was cold, terse and cryptic. That did not seem like Nathan. Her mind began to run through all of the possibilities and none of them were pleasant. She wondered if the email was from Nathan at all or some government person setting a trap. She thought they might be holding Nathan hostage and forcing him to send the message, since even he did not know her exact location. White spots appeared before her eyes and she realized she had been holding her breath. She forced herself to breathe slowly and relax. The thought came to her that if they knew where she was, they would not have bothered with Nathan. That thought gave Emily confidence that Nathan was alright, but that he was troubled by something. If their meeting place at the drive-in was compromised, that meant that agents were in Cedar Pike and they suspected she would return there. Still, Emily felt that she should be cautious. She thought for a moment and then sent a return email.

Buddy...what's with all the drama? It's not like our plans were chiseled in stone or anything. We can set another place. Seriously, I think your parents watch over you too closely considering your age. They still treat you like a baby. I have to go right now, but I will email you later... same time if I can. If I can't, I will let you know. Later dude.

Emily waited to see if Nathan would read between her lines. A few moments later another email arrived.

You are right, of course. My parents bug me to death sometimes. Guess I just needed to vent a little. We will talk later. N.

It was going to be a long day, but she relaxed a bit knowing that Nathan seemed okay. The power indicator showed that the battery was down to 16% and she wanted to save it just in case. Emily shut the computer down and placed it back in the case. She moved to the sofa in the retracted living room of the trailer and stared out the window. She played a game with herself, trying to spot a license plate from farthest away. Each time she would spot one that was from a place farther than the last, she would create a story in her head of where they were going and why. Sometimes a mental conversation between the occupants of a car would go on inside her head.

Why in the world would you want to move us from Denver to Iowa? Karl? Are you even listening to me?

I'm sorry. Did you say something Evelyn? I was busy ignoring you. How thoughtless and inconsiderate of me to try to enjoy some peace and quiet. I am such a jerk.

Your sarcasm isn't funny you know. You think it is, but it isn't.

I think it's pretty funny.

You are a jerk. You said it yourself.

I was being sarcastic. You said it YOURself.

There is just no talking to you.

I wish.

What did you say?

I said I wish...the traffic would lighten up. It would make the ride much more pleasant.

Yeah, right. Now that was sarcasm.

Oh, great! The traffic is stopped ahead. We get to enjoy each other's company while the car overheats.

Like that is my fault? Whose idea was it to move to Des Moines anyway?

Emily snapped out of the mental dialog. The traffic really was coming to a stop. Something was going on up ahead and it worried her. Every time she heard a siren or saw flashing lights, she was certain it was because the authorities were looking for her. Major paranoia seemed to be a side-effect of her captivity; that and the warnings her parents had impressed on her about keeping her secret. They would never have approved of her relationship with Nathan. At least, she thought they wouldn't approve. They were very protective. She now wished she had given them the chance.

The traffic moved at a snail's pace...if the snail took frequent breaks and cursed the cause of the delay. Emily could see restless children fighting, playing and just looking out the windows of various vehicles on the steaming, newly laid asphalt. The parents of the children tried to keep them occupied, but with no success. It was tough enough to transport kids when the traffic was running smoothly; but when it was stalled, it was next to impossible. Those with DVD players showed movies made by Pixar or some other creator of children's programming. One unfortunate driver must have forgotten to bring his kids' favorites and had resorted to playing an orientation DVD he had from work. It did the opposite of pacifying his children. Emily felt sorry for him. She was even thinking of using her invisibility to help him out. She was about to go outside and knock on the windows to distract the kids when the door of the fifth-wheel opened, flooding the trailer with light. Emily nearly panicked as the silhouette of an individual filled the doorway. She relaxed when Paige entered and made her way to the refrigerator. The young girl took two diet sodas from the door, looked through the shelves to see if anything appealed to her and then closed it…making sure it was latched. Paige stopped for a moment, having the eerie feeling that she was being watched. Emily was still holding her breath. White spots were appearing before her eyes again. Paige gave the slightest of shrugs and went back to the truck. Emily had just breathed out when the door opened again and then closed hard because the step had not retracted properly the first time. Paige had to help it with her foot.

The traffic began to move at about fifteen miles per hour, which seemed like racing down the road compared to the complete standstill they had been experiencing. Ahead, Emily could see the reason for the delay. There had been a perfect storm of road construction coupled with an accident that had blocked the only accessible lane on the highway. The truck and trailer merged into the open lane because of the kindness of an older gentleman and his wife who happened to be named Karl and Evelyn. Emily looked ahead at all the flashing lights. An ambulance sat on a slight slant along the side of the road. A man with a fresh bandage around his head seemed to be explaining something to an officer. Behind him was a yellow late-model Mustang. The hood was tragically crumpled to a point that it totally obscured the windshield. Next to it was a blue Volvo with a crushed rear quarter panel. The trunk was sprung at an askew angle and the rear bumper was lying on the ground. Inside the ambulance, a body was covered completely by a sheet. Emily felt guilty for fretting about the delay. She accepted that things could be much worse and continued to observe the scene.

More flashing lights and road flares lined the road. A police officer, probably a deputy sheriff, was wearing a wide-brimmed hat and was motioning traffic to move along. He was wearing what Emily thought might be special dark glasses instead of the mirrored Ray-Bans she had seen on TV. She ducked back behind the curtain as he looked at the window and she held her breath again. Emily decided that she really needed to learn to control her breathing. After they had passed him and she felt it was safe to look out again, she looked back. He reached up and touched the earpiece of his glasses and she thought he might be adjusting the settings. Her paranoia was in overdrive.

A quarter of a mile later the single line of traffic spread out onto the three open lanes before it. To Emily, it felt like being freed from captivity. She continued to look back however, fearing an approach of federal agents intent on taking her into custody once again. The agents never appeared and soon they crossed over into Iowa. Emily felt a strange mixture of relief and foreboding that comes with not knowing what the future holds. She concentrated on all things positive and practiced her breathing control. She stiffened as she felt the trailer lurch forward and change lanes abruptly. She looked out the window to see if there was a roadblock, another accident or if they were being pulled over. It was none of the above. Ellen must have decided to make an unscheduled gas station stop. She ran over the painted lines of the exit and cut off a teenager in a Kia that cursed her and made a lot of unfamiliar hand gestures. When Ellen got to the first light after the exit, he pulled up next to her and motioned for her to roll her window down. She pretended not to see him and when the light changed, he pulled in front of her and applied his brakes. When Ellen didn't look like she was stopping, he sped up to avoid being crushed in his little car. He hadn't considered the stopping distance of a large truck pulling a large trailer and figured he was no match for the size and weight. He gave her the finger as he drove away and Ellen just waved with a friendly smile. She pulled into the gas station and up to the pump. It was one of the pumps that could reach both sides of a vehicle no matter which side of the pump it was on. This was fortunate because Ellen was going to fill both the main and the reserve tank this time; something she had failed to do at the last fuel stop. She breathed a little sigh of relief that she had made it. A Silverado pulling a fifth-wheel did not get great gas mileage and she was coasting on fumes as she pulled into the station.

Paige went inside to look for snacks while Ellen was fueling the truck. Emily cautiously opened the door of the trailer and peeked out. While Ellen had her back turned, she opened the door wider and stepped out. The automatic step engaged and Ellen turned around sharply to see an open door and the step extended. "Dammit Paige..." she muttered under her breath. She tried not to be too hard on Paige. Her daughter was going through a lot. Not only was her family unit shattered, but she had to pack up and leave everything behind that she knew; and all at the critical age of nine years old. Nine was an especially difficult age for a girl. Her body began to change and not in a way she wanted. Paige felt gawky and her mood changed constantly. She needed stability in her life and that had been ripped from her. Emily related to this and could have told her some stories, but she wouldn't get the chance. Before long, they would part ways. Ellen and Paige would never know they had transported a fugitive across state lines.

Emily went into the gas station convenience store to look around. She was tired of the road and needed a little distraction. Inside, the air was cool because of an air conditioner that did not know how to adjust to the unseasonably warm weather. Emily "borrowed" a bottle of spring water, a banana, a chicken salad sandwich wrapped in cellophane and a solar cellphone charger that she thought might come in handy. She really wanted a slice of pizza that she saw in the case behind the counter. It smelled so good and looked even better. However, she was sure she could not navigate the narrow aisle behind the counter without being detected. Maybe at the next stop, she thought. She could also use a change of clothes, but this convenience store did not have a lot to offer in that department. She was about to leave and head back to the trailer when a state trooper came through the door.

Emily froze like a kid who had found the magazine in his dad's sock drawer. The trooper was wearing what looked like special dark glasses. He didn't take them off as he looked around the convenience store. He panned across the interior and stopped. He was looking directly at Emily. He touched the earpiece of the glasses and began walking straight toward her. She began to shiver. She didn't want to go back, especially after coming this far. The trooper walked a little faster and was less than two feet from her when she stepped to the side and bumped into a man holding a bag of chips and a gigantic fountain drink. "Excuse me officer," the man said in a sarcastic tone. The trooper didn't appear to notice. He continued to walk and took the glasses off when he got to a refrigerated case. He opened it and took out a bottle of orange soda. He then closed the door to the case, looked around in the reflection in the glass, put his glasses back on and proceeded to the register. He paid for his drink and left though a group of customers that parted like the Red Sea for Moses. The trooper looked back once after he was outside and then was gone.

Emily was frightened. She wasn't sure why. He apparently hadn't seen her or he would have taken her into custody right then. But there was something nagging at her. She couldn't put her finger on it, but something was really wrong. She looked around cautiously as she left the convenience store and carefully made her way back to the fifth-wheel. She looked around a few more times before she dared to open the door again and get back inside. Emily didn't feel safe even after the latch to the door was secure. She sat on the couch once again and nearly jumped out of her skin when the door opened and Paige came in with a two-liter bottle of diet root beer. She placed it in the larger lower door shelf of the refrigerator and went back out. Emily could hear Ellen telling her to make sure the door was closed this time in a way that seemed less like an admonishment and more like a public service announcement. Paige opened the door and closed it hard…twice. Emily heard the step retract and the engine of the Silverado start. It made her feel a little better, but she would not feel very secure until they were on the road again.

Getting back to the highway seemed like it was taking forever. The traffic signals that were on a thirty-second timer seemed like they were taking every bit of ten minutes. As they finally made their way down the on-ramp of the highway, Emily started to relax and process what had happened. She began to assess what might be fact and what might be paranoia. There was no evidence to suggest that the dark glasses worn by the trooper were *special* dark glasses. After all, he had walked right past her. He was probably just a state trooper who needed a refreshing orange soda. He probably got one every day at the same time. It may have been part of his routine. Emily began to feel better, but her mind kept running though the event…like a YouTube video running on a loop. The fourth time it played in her head, she saw what she had missed. She saw the thing that was troubling her in the back of her mind. The patch on his uniform said Missouri Highway Patrol. They were in Iowa.

"Hello, Emily," said a voice from the shadows.

CHAPTER 9: SO CLOSE

Emily bolted for the door of the trailer, but it was too late. The Silverado was already headed down the highway. The speed was too fast to risk jumping from a moving vehicle.

"It wouldn't matter anyway Emily," said the man in the shadows. "We have people following us that would have picked you up as soon as you got out the door." Emily closed the door of the fifth-wheel hard. She heard the step retract under her feet. The man in the shadows moved into the dim light of the kitchenette. He was tall, had broad shoulders and was wearing special dark glasses. Emily signed to him, *Why can't you just leave me alone?*

"I'm sorry," he said. "I was assigned to this case because of my tracking skills. I am afraid I don't read sign language." Emily threw up her hands and considered the door once more.

"From what I understand, you have obtained a way to verbally communicate. Maybe you could use that. We have a little time to chat. That is, unless you want to involve your unwitting adopted family in the Silverado." The calmness in the man's voice was as unnerving as it was hypnotic. Emily really didn't like him. She sat down on the couch heavily, reached in her pocket and placed the voice generator on her throat.

"What do you…?" Emily adjusted the generator until the voice sounded less like Christopher Walken and more like Scarlett Johansson. She wanted to sound feminine, yet tough.

The controls were surprisingly easy to work and after a couple of test words, she was ready to continue. "What do you want to talk about?" The man in the shadows was a bit impressed by the sultry quality of her manufactured voice.

"To start with," he said as he slid into the bench seat of the kitchen table, "I would like to know who you have been in contact with. Whoever it is seems to be a genius at keeping his (or hers) IP address cloaked. We might even want to recruit him." Emily forced herself not to smile. She was very proud of Nathan at that moment and relieved that they did not know his identity.

"You really don't think I am going to give him (or her) up, do you?" asked Emily. She marveled at the way she sounded. She had never had a real girl's voice before. She wasn't even sure she could use inflections. Emily smiled at herself, but turned it into an ironic smile since she was dealing with a government thug.

"It was worth a try," said the man in the shadows. "After all, it might keep him from getting hurt later. You know, by accident." Emily hid her rising anger.

"So what are you going to do if I tell you?" she asked, matching his hypnotic tone.

"We will pick him up and question him," he said. "If he doesn't know too much, he will be released."

"Now why don't I believe you?" she countered.

"Trust is a hard thing to come by," he replied. "For instance, how did you manage to persuade anyone to help you escape from our facility? There is no way you could have done it on your own."

"Maybe you underestimate me," she responded. "Maybe there is more to me than meets the eye." Emily smiled ironically again.

"I see what you did there," he said. "Very clever. Somehow I don't think you could have convinced Dr. Spencer to help you, in spite of the evidence we found. Still, he has been placed on administrative leave and is on our watch list just in case." Emily had been hoping for a more severe form of punishment for Dr. Spencer, but she appreciated that something had happened to him.

"You're right," she said unconvincingly. "He had nothing to do with my escaping. I just stole his pass." The man in the shadows stared at Emily for a moment. She thought he had a curious expression on his face; as if he was trying to decide if she was lying or not. But it was hard to tell because of the special dark glasses.

"I suppose to find out what I need to know, I will need to use this." He took a small cylinder from his jacket pocket. He removed a syringe from it and discarded the plastic sheath protecting the needle.

"What's that?" asked Emily in a worried tone.

"A truth agent," said the man in the shadows. "It's a genetically engineered version of sodium amytal. It will relax you and make you as docile as a kitten." He held the syringe up and flicked the side with his finger to bring the bubbles to the top. A small trace of liquid spurted from the end of the needle. "Now if you cooperate, this will all be over in a few minutes and then you will sleep like a baby." He rose from the bench seat and moved toward Emily. She drew her legs up and adopted a fetal position for a moment. Then she seemed to give up. She pushed her sleeve up, closed her eyes and gritted her teeth in preparation for the needle. "That's good. Now just relax."

Emily stretched her arm out in defense. But instead of grabbing at the hand holding the needle, she reached up and ripped the special dark glasses from the face of the agent.

For the briefest of seconds, he was stunned. The image of the young girl before him had disappeared. His mind tried to process what he was seeing; or more accurately, what he wasn't seeing. That moment of hesitation was all that Emily needed. She twisted the needle from his hand during his confusion and jabbed it into his neck, injecting the chemical directly into his bloodstream. The substance was designed to enter the bloodstream slowly through muscle tissue. Being injected into a main artery caused the agent to go out like a light. Emily pulled the needle out, broke it off and deposited it in a small trash can that she knew was under the sink. Then she searched the agent and found what she was looking for...his radio and his wallet. His government ID didn't have an acronym that she would have recognized. It didn't have an acronym at all. It only had a symbol. The symbol was an eagle in a circle surrounded by black stars. On the eagle's chest was a black shield with a red chevron across the center. To the side was his picture and his name was printed below the symbol: AGENT BAXTER. She found his special dark glasses and smashed them on the counter with the bottom of a coffee cup. She took his firearm out of its holster and put it in her bag along with her laptop. She didn't like guns but she wasn't going to leave it for Paige to find; and she certainly wasn't going to let the man who was trying to drug her keep it.

Emily thought about what she needed to do. She knew the truck and the fifth-wheel were being followed and didn't seem to have many options. Then she began to think outside the box, since she was in a box of sorts. She played with the adjustments on the voice generator until she got the sound she wanted. She half-cleared her throat for the proper effect and spoke with slurred speech into the radio.

"This is Baxter... (pause) She...escaped," said Emily in the agent's voice.

"What?" said the voice over the radio. "That's impossible. We have been watching the whole time."

"She got the drop on me back at the...gas ssst...ation," she said. "Injected me with my ownnn...needle. She jumped out at the on-ramp."

"I'm telling you we would have seen her!" demanded the voice.

"Are you going to argue or are you going to find her?" said Emily.

"Do you want us to get you first?" the voice asked.

"I wouldn't be any use to you in the shape I'm in," Emily said smiling. "I probably won't even remember this conversation. Just come...back...and get... me when...you...find..." Emily trailed off hoping the voice on the other end of the radio would take the bait. Immediately after she ended her transmission, she heard a siren start up on the highway behind her. Ellen slowed the Silverado and the other cars on the highway pulled into the right lane. An Iowa State Trooper vehicle sped past them and threw up dust as it made a U-turn into the southbound lane using the utility road. It sped back to the gas station that was now twenty-five miles away. By the time Ellen got back up to speed, Emily was crouching in the ditch next to the highway, headed for the next exit.

The next exit was six miles away and Emily did not have that much time. She knew that the trooper could be back before she could get there. On the other side of the fence and across a half-harvested corn field, Emily could see the top of a white farmhouse. It seemed more promising to her than remaining on the highway. She scaled the rusty metal fence and sprinted across the harvested part of the field. Then she placed her arms out in front of her to separate a path in the corn stalks. The dried leaves rustled like wrapping paper on

Christmas morning. She just knew that someone was going to hear her, but the corn made a natural baffle and she really didn't have to worry about it until she got near the edge of the field.

Emily came out of the field before she realized it. She had been protecting her face from the cornstalks. She was faced with another farm fence, but it was not as high as the one next to the highway. It was attached to a tall galvanized post that was at least ten inches in diameter. Emily used it to support herself as she climbed the fence. It was open at the top and she got an idea. The post was about five feet tall and was probably used as a gatepost at one time. Emily took the government-issued automatic from her bag and dropped it into the opening. The post was half filled with water and the gun made a *glump* sound as it sank to the bottom. *Good luck finding that*, she thought.

Emily walked across the barn lot to the house. She felt a little more confident that she had eluded her pursuers, but she didn't want to take any chances. She needed to get undercover, but she needed to contact Nathan. She could call him if he was home. His family had installed a telephone that translates conversations into text, but Emily wasn't sure that would be safe. She might use it as a last resort, but for now she wanted to consider other options.

The tall white farmhouse reminded Emily a little of her own home. It was friendly looking and looked...stable. Lately, stability seemed somewhat lacking in her life. The barn was not very far from the house and she thought there might be a chance she could get a Wi-Fi signal; if these people had Wi-Fi. Their farm seemed like a picture perfect example of the 1950's. She huddled into a corner and opened the laptop. The power indicator said it was down to 12% and that she needed to plug into a power source. She saw an old outlet at the other end of the barn beneath a window. As she crept to it, a horse in a stall snorted and startled her. Emily hadn't even noticed a horse, but she had noticed the smell. She plugged the power source in and the battery began to charge. There was a Wi-Fi signal, but it was very weak. It addition, it was password protected and Emily decided it was a blessing in disguise. The government seemed to have traced her through her emails and instant messages. It was Nathan's skill at masking his IP addresses that allowed him to avoid detection. She decided that it might be time to part company with Kyle's laptop. She kept the power source just in case and took the laptop outside. She had noticed a burn pile across from the farm's gravel driveway. Emily used the laptop to dig a horizontal trench in the ash and slid it in. Then she scooped ash over it and patted it down with her hands. She wiped her hands on her sweatshirt, even though the act made her cringe.

Lunch or dinner was on the kitchen table when Emily feloniously entered the home. She wasn't sure which because she had lost track of time. She wasn't used to long road trips, so parts of it were exciting and seemed to pass by quickly; other parts seemed to drag. As it was, it was a little after four in the afternoon. Emily had missed her appointed time with Nathan and he would be worried. Maybe he had good reason to be. The government had been closer on her trail than Emily had suspected. She passed though the kitchen and seriously considered stealing a piece of cornbread from the table. Her stomach rumbled a little when she smelled the food. It wasn't her favorite. It was ham and cabbage, but she was pretty hungry. She made her way to the living room and found a computer on an open secretary. She quietly logged on and was relieved to discover that the computer saved the internet password. She sent Nathan an email by way of his secondary address. Emily knew it would be automatically forwarded to the primary address they had been using. He had set it up that way. His penchant for redundant security protocols was why he had not been detected yet. She knew she still had to be careful though. She thought for a few moments while occasionally looking over her shoulder toward the kitchen. The quaint farm couple talked over their events of the day while enjoying their early dinner. His name was Gary; hers was Dotty. They must have been the types to be in bed by dusk and up before dawn. Emily did not want to lead government agents to their peaceful home, but she needed to make sure Nathan knew the message was from her and yet remain undetected. Finally, she decided on the text.

Good News for those who suffer from E rectile Dysfunc T ion

Maybe you haven't heard of it, but it is a serious affliction. This patented medication has been proven to help patients in 90% of cases studied. Forget about the blue or yellow tablets. Our pink tablets are approved by the GOVERNMENT and SAFE for use.

We have a testimonial:

KYLE from Kansas says: This is the best thing that has ever happened to me. It has taken my life in a whole new direction.

So contact us RIGHT AWAY for your free sample. No obligation.

Emily would've liked to have been more clever, but she was afraid the message would get sent to Nathan's spam filter. That was why she avoided using a product name. She also hoped that Nathan would spot her initials in the subject line. Now she had to wait and hope Gary and Dotty did not finish their meal too soon.

Emily stared at the blank screen, waiting for a response. It hypnotized her to a point that when the response came back, she almost missed it. She never ceased to be amazed by Nathan's analytical brain. She opened the email and nearly gasped out loud. She was still wearing the voice generator and it was still set to Agent Baxter's voice. Emily turned it off and continued to read.

E. I have been so worried. I didn't hear from you and I thought something had happened. I have a lot to tell you. I saw your dad. The government has him. They are keeping him at the abandoned drive-in. He broke into Dr. Cornell's office to try to find your records before the government could get them. They think he got them already and are trying to find out where he hid them. No word on your mom. I hope she is safe. I don't know what we should do. Do you have any ideas?

Love. N.

Emily's eyes misted a little. Nathan didn't usually use the "L" word in his messages. He said it in sign language a few times, but seldom in writing. She was relieved that her dad was alive, but frightened because he was in custody. She wasn't sure what those people were capable of. It had been her intention to head in a different direction and have Nathan meet her in another state. This new development changed those plans. Her dad needed her and she still knew very little about her mother. Emily was still a hundred and sixty miles from Cedar Pike if she went by the main interstates; less if she used a network of state highways. Freight trains going to Cedar Rapids passed through the town, but that would be risky. Even if she could board one, she would have to be sure it was the right one; and getting off of it could prove to be problematic. An email popped up on the screen.

Any ideas? was all it said.

I'm thinking, she typed back.

Emily looked at the subject lines on Gary and Dotty's computer. From what she could tell without opening them, they were in the market to buy livestock; specifically, a stud bull. They appeared a little desperate. That gave Emily an idea. It was a longshot, but that was all she had lately.

N. Write this email and address it to Gary Schuller. Tell him you have a prize Angus bull for sale. Tell him your farm is being foreclosed on and you need to sell right away. Look up a reasonable offer and quote him 20% less, but only if it can happen tomorrow. Have him meet you downtown in Cedar Pike. Be there, but don't acknowledge him. I hate to do it to him, but I have done a lot of things I regret in the past few days. I will hitch a ride and will meet up with you after he leaves. I am going to stay here tonight. I will contact you again after they go to bed. For now, I will delete our messages so he doesn't get suspicious.

Love E.

Nathan didn't respond to her directly. A few minutes later, an email popped up to Gary with PRIZE ANGUS BULL FOR SALE in the subject line. Emily hoped her plan would work. She deleted all of the messages that she and Nathan had exchanged and was careful to empty the TRASH folder. Then she slipped back into the kitchen for a piece of cornbread. No one noticed when she took it.

As was his custom, Gary checked his emails after his meal. He whooped loudly when he read the email. Nathan posing as a farmer named *Jason Barnes* offered him a prize Angus bull for twenty-two hundred dollars. Gary had been willing to go three thousand, so the offer was too good not to at least check out. He talked the prospect over with Dotty and struggled with whether he should take the trailer or not.

"If I take it, I will look too anxious and I think that is bad," he said.

"If you don't take it, you will have to make two trips and THAT is bad," said Dotty.

"You don't understand business," said Gary.

"Apparently, you don't understand gas prices," replied Dotty. "Besides, who does the books for this farm?"

"You do," said Gary sheepishly. He was only playing with her anyway. He trusted her business sense and financial acumen. Before they were married, she used to work at a credit union. He kissed her on the forehead and said, "You're always right. Do you know that?"

"Of course I do," she said. "Do you?"

"Of course. You married me, didn't you?"

"So you have to bring up my one mistake," she said with a grin.

"I'll go get the trailer hooked up and ready for an early start," said Gary. "This Jason Barnes wants to meet at nine o'clock in Cedar Pike. There is no short way to get there from here. Looks like we will be going to bed early…if you get my drift." He winked at Dotty.

"I get your drift," she replied. "You are a dirty old man."

"I am not that old," said Gary. "I have to concede the dirty part."

"That's one of the reasons I married you," said Dotty.

"What is another reason?" asked Gary.

"Well…you said yes when I asked," replied Dotty.

"I thought I asked YOU?"

"That was just what I wanted you to think," said Dotty.

The two embraced and Gary went out to make his preparations. Emily slipped back into the kitchen to see if there was something she could forage from the table. Besides cornbread, there was a bowl of green beans that looked as though they had been canned by Dotty herself. There were little pieces of bacon and onion throughout. Emily grabbed a spoon and helped herself right out of the bowl. They were heavenly. There was also a bowl of mashed potatoes that were made from real potatoes…not out of a box. Dotty had left the peels on when she mashed them and used whole milk and real butter in the recipe. Emily used the same spoon and ate several bites. She promised to punish herself later for her bad table manners. Then she finished off with a slice of the best apple pie she had ever had. The crust was made from scratch, the apples from home-canned and the top crust was made from homemade biscuits. It had the perfect amount of cinnamon and spices. Emily could not eat another bite after finishing it. She wondered how Gary and Dotty stayed so thin. They either had very fast metabolisms or they worked a lot; probably the latter.

As the late afternoon sun began to fail, Emily found an unobtrusive place in the corner of the living room to wait. Gary watched the evening news as was probably his usual habit. He seemed calm and relaxed, but his right foot kept tapping softly on the living room carpet. Emily couldn't tell if he was excited about the prospect of the new bull or the romance he would share with Dotty in a few minutes. In reality, it was both. As the news was airing its last story of the evening, a human interest story about ducks, Gary stretched, yawned loudly and said, "Well…I guess it is about time for bed." Dotty responded, "Well…if you're tired… go on then." Gary looked at her with his eyebrows furrowed. Then he raised and lowered one and it made her laugh.

"Alright... if you insist," she said. Emily really liked this couple. She resolved to do something nice for them someday...to pay them back for their unwitting hospitality.

Dotty turned out the lights downstairs and Emily heard the water running in the bathroom upstairs. She guessed the dirty old man wasn't that dirty after all. She smiled when she saw Dotty do a little dance as she ascended the stairs. She was looking forward to the romance as much as Gary. He came out of the bathroom just as she reached the top of the stairs. He grabbed her, twirled her around once and dipped her. Then he turned off the upstairs hall light and closed the bedroom door behind them. Emily thought it was as if they could sense that they were not alone. That thought perished when she heard the noises that were coming from the bedroom a few minutes later. There was no way that people would make those kinds of noises if they thought anyone could hear them. Emily booted up the computer and the glow of the screen softly illuminated the living room.

Emily had to content herself with emails because she wasn't sure if she could delete instant messaging. It was something Nathan would have to teach her later if they got the chance. Nathan responded right away but the responses took a few moments bouncing through a series of dummy email accounts before they got to Emily. It was a system Nathan developed himself. The delay was worth it because he could converse with Emily freely without the need for codes or subterfuge. He still referred to her as E though. It was his affectionate nickname for her.

E. Everything is set. I am looking forward to seeing you again tomorrow. I have good news. We will meet up with your mom day after tomorrow. I will let you know the time and place when I see you. I checked and your dad is still being held at the drive-in. It doesn't look like he is being mistreated, but I could be wrong.

We will deal with that tomorrow. Is everything set on your end?

N.

Emily was very excited to hear about her mom and the news about her dad wasn't terrible. She felt a spark of hope that everything would work out.

N. Everything is set here. We should be there by nine tomorrow. I suspect Gary is the punctual type. Besides, he is motivated. I think he is upstairs getting motivated right now. I am excited to see you too. It seems like forever. I want this to all be over. I wish it could go back to the way it used to be.

Love E.

Nathan's response seemed quicker for some reason.

E. Things happen for a reason. If things had stayed the same, we would have had to change them ourselves. We couldn't go on the way we were going. I finally had the courage to tell my mom that I could see you. I think she knew all along. I still haven't told my dad. I am not sure what he would do. I don't really trust him. Once all this is behind us, we can sit down and make our plans for the future.

Love N.

Emily's eyes filled with tears. She wanted them to be happy and it sounded wonderful; but there were so many obstacles in the way, it just seemed impossible.

N. I want that more than anything. You are a beacon of hope in my life. I never thought I could ever be happy before you. I guess there really is someone for everybody.

Love E.

The exchange went on for another forty-five minutes. Emily noticed that the noises coming from the bedroom had ceased. She signed off swiftly but sweetly and closed the lid of the laptop just as she heard the hinges of the bedroom door squeak. She moved to the end of the couch and waited. A large figure that Emily presumed to be Gary came down the stairs and headed for the kitchen. As he passed the secretary he paused and touched the top of the laptop. "Why is this thing so warm?" he muttered. "Damned thing. Probably have to buy a new one soon." He flipped the light on in the kitchen and Emily could see that he was only wearing a t-shirt. In her opinion, she had seen far too many naked men in the last few days. She covered her eyes when he appeared in the doorway again with a large slice of homemade apple pie. Thankfully, he turned the light off and Emily was spared full disclosure of his nether region. She hoped that would be the last intrusion of the night and snuggled with a throw pillow to get some sleep.

Emily awoke to the smell of sausage patties. Even the sound of them sizzling in a pan seemed to have a heavenly aroma of its own. The sausage had just the right amount of seasoning and a hint of crushed red pepper. She could tell just from smelling it. Homemade biscuits were baking in the oven and Dotty was scrambling eggs. She was making Gary sausage and egg biscuit breakfast sandwiches for the road. She wrapped them in paper towels and set them on the table as she completed them. When she had finished two, she prepared one for herself; except hers was on a sandwich plate. When she turned back to the table, there was only one. Dotty looked around to see if Gary had stolen one when she wasn't looking. She could see him out the window. He was in the barn lot checking his trailer connections one last time. She looked on the floor, shrugged and said, "Alright you gremlins...I hope you enjoy it." Then she prepared another sandwich and wrapped it. This time, she didn't take her eyes off of it.

Emily pocketed her purloined breakfast sandwich to eat on the road. She quietly slid into the back seat of Gary's extended cab Chevy pickup and waited. Gary came out of the house, kissed Dotty for a long time and thanked her for the breakfast. He also thanked her for last night. She handed him a thermos of coffee and said, "No...it is I who should be thanking you." She smiled at him and imitated his eyebrow trick. If he was not so anxious to get to Cedar Pike, he would have given her an encore performance that morning. But business was business, so he promised her to be even better when he got back. Dotty stroked his face and went back inside.

Gary surprised Emily with his choice of music. She expected a country station or at the very least, 50's Rock and Roll. Instead she was treated to the likes of *Maroon 5* and *Carly Rae Jepsen.* After a while, he inserted a compact disc and for the next hour he listened to Vivaldi concertos. It was very relaxing and the drive passed quickly. Before long, Emily was seeing landmarks that were familiar to her. Finally, the outskirts of town appeared and Gary drove on a road from which Emily could see her house. It filled her with a lot of mixed emotions. He then turned onto Main Street of downtown Cedar Pike, which was also uptown Cedar Pike. Nathan was nowhere to be seen, which was good. That was according to plan. Emily just needed an opportunity to get out without being noticed.

Gary waited, looked at his watch and waited some more. He didn't know why he hadn't just agreed to meet Jason Barnes at his farm. He suspected Jason Barnes had a farm that was hard to find and so he would need to guide him in. Gary was starting to worry that he was being scammed. He waited another few minutes before getting out of his truck to look for someone who could help him. Jason Barnes had given him all the information he needed about pedigrees, but no other contact information except for an email address. If he had asked for money, Gary would have been sure it was a scam. But he hadn't. Gary decided to give him the benefit of the doubt and ask someone for directions. Dr. Bethany Hertz was just going into the office when Gary stopped her and apologized for being abrupt. He asked where he could find Jason Barnes. His heart sank a bit when she said "Who?" If the town doctor didn't know someone, they didn't exist. Gary thanked her as kindly as he could, considering his mood. He squealed his tires as he drove off; his empty trailer rattling and calling attention to his shame.

Emily crouched behind a dumpster in an alley between two buildings. She wasn't sure who might be watching and she needed to be cautious. Her clothes felt dirty and she wished she had had the opportunity to change them. She considered borrowing something from Dotty, but they were not really the same size; and besides, the couple had been so generous already without their knowledge. Main Street got a little busier and Emily ventured to the corner to look for Nathan. He should have been there by now. She saw him on the other side of the street, walking nervously towards the post office. He saw Emily peeking out and darted his eyes sharply to the right several times. She dared to peek out a little farther and saw a black SUV parked less than a block from her.

CHAPTER 10: SURVEILLANCE

Nathan had been up since before dawn. He paced nervously in his room and with good reason. Emily had filled him in on her entire ordeal of the previous few days. He didn't know who to trust or how much risk he should take. He desperately wanted to control his anxiousness to see Emily, but he was afraid his excitement would get the better of him. David was up and gone already. He had wanted to get an early start at his job. Sue might have been up or she might have stayed in bed. Nathan had no way of knowing without checking. He was born deaf so he didn't know how dependent others were on their sense of hearing. They didn't fully appreciate it unless they lost it; and then it was too late. Some people lose their hearing over time, so they still never fully appreciate it.

    Nathan watched the second hand of his clock move slowly around the face until it came full circle. It reminded him of the rotation of the earth around the sun. It seemed like it was taking that long too. He considered showing up early, but was afraid that would look too suspicious. In the small town of Cedar Pike, there was nothing to do downtown until at least nine. He thought about going to the kitchen and getting something to eat, but he had no appetite. There were just too many dynamics at work in his head. Reading was out of the question so Nathan logged on to his email, checked his security protocols, checked to see if his dummy emails were still in place and tried to compose a message that he could send just in case plans fell through for today. His heart sank a little when there were no messages in his inbox. He didn't expect any, but that didn't stop him from hoping. His mind drifted back to the first time he met with Emily alone.

If two people were ever meant to be together, it was Nathan and Emily. He didn't know why he could see her when others couldn't. He didn't dwell on it. For him, it felt like a gift; for Emily, it was an answer to a prayer. If they had revealed their secret to their parents, Dr. Cornell might have been able to tell them the reason. But they preferred not to know. It seemed more like magic that way, instead of Nathan's immunity to Emily's sphere of influence. He was also immune to the field of influence that caused others to become so loyal to Emily, but you could never have convinced Nathan of that. His love for her was sincere and not chemically induced.

Nathan was careful not to be seen apparently signing to himself and Emily was careful not to walk around naked so freely anymore. Since no one could see her, it had not been unusual for her to walk all the way to the mailbox without a stitch on. The first few times, it felt naughty and exhilarating; but after a while, it meant nothing. She suspected it was the feeling that people in nudist resorts feel. Not that she would know such things or ever visited those websites…much. When Nathan first indicated that he could see her, she was surprised and excited. Later in the evening, when she had time to think about it, she wondered if others could see her also. Emily thought about cars driving by while she was standing next to the mailbox completely naked. Could they have seen her and just pretended not to notice? She had blushed at the thought. Then she drove the thought from her head, rationalizing what's done was done and it was too late to worry about it now. She turned her thoughts toward Nathan and what their life could be like together.

Nathan literally had never known anyone like Emily. Her image changed as he thought about her. Sometimes, she was as solid as any other person; other times, she looked like a moving crystal figurine to him. Most of the time, he saw her as an angel. That thought troubled him the most. Angels were supposed to protect…to guard. Angels were not supposed to be the ones in trouble. Seeing her as a crystal figurine filled him with the sense of how fragile she was. Nathan didn't think she could take care of herself and she needed him. He was right and wrong at the same time. Emily's condition had made her strong, but left her with terrible insecurity and doubt. Perhaps if she had been able to speak, things would have been different. Nathan had no way of knowing she had obtained a way to speak. It didn't matter. In his world, everyone was silent.

Nathan jumped up startled. The clock seemed to have sped up while he was daydreaming. He was going to be late. He rushed out of the house and headed for Main Street. About half a block away, he forced himself to slow down. He was on time and didn't want to appear to be in a hurry. A person in a rush stands out like a sore thumb in a lazy little town like Cedar Pike. He got to Main Street and crossed to the opposite side of it as a precautionary measure. Nathan tried to look casual as he looked into windows of businesses along the street. He was failing. Most people do not find a lot of interesting things to look at in the window of a Laundromat or an attorney's office. The windows to one of Cedar Pike's two Main Street bars were painted black, so there was nothing to see there. He was considering going up to the door of the post office to check its hours when a black SUV pulled up to the curb across the street from him. The driver looked over at him, but didn't appear suspicious. He was wearing a plaid shirt and a Chicago Cubs baseball cap. The man didn't seem out of the ordinary until he waited until he was parked to don a pair of sunglasses. The morning was very sunny and Nathan wondered why he wasn't wearing them already while he was driving. At that moment, he saw Emily peeking out from the side of a building across the street.

It dawned on Nathan what the glasses were and he fought his natural instinct to wave her off. The driver of the SUV was looking at himself in his visor mirror and didn't notice Emily. Nathan began to walk slowly toward the post office averting his eyes toward the SUV and hoping Emily would notice. She did, but not before the man closed the visor mirror and looked directly at her. His special dark glasses, if they were special, didn't appear to be calibrated properly because he didn't seem to notice her. She slowly retreated back into the alley and returned to her hiding place behind the dumpster. Nathan walked on to the post office. The building was recessed from the road and had a green lawn and three angled sidewalks that met at the door. By standing in the corner of the lawn, he remained out of sight of the SUV driver, but could see the small dumpster in the reflection of the post office window. Emily peeked out and could see Nathan facing the window and quickly realized he was signing to her through the reflection.

That was close, he signed.

I know, signed Emily. *What are we going to do?*

We need to go somewhere else, signed Nathan. *Any ideas?*

I am not sure I can get out of the alley, signed Emily. Nathan moved casually to the other window to check out the situation. She was in a blind alley; both of the doors in it appeared to be locked. Nathan moved back to his original position and shrugged. He hated feeling helpless. He began to rationalize the circumstances of the morning and consider his options. Nathan had a very analytical mind. Images coalesced in his head which played out in scenarios. In his mind's eye, he saw the black SUV pull up and the driver don dark glasses. *That meant he wasn't expecting Emily to be there or he would have had them on already.* He didn't pursue Gary the farmer, so it meant that he probably didn't know about his connection to Emily. That thought made Nathan relax a little. *That means the driver is just a scout; someone to keep watch just in case Emily shows up.*

Nathan went into the post office and bought a book of Forever stamps to keep from looking suspicious. He walked back to the corner and signed to Emily that he was going to walk up the block so he wouldn't tip their hand to the government man. As he finished signing, he noticed a woman standing on the other side of the window. She was staring at him with a curious, almost amused, expression. She had raised the window blind while Nathan was signing and he hadn't noticed because he was so focused on Emily. Nathan blushed, waved meekly and began walking down the block. There were four businesses at the corner of the town's 4-way stop. The only bank in town occupied the nearest corner. Across the street was a Masonic Lodge. It was almost the newest building in town, even though it had been there for five decades. The funeral home that stood diagonal from the bank was actually the newest, but that was because the original building that housed it had burned down a few years ago and was reconstructed on the same site. The vintage drugstore stood nobly across from the bank.

Nathan crossed the street to the drugstore and entered the heavy wooden door with beveled glass panes; a polished brass bell jingled announcing him. The pleasant sound was lost on him, but several customers turned to see who had just come in. The drugstore looked bigger on the inside than the exterior would seem to indicate. Along the left side was a soda fountain with red vinyl stools and an enormous mirror behind it. The mirror gave the illusion that the room was twice as big as it actually was. On the right side was a row of greeting card racks with cards for every conceivable and inconceivable occasion. The black and while tiled floor led back to the ancient pharmacy window. The rich, dark brown wood and wrought-iron bars seemed to imprison the pharmacist. Frosted glass kept most of the pharmacy hidden from the public and Nathan wondered what kind of alchemy might go on back there when no one was around.

    Nathan hopped up on a stool and took a menu from the condiment rack. The *Soda Jerk,* who was actually one of the owners of the drugstore, came over to take his order. He wore a white shirt, a red bowtie and garters on his sleeves as if it was the Fifties. Gerald, the half-owner, knew that a major drugstore chain could locate in town at any given year. So, he wanted to insure that customers had a reason to keep coming to his drugstore. Nathan pointed to a chocolate milkshake on the menu. Gerald held one hand over the other and indicated various heights to Nathan. Nathan mimicked the last height indicating he wanted a large shake. Gerald smiled and began concocting the shake the old fashioned way; hand-dipped ice cream, rich chocolate syrup and whole milk. He topped it with whipped cream and a green cherry just to be different. He presented it to Nathan on a perfectly folded paper napkin triangle in a vintage footed soda glass. It was so perfect that Nathan felt terrible when he pointed to a stack of paper cups indicating he wanted the shake *to go.* Gerald smiled cordially, but there was obvious disappointment in his eyes. He took great pride in recreating a bygone era. He politely took the shake, scraped the whipped cream and cherry off of the top and poured it into a tall paper cup. Then he squirted a fresh dollop of whipped cream into the cup and placed another green cherry on its peak. Then he smashed the whole thing down with a plastic lid and impaled it with an extra wide straw. Nathan paid Gerald, thanked him in sign language and left the drugstore.

The jingling bell attracted attention again as he left. Small town people are easily entertained sometimes.

Nathan pretended to sip the shake as he checked to see if the SUV was still there. It was. He looked diagonally across the street at the Masonic Lodge. A half-block behind it towered a grain elevator. Nathan crossed the street diagonally after checking all four ways…twice. He stayed close to the red brick façade of the lodge until he reached the back. Rounding the corner, he could see that no expense had been made to keep the rear of the building looking presentable. It looked as though the wall was constructed of the original cinderblock. Paint had chipped off in most places and what windows there were had been painted over. The building was almost three stories tall and had a fire escape even though building codes probably didn't require one. Next to the back of Masonic Lodge was Angelo's Pizza. Its street address was on Second Street and had been built adjacent to buildings on Main. Angelo, whose real name was Terry, had bricked over the alley to make a patio area for his customers. It was very nice and actually brought in a lot of business from out of town. He had constructed it with used bricks and the walls had arched brick windows with wrought-iron bars. Nathan thought the town seemed obsessed with iron bars. He made sure he was not being watched and walked around the corner to the center of the lodge.

The grain elevator was busy, but everyone there seemed occupied with their own granary needs. He looked up at the retractable metal fire escape ladder. It looked too high for him to reach. Nathan's height was only slightly above average and the ladder looked to be ten feet away from the ground. He took a gulp of his chocolate shake and was immediately seized by an ice cream headache that felt like an aneurysm. Pressing his tongue to the roof of his mouth helped to relieve the pressure, but he was done with the shake. He set it down next to the wall and turned his attention back to the ladder. Nathan tried jumping up to grab it, but missed it by about six inches. He looked around again to be sure no one was watching. He jumped again and got a little closer, but it was still too far. Looking around on the ground, Nathan spotted a broken cinderblock that was probably used to prop the back door open for deliveries. He placed it under the ladder, balanced on it and jumped again. One of his hands grasped the bottom rung of the ladder, but the other slipped off. He held on as it dislodged and descended. He fell back, but kept hold of the rung. His feet slid forward and he stiffened. He grabbed the rung with his other hand and maintained a comical slanted pose until he walked backwards to right himself. The ladder had vibrated so hard in Nathan's hand that he was sure it must have made an enormous amount of noise. He was right; but what he failed to consider was that the grain elevator was also making an ironically deafening amount of noise that time of day. No one had noticed at all.

    Nathan stepped back onto the broken cinderblock and hoisted himself up on the metal ladder. It retracted with another unnoticed loud clunk when he stepped onto the metal fire escape. A metal ladder next to it led to the roof. He climbed it quickly so as not to be spotted. The top of the Masonic Lodge had been tarred some time ago and the black tar had turned dark gray. Nathan crouched behind the ledge of the building until he was sure that he was out of sight. He duck-walked to the left side of the building and looked over the ledge into the alley below. Emily was still crotched behind the small dumpster waiting for him to rescue her. The building across the alley was half a story lower than the Masonic lodge and was even with the height of Angelo's Pizza. The brick wall blocking the alley was about nine feet lower than the ledge Nathan was looking over. He considered his options. He couldn't scale the wall down to the alley so one of his only options was to climb back down the fire escape and look for another way to rescue Emily. Or he was going to have to drop down nine feet onto the top of a two story brick wall, tightrope across it and climb down the drain pipe from the roof on the other side. Nathan wasn't sure, but he thought that he might be afraid of heights.

Looking down from the ledge of the Masonic Lodge, the brick wall looked as though it was only the width of a shoelace even though it was just nine feet lower than the roof. Shaking, Nathan got on his hands and knees and backed to the corner of the ledge. To his right was the sheer drop of the back wall. While it was only a little under three stories high, it looked like the Cliffs of Moher to him from his vantage point. The view made him a little dizzy, so he closed his eyes. That made it worse and he opened them again. He backed to the edge until he couldn't feel the ledge under his feet. Then he lay down on the ledge and scooted farther back using his arms until his knees were over the edge. The Law of Gravity seemed to be playing games with Nathan. It wanted to pull him over the right side of the wall and was working extra hard to do so. He fought the impulse to overcompensate and continued to move back until his legs hung over the side. He knew that the fall probably wouldn't kill him, but an injury from that height could be debilitating and possibly permanent.

The hardest part was yet to come. As soon as Nathan moved his center of gravity over the edge of the ledge, he began to slip and scraped his chest as he went over the side. He caught the ledge with the tips of his fingers and hung flat against the wall. He knew that he needed to let go and he knew the wall was only inches below his feet, but he could not force his body to respond to his demands. The wall was in his blind spot and he would have to trust that he would be able to land on it and maintain his balance. Gravity began to aid him in a sadistic way. The strength was leaving his fingers and he had to make the choice between letting nature takes its course or being proactive and just letting go. At the very last second possible, one or the other happened. Nathan was not sure which, but he suddenly found himself standing on the top of the wall with his arms outstretched in either direction. Gravity was having a tug of war with him, trying to pull him to one side or the other. He placed one hand against the wall of the Masonic Lodge and the other on the corner. Taking the tiniest of baby steps, he turned one hundred and eighty degrees to face the opposite side of the alley.

The narrow strip of brick on which he stood seemed to stretch on forever. In fact, it was only ten feet. Nathan tried to look down at Emily, but doing so seemed to shift his center of gravity to the right. Had he seen her, he would have panicked at the look of horror on her face. She had watched him as he slid off the building and was horribly frightened by his lack of acrobatic skills. Nathan had to make a decision whether to rush across the wall or to balance-walk with his arms outstretched. He surprised himself that he needed to force his eyes to stay open. He tried to take a deep breath only to find that he had been holding it for some time. He let it out slowly and hoped that his heart would stop beating so fast. When that didn't happen, he proceeded forward in a mixed rush and balance-walk that made him look a little like a ballerina. Three feet from the opposing wall, he lost his balance and was about to fall into the alley. He used the forward inertia to his advantage, bent his knees and dove for the wall. His adrenalin must have been stockpiling because he leapt six feet and executed a somersault onto the other rooftop. Emily looked somewhat impressed by the action, but Nathan never saw her expression. He lay on the roof with his face pressed against the surface until he could catch his breath.

Nathan's face finally appeared over the edge of the roof and Emily breathed a sigh of relief. She did a silent clap of her hands and smiled; but Nathan could tell she was still nervous. He held up one finger indicating for her to wait and he disappeared once again over the edge. The next time she saw him, he was climbing down the drainpipe with confidence. Apparently, walking a ledge precariously made everything else seem easy. He reached the ground and felt secure for the first time in a long while. Emily embraced him and it all seemed worth it. She kissed Nathan long and passionately. Then they ducked back behind the small dumpster and made plans.

There is another drain pipe on the other side of the building, he signed. We *can climb this one and climb down the other side.*

Emily signed, *I'm not sure I can.*

I will help you, signed Nathan. *You will be fine.*

Nathan positioned Emily on the drainpipe and showed her how to grip with her knees while pulling herself up hand over hand. Once she was up a few feet, he climbed up directly below her to make her feel secure. She reached the top and he pushed her over the building's ledge by placing his hand on her butt. Her eyes widened, but she didn't hate it. She was smiling as she rolled onto the roof and waited for Nathan. He had not realized what he had done until it was too late and chose to pretend that it was no big deal; but he liked it too. Emily crouched low and went to the front of the building. Of course, the SUV was still there. *Your tax dollars at work,* she thought. The two of them went to the back corner of the roof. Nathan climbed down a few feet and motioned for Emily to join him. Getting down was easier than the trip up and they were soon on the ground. They turned around to find that a man had been standing there the whole time.

Mr. Ellinwood was a decorated veteran of the Korean War. He was out walking his dog Muffin, a Cairn Terrier. Muffin had really been Mrs. Ellinwood's dog, but she had passed away a year ago. Mr. Ellinwood considered giving the dog up, but Muffin seemed to channel his late wife sometimes; so she stayed.

"What were you doing up there kid?" he asked in a gruff tone. Emily stood perfectly still while Nathan pointed to his ears and shook his head. Muffin began to bark at Emily and then wagged her tail and sniffed at her shoes. Emily stiffened and tried to shoo her away.

"Oh, I'm sorry," he continued. "I know who you are. That's okay. You can go on." Emily breathed yet another sigh of relief but Nathan was a little angry. Mr. Ellinwood seemed to be equating deafness with being mentally challenged. Nathan just wanted to be treated like everyone else and if that meant getting in trouble for mischief, so be it. Mr. Ellinwood began to walk away and had to pull Muffin along against her will. She wanted to stay with Emily. The aura that inspired loyalty to Emily must have been working on her.

The silent couple cut though alleys and between houses until they came to the town cemetery. There were no Wi-Fi connections or technology, so there was no real reason for them to be there. For that reason, they figured no one would be looking for them there. They hid out in the modest mausoleum near the middle of the graveyard. No one seemed to have visited it in quite some time. Cobwebs hung from the vaulted ceiling and dried leaves littered the floor. Emily and Nathan sat on a stone bench in the center of the building and considered their next step. Nathan held her hand reassuringly, but he had no idea as to how to proceed.

We need to rescue your dad, signed Nathan.

I think we should contact my mom first, signed Emily. *We will need to know how to get to her when we rescue my dad.*

You're right as always, signed Nathan. Emily smiled at him and kissed him again. He had been so great and she couldn't believe she was back with him. She was afraid that at any moment she would wake up and find herself back in the government facility. She comforted herself by knowing that if she was going to dream about reuniting with Nathan, she would not have made it take place in a creepy mausoleum.

Do you know of any way we can contact my mom? she signed.

I might have a way, he signed back. *Patty.*

Patty? signed Emily. She had one eyebrow raised slightly higher than the other.

Yes, Patty. She was a friend from school, signed Nathan. Emily wondered why she had never heard about this *Patty.*

Patty wasn't born deaf, he continued, ignoring the signs of jealousy. *She got an infection when she was four. It turned serious and she lost her hearing. She can talk and she translated for me to the teachers and others.* Emily wanted to ask a lot of questions about Patty, but instead she stayed on track.

How do you think she can help? she signed.

I think we can use her computer to contact your mom, Nathan signed. *No one would consider looking for you there.*

Can we trust her? That question had a double meaning.

Yes. Nathan was looking directly into Emily's eyes when he answered with fierce conviction. Emily did not want to be the petty, untrusting girlfriend; so she smiled and stroked his cheek. *Let's go see Patty then*, she signed.

CHAPTER 11: HIDING IN PLAIN SIGHT

The Carlstone County Library had only been open for six minutes when a small group of individuals passed through the large automatic doors, through the electronic sensors that detect when books are being stolen and into the main lobby. Six women and two men that looked as though they had been together, spread out to various destinations in the library. Two women headed upstairs to the records room. One was intent on tracing her family tree; the other needed to look through the microfilm archives. She needed a newspaper article about a courthouse fire that occurred fifty-seven years ago.

One of the men went to the video room to see what new DVDs had been donated or purchased. The rest of the group went through a second set of glass doors to the main library floor before breaking off into smaller groups. The man and two of the women went to the high tables with the high stools where the library's reference computers rested. The other two women appeared to be a couple. One of them was a young, attractive brunette. She was dressed in tight blue jeans and a form-fitting sweater top. The other was dressed like a workman. She wore a flannel shirt over an olive drab military-type tee shirt and painter's pants that were anything but form-fitting. Her blond, almost white hair was only an inch long and was spiked. Work boots completed her ensemble that almost caused Madelyn, the librarian, to mistake her for a man. The couple went directly to the service desk to register to use the computers; they then went to opposite sides of the computer bank circle. The brunette logged on, checked her email messages and then brought up a few celebrity gossip pages that interested her.

The other woman logged onto an email account identifying her as Willee Drake. There was a single email in her inbox. It was from Dante Muller and originated in Hapsburg Austria. The email was in German and translated it read:

```
     Willee.   Your   package   finally
arrived.   It took the long way around to
get here, but I am glad that I was there
to pick it up.   It is perfect.   I have
information about the item you have been
looking for.   I know where you can find
it, but getting it past customs might take
a long time.  When do you think you might
be able to pay me a visit in person?  Your
friend, Dante.
```

Willee Drake understood the coded message. She inserted a flash drive into the computer and responded to the email.

```
     Dear Dante.   Thank you so much for
all your help.   I will travel to meet you
as soon as I can work a few things out
here.   I am glad you got the package.  Be
careful with it; it is fragile.   I have
attached  a  jpeg  I think you will find
amusing.   Have a great day.    Willee.
```

Willee copied her message and pasted it into a translator window to translate it into German. Then she copied the result, pasted it back into her message and attached an encrypted file from the flash drive. She pushed SEND, removed the flash drive and deleted her browser history. She looked up a few videos of puppies and kittens before logging off. The brunette logged off as well and Willee followed her out the door. The couple stayed together for almost a block from the library until Willee ducked down a side street and disappeared.

Forty miles away, Nathan received the email from Willee almost twenty minutes after it had been sent. He had routed several dummy emails to go through Brazil to England to Denmark to Italy to India before arriving in Austria. Sometimes there was a delay due to servers in one of those countries. It was an unpredictable way to communicate, but Nathan didn't take chances or shortcuts when it came to security. He put the message through a translator as Willee had done and read what she had written. Then he opened the encrypted jpeg file using the code they had prearranged. It was not a large file, but Patty's computer was slow and it took a while to download. Nathan mentally vowed to overhaul it for her when all of the drama in his life was over. Patty had been kind enough to allow Nathan to use it without asking a lot of difficult questions. She suspected his actions had something to do with pirating games or something, but she never asked. She had a bit of a crush on Nathan and had welcomed him in when he showed up on her doorstep. She wasn't aware that he was not alone.

Emily had watched her closely when she ushered Nathan into her home. Patty almost closed the door on Emily; and she would have thought it to be intentional if she hadn't known better. Nathan's attitude towards Patty had been friendly but not flirtatious, so she relaxed and followed the two of them to the kitchen. Patty moved out of her parents' home after high school and went to work in the local nursery during the summer months and as a lunch lady when school was in session. Her ability to read lips was very useful in both jobs and proved to be quite a challenge when trying to interpret the words of grade school children who were missing their front teeth. Fortunately, they could point and that resolved any breakdowns in communication.

Emily watched Nathan work his magic on the computer. Patty moved behind him to look over his shoulder. She raised her hands in a way that relayed her intentions to rub his shoulders, but she lost her nerve and put them back down to her sides. Emily huffed and folded her arms. Nathan continued to wait for the download to complete and checked to make sure his personal security protocols were still in place. He smiled a satisfied smile when they were. The download completed and a window popped up asking which application Nathan wanted to use to view the file. He chose from a list presented to him and the jpeg file revealed a message that had been imbedded into it.

It read: I HOPE BY THE TIME YOU READ THIS THAT YOU HAVE SOME NEWS ABOUT EMILY AND CHARLES. I HAVE BEEN AFRAID TO GO OUT FOR FEAR OF BEING DISCOVERED, EVEN THOUGH I KNOW I AM MILES AWAY. I CHANGED MY APPEARANCE AND I AM USING THE FALSE ID YOU PROVIDED FOR ME. I CANNOT TELL YOU HOW MUCH I APPRECIATE ALL YOU ARE DOING FOR US. I HOPE YOU KNOW SOMETHING ABOUT CHARLES BY NOW AND THAT IT IS GOOD. IF YOU CAN GET AWAY, I AM IN THE COUNTY SEAT TO THE NORTH. I CAN MEET UP WITH YOU WHERE I GET MY INFORMATION. I WILL BE THERE TOMORROW AS SOON AS THEY OPEN. THANK YOU SO MUCH.

Who's Emily? Patty signed as Nathan erased the file. She had a suspicious, possibly hurt look on her face.

She's a friend who is in trouble, he signed. *I need to help her and you are the best for helping me.* Patty relaxed a little as Emily began to bristle. Nathan casually stroked her arm, which looked like an unusual motion to Patty. To her, it seemed that he had just stroked the air.

I hate to do it, but I have another favor to ask, he signed. Patty wasn't sure if she was being used or not, but it was hard for her to refuse anything to Nathan. *I need to borrow your car.* Patty's eyes grew wide. That was a pretty big favor and there was no promise of any commitment in the future.

You're going to Carlstone County, aren't you? she signed.

How did you know? asked Nathan.

It's the next county to the North, she responded. *Do you even have a license?* Nathan nodded. *I think that I should go with you,* she signed with determination.

You can't, signed Nathan.

Why not? Patty was getting angry.

Your job, he signed. Patty hated that he was right. It would be too short of notice not to show up for work.

Alright. You take the car, she signed. *I will take my bicycle to work tomorrow. But have it back by evening...and with a full tank of gas.* Patty had been speaking while she signed. Emily could hear tears in her voice and felt a little sorry for her. Patty and Nathan would have made a good couple, but SHE and Nathan made a perfect couple. Emily felt enough pity that it eased the jealousy she felt when Nathan hugged Patty. Patty signed that she would get her car keys and left the kitchen. Nathan started to sign an apology to Emily, but she shook her hand and head indicating that there was no need. He was about to kiss her when Patty returned and looked at him curiously. He realized his lips were still pursed to form a kiss. He smacked his lips a couple of times and ran his finger across them. Then he signed, *dry*. Patty shook her head and handed him the keys. Nathan held her hand with both hands and thanked her with the expression in his eyes. It was enough for Patty...for now.

Nathan didn't go home. He did not want there to be a connection between him and Patty's car just in case his house was being watched. He had sent an email to a friend from Patty's computer before erasing everything on it that tied her to him. The friend was Galen Phillips. Galen had been friends with Nathan for a long time. He had stood up for Nathan when some of the other students had been taunting him. Galen was no stranger to taunts himself. Before he had a middle school growth spurt, he had been small, skinny and weak. Add to that all the name variations students could think of and Galen's childhood was miserable. He wasn't about to stand around while others put Nathan through the type of torture he had known. He stepped in with his six foot one, two-hundred and ten pound frame and made it very clear that Nathan was under his protection. That was all it took. No one ever bothered Nathan again and he never forgot it. He helped Galen with subjects he was having trouble with and downloaded games for him before they became available in stores. They communicated through notes until Galen surprised Nathan one day by showing him that he had learned sign language. He was not very good and got a lot of things wrong; but Nathan thought he was amusing and helped him correct his mistakes.

Nathan instructed Galen to call his mother and tell her they were going to a party and probably wouldn't be home. He knew his mother would be concerned and confused, but he was of legal age so she couldn't say too much. He didn't want to give too much away and thought it best to keep the story simple. Galen was curious about all the cloak and dagger behavior. Nathan had satisfied him with a simple sentence: *It's about a girl.* Galen had responded with a single word. *Nice.* He carried out his instructions and Nathan had Emily to himself for the first time in a long time.

They drove to the county line…of the county due west of the one they were in. It wouldn't be a good idea to get careless when they were getting so close. Nathan timidly suggested that they check into a motel...under an assumed name of course. Emily was much more receptive than he thought she was going to be. They pulled into one that did not look like the proprietor was a serial killer and Emily motioned to Nathan. She had an idea. His mouth dropped open as he listened to her proposal. Then he shrugged and smiled. But then his brow furrowed. *How are we going to pay for this?* he signed. Emily held out some folded bills that amounted to two-hundred and sixty dollars. It was money she had liberated from Agent Baxter's wallet. She explained it was best not to leave a paper trail. Nathan did his part by producing a fake driver's license. Producing fake identification for others was one of his means of making money. He was very good at it. He nodded to Emily, kissed her on the cheek when he was sure that no one was looking and went into the lobby of the motel. It was a national chain that advertised breakfast as one of its amenities. To his right was the dining area with plastic containers of cereal, coffee urns that would be filled in the morning and a self-serve Belgian waffle maker. To his right was the check-in desk.

"Can I help you?" asked the man behind the counter. Nathan held a tissue up to his face and said, "Yes, I would like a room please."

"For how many?" asked the clerk.

"Just one," said Nathan. "One night only."

"How will you be paying?" he asked.

"Cash," replied Nathan.

"Very good, sir. I will need to make a copy of your driver's license," said the clerk. Nathan handed him his fake license with his free hand. "Excuse me sir, but do you have a cold or something?"

"Yes," said Nathan. "Must be this roller coaster weather we have been having. Can't seem to shake it."

"I understand completely," replied the clerk, handing the license back to Nathan. "We have a small selection of cold relief products in the vending machine if you need it. Here is your key and your change. You are in Room #208. Enjoy your stay with us." Nathan said, "Thank you," and turned to find the elevator. The clerk called after him and he stopped in his tracks.

"Sir, can I ask you something?"

"Yes?" responded Nathan.

"Has anyone ever told you that you sound a lot like Christopher Walken?"

"All the time," he said and continued on.

Nathan waited until they were in their room before acknowledging Emily's presence. He wasn't sure about the security camera in the elevator, so he acted casual. It was not easy after the performance they had just executed. They broke into silent laughter that took their breaths. Part of it was because of the humor and part of it was the release of tension. Emily had considered that a deaf man checking into a room might be something that could be a red flag to someone. It wasn't that deaf people do not check into rooms, but they did not want to point anyone in their direction if they could avoid it. Emily's brilliant plan was to talk for Nathan, giving the impression that he could speak. At first she considered having Nathan wear the voice generator, but they decided it would take too long for him to master the device. Instead, he pretended to have a cold so his lips did not have to match up to the words. Since he could read lips, he knew what he was being asked so he could do all the physical responses without prompting. The only exception was when he was headed for the elevator. It was necessary for Emily to tap him on the shoulder to get him to stop and half-acknowledge the clerk. The whole plan worked like a charm.

What do you want to do now? he signed.

I don't know, signed Emily. *We could watch TV...or something.* She involuntarily looked over at the bed. Nathan blushed and his throat went dry. It was not his intention to take advantage of Emily and he wasn't even sure he was reading her correctly. He wanted their first night together to be special. Emily blushed when she saw the look on his face. Nathan saw her appearance change for a fleeting moment. For the briefest of seconds, she looked normal to him. She was not the shimmering angel or glass figurine; she looked like a normal young woman.

What's wrong? Emily signed.

Nothing. Nothing is wrong. You looked different for a second, he signed.

Different how?

I don't know...different like...normal. Nathan tried to convey what he had seen and he knew that it was significant. He just couldn't put his finger on why.

The confusion broke the mood for the time being and Emily suggested that they get some food. On the back of the keycard was an ad and phone number for a pizza chain. Emily asked Nathan if that was alright and he nodded. She used the voice generator to place the order. It arrived at their door in a little over thirty minutes, along with a two-liter of soda. Nathan thanked the delivery guy and gave him a fair, but not too generous tip. Before leaving, the delivery guy asked, "Do you know who...?"

"I know...I know...Christopher Walken," said Emily as Nathan covered his mouth. *I really need to change that voice setting*, she thought. They were beginning to attract too much attention. They sat on the end of the bed and dined. Both of them thought that sitting in the chairs and at the writing desk seemed too impersonal; but propped up on pillows at the head of the bed seemed too forward. So they sat at the end of the bed like two teenagers on their first date. They watched television after Nathan fumbled with the remote to find the closed-caption setting. He flipped through the channels, passing up several programs that Emily thought looked interesting. She stared at him in mild disbelief. They had gone from looking like kids on their first date to a seasoned married couple arguing about what program to watch. Emily stroked his hand lightly and it sent pleasant chills through him. She used the distraction to wrest the remote from him and pushed the buttons until she found what she was looking for…Sleepless in Seattle. It was her favorite movie. There was something about Tom Hanks falling in love with Meg Ryan while having never seen her that spoke to Emily. The movie gave her hope. Nathan reached for the remote, but Emily held up her finger and gave him a stern look that he found adorable.

The movie ended and Emily cried as usual. This time she was crying because the music and the inflection of the dialog were lost on Nathan and that made her sad. He wiped a tear from her cheek and somehow she knew that he enjoyed the story and the imagery. She knew that the lights, colors, shadows and movements in the movie formed their own kind of soundtrack in his mind. The credits ran and the light of the room dimmed. The glow from the TV seemed to bathe Nathan in starlight. Nathan thought Emily seemed to be *made* of starlight. He leaned over to kiss her and she met him more than half way. They stood, embraced and kissed again. No words, sign language or indications of any kind were necessary at that point. They were of one mind and moved as though they had been choreographed. Emily turned down the bed from one side; Nathan did the same from the other.

Then he joined her on her side of the bed and pulled her sweatshirt over her head. She unbuttoned his shirt and ran her hand down his chest. He resisted the temptation to caress her breasts right away. His restraint took superhuman strength. An awkward moment in the otherwise perfect movie scene came as they removed the rest of their clothes. It was nearly impossible to remove socks and tennis shoes in a romantic way. Once they were undressed, modesty kicked in. But instead of diving under the covers, they embraced once more, kissing long and passionately. Then Emily sat on the bed, slid back to the middle and shyly beckoned Nathan to join her. It puzzled her for a moment when he hesitated, but his intentions became clear when he retrieved the remote and turned the television off.

The room was black as ink, but as Nathan's eyes adjusted he could see Emily in the middle of the bed. He could see the slightest of ambient glows about her. He could not imagine that everyone couldn't see the glow. At that moment, he didn't want them to. They were together and alone. It was the first time for both of them and it was perfect. They had read that first times can be clumsy and awful. This was neither. Nathan held Emily in his arms afterwards. He thought she might regret the loss of her virginity, but she smiled and snuggled in tighter. It was the greatest experience of her life. Nothing could ruin it and nothing did.

Breakfast the next morning consisted of the remainder of the pizza. They showered together and dressed after considering another lovemaking session. They determined they did not have enough time, left the keycard in the room and locked the door behind them. Nathan had the sick feeling they had left something behind, even though they had brought nothing with them. He decided that the only thing he left behind was his innocence and he grinned widely. Emily looked at him curiously in the elevator, but she knew what the grin was about. She felt the same way. They walked past the morning desk clerk and she seemed to stare at Emily as she walked past. It made her nervous and she pushed Nathan so he would speed up. The desk clerk only saw a slight shimmer that looked a little like a rainbow created by light through a prism. Her look was more of curiosity than suspicion, but Emily felt she was doing the walk of shame...after a fashion.

Heading toward their rendezvous with Emily's mother, the couple held hands. Now more than ever, Emily wanted their ordeal to be over. She had a taste of what a normal life was like and she wanted more of it. Nathan looked over at Emily from time to time. She looked different to him somehow, but he couldn't explain it if he tried. He decided that he was just looking at her with new eyes; eyes that had matured in the last twenty-four hours. They took a state highway to the county seat rather than risk the interstate. They also needed to eat up some time. It wouldn't do to be sitting suspiciously outside of a closed library for an extended period of time. The road had a few cars on it, but traffic wasn't heavy and it was a pleasant drive. Then, an idiot completely ignored a stop sign and pulled onto the highway causing Nathan to slam on the brakes and swerve to avoid hitting him. He flipped Nathan the bird as he drove off laughing. Nathan became consumed with road rage and sped up to pursue him. Emily signed that it would not be a good idea to get pulled over and he slowed down in spite of his anger-impaired judgment. It proved to be good advice because they went through a speed trap less than ten minutes later.

They had hoped they would have seen the idiot in the Mazda pulled over by the local law enforcement, but he had apparently noticed and slowed down. Nathan and Emily caught up with him as he was pulling into a gas station. Emily motioned to Nathan to follow him in. Nathan looked at her curiously, but was obedient. He would do anything for her right now. The idiot pulled squarely between the two pump islands, preventing anyone from getting gas from four different pumps. Then he went inside without getting gas himself. Emily thought that he must have had a lot of anger issues; what's one more? She smiled an evil grin as she instructed Nathan to go inside and make sure he was seen. He didn't understand but he followed her instructions. They parked near the dumpster where the manager parked his car and Nathan went in. Emily took the keys from the ignition, adjusted the setting on the voice generator and went to the driver's side of the Mazda. On the door, in deep scratches she wrote STOP MEANS STOP. She underlined STOP twice. Then, as an afterthought she scratched RAPIST into the trunk lid. She regretted the last act of vandalism right after she did it, but it was too late to do anything about it now. She waited until he came out to see his reaction. It was exactly what she had hoped for and it was priceless.

"Son of a bitch!" he shouted. "Who the hell did this? I will kill you! Who the f…"

"Sir, could you please come back inside and pay for your gas purchase?" Emily interrupted in an echoing metallic voice.

"I didn't make a gas purchase, you son of a bitch," the idiot yelled up at the speaker. "Who did this to my car?"

"Sir, if you don't pay for your gas purchase I will have to call the police." Emily tried to keep from giggling.

"I told you I didn't get any gas, you…!" He stormed back into the gas station. Emily followed him in and watched the heated argument unfold. The attendant denied saying anything over the speaker and the idiot called him a liar among a few other choice derogatory terms. The attendant put up with it for as long as a person working for minimum wage might be expected to before releasing a barrage of his own expletives and defamations. This enflamed the idiot's rage and he reached across the counter and grabbed the attendant's collar. He pulled him close and drew back his fist just as a voice came from the door.

"Who does this car belong to," said the police officer who had just tried to fuel up. "The one blocking all the pumps." He walked straight up to the idiot and said, "Let me guess." The idiot was caught off guard and didn't think to release the attendant.

"You want to let him go, son? I think we need to talk." The officer placed his hand on the butt of his pistol and the idiot forced his fingers to loosen their grip on the attendant.

"Officer, I think I want to press charges," said the attendant.

"First things first...uh, Jack," he said, looking at the attendant's nametag. "I think junior here and I need to discuss his detailing...along with his parking methods."

"I didn't do anything wrong!" the idiot yelled.

"We'll see about that," said the officer as he led him outside. "First, I need your keys."

"Why?" he asked with a mix of nervousness and anger.

"Because I said so," said the officer with anger only.

"Well, at least let me move my car first," said the idiot.

"Oh, it's going to get moved alright. I already called for the tow truck."

"You can't do that! I didn't do anything wrong." The idiot was almost in tears, but he held them back and tried to look tough.

"I am not so sure about that," said the officer. "When I saw the word RAPIST and STOP MEANS STOP scratched into your paint, I got to thinking there is more to this story than just some bad parking. The station is running a background check on you as we speak. Oh…and since this was obviously vandalism, I am going to search your car to make sure nothing else was damaged."

"You can't do that!" yelled the idiot. He began to panic; mainly because he knew that a background check would reveal a suspended sentence for date rape. But mostly it was because of the *blunts* he had hidden in the cup holder under a lottery ticket.

Emily would have liked to stay and find out how the whole drama played out, but they needed to go if they were going to be on time. Nathan followed her to the car and cautiously signed to her, *Remind me never to get on your bad side.*

Karma's a bitch, she signed. *…and I helped!* Nathan was seeing a side of Emily he never knew existed. It was going to take some getting used to. They pulled out of the gas station lot and got back on the road, never knowing the fate of the idiot who had almost killed them. If they had been able to read the local paper the next day, they would have found out his name was Tony and he had been charged with possession of marijuana. The courts would decide just how much of a bitch Karma was going to be.

Emily and Nathan arrived at the Carlstone County Library at twenty minutes after nine. They had hoped to be there when it opened but the Karma detour delayed them a bit. They were not sure how to find Alma Troy. All they knew was the alias she was using and they couldn't just ask around. Instead, they decided to look for her. No one in the library seemed to fit her description but Emily remembered that she had written about changing her appearance. She finally saw her mother's familiar profile on a person sitting in the periodical section. At first, she wasn't sure it was her. Emily thought she was a guy. So she moved to the table where Alma was and sat across for her. Looking around to make sure they were alone, she whispered "mom?" using the voice generator. Alma jumped so hard that her knees hit the bottom of the table, causing heads in the library to turn. She buried her face in a magazine and everyone returned to their own business.

"Emily?" she whispered. "How are you talking to me?"

"It's a voice generator," she said softly. "A gift from a friend."

"Where is Nathan?" asked Alma.

"I had him look up some stuff on the reference computers so he wouldn't look suspicious," Emily whispered. "We have a lot to tell you."

"Emily," said Alma softly. "Something is different about you…and I don't mean that you are speaking. There is something different. It only looks like tricks of the light, but I would almost swear that I can see you."

CHAPTER 12: NEW OBJECTIVE

Emily and her mother left the library together and walked to the next block. Nathan left a few minutes later to avoid suspicion. He met them around the corner with the car when he was sure he wasn't being followed or observed. Alma and Emily sat in the back seat on the way back to Cedar Pike. Alma conversed with Nathan by way of the rear view mirror when the conversation wasn't distracting to his driving. After he drove off the edge of the road a couple of times, he decided he needed to find a place to stop for a few minutes. The group needed to plan their next move carefully. They had avoided detection for too long and couldn't afford to get careless. A supermarket parking lot provided a place for them to talk. Nathan informed Alma of Charles' capture. Her eyes filled with tears as his hands formed the symbols conveying the message. Emily was already aware of her father's situation, but that didn't stop tears from rolling down her cheeks as well.

Do we have a plan? Alma signed to Nathan as she looked hopefully to Emily.

There is a risk with any plan, signed Nathan. *I don't want to lose Emily again.* Alma smiled and caressed his hand. She liked Nathan. She thought he was perfect for Emily. She only wished he had told her that he could see her sooner. She would have approved of most of their contact. But she understood why he had kept it a secret from everyone.

"I want to be involved," said Emily with the voice generator. She signed as she talked for Nathan's benefit. He started to protest, but he knew Emily. He knew she was stubborn and would win out in the end. Alma could not deny that Emily's condition could aid them in Charles' rescue.

"We just need a few hours to get a head start," Emily said. "If we can do that, we can disappear…so to speak." She smiled at her own half-intended pun. Nathan smiled a worried smile and Alma got a sick feeling in the pit of her stomach.

"I'm not sure," she said. "They have guns and equipment. I don't mean to be rude or anything sweetheart; but all we have…is you."

"…and –I– am what they want so badly," said Emily. "They fear what they cannot see."

But with their glasses, signed Nathan, …they *can see you. You told me that.*

"But they will only be wearing them if they know I am coming," said Emily. "As long as I don't give them a reason to suspect I am there, they will keep them in their pockets." Nathan and Alma still didn't like it, but they felt that they had no other options. When the government is involved, there is no one to run to.

"You said you saw cots," Emily said and signed to Nathan. "That means they sleep there. Most, if not all of them, will either be asleep or at least caught off guard. If I can sneak in, I can free daddy and be out before they know he is gone. I will steal their keys and we can take one of their vehicles after disabling the others. It's not a perfect plan, but we may need to make some things up as we go along."

The others nodded solemnly in agreement and they got back on the road for Cedar Pike. Patty would start looking for her car around four, so they had a little time to spare when they got to the edge of town. Figuring that no one knew what her car looked like, Nathan thought it might not be too great a risk to go past the drive-in for some reconnaissance. He had not intended to slow down, but what he saw puzzled him. From the road, he could see the boarded-up concession stand. The night he had been there, three SUVs were parked outside. Now, there were none. Emily tapped him on the shoulder and motioned for him to pull off the road when he got past the line of windbreaker trees. Nathan shook his head in protest but obediently pulled over anyway. Emily's mother only told her to be careful. Emily slid out of the car quietly and softly padded across the desolate drive-in lot. In the afternoon light, the rows of speaker posts reminded her of grave markers in a bleak cemetery. The stark silence made her feel uneasy and her stomach was a little upset. A sudden gust of wind blew up a small dust devil that startled her and she froze in her tracks.

When she realized it wasn't a threat, she continued to the projection window that Nathan had told her about. She paused for a second before looking in. She was barely tall enough to see through the window and then only by standing on her toes. Emily looked in and saw…nothing. The room was pitch-black. If anyone was in there, they would have to be using night vision goggles to see. Her eyes had just begun to adjust to the darkness when there was a loud noise to her right. She dropped to one knee and held her breath. She waited…not sure what the noise was. Another dust devil blew up and the plywood sheet that served as the men's room door clapped loudly against the doorframe. Emily allowed herself to breathe and moved around to the side of the concession stand. Cautiously, she opened the door just a crack and peered in. She could only see the light from the projection window. She opened the door wider and let the daylight spill into the room. Dust particles played in the ray of sunlight that streamed through the small projection window. The sun cast a distorted rectangle on the back wall. The room contained an old chair and a weathered table. Other than that, there was no sign anyone had ever been there.

Emily was a little relieved, but her heart was heavy. She wasn't really ready for a confrontation, but now she was no closer to finding her dad. Feeling that she had no need to sneak, she ran back to the SUV and informed the others of what she had found out. Alma uttered a muffled whimper before composing herself and exploring their next move. Nathan was glad Emily was safe. He didn't like the fact that she had to check out the concession stand alone; even if it was dictated by logic. Donning the voice generator again, Emily spoke in a mix of spoken words and sign language that to an outside observer would have sounded like a weak signal on a satellite radio channel. Her words were frantic and a little jumbled, but she finally took a deep breath and closed her eyes. When she opened them, her demeanor had changed. She had transformed into someone who was logical and determined. It was a side of Emily that Nathan liked. Alma looked at her daughter with renewed admiration.

"We have to think how they think," said Emily. "Where would we have taken daddy if we were them?" The first thought that popped into Nathan's head was that they would have killed him and disposed of the body somewhere. He kept that thought to himself and turned his mind to more positive possibilities.

We should consider why they brought him here in the first place, he signed. *They were trying to find Dr. Cornell's journals. They thought your father had stolen them from his office. If he had an idea of where the records might be, they would probably have taken him there.*

Emily and Alma looked at each other. Nathan had hit the ball out of the park on his first time at bat. They were sure they knew where Charles was being held. At least they hoped they knew. The idea that they had disposed of him had crossed their minds too, but they had dismissed the thought even quicker than Nathan had. Emily touched Nathan on the shoulder and signed, *Take me home*.

Dr. Cornell was a fantastic note-taker. As far as the Troy family knew, he never transferred any of his findings to a hard drive anywhere. The downside of his method was that over the years, the volume of college-ruled notebooks became downright ponderous. His findings over the years made some of the earlier ones useless, as most of his research was conjecture. They were the results of trial and error experiments that had usually produced negative results. He had almost given up and was about to concede that Emily would have to live her life silent and invisible, when a breakthrough happened. Emily had just turned fifteen and the chemistry of her body was changing. In normal adolescents, there are growth spurts and hormonal changes. In Emily, the chemical composition of her bodily fluids such as blood, sweat and saliva changed in such a way that they could be compared to previous samples. The changes were subtle, yet remarkable. Dr. Cornell could see that her cells were evolving as she matured. Not only was he able to determine that her invisibility was caused by a chemical similar to a pheromone that she excreted, but he also found that her cells themselves generated a form of energy that caused the air around her to absorb light instead of allowing it to reach her. The result was the creation of a field of invisibility. It seemed to be a recessive trait that some primates might have possessed as a defense mechanism.

Dr. Cornell knew that his earlier findings were useless and he gave eleven of his earlier journals to Alma and had asked her to burn them. Alma would have complied had she not read some of the notes first. Not only were the notes concise about Dr. Cornell's medical findings; they also painted a detailed portrait of Emily's childhood and his observations of her personality. To Alma, burning them would have been like burning a family album. There were no pictures of Emily past age six and Alma could not bear the thought of destroying the only record of the rest of her childhood. Dr. Cornell had only named the journals by year with no reference to Emily or her condition. Alma had bought adhesive labels and placed them over the year. Then she wrote RECIPES on each of them and placed them on a shelf in the kitchen along with the collected works of Rachael Ray and Martha Stewart. The rest of the journals, Dr. Cornell had kept. Alma hoped he would make more discoveries that would render his earlier findings obsolete so she could keep those journals too.

Dr. Cornell kept the rest of his journals in an unassuming file case which he kept in the trunk of his car. It was covered in a drab brown fabric and looked like something a salesman or insurance adjuster might carry. As a precaution, he carried two more just like it. One contained clothes and toiletries; the other contained medical reference books. He also carried an antique medical bag made of dark brown leather. Its outward appearance gave the impression that it belonged to an aged country doctor who still prescribed poultices and leeches to his patients. But inside were some of the most up-to-date instruments and experimental drugs available, if one knew the right people. Dr. Cornell knew the right people. He also knew at least one of the *wrong people*. One of his former colleagues, whom Dr. Cornell had trusted with a small amount of information about Emily, had betrayed him to the government. His colleague had traded what he knew for immunity from a transgression that was about to blow up in his face. Even though he sold out Emily, her family and his former friend, the transgression blew up in his face anyway.

The shadier departments of government were not exempt from bureaucratic red tape it seemed. It was a full month before agents showed up at Dr. Cornell's office. He was taken into custody under the auspice of Homeland Security which followed some relaxed rules about detaining civilians. The agents searched his office and found nothing. They searched his car and found only two of the three cases. The one they were actually looking for was missing. He and his car were removed from town. An email was sent to Dr. Hertz indicating that she would have to take over the practice for an extended period due to an unexpected family emergency.

Dr. Cornell did not like the way his former colleague had responded to some of the requests he had made. The colleague had been working in a related field and had actually secured a government grant to study a finding very similar to Emily's case. He seemed a little too anxious to help and wanted to know a lot about the case. Dr. Cornell had told him that it was just an experiment that he was working on, but his colleague insisted on knowing more…even to the point of raising his voice. Warning bells went off in Dr. Cornell's head and he ended the phone call as quickly and politely as possible. He didn't return messages and sent his former colleague an email stating that his experiment had stalled and he was abandoning it. The colleague then insisted that Dr. Cornell turn over his research to him in spite of the fact that he had no legitimate claim to it. Instead of answering the demand, the doctor hid the journals and told no one what he had done with them. He also warned Alma and Charles to leave Cedar Pike and find someplace safe for Emily. He told them that he had made a terrible mistake and they were in danger of being apprehended and detained…maybe indefinitely. They trusted Dr. Cornell and had made preparations to move during the night to another state. Emily didn't want to go. She didn't want to leave Nathan. Her parents didn't know about their relationship. She pretended to go to sleep in the backseat of their car. They were in the next county before they realized she had slipped out and stayed behind; yet one more disadvantage of having an invisible child. Even though she had grown into a young woman who could make her own decisions, they still sheltered her; almost to the point of smothering.

Emily was captured. She never considered that the government might have glasses that would allow them to see her. She had been imperceptible for so long, she had become complacent. She didn't even know they had found her until she woke up in the research facility, recovering from the effects of a tranquilizer dart. Her father went back for her, leaving Alma behind to look for her in the event anything happened to him. He never contacted Alma and she went into hiding; disguising herself as well as she could. When she didn't hear from Charles, she contacted the only person she thought might be able to help her. She and Charles were friends with David and Sue Saunders. Emily had finally confided to Alma that Nathan could see her for some reason and that she had feelings for him. She also had some female questions that she needed answered and she had nowhere else to turn. The internet was not a place one could go and get guaranteed accurate information about some things. Alma had contacted Nathan using a fake email address from the Carlstone County Library computer bank. She got the address from Emily when she had asked her how she and Nathan managed to communicate. Alma used a passive email message with some key words that he would recognize. He was anxious to respond because at first he thought it was Emily contacting him. When he discovered it was Alma, he set up a series of dummy accounts to prevent them from being detected. He also forged some fake IDs for her using a picture she sent him on the cell phone he used for text messaging. Forging fake IDs was one of the more dubious services Nathan provided for the high school crowd. No one ever seemed to suspect the deaf kid of wrongdoing. Alma had hitchhiked back to Cedar Pike to pick up the documents at the edge of town. Her dowdy appearance seemed like the perfect cover; she looked like someone who would hitchhike to get around.

Nathan left the false identifications at a drop near a gas station that went out of business when an interstate took traffic in another direction. He also left detailed instructions of how to set up secure accounts and how he would bounce signals around the globe to remain anonymous. Alma didn't need to know all the details. It was best that she didn't. It actually filled her with hope when she was notified that Charles was being held at the drive-in. She thought there might be a chance that he could escape and join her. After the nightmares she had about Charles being water-boarded at Guantanamo, it was like she had been told they were keeping him at the Holiday Inn. Alma was ecstatic when she learned Emily had escaped. For the past few days she had felt like a victim. Now she was with her daughter again, ready to rescue her husband. She felt it was time to go on the offense and get her family back together.

Alma and Charles had an almost psychic connection. Maybe it was because of the years of having to anticipate Emily's needs or maybe it was because they really were meant for each other. It went beyond just finishing each other's sentences. They could really feel what the other was feeling. The couple never argued because they were always in sync. Alma just needed to ask herself what she would have done if she had been in Charles' place at the abandoned drive-in. When he found out Emily had escaped, he knew that she would try to go back to the house. They were going to be there waiting for her. He didn't know why, but he needed to be there too. It was as if Alma could see what played out. In her mind, she saw an agent answer his phone. He announced to the others that Emily was free and was probably headed their way. They were ordered to get to the house. One must have said, "What about him?" They would probably have arranged transport to the dreaded secure facility…or worse. Charles probably spoke up with the only card he had left to play; the journals. He knew the ones in the kitchen would do them no good, so he bluffed the agents into taking him with them to the house. There he would send them on a search of the premises by showing them the disguised notebooks and saying in an unconvincing voice, "That's all I have." They would be tearing the house apart, trying to find the latest journals. They might even be torturing Charles.

Alma felt a sudden sense of urgency and signed for Nathan to hurry, but not speed. Nathan looked confused but tried to comply. Emily put her hand on her mother's shoulder as they approached the Welcome to Cedar Pike sign. A feeling came over her and she suddenly dropped onto the floorboard of the backseat. Alma pretended to be smoothing her short hair as they passed a local deputy behind the sign. He seemed to be wearing special dark glasses.

CHAPTER 13: REUNION

The farmhouse looked cold, uninviting...and somehow, sad. It was a stark contrast from the home that Emily had shared with her parents for two decades. It appeared to be empty. Nathan drove past the long gravel drive at a comfortable speed that did not look like he was casing the place. Alma sat low in the passenger seat and Emily stayed on the floorboard of the backseat. Nathan observed as much as he could with his peripheral vision while Alma adjusted the visor mirror in such a way that allowed her to observe without being noticed. Nathan drove to the four-way stop at the corner of the property and turned left. From there, the side and some of the back of the house could be observed, even though it was from quite a distance. Alma felt a wave of depression wash over her when nothing was out of the ordinary. Nathan stepped on the accelerator to get out of the area before they looked suspicious. As he did, Emily noticed a reflection in their barn. She had risked peeking up over the door after they had turned the corner. Her mother saw it too. They both knew that the only thing that would reflect in the barn was an automobile.

Nathan pulled the car into a dirt access road between a tree-lined fencerow and a field of withered cornstalks. They all began to converse simultaneously; Nathan in sign language and Alma and Emily in a mix of spoken word-sign language blend. Once they relaxed and began taking turns, logic and order began to prevail.

"Could you see what kind of car it was?" asked Emily.

"All I could tell is that it was a vehicle of some kind," said Alma. "The interior of the barn was too dark to see anything else."

I didn't see a car at all, signed Nathan. *Are you sure it wasn't something else?*

"I know what was in the barn," said Alma. "Everything in there was either wood or rusted metal. Even the windows are frosted with dust. There was never a point in cleaning them. They were dirty again within a week."

"I think we are getting off the subject," said Emily. "Who do you think is there?"

Nathan was quick to take the lead in the conversation. *If it is your dad's car,* he signed *...it means they hid it there while they kept him at the drive-in. If it was one or more of their cars, it means they probably have him there.* Emily kissed him on the cheek and nodded agreement.

"So what now?" Emily finally asked.

"Simple," said Alma. "We have to find out what is in that barn. The only way to do that is to come up behind it. That way, the barn provides cover so we won't be seen."

Then what? signed Nathan.

"Well, if it is Charles' car, there's a chance the house is empty," she signed and said. "If it is a government car, we will have to think of something."

"It also means we have to cross the field adjacent to ours," said Emily. "Mr. Booth doesn't like trespassers."

"We could wait until it gets dark," suggested Alma.

Nathan seemed more than a little concerned. *I have to get Patty's car back to her. She was nice to let me borrow it. I don't want to make an enemy of her.*

Emily bared her teeth and said, "Patty" softly and in a disparaging tone. Alma couldn't see her expression, but she knew the tone. Emily was unknowingly mimicking her. She hid her smile and thought for a moment.

"We can stay here," she said finally, when she was sure she wouldn't break into a chuckle. "We can hide here in the corn while you take the car back. You can check in with your parents and meet us back here if you like." Nathan seemed a little offended by the last part of her sentence. Alma grasped the meaning of his expression right away. *What I mean is*, she signed, *you have done so much for us already. This isn't your fight and you shouldn't put yourself at risk.*

As long as it is her fight, he signed, *it is MY fight.* Nathan intentionally spelled out *M-Y* to emphasize it. *I will come back. Nothing can stop me.* Alma hoped that was true. She touched his hand softly and nodded. Emily put her arms around his neck from the backseat and kissed him on the cheek. She shoved her jealousy to the very back of her mind. She had more important things to think of. She and Alma got out of the car. Emily signed, *Be careful* and gave Nathan a passionate kiss that Alma was grateful she couldn't see. Nathan smiled and signed, *Y-O-U be careful.* Emily nodded and Nathan backed out onto the road and drove away.

Alma looked at the position of the sun. It would probably be two hours before it would go down. She motioned to Emily that they should make themselves comfortable. Emily did not want to embarrass her mother by informing her that she had just motioned to empty space; so she got into position before agreeing. They sat under a moderately-sized elm tree. They talked about everything that had transpired in the last few days. Emily was sorry she didn't keep the special dark glasses she had stolen so that her mother could see her. They sat under the tree and talked for half an hour before Emily began to notice that the voice generator was getting hot. She had been warned that excessive use would cause the battery to overheat. She told her mother that she had to go silent for a while and put the device in her pocket. Alma suddenly felt alone and a chill went through her. It was a feeling she got whenever she felt as though Emily wasn't safe. She reached out, held her daughter's hand and relaxed somewhat.

Emily began to tug Alma's hand, urging her to stand up. Alma didn't understand, but she complied and followed Emily's lead into the cornfield. Four or five rows in, Emily pulled her down to a crouched position and they waited. A rush of wind indicated a car was passing the field. Peering between the stalks, Alma could barely make out the markings of the deputy town marshal's patrol car. She wanted to ask Emily how she had known to hide in the field, but she knew she could not get an answer right away; so she saved her questions for later. They didn't know whether the deputy was looking for them or if he was just making his routine rounds. It didn't matter. It was better to be safe than sorry.

The sun had dropped to a place where it shined though the corn tassels, creating a striking starburst effect. Alma was usually afraid of spiders, but the sight of an intricate web strung between two stalks fascinated her. The way the sun played on the elegant symmetrical design was mesmerizing. In fact she was so mesmerized, she didn't notice that Nathan had returned until he touched her on the shoulder. Alma squealed and then quickly clasped her hand over her mouth. She worried that someone might have heard her, but rows of corn served as a natural sound baffle. Emily was glad to see him back. She mentally congratulated herself on suppressing her jealousy of Patty, but she still calculated how long he had been gone to see how much time he might have spent with her. When she realized he had walked all the way back to them, the time he must have spent with her would have been insignificant. She felt a pang of guilt. Patty had been so kind to lend him her car. Emily didn't want him to seem unappreciative. She hugged him tightly to let him know she was glad he was back and safe.

How did you know we were in the field? she signed.

I followed your footprints, he responded. *The soil in the field is very soft.*

You are a genius, signed Emily.

I know. Nathan grinned as he signed. Emily punched him softly in the chest. *Don't get a big head,* she signed.

Emily began to get impatient and the voice generator in her pocket seemed to have cooled down. She put it in place, making sure the settings were still adjusted properly and spoke softly.

"I think I want to go ahead," she said. "We don't have any light sources and waiting until dark might put us at a disadvantage."

"But what if they see you?" asked Alma. She was trying to come up with a good reason to stay together.

"With those glasses, they can see me in the dark too. The risk isn't any greater," she argued. "Actually, there is less risk if I go now. If they aren't wearing the glasses, no one will be able to see me. I can scout out the farm and report back when it is safe."

How are you going to do that? signed Nathan. Emily looked him in the eyes, but took her mother's hand. In it she placed a cell phone. From Alma's perspective, the phone seemed to magically appear in her hand.

"Where did you get this?" she whispered.

"I borrowed it from a lady at the library," she answered. "I got another one from the guy at the reference computer. We can text and they can't trace them to us."

"You and I are going to have to sit down and talk about boundaries, young lady," said Alma. Emily smiled. She knew Alma was impressed with her.

"You have to promise me that you will be really careful," Alma said.

"I have always been careful," replied Emily. "I won't take any unnecessary chances." Alma searched for her to hug her. The setting on the voice generator seemed to be a little off and it threw her voice a little. Emily took her mother's arms and guided them to her. They embraced for a long time while Nathan stood by, patiently awaiting his turn. Emily gave him more than a long embrace. She kissed him with the same passion she had done earlier that day. Alma was glad that Emily's invisibility had the strange effect it did on objects she touched. Otherwise, Nathan would have looked as though he was kissing the side of an aquarium. It would not have been pretty. Emily got down to business and obtained the numbers of the two phones from their directories. Then she tested them to make sure they both had texting capabilities. She would have been surprised if they didn't. Alma kissed her cheek and Emily left the field.

Alma and Nathan moved closer to the road to observe Emily's trek across Mr. Booth's field. Nathan could make out her celestial form moving in a half-crouched manner up the subtle grade to the barn. Alma saw almost nothing. Occasionally she saw shimmers of light that looked like sunlight reflecting off the surface of a pond. It worried her, but filled her with hope at the same time. She felt there might be a chance she could someday actually see her daughter again. But the condition she had come to hate was keeping

Emily safe for the time being. Emily reached the barn and stopped. Alma felt the cell phone vibrate in her hand.

SO FAR SO GOOD, she texted. NOT SURE HOW I SHOULD GO IN.

ONE OF THE WINDOWS NEAR THE BACK OF THE SOUTH SIDE HAS A LOOSE LATCH, Alma responded. YOU MIGHT BE ABLE TO JIGGLE IT LOOSE.

I WILL TRY. Alma saw a brief flash of light at the corner of the barn. It was the wrong corner. Another text came in. WHOOPSIE. Alma smiled. Emily had never been very good at determining directions without a map. Emily slipped to the other side of the barn. The window was attached to the barn by hinges at the top. It had replaced wooden shutters a number of years before. It was a relatively high window and getting in was not going to be easy. It was open about an inch at the bottom. Emily opened it the rest of the way and was surprised that the oxidized hinges made no noise. A stick lay in the window sill. Emily used it to prop the window open. She turned around with her back to the barn and grabbed the wooden support above the window on the inside. She hoisted herself up in a pull-up fashion, lifted her knees and dropped down quietly inside one of the stalls. The stalls were used for storage as the Troy's had little need for livestock.

A collection of rusty primitive farm implements hung on the rustic barn walls. It looked like a museum display and gave more of an impression of respect than of neglect. Beams from the waning sun filtered in between the boards of the barn. Dust particles stirred up by Emily's entrance through the open window danced in the sunbeams in a free-style dust particle ballet. Emily covered her mouth when she realized the dust that swirled around the interior of the barn was not confined to the beams of light. The barn was dark by comparison and it took a little while for her eyes to adjust. The outline of a vehicle became apparent. It appeared to be a black SUV like the one that Nathan had described to her. As her eyes became more adjusted to the light, the black exterior seemed to morph into the dark burgundy of her family's Chevy Equinox. Emily was expecting either one to be in the barn, so knowing did not stop her uneasiness. All finding it meant was that *they* had brought the vehicle here to keep it out of sight. She moved to the large barn doors and peered out. The right door was slightly ajar due to a faulty lock that Emily's dad had never gotten around to fixing. She was a half second away from exiting the barn to investigate the house, when a black SUV pulled into the yard behind the house and parked. It was positioned strategically to be hidden from all of the main roads. A short man wearing special dark glasses got out. He carried white paper bags from a fast food chain that was not located in Cedar Pike. He pushed a button on his key fob and a double bleep let him know his ride was secure. He looked around and appeared to shake off the feeling that he was being watched. Then he entered the back door of the house. Emily was pondering her next move when a vibration in her pocket startled her.

WHAT'S GOING ON? CAN YOU TELL ANYTHING? Alma texted.

SOMEBODY IS HERE, Emily responded. A GUY IN A SUV JUST TOOK FOOD INTO THE HOUSE. LOOKED LIKE TOO MUCH FOOD FOR JUST ONE PERSON.

WHAT DO YOU PLAN TO DO? –MOM–

NOT SURE. HE WAS WEARING THE DARK GLASSES. THEY CAN SEE ME. –E–

OUR CAR IS HERE. MAYBE DADDY IS HERE TOO. Emily tried to sound as positive as possible in her text message.

BE CAREFUL. I CAN'T LOSE YOU. –MOM–

I AM ALWAYS CAREFUL. I THINK I MIGHT...
Emily hit SEND without thinking. Someone was coming out of the house. It was the short man in the special dark glasses. He walked around to the passenger side of the SUV and clicked the fob again. Another bleep told him the vehicle was unlocked and he retrieved a small white bag from the front seat. Emily suspected it was a bag of condiment packets and napkins from the fast food restaurant. The agent closed the door and turned suddenly, looking directly at the barn. He began to slowly walk in Emily's direction. She had moved to a place where she could look between the cracks in the planks that made up the door. She was sure he couldn't see her, but he was headed right for her. Emily was too scared to move. As he got closer, he took out his service weapon. He gripped the barn door that was open slightly and pulled it back abruptly. The short agent surveyed the barn. Nothing seemed out of the ordinary, but something was out of place. He couldn't put his finger on it. He was about to perform a thorough investigation when an impatient voice from the house yelled, "Roy! Where's the mustard? What's the holdup?" Roy paused, considered his next move and reluctantly returned to the house. "Now go back and close the door. Were you brought up in a barn?" Laughter came from inside the house. Roy fumed as he went back to close the barn door. He didn't like being pushed around and he didn't like being the butt of jokes which the other agents aimed at him. He looked at the dark-tinted windows of the Equinox as he closed the barn door. Roy imagined he saw movement, but he wasn't about to investigate now. *Screw it!* he thought and went back to the house...wishing he had spit in their sandwiches.

Emily lay on the back seat of the Equinox shaking. That had been too close and she did not want to go back to the research facility. This time, they would make sure she never escaped again. Her mother had been frantically texting since Emily's last text had been cut off. Emily texted her and told her how the events had unfolded. Alma wanted her to come back to the relative safety of the cornfield, but Emily assured her that she was alright for the moment. She wasn't sure what she was going to do, but she was too close now to just quit. She had just pushed SEND when a voice behind her said, "Emily?"

She threw herself against the back of the front seat as she turned around. A black silhouette loomed behind the backseat of the Equinox. Emily strained to force her eyes to see in the near darkness. Finally, she aimed the light from the cell phone at the figure. She tried to talk, forgetting that she had removed the voice generator. She quickly replaced it and softly, but enthusiastically said, "Doctor Dave?"

CHAPTER 14: A PLAN OF ACTION

Doctor David Cornell could barely see the light from the cell phone. Emily's invisibility did not completely hide light for some reason. The soft glow illuminated his face in the dark interior of the vehicle. His eyes were wide with astonishment. He had grown used to Emily's invisibility, but hearing a voice come from an empty space was unsettling.

"How are you speaking?" He had heard her voice through the throat back of course, but this time she sounded different; like someone on the other end of a very loud phone conversation. Emily had chosen the setting to help her remain undetected.

"I got a gift from a friend," she said. "What are you doing here?"

"I suspected they would come here after I found out my office had been broken into," he said. "I thought it might be a good idea if I came here to collect my other journals. I barely made it into the barn when I saw them drive up with your father."

"Daddy's inside?" she exclaimed. Dr. Cornell was surprised to hear inflection in her voice. He was used to the mechanical monotone of the throat back.

"Yes," he responded. "They brought him here before dawn this morning. He seems to be in good health, but he looks tired. They must have been interrogating him a lot before he finally told them about my journals." Emily was silent for a few moments and Dr. Cornell suspected she was either fuming or sobbing. In reality, she was doing a bit of both. She regained her composure and began to formulate a plan.

"I should have mom and Nathan join us," she said finally. "They are waiting across the field for word from me."

"Nathan? The deaf boy?"

"Deaf *man*," corrected Emily. "He has been wonderful through this whole thing. I will have to fill you in later. I can't wait for you to meet him. They are waiting until dark so they can cross the field undetected." The sun had dipped below the horizon, evident by the pinkish glow through the barn window. Emily texted Alma and told her who she had met in the barn. Alma wasn't sure how to respond. She hadn't expected anyone to be in the barn and she had not even been certain of the fate of Dr. Cornell. She was glad he was alive and not in custody; but she feared his presence might be a complication. He was a factor she had not considered.

Nathan and Alma stealthily moved across the harvested field behind the barn. The subtle glow of twilight gave them enough light to see without being observed. Once at the rear window of the barn, Nathan helped Alma up and through the opening. His hand accidentally groped her in the near-darkness and she muffled an exclamation of surprise with her hand. She tumbled into the stall, bruising her shoulder on the hard surface of the floor…or more accurately, ground. Nathan followed her in, hoping his accidental slip would be ignored. The interior of the barn was filled with a gloomy darkness, interspersed with shadowy silhouettes. Nathan moved forward and bumped into Alma who had just risen to her feet. He signed an apology, but it was lost in the darkness like smoke in fog. Alma patted his shoulder to reassure him that there was no harm done and the two navigated the obstacles to the vehicle. Alma opened the passenger door of the Equinox carefully, worried that the dome light would come on. Dr. Cornell had taken the precaution of overriding the dome light while it was still light out. Nathan entered on the driver's side, reached back and softly stroked Emily's face.

"Wait! He can see you?" asked Dr. Cornell.

"I don't know how, but yes," said Emily.

"This could put a whole new slant on my research," said Dr. Cornell.

"No more tests!" demanded Emily. "Not for a while at least. I have had enough tests and those bastar....*individuals* don't need anything else to work with. We need to solve the problem at hand."

"I am not sure what we can do," said Alma. "They have your father; and while they have those glasses, you can't even sneak up on them."

"I have an idea that might work," said Emily. "It is kind of a longshot, but I saw it on TV one time."

"This isn't TV," responded Dr. Cornell. "If we get caught, they might just make us all disappear...no offense." Emily's smile was lost on him, but Nathan could see that she was amused by Dr. Cornell's faux pas.

"We don't have a lot of choices," she said. "...unless we just plan to leave daddy behind. I, for one, am not willing to do that."

"No one is suggesting that," said the doctor. "We just need to be cautious."

"Maybe not," said Emily. Dr. Cornell was almost certain he could see a smile illuminated in the glow of the cell phone. He was sure he was imagining it, but it reminded him of the Cheshire Cat. The next instant, a frantic voice filled the interior of the Equinox. It was not the voice they had heard coming from Emily; it was the voice of Agent Baxter. Everyone jumped except for Nathan. Alma and Dr. Cornell looked around, sure that they had been discovered. Emily remained calm, even though her voice was still frantic.

"...repeat! Officer down! Be advised...there are an unknown number of assailants in the house. I am certain they have at least one hostage. Use force only as a last resort." The 911 operator became a bit frantic herself. She was used to house fires and heart attacks. This was her first hostage crisis. She passed along the information to every local, county and State Police agency on her list, without ever checking the authenticity of the call. Within minutes, all manner of patrol cars had surrounded the house, taking the government agents completely off guard. The red and blue flashing lights, mixed with intermittent flashes of yellow and white made the house, barn, trees and surrounding fields look like a psychotic carnival from hell.

Inside the house, the agents began to panic. This was one contingency they had not planned on. Every step of the operation had gone smoothly until now and no one currently in the group had the authority to act. Finally, one of the agents (Agent Carmichael) decided to be proactive and made an executive decision. He stepped out of the back door with his arms raised high in the air. He moved his arm in front of his face to shield his eyes from the spotlights that shined upon him. In doing so, his sport coat shifted revealing his service weapon in its shoulder holster. One of the younger officers shouted "Gun!" and Agent Carmichael froze in his tracks. His knees weakened as a multitude of weapons were trained upon him, which made it easier for the members of the volunteer SWAT team to take him down. Before he could speak, they had him on the ground with his face planted in the dust. He was handcuffed and forced into the back of a patrol car as his protests went unheeded.

Emily and the others had exited the Equinox and moved to the back of the barn. There they climbed out the back window just in case the barn was to be searched. Emily told the others to stay out of sight and she moved to the front corner of the barn. Two officers were positioned on either side of the back door, preparing to rush the farmhouse. Obviously, the team had not been instructed in hostage negotiations and Emily was worried that she might have made a mistake. She thought that since her abduction by the agents and the abduction of her father had been a covert operation, they would probably not be forthcoming about their motives for detaining them.

Emily strolled boldly across the barn lot, careful to avoid getting in anyone's line of fire, went to the kitchen window and peered in. At first, she could see nothing. But the spotlights cast enough light to make the interior rooms look like a diorama decorated with black cardboard cutouts. She could make out the silhouette of her father bound to a chair and two other individuals crouched behind furniture. On the kitchen table were two pairs of special dark glasses as well as what Emily inferred were specialized night-vision binoculars. The two officers next to the door seemed to be waiting for instructions. She adjusted the controls on the voice generator and said, "Stand down, but hold your position," in a metallic voice that sounded like it came from the radio on one of the officer's belt. "We are in contact with those inside the house…repeat…stand down!"

The two officers were startled and confused as the back door of the farmhouse opened by itself. The one of the left reached out and grabbed it, but Emily was already inside. A voice came over the radio saying, "What are you idiots doing? Leave that door alone." The officer who was holding the door was about to make an explanation, but decided he wasn't quite sure what to say; so he simply closed the door. Emily moved to the table and pocketed the special dark glasses. She suspected that the other agent had his pair in his pocket when he was apprehended. Since his hands had been cuffed behind him, she knew he was no longer a threat and that she now had the upper hand. She took the night-vision binoculars and deposited them in the trashcan under some empty Chinese food containers. On the kitchen counter was a radio like the one Agent Baxter had with him. There was also a shiny metal case that had five syringes in it containing a substance that Emily recognized as the drug Agent Baxter had tried to give her. She removed three of them and placed the remainder in her pocket. Moving to the next room, she found the other agents strategically positioned on each side of the living room window. They were speaking in low whispers, but it was obvious they did not know what to do. Emily moved to the one on the right, jammed the needle into his neck and pressed the plunger down. He tried to say "ouch" but it came out as only "uh" before he slumped forward. The other agent thought that his partner had been shot by a sniper with a suppressed rifle. He dropped prostrate on the floor and was an easy target for Emily. With the two agents dispatched, she moved to the chair where her father was bound.

"I'm sorry I have to do this, Daddy," said Emily. "...but the only way to get you out is to let them take you out."

"Emily?" he gasped. "How? What? How are you talking?"

"It's a long story, Daddy," she said. "Just know that mom is safe and we have a plan....sort of."

"I don't understand," said Charles.

"I need you to trust me," said Emily, as she gently injected her father in the neck.

"Wha…" said Charles as he slumped in the chair. Emily moved to the back door, adjusted the voice generator again and said, "All units! Converge on the house. You two men by the door. Enter the house but use caution. There is a hostage bound to a chair. He is not to be harmed! The terrorists are in the living room. Use extreme caution as they are armed." The two officers next to the door rushed the farmhouse, expecting to be followed by every other individual present. They didn't notice that they had entered alone, but their commander did and he reprimanded them later for their careless disregard for the safety of the hostage. When they found the two agents unconscious in the living room, they were not sure what to think. They called their commander on the radio and said, "Two terrorists down in the living room. They look dead. Should we cuff them or what?"

"Who said they were terrorists?" asked the commander. "Check their pulses, you idiot. If they have one, cuff them. Is the house secure?"

"As far as we can tell, sir," said the officer.

"Hold your position, we are coming in." The officer was not sure why the others were not in already. A team of officers swept the house to make sure the situation had been defused. Emily could hear sirens approaching from the east and suspected that an ambulance had been called as she had hoped. She texted her mother with instructions for Dr. Cornell; then she remained near her father to make sure he was treated well.

"They are all still alive sir," said one of the officers. "I am not sure what happened here…and I can't find any 'officer down' like we were told on the radio."

"We will sort it all out when we get back to the station," said the commander. "For now, get this one in the ambulance and these two in the back of one of the patrol cars. I want to have a long talk with them." Two paramedics brought a gurney in through the front door and lifted Charles onto it. Emily followed as they took him to the back of the ambulance and climbed in after the gurney was secured to the floor. One of the paramedics sat next to him as the ambulance pulled down the long gravel driveway. It turned onto the county road and made its way to the corner. It turned left instead of right, but none of the officers seemed to notice. They were too busy with their "prizes" that were now being called terrorists by almost everybody there.

"Pull up here for a second, will you boys?"

"Sure thing Doctor Dave," said the driver. "We aren't going to get in trouble for this, are we?"

"No. You will be fine," replied Dr. Cornell. "We will head for the hospital in just a second…just like you are supposed to do." He opened the back door. Alma and Nathan climbed inside. It was a little crowded, but everyone was finally back together.

"How are your parents, Darnell?" Dr. Cornell asked. "Does your dad still fish?"

"Only every chance he gets, Doctor Dave," said Darnell, the paramedic whose place Dr. Cornell had taken. "Can you tell us what is going on here?"

"I wish I could guys," he said. "But this is one of those cases in which it is better not to know very much about what is going on. If I get the chance, I will explain it all to you later." Dr. Cornell knew he would never get the chance. He liked the boys. He didn't want them to get in trouble. It was because of him that they became paramedics in the first place. Darnell Watson was a good student, but not good enough for a scholarship. He would have made a great doctor and might still someday; but for now, being a paramedic was as close as he was going to get.

"What about you, Dallas?" Dr. Cornell asked. "Any big plans for the future?"

"I don't know, Doctor David," he said. "I've been thinking of entering the military. They pay for your college when you get out and I could get medical training and experience while I am in."

"Sounds like a plan," said Dr. Cornell. "…if you are sure that is what you want to do."

"I don't know," said Dallas. "I figure I got time. Right now, I've got this job and I like it pretty well." Dallas Ferguson was also a fair student, but he had a passion for helping people. Like Darnell, he didn't have the money or the grades to go to a good college. Dr. Cornell had known them since they were kids. He even treated a few of their skateboard injuries on the *down-low* so their parents wouldn't find out. It wasn't an ethical thing to do, but it instilled a fierce loyalty to the doctor into them. The boys never forgot what he had done for them, so they were ready to help him when they got his call about Charles.

"Now," said Dr. Cornell. "Here is what you say. When they ask you what happened to Charles here, you say that a doctor at the hospital took charge of him and that was the end of your responsibility. Describe me as the doctor. It will make things easier for you later. Trust me."

"What are you going to do?" asked Darnell.

"That's something else," said Dr. Cornell. "You guys have been great…and I hate to ask anything else; but could one of you lend us his car?"

"You know I would do about anything for you, Dr. Cornell," said Darnell. "…but I just got my car painted and detailed. I would hate for anything to happen to it."

"Did you finally get the flames on the hood and the blue neon undercar lights?" the doctor asked. "That might be a bit more ostentatious than we need right now anyway. We would like to keep a low profile."

"You can use my car," said Dallas. "It's a 1980 Oldsmobile Custom Cruiser station wagon. I don't think you can hurt it."

"We really appreciate it, Dallas," said Dr. Cornell. "Where is it?"

"Not far from the hospital," replied Dallas. "Would you like us to take you there?"

"No," said Dr. Cornell. "Go ahead and take us to the hospital. We will find our way to the car if you tell us where it is. That way, your story will seem more plausible."

"You got it Doc!" said Dallas.

Dallas had turned off the flashing lights and silenced the siren about a mile from the hospital at Dr. Cornell's suggestion. The ambulance pulled up to the edge of the parking lot and stopped. Emily wished she had encumbered herself with the night-vision binoculars as she strained her eyes to see across the lot to the emergency entrance. There was a man standing outside looking around suspiciously. He was wearing dark glasses and Emily felt her heart sink. Charles was not yet close to coming around and their options were fading swiftly.

"I've got an idea," said Darnell. Dr. Cornell smiled, knowing what he had in mind. Dallas flipped on the lights and pulled into the drive leading up to the entrance. He shifted the ambulance into park, got out and went around to the back. There, he and Dr. Cornell unloaded their passenger and transported him inside. The man in the dark glasses and hospital scrubs watched them suspiciously as they went past. Darnell lay on the gurney pretending to be unconscious. While the man in the dark glasses and scrubs watched them, Emily approached him from his blind side. She had the needle poised to plunge into his neck when another man in scrubs came out of the entrance and said, "Doug! What are you doing? You know you are on probation around here. You aren't supposed to be smoking around the hospital at all…let alone those!" The second man pointed to the *roach* Doug had palmed when the ambulance had arrived.

"I just needed to mellow," said Doug. "It has been a tough night."

"Tough my ass," said the other man. "You have hardly done anything. Now get back inside and get to work. But take off those sunglasses first. God! You might as well wear a sign that says you are high." Doug removed the glasses, took a discrete hit off the joint and reluctantly discarded it in the shrubs. Emily breathed a sigh of relief, replaced the cap on the syringe and placed it back in its case. She joined the others in the ambulance and waited. Charles sat slumped on the seat while Alma supported him in a caress. Emily wished the whole ordeal was over.

Dr. Cornell and Dallas rejoined them, replaced the gurney in the back and they drove down the exit ramp to the front entrance of the hospital. There they were joined by Darnell and they quickly departed the hospital property. Dallas drove them to where he lived; an upstairs apartment about a mile from the hospital. He pulled the ambulance into the alley behind the apartment house and up next to a beat up green Olds station wagon with rusted wood-grained panels on the sides. The front fender was primed only, ready for paint. The luggage rack on top was missing a runner and one of the taillights had been repaired with red plastic and duct tape.

"This is your car?" asked Dr. Cornell.

"That's it," answered Dallas. "It doesn't look like much, but it will get you where you want to go….as long as you put gas in it. By the way, it needs gas…and maybe oil."

"I can't tell you how much we appreciate this," said Dr. Cornell, trying to sound genuine. He felt that his words sounded sarcastic in light of the appearance of the vehicle, but he really was appreciative.

"Don't worry, Doc," said Dallas. "I am glad to help you out."

"I guess we will need the keys," said the doctor.

"Not really," replied Dallas. "I don't have any keys. I installed a toggle switch for the ignition and the door locks don't work. I have never worried about installing new locks. The only reason somebody would steal this piece of junk is for a joke."

"That's reassuring," said Dr. Cornell. He smiled and thanked Dallas as he shook his hand. "I will let you know where you can pick the car up."

"You're not coming back?" asked Darnell.

"I'm not sure," said Dr. Cornell. "Not anytime soon, I suspect."

"What about the hospital?" asked Dallas. "Aren't they going to get suspicious when they find out they lost a patient?"

"What patient is that?" asked Darnell, smiling. "I've got all the paperwork right here. As far as the hospital is concerned, they never got a patient. But as far as our involvement is concerned, we dropped off a patient and left…according to the witnesses, that is. The guy in the dark glasses will vouch that an ambulance pulled up and a patient was taken inside." Emily could not tell them that Doug was probably not reliable enough to remember if he had breakfast. Neither Dallas nor Darnell had any idea that she was a passenger in the ambulance.

The group said their goodbyes, got in the station wagon and Dr. Cornell started the engine. A cloud of thick blue smoke billowed from the tailpipe and the smell of burning motor oil filled the vehicle. Alma tried to roll the window down, but the handle spun comically with her efforts. Emily rolled down the back window as Darnell and Dallas watched.

"I didn't know you had power windows," said Darnell.

"Me either," said Dallas. "I wonder where the button is."

The station wagon drove off as Darnell and Dallas prepared to go back to the EMT headquarters. Dr. Cornell's first stop was a gas station where he not only filled up the tank, but purchased five quarts of motor oil…the cheap stuff. He figured there was no point in using quality oil since the engine was just going to burn it anyway. As they drove off in another cloud of blue smoke, he wondered if they might have looked less suspicious in Darnell's tricked-out hot rod.

CHAPTER 15: ON THE RUN AGAIN

Charles Troy slept comfortably in the back of the Custom Cruiser station wagon. His dreams were tranquil and filled with images of Emily's early childhood; before she became invisible. It didn't matter that she wasn't able to speak. Her personality and adorable expressions more than made up for her lack of communication skills. The part that troubled him was her inability to tell him when something was wrong. When she cried, the noise that emanated from her throat sounded like someone blowing through a long pipe. It was pitiful and heartbreaking...but terribly cute. She made the same noise when he made her laugh. It made him laugh also, which caused her to laugh again until she snorted. Tears would run down his face from laughter. Then the tears would turn to tears of regret. Somehow, he blamed himself for Emily's disability. There was nothing he could have done about it. He just felt it was his responsibility to feel guilty. Charles Troy's sleep became troubled and he began to stir.

"Weirdest thing," he said in a half-drugged state. "I dreamed that Emily spoke to me." No one in the station wagon knew what to say. No one felt authorized to speak on Emily's behalf and she didn't quite know how to begin. In an ironic twist, it was Nathan who took control of the conversation and signed to Charles that he might want to prepare himself for a surprise. He then signed to Emily that she should say something to her father.

"Daddy? You weren't dreaming," she said. "I have a devise that lets me talk now." Charles looked around and stretched out his hand. He had been lying in the back of the station wagon and reached over the seat to where the voice seemed to be coming from. Emily took his hand and placed it on the side of her face. He could feel her smile and he shuddered instead of breaking down in tears. He stroked her face for a moment before becoming fully aware of his surroundings. Alma sat in the front passenger seat and Dr. Cornell was driving. The scene seemed very surreal and Charles was not sure he was really awake.

"I guess I should ask where we are going," he said finally.

"We are not really sure," said Alma. "There is a lot that we need to sort out."

"I don't want to be offensive," he said. "...but why is Nathan here and how long has he known about Emily?"

"He does more than know about her," said Alma. "He can see her."

"Don't joke with me," said Charles. "I've had a rough week."

"She's not joking, Daddy," said Emily. "He could always see me. We love each other."

"Okay...this is just too much to process," said Charles. "My head is starting to spin. I think I might be sick."

"If you can hold on for a few minutes," said Dr. Cornell. "There is a rest stop up ahead. We can get our bearings there and you can splash some water on your face."

"I'm okay...just need a little air," said Charles. "The rest stop sounds good though."

The rest stop wasn't very busy. It was about four in the morning and traffic was light. A few semis were parked in the huge lot and the truckers were probably sleeping in their sleeper cabs. Dr. Cornell pulled the station wagon into a parking place next to the curb near the dog walk. He got out and stretched his legs like anyone on a long road trip would have. Alma got out next, followed by Nathan and Emily. Charles climbed over the seat and got out. He stood unsteadily next to the station wagon for a couple of minutes while his legs remembered what they were for. Finally, he took a few wobbly steps like a newborn calf and the act of walking came back to him. They all headed to the building that housed the restrooms. There was a chill in the night air and they could see their breaths. The men went in the men's room and Emily followed her mother into the ladies' room. As is customary, the men took less time to accomplish their business and came out to investigate what the lobby had to offer. A shriek came from the ladies' room and Charles charged in before realizing what he was doing. Alma stood next to the sink with her mouth open and her lower lip quivering. She was apparently in shock. She was wearing a pair of special dark glasses.

"I can see her!" she exclaimed. "I can see my baby! She is so beautiful!" Her head followed an unseen image across the room to where Charles stood. Emily touched his face and then placed something in his hand. "These are for you, Daddy," she said softly. Charles looked at the second pair of special dark glasses she had given him before putting them on. The room became bathed in a luminescent green glow for a moment until adjusting to the ambient light. At first, he saw only Alma standing next to the sink, supporting herself on the counter. She seemed uncertain and elated at the same time. Emily could tell that he couldn't see her and she guided his hand to the control on the earpiece of the glasses. It only took a slight adjustment before she began to materialize. His throat became dry and his knees weakened. Charles forced himself to remain standing as her image came into focus. Over the years, he tried to imagine what she looked like. He remembered her as an awkward child who was all arms and legs. Before him, bathed in lime green light, was a beautiful young woman dressed in sweat clothes and tennis shoes. Emily began to feel uncomfortable with her parents staring at her. Without realizing it, they were both trying to memorize every aspect of her image; just in case they never got to see it again. Dr. Cornell finally broke the spell that had been cast upon them.

"Do you think that maybe we should continue this someplace other than the women's restroom?" Reality came crashing down and they made a hasty retreat. Once in the lobby of the rest stop, they realized they were not alone. A retired couple stood next to the large map of South Dakota, looking disoriented and a little frightened. They had seen a lot of things in their travels, but never three men and one woman exiting a ladies' room. They all stared at each other for a moment until, again, Dr. Cornell came to the rescue.

"It's okay," he said. "I'm a doctor." The silence that followed was palpable. Finally, Alma, Charles and Emily broke into almost hysterical laughter. Emily's voice generator caused her laughter to sound spectral and evil in the echoing lobby. The couple rapidly returned to their motorhome without a word and drove out of the parking lot at the maximum recommended speed limit.

"We should get moving," said Charles, whose head was finally starting to clear from the drug and long sleep. "We don't need any trouble right now."

"You're right," said Dr. Cornell. "…but we should have some kind of plan of action. Our only plus right now is that no one knows where we are headed because we don't know ourselves."

"And what about Nathan?" asked Alma. "His parents are going to be worried about him. How are we going to make sure he gets home?"

I am not going anywhere without Emily, signed Nathan. *Besides, I think you are going to need me.* Emily touched him on the shoulder and smiled. She signed to him, *I am going to always need you.*

"Well, we're going to need to contact them somehow," said Alma. "We can't have the authorities looking for us for kidnapping too." Nathan read her lips and signed, *We just need to find a library. I will tell my mother that some friends and I are going on a road trip. She suspects something anyway, so she will accept the explanation rather than getting my dad angry.* Emily touched his shoulder again as a sign of support and a little sympathy. She knew of the friction between Nathan and his step-father. She hated that he was never able to confide in anyone until he met her. She felt obligated to help maintain his morale for that reason.

"Well," said Charles. "We should see what we can do about getting another mode of transportation. Dallas will need his car back and, to be honest, I am not sure how much farther it will make it." The old beater had been reliable thus far, but they all felt it was better not to take chances. Getting another vehicle was going to be a problem. Most of the parties were opposed to just stealing a car, in spite of Emily's natural aptitude for it. Nathan came to their rescue again with a plan that was simple and perfect.

In Sioux Falls, they parked the station wagon two blocks from a *Buy Here, Pay Here* lot that was conveniently close to a Starbucks. Nathan used an *acquired* laptop to access his bank account, routing the connection through several dummy accounts to avoid a trace. He then transferred a considerable amount of money into a different bank account that he had set up under a false name. The second account had been part of a failsafe plan in the event things got too bad at home. The money had come from an insurance policy which his biological father had set up for Nathan so he could go to college. In twenty years of compounding interest, it amounted to a little over two-hundred thousand dollars. Nathan transferred just over nine thousand into the false account, so as not to alert the IRS. Nathan also contacted his mother through a dummy email and let her know that he was safe and would be going away for a while. He told her he was sorry for the difficulty his step-dad would put her through, but it was necessary. She knew what he meant and told him only to be safe and that she loved him. Then she deleted the message and put a block on Nathan's fake email address as he had instructed her to do. He had other accounts with which to contact her. He felt it would be best to take every precaution possible.

Nathan's next step was to go to an ATM and withdraw money for a down payment. The first ATM only allowed a withdrawal of three hundred dollars. The second and the third only allowed two hundred dollar withdrawals; and they charged a four dollar service fee because he did not have an account at their banks. With seven hundred dollars in his pocket, Nathan and his "team" headed for the car lot. He looked over the selection of vehicles, trying to determine which one would best suit their immediate needs. Emily made her way to the office to spy on the car dealers' assessments of Nathan and to gather *Intel*. It was as expected. They suspected that he knew nothing about cars and plotted ways to take advantage of him. Nathan played his part perfectly, kicking the tires and looking generally confused. In reality, he knew a great deal about cars. A salesman with a nametag that read *Bill* came over to him with an attitude that was less friendly and more condescending. Nathan was looking at a 1990 Ford Taurus that had significant rust around the fenders and torn upholstery. Bill walked up behind him and stood for a moment.

"She's a beauty isn't she," he said in a pre-rehearsed tone. "Yeah, I doubt this baby is going to stay on the lot very long. It's got low miles and was properly maintained. It's also priced right for a young man like you. Easy payment plan, but you will have to decide quickly. I've got a couple just dying to buy this car as soon as they can get the down payment together. Whaddaya say…shall we write it up right now, or do you want a test drive?" Bill was used to getting results with his high-pressure pitch…at least with first-time buyers. Nathan turned around and acted surprised to see him standing there. He handed Bill a card informing him that he was deaf. He signed asking Bill if he understood sign language. When Bill stood there with a confused expression on his face, he knew he did not. Nathan motioned with his hands indicating he would like to have a pen and paper. Bill began to roll his eyes and then caught himself. He donned a superficial smile and held up his index finger before heading for the office. Emily followed him.

"Son of a bitch!" he said, once he was inside. "My first customer of the week and it's a deaf-mute. Where is that legal pad that was on my desk Friday?"

"Check your briefcase," said Roger, the other salesman on duty. "Take it easy. He looks like a nice kid."

"He's an idiot," said Bill. "I can tell by looking. I am about to sell him the worst piece of crap on the lot." Emily had to control herself to keep from punching him in the throat. Bill stopped at the door, took a deep breath and resumed his artificial countenance. He returned to Nathan and hastily scribbled something on the legal pad. *So what do you say…* he wrote. *Ready to take this baby home?*

I don't think so, wrote Nathan. *This looks like the worst piece of crap on the lot.* Bill's eyes widened. He measured the distance from the Taurus to the office. He turned his head away from Nathan and muttered, "There is no way you could have read my lips from this distance." He turned back, smiled a fake smile and asked in a deliberate manner, "CAN YOU READ LIPS?" Although Nathan could not hear him, even his expression was condescending. He took the pad and wrote, *What?* Bill planted his face in his palm, regained his composure and wrote, *If you aren't interested in this one, did any of these others catch your eye?* Nathan pointed to a black Chevy SUV parked near the office. Bill's eyes narrowed and his brow furrowed. The SUV was the vehicle he had been using as a personal car. Bill wondered if there was some way the guy could have known that. He forced a smile and wrote, *I think that one might be a bit out of your price range.* Nathan took the tablet back and wrote, *How do you know what my price range is? Is it because I am deaf? Do you think I don't have any money because I am deaf?* Nathan began to write with purpose. His letters dug into the paper and made impressions several layers deep. *No,* Bill wrote. *I didn't mean anything like that at all.* But it was exactly what he meant.

I think I want a test-drive, wrote Nathan. He folded his arms in a way that said he was not going to take no for an answer. Bill knew there was no point in arguing. He went back to the office to get the keys. Nathan winked at Emily who had witnessed the entire performance.

"He thinks he wants my SUV," Bill said as he angrily entered the office.

"Actually, it's my SUV," said Roger, who was half-owner of the lot. "We are here to sell the cars, you know."

"But if he buys the SUV, that leaves me driving the Taurus to get around!"

"Here's a crazy idea," suggested Roger. "You could actually BUY a car. We are a car lot after all."

"You are a funny guy, Roger," said Bill.

He stormed out and made no pretense of congeniality anymore. He hoped he would offend Nathan and that he would leave. Emily had witnessed the entire exchange in the office and conveyed the information to Nathan. Nathan just smiled and took the keys. Bill had refused to release his grip on them for a couple of seconds, just to get his point across.

"Wait a minute," he said, forgetting Nathan was deaf for a moment. "I will need to see a driver's license." Nathan feigned understanding again and Bill took out his own license and showed it to him. Nathan looked at it for a moment, took the legal pad and wrote, *Nice picture.* It wasn't. Bill ground his teeth, took the pad and wrote, *I NEED YOUR LICENSE!* Nathan nodded, smiled like he finally understood and took one of his licenses from his wallet. Bill looked at it and wrote down some of the information. He was sure he wouldn't need it. He had no intention of selling the SUV.

The test-drive was unpleasant for Bill, but delightful for Nathan. Bill was used to talking about the selling points of various vehicles. On this drive, he had to sit in awkward silence while Nathan pointed at various features of the SUV, nodded and smiled. Bill suspected Nathan was mocking him when he pointed to the radio and smiled, but he couldn't do anything about it. When they finally returned to the lot, Nathan got out, looked the SUV over again and then rubbed two fingers and his thumb together making the international sign for "money" or "how much?" Bill grinned in a way that could only be described as dastardly. If he had had a handlebar mustache, Nathan and Emily just knew he would have twilled the tip. He wrote down a clearly inflated price for the SUV and handed it to Nathan, who he now knew as *Kyle Marx.* Nathan looked at the price, smiled and handed him back a counter offer that was eight hundred dollars below book value. Emily had conveniently borrowed *the book* while she was in the office. Bill got angry and was about to storm off when he saw Roger standing at the door of the office watching him. He took the pad and hastily scribbled that the boss would not let him sell the car at that price; that the price of the SUV was firm. Nathan calmly smiled and pointed to the sign that said NO REASONABLE OFFER REFUSED. Then he suggested that Bill go inside to ask Roger about the offer. Bill nodded and headed back to the office.

After what appeared to be a heated exchange, Bill returned with a counter-counter offer. Roger had told him to sell the SUV to Nathan or he would do it himself; and that Bill would lose the commission if he did. Nathan shook his head, wrote down a final offer of two hundred dollars below book and that he had a five hundred dollar down payment in cash. Bill was tired and really didn't want to settle, but cutting a deal might teach Roger a lesson about trying to thwart his sales technique. He nodded begrudgingly and motioned for Nathan to return with him to the office so they could draw up the papers. Emily hugged Nathan as they walked back to the office. Forty-five minutes later, they were driving off the lot in the SUV with a temporary plate.

Alma and Charles panicked when they saw the black SUV approaching them. The windows were tinted and they could not see that Nathan was driving. They were about to make a run for it when the passenger door opened and no one got out. Then Nathan appeared and they knew that the SUV was the vehicle he had acquired. *Why did you pick this?* Alma signed.

It is a case of hiding in plain sight, signed Nathan. *If they are looking for us, they will be looking for just about any kind of vehicle but this one. We could practically park on the street next to them and they would think we were one of their own.*

That is kind of brilliant, signed Alma. She informed Dr. Cornell and Charles of Nathan's ingenuity and the deal he got on the SUV.

"Won't they be checking bank transactions and stuff?" asked Charles.

"From whom?" asked Emily, using the voice generator. It was still a little freaky to have one's questions answered by a disembodied voice. "They don't know anything about Nathan and they really don't know anything about *Kyle Marx*. As long as we all stay off the grid, we should be fine." She thought she sounded like a TV detective.

"Okay...so what is our next move?" asked Dr. Cornell.

"I think we should get something to eat and decide on a direction to head," said Alma taking command. "Then we need to arrange accommodations for the time being."

"I can go for that," said Emily. "I am really in the mood for Chinese...and strawberry cheesecake... or waffles."

"Are you okay sweetie?" asked Alma.

"I'm fine," replied Emily. "There are just a lot of things that sound good to me. It's funny though. I was never a big fan of cheesecake."

They grabbed some fast food and headed out of town. Charles didn't like staying in one place too long. They found a hotel about ninety minutes west of town and got two adjoining rooms and a single across the hall for Dr. Cornell. They ordered Chinese takeout and Nathan made a special trip to a *Big Boy* for strawberry cheesecake. He decided Emily would just have to wait for waffles. Her mother warned her about getting fat. She responded by saying, "I'm invisible. Who cares if I'm fat?" Alma indicated Nathan slyly and said, "He can see you," and smiled. Emily smiled back.

It had been a long day and everyone was tired. Dr. Cornell bid them all good-night and went to his room. Nathan did the same and tried to look normal as an invisible Emily passionately kissed him. As she did, a brief shimmer of light cascaded down her body and then was gone. He breathed deeply, waved at Alma and Charles and closed the adjoining door behind him. Charles got into one of the double beds and was asleep almost immediately. Alma got into bed and propped herself up on the extra pillows she had found in the dresser. She flipped through the TV channels, looked in Emily's direction and signed, *You might want to be back in your own bed by the time your father wakes up. No need to shatter his illusions just yet.* She felt Emily embrace her and kiss her on the cheek. Then the door to Nathan's room opened and closed. She was confident she would hear no noises coming from their room. She swept such thoughts from her mind and turned the TV off.

CHAPTER 16: STORMING THE BEACH

 The weather was cold and depressing. A layer of fog drifted in from the Pacific and floated just above the surf and sand. There was an ethereal feeling as Doctor Cornell walked along the deserted beach. The past few weeks were a blur and the days blended into one another. He needed to clear his head; to sort things out and develop a plan of action. The condo they had secured on the beach was alright for the time being, but it was by no means a permanent arrangement. It was designed for tourists who would only be staying for a few days or even a season. Suspicions would be raised if they stayed longer.

 The trek to the ocean had been long and circuitous. Several times, the party had backtracked to avoid potential government confrontations. The route they took made the Lewis and Clark expedition seem like a sightseeing tour. At one point, they found themselves in West Texas near the Mexican border. By the following week, they were camped in the Big Horn Mountains in Wyoming...only six hundred miles from where they had acquired the SUV. The path they took had been necessary; not only to avoid being caught, but also to acquire a few things they would need. Nathan proved to be an absolute genius when it came to computer hacking and obtaining false documents. Everyone had new identities; even Emily. Armed with passwords and account numbers, he was even able to transfer funds from their personal accounts in small, innocent-looking withdrawals. The movement of money was always in odd amounts and never over a hundred dollars at a time. He managed to make them look like automatic bill payments. Nathan organized and funded his own personal witness protection program that nearly rivaled anything the government could have put in place. Unlike the government however, he kept everything moving and changing. That way, even if Agent Baxter and his group got on the trail of something, it would lead to a dead end.

  The SUV was paid off in full to avoid further connection with Sioux Falls and was promptly "sold" to another identity Nathan had created. Alma and Charles enjoyed setting up house in the beautiful condo near the beach. It was large enough to accommodate everyone in the party without seeming cramped. Emily liked to listen to the surf softly pound the beach at night. When it rained, the rain seemed to fall straight down. There was seldom thunder and lightning. Alma liked to get up early and walk on the beach when the weather was nice. One morning, she stood in the driveway of the condo waiting for the sun to peak over a rise behind her. She turned to find two small Black-tailed Deer standing on the drive between her and the condo. They looked at her curiously, as though she was the one who was out of place. She thought that maybe they were right. She reached to get her phone to take a picture. When she looked back, they had vanished. She decided that some things were just to be enjoyed…not shared. She walked on the sandy pathway through an opening in the sea grass down to the beach. The sun had not yet breeched the rise and the ocean was as blue as sapphire. Fishing boats had moved in closer to the shore with the tide. Seagulls greedily dove down to obtain chum thrown in by the fishermen. The setting was so perfect; Alma thought it felt like a scene from a movie or an oil painting. It was easy to imagine that she was on the coast of New England, especially this time of year. The weather was brisk, but not unpleasant. Late autumn on the Oregon coast seemed different than in other parts of the country; and they had seen a lot of the country in the last few weeks.

Doctor Cornell sat on the bed next to Emily in her room. An iridescent shimmer washed across her body. The flashes of light were becoming more frequent and were putting her at risk of being discovered. He took her pulse, blood pressure and temperature. Then he recorded his readings, put away his instruments and held both of her hands.

"Don't you think it is time to tell your parents," he asked.

"I don't think I can," she said. The voice generator was weakening and had begun to grow hot sooner than usual. "I don't know how to tell them."

"We could tell them together. Would that help?" Doctor Cornell looked into where he suspected her eyes were.

"They'll hate me," she replied.

"There is no way they are EVER going to hate you," he said. "You mean too much to them. They have sacrificed so much for you. You really should tell them."

"Then we should do it soon," she said, suppressing tears. "This thing is getting hot and I don't know if I can keep my courage up."

"What about Nathan?" he asked.

"He should be there too," said Emily. Her voice crackled and Doctor Cornell suspected it was the speaker of the voice generator giving out.

"Then I guess we should call a family meeting," he said smiling. "Don't worry, Emily. Things are usually never as bad as you suspect they are going to be."

"It's been my experience that they can be even worse." She rose, took Doctor Cornell's hand and led him downstairs to the enormous common room. The room had a high, vaulted ceiling and a fireplace in the corner. The large picture window looked out at the ocean and the room was separated from the kitchen by a cooking island and bar. The family was assembled in the chairs around the lit fireplace, completely unprepared for the news Emily was about to share. She stood for a moment next to the doctor as the family looked at her curiously. Light flashed across her body like sunlight through stained glass. She cleared her throat and spoke in a raspy whisper. "I think I need to tell you all something. You may have noticed…"

"Are you talking?" asked an astonished Charles.

"What?" asked Emily.

"That doesn't sound like the voice generator." Charles and Alma got to their feet. Nathan looked around curiously. Emily removed the voice generator from her throat and spoke again. "I don't know what is going on. How is it I can talk now?" They all turned to Doctor Cornell who was as confused as the rest of them. Alma signed to Nathan that they could hear what Emily was saying without the appliance. He smiled a sad smile. He wished he could hear her voice; her real voice. Finally, Doctor Cornell spoke up.

"You may not remember, but I told you when she was born that her condition might correct itself in time." He thought for a moment and said, "It is also possible that the time she spent using the voice generator strengthened her throat muscles and caused her brain to bypass the neural pathways that were preventing speech. Actually, to be totally honest, I have no idea why she can talk now."

Charles and Alma embraced her and Charles said, "So that is what you wanted to tell us; that you can talk?"

Alma felt Emily's stomach and said, "You'd better sit down, Charles." Charles looked puzzled but was an obedient husband. Alma began to cry and kissed Emily's face again and again.

"I thought you would be mad at me," she whispered.

"Never!" said Alma.

"Is somebody going to tell me what is going on?" asked Charles, who was getting a bit perturbed.

"It's simple, Charles," said Alma in hushed tones. "We are going to be grandparents." Charles was glad he was sitting because he felt the weight of his body double.

"How is that possible?" he asked finally. "That would mean she would have to…" He looked at Nathan who was still confused by the whole scene. Doctor Cornell thought he might need to position himself between Charles and Nathan for safety reasons. It proved to be necessary. Charles shook his head to collect his thoughts and signed (poorly), *Congratulations son. You are going to be a father.* Nathan wasn't sure Charles had communicated correctly and he asked him to repeat it. Alma came to the rescue and repeated Charles' sentiments. She held Nathan's hand and kissed him on the cheek. He reached for a chair behind him and found none. The Law of Gravity was strictly enforced and he sat down heavily on the floor. Emily's tears turned to an uncontrollable whispering laughter. She went to him, kissed him and signed that she loved him so very much. Alma joined Charles, sat on the arm of his chair and put her arms around him.

"Thank you for being so understanding," she whispered.

"What is to understand?" he asked. "I would die for her. I think I can handle this." Alma hugged him tighter. Doctor Cornell seemed to be lost in thought. There were so many revelations that had taken place in the last few minutes; some thoughts that had been rummaging around in his brain for the past few months were beginning to coalesce.

"I think I need to run some tests," he said finally.

"What kind of tests?" asked Alma. "Emily has had about every kind of test anyone could think of. Being pregnant probably hasn't changed anything that much."

"I not so sure," he replied. "But I wasn't talking about testing her. I want to do a few tests on Nathan."

"For Heaven's sake, why?" she asked.

"Haven't you noticed that Emily has begun to shimmer more frequently?" the doctor asked. "Nathan is the only one who can see her. I think this boy's DNA is starting to react with hers. I can't explain it, but I think these two really were meant for each other; even down to a genetic level."

"So should we start hoping?" asked Alma.

"Don't do anything yet," said Doctor Cornell. "Everything right now is conjecture; and if our experiences have taught us anything, it's that we really don't know much of nuthin'." He placed his thumbs in imaginary suspenders like the old country doctor he felt like sometimes.

Emily helped Nathan to a chair. He had a glow about him that was hard to read. It could have been shame, embarrassment, excitement or a combination of the three. He also felt dread. He was excited about the prospect of a child, but he was worried that it might possess the traits of its parents. He imagined what it would be like if the child was born deaf, mute AND invisible. His stomach churned and he felt nauseated. Emily took his hand and placed it on her belly. Suddenly, everything was right with the world. He didn't know why. He just knew they would overcome any problems they might have to face. After all, they had done it before.

The stretch of beach near the condo was over three miles long. Rocks jutted out from the shore creating natural cliff barriers at both ends. Even though it was open to the public, only those who lived along the shore knew it was there. Emily and Nathan took long walks on the beach. When they first came there, they tried walking close to the surf in bare feet. The ocean temperature was roughly fifty-five degrees, yet the sand was as warm as in California. In the ocean was a haystack-shaped monolith. It was one of several Haystack Rocks along the Oregon coast. It made for beautiful sunsets over the ocean and seals would sun themselves on it during the afternoon. The seals attracted sharks though; occasionally a hearty surfer in a black wetsuit would be attacked. Usually, the bites were not life-threatening. The sharks didn't much like the taste of humans...surfers, anyway.

Sometimes Emily would walk alone on the beach. This caused rumors to arise that the beach had become haunted. Footprints appeared in the sand where no one had been seen walking. When a fogbank rolled in, the figure of a girl could sometimes be seen gliding through the mist. Occasionally, people reported seeing flashes of iridescent light in the fog. Some reports came in that they could actually see the transparent image of a young girl; but they were dismissed as coming from overactive imaginations. When Nathan walked with her, residents of the area saw him as lonely and sad. They could not possibly know that he was walking with the love of his life and the mother of his child yet to be born.

Doctor Cornell ran tests on Nathan's blood. It didn't reveal very much, but he didn't expect it to. He needed access to a facility that would allow him to study Nathan's DNA and compare it to Emily's. There was a facility about six hours south in Northern California, but Doctor Cornell was hesitant to go there. Even with his nearly-flawless credentials that Nathan had secured for him, he worried that the area of research he would be conducting could set off red flags with the government and bring Agent Baxter down on them again. The doctor was even cautious about how much internet research he did.

Emily went through a spell of morning sickness that disappeared almost as quickly as it came on. Her desire for certain types of unusual food combinations were deemed normal by their resident doctor; a perk that usually only the wealthy could afford. Emily's voice didn't get louder, but got less raspy. She spoke in a sweet, low voice that was only slightly louder than a whisper. It would have been possible to equip her with some sort of amplifier, but her parents enjoyed hearing her natural voice too much to suggest it. They were just happy they could hear her at all.

Emily was also concerned about her pregnancy. Like most expectant mothers, she didn't know what to expect. She had no idea which of their traits her child might be born with. She also was concerned as to how Doctor Cornell was going to be able to manage a delivery with a mother who would be unseen. The doctor reminded her that he still had the special dark glasses and that everything would be fine. He tried to keep any doubts out of his voice when he talked to her, but he was concerned about what would happen if the baby should need some kind of postnatal medical treatment. He decided that the best thing he could do was prepare for what he could and cross that bridge when he came to it. Emily sat on the window seat, looking out at the ocean for hours sometimes. The moods of a pregnant woman can be an emotional rollercoaster anyway. Emily's mood was compounded by her invisibility and the constant threat of government intervention. For so long, she had just wanted to be seen. Now she wished she could disappear for real.

Alma arose one morning to take a walk on the beach before dawn. She quietly slipped down the stairs and went to the kitchen to make coffee. She looked across the room and out the large picture window. The beach looked so sad…so desolate. Light patches of fog rested in low-lying indentations in the sand. There was something about the scene that cheered her up instead of depressing her. As she stood staring out the window, her imagination began to play tricks on her. The hood light over the stove reflected in the glass. Within the glow, she could see the reflection of Emily. Alma was sure it was an optical illusion or her imagination. She softly whispered, "Emily?" The reflection turned away from her. A soft, quiet voice came from its direction. "Mom? How did you know I was here?" A shimmer cascaded down Emily's form as she sat on the window seat.

"I…I can see your reflection in the window," Alma gasped. "Can't you see it?"

"I can always see it," said Emily. "You're telling me you can see it?"

"Yes," she replied. "It was transparent at first, but now it seems almost solid."

"I don't understand," said Emily.

"Neither do I," said Alma. "…but there are so many things I don't understand. I think I should wake Doctor Cornell. You stay right there. Do not move!" Alma raced upstairs to wake the doctor. Nathan came out of the bedroom to look for Emily. No one objected to them sharing a room since there was little damage that could be done by it now. He signed to Emily asking what was going on. She signed back that her mother had just seen her reflection. Nathan was surprised, but the news was not earth-shattering to him since he could always see her. Doctor Cornell came down the stairs rubbing his eyes, followed by Alma who was in turn followed by Charles. They all stood in front of the cooking island looking at Emily, who felt as though she was on trial. Charles rubbed his own eyes to make sure he was seeing what he was seeing. Doctor Cornell's mouth was open and his mind was racing with confusion and conjecture. Alma was the first to act by going to Emily and hugging her. She looked at her own reflection hugging Emily's in the glass. It was another first for her and she wept openly; not even trying to suppress her joy. Emily, she thought, does not have a monopoly on rollercoaster emotions.

Doctor Cornell composed himself and spoke a phrase that was pretty common to him. "I need coffee." Alma realized that she hadn't made any after she had spotted Emily's reflection. She hugged her daughter extra tightly, kissed her on the cheek and headed to the kitchen. Charles could have made the coffee, but Alma thought he just didn't measure it correctly. After a few minutes and the introduction of caffeine to his system, Doctor Cornell was thinking more clearly. Something about the events of the morning intrigued him.

"Emily, I know this is going to sound funny…but do you think you could try to will yourself visible?" He felt almost foolish asking.

"I'm not sure I would know how," said Emily.

"Your mother said your image became more solid the longer you talked with her," he said. "I think there may be something in the bond you have with your family. Could you give it a try?"

"I can try…but don't expect too much," she replied. Emily tensed up and tried to clear her mind. Nothing happened. If anything, her image in the glass became slightly less opaque. She tried again. Nothing.

"Maybe trying too hard is the problem," suggested Doctor Cornell. "Try clearing your mind."

"That's a little hard with everyone looking at me," said Emily.

"We can fix that," he said. "We will just go about our business as usual." At first, everyone looked comical; like people trying to act nonchalant without succeeding. After a few moments, everyone settled into their usual morning routine and almost forgot Emily was there. Emily tried to clear her mind, but it was impossible. Thoughts kept coming to mind that she had to shove back into her mental trash bin. Instead, she let her mind drift to a more pleasant time; a time when she could stand in the sun and no one noticed. She thought of the times she would stand and watch her mother around the house. She remembered waiting for her father to come home and ambushing him with hugs and kisses on the big front porch. He never failed to appreciate it. She thought to when she first saw Nathan, and how it had frightened her when she realized that he could see her. She thought about the first time they had kissed and then their first night together. She thought about....the baby kicked.

Alma, Charles and Doctor Cornell watched in amazement as the scene unfolded in front of them. It was as if Emily's image had been cut out of a sheet of black felt and a shiny metal color wheel spun behind it. It wasn't just an optical illusion because the light reflected from the large picture window as well. Even Nathan, who could always see her, could see the light. It was almost blinding in its intensity. As it began to subside, it melded into flesh tones and fabric, highlights and hair color. Emily sat before them on the window seat, looking as normal as anyone anywhere. Her flowing light blond hair cascaded down her bare shoulders.

Her nightgown clung to the petite form of the expectant mother. She looked at them all with wide, innocent eyes. Nathan still thought that she looked like an angel. Alma cried out and Emily's image flickered slightly. Doctor Cornell went across the room and dropped to one knee in front of her. He took her pulse and held up her arm. There was only the slightest hint of transparency in it; something that could be easily concealed if need be. He held back his own tears. He had invested so much of his life in Emily and her condition. This turning point was emotionally draining for him and he began to feel light-headed. Emily didn't know what to say. She felt excited and a bit embarrassed. No one had seen her like they were seeing her now…not even Nathan. When she finally spoke, she felt silly for what she said. It was something that girls say all the time. Emily had never said it because she couldn't talk and because there was no need. Both of those things had changed. Her eyes filled with tears when she asked, "Do you think I'm pretty?"

CHAPTER 17: THE SERPENT IN THE GARDEN

In a manner of speaking, Joseph Oliver Baxter had gone off the rails. He maintained his composed exterior; but inside, he was seething with fury, humiliation and thoughts of retribution. Being subdued by a girl who was, in essence, an untrained recluse had been difficult enough to explain to his superiors. But the subtle yet relentless taunting by his fellow agents angered him to no end. He had always been plagued by feelings of inadequacy. He barely passed the height requirement for the agency and had begun to lose his hair at an early age. His relationship with his parents had been strained at best and the strict discipline of the agency actually gave him confidence and a sense of purpose. His past life was buried in the agency's extensive encrypted records and he was free to reinvent himself in a way that was acceptable to his own ego.

The *Emily Troy* assignment was the first case in which he had been given a higher security clearance. At first, he thought the agency was messing with him, or maybe testing his gullibility. When he read the lab work that had been obtained from Doctor Cornell, Agent Baxter realized that it was a real case and he was honored that he was being entrusted with such a crucial assignment. It was hard for him to keep from showing emotion while in the presence of his superior. Instead, he had adopted a nonchalant, professional posture as he thanked him for the assignment. Baxter's demeanor changed dramatically when he had to return to the same office and inform his supervisor that his charge had escaped. It took a lot of explaining on his part to convince his superiors to allow him to go after Emily. But in reality, they were short-staffed as it was and elevating someone else's security clearance didn't seem like a good idea at the time.

Agent Baxter, using the team that was put at his disposal, staked out the town of Cedar Pike, expecting that Emily would return to find her parents. It was difficult to acquire assistance in the field, but he was able to contact a few agents who were working undercover as law enforcement officers. They were more than happy to help him when he elevated their security clearances...something he did not have the authority to do. He managed to track Emily Troy through the Midwest and finally caught up with her near the Iowa border. That proved to be the turning point of his career in espionage. In essence, she had blinded him and then subdued him. He was sure he would never live it down and he was right. By the time he regained consciousness, he was already being transported back to the facility in Ohio. This time, as he sat in his supervisor's office, he felt like a student being called down to see the principal. His security clearance wasn't revoked, but he was confined to a desk job for the time being; pending further evaluation. The hazing from his fellow agents continued until word came back that an entire team of agents had been subdued by this frail, introverted, invisible mute girl. Agent Baxter still wasn't released to go back out into the field. He was, however, given the results of the medical findings of Emily Troy's condition. The studies showed that while the initial results had been promising, synthesizing the exact compounds in her system would be tricky at best. While a few samples of a serum had been produced, Agent Baxter's investigation had been shelved. The agency he worked for simply didn't have the funding or the manpower to pursue a course that only promised a modicum of success. But that was not about to stop Agent Baxter.

Baxter sat at his office window looking out over the base. The pavement was slick with rain and the cars in the lot all looked freshly washed. The cloud cover was low and made the base look as though it was located underground. The rain had been steady for the last few days, but the storms produced no lightning or thunder. There was only depressing straight-down rain and it perfectly matched his mood. He was a beaten man. He imagined it was what his father had felt like. His mother had been a domineering woman who was quick to criticize and refused to praise. His father sat by impotent as she picked away at her son's confidence, one criticism at a time. She had destroyed his father's ego and self-confidence some time before. When Baxter was very young, he became the next victim of her own self-loathing and discontent. Even though he had graduated at the top of his class, his mother did not attend the ceremony or hear his valedictorian speech. Nor was his father allowed to attend. His failure in the Emily Troy case reinforced the feelings of inadequacy his mother had instilled in him. Her words came back to him as he stood staring out the window at the rain.

"Of course you failed." The voice in his head was as audible as if it had been spoken directly into his ear. "You're a loser! You always were. You always will be! What were you thinking? Did you really think you were going to be a success at anything? Get out of my sight!" Baxter actually looked around the office to make sure he was alone. Even though the denigrations had been uttered years ago, he felt they still applied to him. Baxter knew he had failed. A psychologist might tell him that he had failed because he suffered from a complex which prevented him from being successful when dealing with a woman. She would represent his mother in his psyche. He had read enough profiles of others to know what to apply to himself. He knew it was probably true. But knowing was half the battle.

Agent Baxter picked up the file on Emily Troy again. He had other assignments and paperwork, of course. But he just couldn't let her case go; even if he had to resign. He didn't have much vacation time left on the books, but it was enough to get him started. He sat down at his desk and took out an application for vacation leave. After filling out all the mundane lines with his name, his social security number, address, dates and so forth, he paused. He needed a reason for his absence. The word *personal* came to mind, but everyone used that. It might raise red flags in his case. He thought he might be followed. Baxter knew he was being paranoid. If the department did not have the resources to pursue a girl who possessed the secrets to invisibility, they surely didn't have someone who could tail him while on vacation. Finally, he wrote *fishing trip* on the line, signed and folded the application and placed it in a box marked Interoffice Mail. He knew he would hear back by the end of the day. The agency was efficient in that way at least.

In the meantime, he went to the surveillance section and the lab to secure a few things he would need. Among them were another pair of special dark glasses *and* a backup pair. He also obtained a voice generator as well as a tranquilizer dart gun. He pilfered a selection of chemical compounds and hypodermics from the lab that he would need for his *fishing trip*; including an experimental compound that was yet to be tested on humans. Baxter replaced the chemicals with bottles containing distilled water. He suspected his career with the agency would be over after his trip anyway. He casually visited several different sections that day so as not to arouse suspicion. In all, he amassed enough equipment for an extended covert surveillance operation; yet it all fit conveniently in his pockets and a single briefcase. He would obtain the final items he needed from sources outside the agency.

By the end of the day, Joseph Oliver Baxter's leave at been approved; just as predicted. He walked confidently through the halls to the secured door leading to the parking lot, swiped his keycard and entered his code. That was it. His high level security building was not supposed to exist. That way, the government could deny all knowledge of their activities if necessary. So, there was not a lot of added security to draw attention to the entrance. He walked calmly to his car, placed his briefcase in the trunk and left the facility…possibly for the last time.

Next, he would visit a few outside contacts to obtain some specialized items. Among them would be a few *old school* items, such as a stainless steel 22 magnum Automag pistol and sound suppressor. The style and make were discontinued more than a decade before and had been modified to be untraceable. The sound suppressor used a combination of a noise dampening gel and a series of synthetic baffles to reduce the report from the pistol to little more than a whisper. The ammunition looked like a box of small crayons. The slugs were designed to split apart on impact, producing what would amount to secondary projectiles. They limited the possibility of exit wounds and increased the likelihood of hitting vital organs. Baxter looked at the box of shells for a moment while a voice in his head asked him why he was going to such extreme measures. He couldn't answer the voice. He didn't know. It felt as though he was being manipulated by chemicals in his system. He wondered if there was something he might have ingested that could be influencing him. It didn't matter. Whatever it was had control of him now and it wasn't about to let him go. He ordered a second box of ammunition and placed it in the case along with the pistol, two extra clips and the suppressor. Next, he needed to visit Grandy.

Lyn Grandy was an electronic wizard. He was the type of wizard that other wizards came to when they were stumped or needed specialized items. He had been responsible for much of the technology used in the special dark glasses which allowed the agency to be able to see Emily Troy. He had worked on a *need-to-know* basis and produced remarkable results considering he didn't know what the technology was actually for. He didn't like the name *Lyn* because he thought it was more feminine than he cared for. Some of the people he had called his friends in grade school mocked his name…mostly because they were threatened by his intelligence and talent. Had his name been *Lyndon* or *Leonard*, he would've at least liked it better than *Lyn*. He thought the name was better suited for a middle name, but he wasn't even given one of those that he could use as an alternate moniker. Just *Lyn*. Instead, he went by the self-dubbed nickname of *Twenty-Grand*. He thought it made him sound gangsta; like a rapper. But he looked less like *Jay-Z* and more like *Johnny Mathis*. Baxter had once suggested *LG* as a nickname, but Grandy rejected it because he thought it might suggest a product endorsement. Baxter just called him Grandy.

The first item on Baxter's shopping list was a custom listening device. It didn't look very professionally constructed. Part of the device was a set of modified laser pointers attached to small tabletop tripods with electrician's tape. The receiver was a bit more sophisticated. It was housed in a small metal case that was a little bigger than a lunchbox. Baxter was surprised how inexpensive it was considering the technical expertise that had to go into it. The system was designed to pick up sounds and conversations in any building with an exposed window by using the glass as an amplifier. The laser relays the vibrations to the receiver which translates them into sound. The downside to the system was that the laser had to be fairly level with the window to calibrate properly.

"I don't know what you're into, Bax," said Grandy. "...but I have known you long enough not to ask. All I care about is that the checks clear." He grinned because Agent Baxter always paid him in cash.

"Just some routine surveillance," he replied. "I am just checking out a boyfriend of a girl I know. I am pretty sure my employer would not approve."

"Hey...I didn't ask and you didn't tell me," said Grandy. "I just thought you might be interested in something I have been working on. It uses a Wi-Fi signal to track movement inside a building. It doesn't emit a signal so it is passive. The system is a prototype though, so it is a little pricey."

"I can use that," said Baxter. "I'll take it."

"Don't you even want to know how much?" asked Grandy.

"Nope," said Baxter. "I know you. You'll give me a fair price. Besides, if it works well, I can recommend it to my bosses. You know they have deep pockets."

"Well, then maybe I will give you a little discount," he said. "...you know, because it's a prototype."

"I appreciate it," said Baxter. "I will have to get some cash together and will be back in the morning to pick it up and let you give me a tutorial."

"That works for me," said Grandy. "Do you need anything else?"

"Not at the moment," replied Baxter. "Besides, you have pretty much cleaned me out as it is."

"Well, you know what my policy is if you are not completely satisfied, right?"

"As I recall, it's 'Baxter who?'"

"As long as we're clear," Grandy said smiling. "Come back when you have some more money."

"See you in the morning," said Baxter as he headed for the door. "Early!"

Agent Baxter left the apartment building where Lyn Grandy did his business. Grandy's clientele usually paid in cash that mostly went unreported to the IRS. Baxter knew that he could trust him to be discrete. He had too much on Grandy and could put him away for a long time, if necessary...or worse.

His last stop of the day would be at a local university sorority house. Baxter changed into jeans and a t-shirt in a public restroom and mussed his hair a bit so that he looked less *establishment*. He parked a block or so away from the large two-story colonial home that had been converted to student housing for the sorority members. He was looking for someone he only identified as Belinda B. She wasn't a student. She was the House Mother; or House Mom as she preferred to be called. He stood on the porch and rang the bell. A girl in bright red sweats and thermal socks answered. She considered his age and looked at him suspiciously.

"I'm here to see Belinda B.," he announced as casually as possible. He felt that the words still came out a little too formal. The girl's suspicious look melted into one of impish approval. Apparently, Belinda B. often entertained gentlemen callers. "I'll tell her you are here," she responded.

"Would you like to come in...?" She paused hoping Baxter would fill in a name for her. He didn't.

"Yes, that would be fine," he said and followed her to the foyer. The house looked considerably bigger on the inside than it appeared on the outside. A grand staircase on his right led to the expansive second floor. The girl motioned Baxter to a small settee on the left. Another girl, also in sweats, rushed past on her way to the back of the house. The first girl pinched the fabric of the other girl's sweatshirt causing her to almost lose her balance.

"Tell mom that her boyfriend is here," she said with a grin. The second girl looked Baxter over, smiled and nodded.

"I'm not her boyfriend," he said in a sort of defense.

"Boyfriend...boy toy... I don't judge," she said smiling. "She will be here in a moment or two. Now if you will excuse me. I have to get ready for a boy toy of my own." Baxter tried to form the words that would explain his visit, but she dashed up the stairs before they coalesced. He sighed and sat back patiently on the settee. After six minutes and forty-two seconds (Baxter was a stickler for timetables), Belinda B. joined him in the foyer. She seemed a little like a relic from the student protest days at Berkley combined with the Yuppie movement of the 80's. She wore a silk long-sleeved white blouse with three buttons on each cuff. The top two buttons were unbuttoned and a gold chain led to a golden ankh that rested in the "V". Her fashionable jeans looked fashionably worn and were embroidered around the bell bottoms. She was barefoot like a hippy but her nails were impeccably done; obviously the result of an expensive mani-pedi. Her salt-and-pepper hair had never been dyed. A lock on each side had been braided and met in the back. Time seemed to have no effect on her beauty. Baxter stood and they embraced in a customary hug. They were not strangers.

He had used her services before. Belinda B. was the best hacker he knew...quite possibly the best in the country.

She led him back to her living quarters that consisted of two rooms and a private bath. The rooms were decorated with the same dichotomy as Belinda B.'s fashion choices. The furniture was richly appointed, but the décor was classic *Woodstock*. Belinda B. motioned Baxter to the couch and sat down next to him.

"What can I help you with this time?" she asked in a friendly but business-like tone. "Same payment arrangement, I hope."

"I will be paying in cash this time," he said. "I can't have a paper trail."

"So should I suspect that this is a personal project you are working on?" she asked.

"The less you know, the better," he answered.

"You know that's not how I work," she said. "If I am going to do the job, I need details...ALL the details. Besides, if you didn't trust me, you wouldn't be here." He knew she was right and told her all the information he had. Belinda B. took everything in stride. She had seen a lot of things over the years that most people thought were urban legends. Nothing really shocked her anymore. She also had developed a moral ambiguity that allowed her to work on nearly anything for a price. She had enough money stashed away that she could have retired a decade ago; but she liked what she did. She liked knowing what was going on behind the scenes. Her job was like the ultimate Backstage Pass.

Belinda B. plugged the flash drive into her laptop and looked over the information Agent Baxter had provided for her. After forty-seven minutes of silence, she spoke.

"She headed home after escaping your facility hiding in the vehicles of strangers," she said, almost to herself. "Smart. Yet she headed back to where she knew you would have people waiting for her. Not smart."

"She was looking for her parents," said Baxter.

"I don't think that was the only reason," replied Belinda. "What about a boyfriend?"

"There is no way that she had a boyfriend," said Baxter in the matter-of-fact tone that annoyed his coworkers. "She is invisible and she can't talk. That doesn't make social interaction very likely."

"Maybe not," said Belinda. "But these false accounts and identities came from somewhere. No one in these files seems to have the expertise to create so many fail-safes to keep them from being detected."

"That was the problem," said Baxter in a somber tone. "They didn't give my assignment enough manpower to follow through with a thorough investigation. That is one reason I am here."

"Okay, so let's do some reasoning," she said. "Let's think of all of this as a magic trick…a disappearing act if you will. The best way to figure out a magic trick is not to figure out how the magician did it. It is to think of a trick and figure out how you would do it. So, to start with, where would you go to get a fake ID?"

"I know where I would go," answered Baxter. "But they don't have access to the same resources I have."

"I know where I went," said Belinda. "I went to the local high school. You can find almost anything you want there. It's the nature of youth to be rebellious."

"I was never rebellious," said Baxter indignantly.

"Yeah...I can tell," said Belinda, touching his leg compassionately, with just a hint of seduction. Baxter's frown softened as her hand softly stroked his inner thigh. With his attitude properly adjusted, she returned to her keyboard.

"There are a few people who were in high school at that time who might have had the connections and expertise which would have been able to help your girl pull off her disappearing act," said Belinda. "Disappearing act, heh heh...I kill me." She laughed at her pun for a few moments while Baxter sat patiently. "Oh, come on. You know it was funny. Alright. Anyway, there were three in the high school there who could have arranged for fake identities and dummy internet accounts. But they would've had to have worked as a team. None of them possess all of the abilities that would be required. Well...unless you want to count the deaf kid."

"Deaf kid?" asked Baxter. "What about the deaf kid?"

"His aptitude for anything cyber-related is off the charts," said Belinda. "...but you said the girl couldn't speak and was invisible. I don't see how they would have ever been able to communicate even if they did make contact somehow." She began to laugh at her second pun. Baxter was not amused.

"Who is the deaf kid?" he asked with just a hint of annoyance. Belinda's hand stroked his thigh again. He hated that she could manipulate him in that way...a little.

"Nathan Saunders," she said, becoming serious again. "He was brilliant. An M.I.T. candidate if ever I saw one. But, as I said, deaf and mute."

"Saunders? His parents are David and Sue Saunders?" asked Baxter, astonished. "They were friends with the Troys. How did we miss that?"

"As you said," replied Belinda in a sympathetic tone. "…lack of resources. I am still not sure he is the one you are looking for. After all, the facts would seem to suggest otherwise."

"There are too many coincidences for it to be anyone else," said Baxter. "What else can you tell me?"

Belinda B. spent the next hour and thirty-seven minutes filtering through false leads and mapping a cyber-trail that Nathan Saunders had followed. The picture she painted was quite detailed until it went cold in South Dakota; but it was a start. Baxter had other resources that could help him from that point on. But first, he was going to return to Cedar Pike, Iowa and collect a little more information from the Saunders; by force, if necessary. Most likely, by force. He thanked Belinda, handed her an envelope that contained an undisclosed amount of cash and started to stand up. She placed her hand on his thigh a little more forcefully than before and sat him back down. When she began to stroke his inner thigh again, she did not stop until she reached her goal. He tensed for a moment until she leaned in and kissed him. She slid her tongue between his lips and had to force his teeth apart. He finally relented. She was twenty years his senior, but she was still desirable…and talented. She escorted him to her bedroom and they made love (quietly) for the next fifty-six minutes. Baxter dressed quickly and prepared to leave. He knew that if he didn't, he might not. She motioned for him to return to the bed for a moment, stroked his face and kissed him passionately one more time. "Be careful," she said. He smiled but didn't respond. He kissed her again and left her quarters.

Even though they both had been very quiet during lovemaking, several girls seemed to be waiting in the foyer as Baxter did his *walk of shame*. He looked straight ahead as he went to the front door. He hoped he was not blushing; his hope was in vain. The girls didn't giggle or whisper as he expected. Instead, those seated stood and they all gave him a faux standing ovation. He knew he was not the first to be awarded this *honor*. He knew he would not be the last. He also knew that he would probably not be returning. Baxter took a deep breath as he stood on the porch of the sorority house. The night air was brisk and his t-shirt was thin. He was shivering by the time he returned to his car. He donned his suit coat and waited for the heater to warm up. It took forever he thought. His final preparation for the evening would be to pack. Tomorrow, he would head once again to Cedar Pike, Iowa. The Saunders had some 'splainin' to do.

CHAPTER 18: THE TRUTH IS WAY OUT THERE

Sue Saunders' head began to clear as her eyes tried to focus. The room was dimly lit and her mouth felt as though it was stuffed with cotton. She became aware of intense pain in her wrists and her hands tingled. She noticed the same sensation in her ankles and her feet were very cold. Her eyes refused to focus beyond the point of the gauze-like blindfold across them. She could make out a dark image of an individual, but that was all. Looking down, she could see under the blindfold. On the floor lay her husband; motionless and in a fetal position. A chill went through her as she considered the possibilities. She knew why she was in the state she was in; it was about Nathan.

"Welcome back," said Agent Baxter in a mock friendly tone. "I am really sorry to inconvenience you, but you have information I need and I intend to get it." Sue tried to speak, but found that her tongue met an obstruction.

"I'm sorry," said Baxter. "We will get to your responses soon. First, I want to lay down a few ground rules. Number one: no yelling. If you cry out, I will shoot your husband in the leg. If you continue to cry out, I will shoot him in the head. After that, I might have to get nasty. Do you understand?" Sue paused and then nodded.

"Good," he continued. "Second: you are going to tell me the truth if you want your son to survive. I will find him...with or without your help. If it is *without*, I do not guarantee his safety. Actually, I don't guarantee his safety either way, but his chances are better with your cooperation. Again, do you understand?" Again, Sue nodded. "So are we agreed on the rules?" Sue breathed out heavily through her nostrils, partly from submission; mostly from annoyance.

"I am going to remove the gag now," he said. "I will leave the blindfold on. That way, I might not have to kill you." Sue tensed up again. Agent Baxter began to untie the knot of the scarf he used as a gag. In doing so, he pulled Sue's hair, but she suppressed the urge to cry out. She spit out the sock that had restricted her tongue in a minor display of defiance and a major display of disgust. She had no idea where he had obtained the sock, but decided it was best not to think about it too much. Agent Baxter pulled up a chair and sat across from Sue. They were in her kitchen; as if they were old friends chatting, except one of the old friends was bound with reinforced pull-ties.

"It's a funny thing about literature and cinema," he began. "They use a lot of fictional elements to speed a story along. Knocking someone unconscious for instance; a character hits somebody in the head and he is conveniently out for the amount of time the character needs. That is completely false. The person would potentially suffer a tremendous amount of head trauma from which he might never recover. Yet, some characters get hit on the head every week." Sue wondered where this story was going.

"Another thing is *truth serum*," Baxter continued. "In reality, there is no such thing. There is no way to determine what is real, what is made up or what is a combination of the two. The secret is to make the person *think* that he or she has to tell the truth. Kind of like hypnosis; but that is easy to beat and thus, unreliable." Sue hoped he would get to the point soon.

"No…the best method we…and by *we,* I mean *you don't need to know*, have found to be the most effective is coercion. Plain, simple and to the point. We rely on the threat of bodily harm to get the results we want. We also make sure there are multiply targets; just in case we have a stubborn subject. You are a mother and would probably do anything to keep your child safe. David here is a step-dad. He might have the same loyalty, but it is a choice for him. For you, it is hardwired into your very being.

"Emily Troy…" Baxter paused to get the full effect of stating her name. "You see? I know everything. Everything except where she is. That is where you come in. You are going to help me find her. That way, you will protect Nathan; the way you always have."

"Why can't you just leave us all alone?" asked Sue, finally finding her voice.

"I am afraid that is a matter of National Security," answered Baxter. "You just need to know that it is imperative that we find her and her family. They are fugitives from the law. You could find yourself living out your days in a cell surrounded by other individuals bent on bringing down our government. Am I being clear enough here?"

"What if I don't know where they are?" Sue asked. She bit her tongue as the last word left her lips. She knew she should have been adamant about not knowing where they were.

"We both know that isn't the case," said Baxter. "This doesn't have to take a long time. I can be out of here in the next half hour if you will cooperate. That way, David here can sleep off the drug that I injected into him instead of waking up just long enough to see your bound corpse and realize he is bleeding out onto your shiny linoleum." Tears rolled down Sue's cheeks from under the blindfold. Her options were limited to betraying Emily or protecting her son. Neither provided her with a guarantee of Nathan's safety.

"The computer," she said finally amidst a shuddering whimper. "I don't know where they are, but I contact them through the computer."

"I am going to need a password I suspect," said Baxter impatiently.

"Lesser Godz," replied Sue. "Godz is G-O-D-Z. You must promise not to hurt Nathan."

"I could promise," said Baxter. "...but I don't make guarantees. It will all be up to how things play out."

"What about us?" she asked in a low voice.

"That will depend," said Baxter. He was enjoying his dominant role too much. "Let me see what I can do with this information before I decide that."

"Just don't..." Sue's words were muffled by the replacement of the sock and scarf gag. More tears rolled down her cheeks as Agent Baxter tied the scarf tightly behind her head. He left her in the kitchen while he checked the information she had given him. After an indeterminable amount of time that was marked by the clicking of a keyboard and the occasional soft chuckle, Agent Baxter returned to the kitchen. Without a word, he moved to a position behind Sue Saunders. She heard a soft click and felt a brief moment of pain. Sue felt nothing as white light surrounded her and then she collapsed into blackness.

* * * * * *

Agent Baxter had a long drive ahead of him. The small amount of information he had gathered was leading him to the west coast. The Saunders would no longer be a problem for him; except maybe for Nathan. He would deal with him when the time came. The route across Wyoming had been touted by Teddy Roosevelt as the most scenic route in the country. Its beauty and grandeur was lost on Baxter. His mission was one of vengeance. In reality, it was less about exacting his twisted image of justice on Emily Troy and more about proving his own mother wrong.

He drove straight through with the aid of an experimental amphetamine. He didn't want Nathan to get suspicious when he didn't hear from his mother. That was likely to spook his quarry. Baxter crossed the Rockies at night and the Cascades at about three in the afternoon. He got to the ocean in time to watch the sunset. He checked into a motel after making certain it had a Wi-Fi connection. The amphetamine had about worn off and he was starting to feel the fatigue that his muscles had been experiencing the last eight hundred miles. He walked a block to a restaurant and microbrewery that looked out over the beach. An almost full moon was beginning to set and it balanced on the horizon like a balloon balanced on a string. A waitress brought Baxter his order which consisted of breaded flounder, onion strings and a dark microbrew. Its bitter hops seemed to fit his mood. After he finished his meal, he ordered a second beer and went out on the restaurant's deck to look at the night sky. There was nothing left of the moon but a faint glow on the horizon and a light film of clouds that obscured most of the stars. The clouds reminded Baxter of the scarf tied around Sue Saunders' eyes. He thought for a moment that he might feel remorse. The moment and the feeling passed.

Agent Baxter walked back to his motel room and sent an encrypted message to Nathan Saunders that would be accepted as being from Sue. He was very careful with the wording of the conversation. He was trying to get a clue as to where in Oregon Nathan was located without tipping him off. There was not much information forthcoming. Baxter didn't mind. At the present, he was only laying a foundation for communication. He was tired and his body needed rest. He stripped down to his t-shirt and boxers. As he turned out the light and lay back waiting for sleep to overtake him, he considered if he might be a sociopath. *Probably,* he thought as he drifted into darkness.

* * * * * * * * *

Morning did not come for Agent Baxter. He awoke at twenty-one past twelve. He could smell the ocean and forgot where he was for a moment. He dressed casually, like a tourist and walked to the motel office to pay for an additional day. Somehow, he had slept through the persistent knocking of housekeeping and her intrusion into his room before retreating. She was lucky he didn't shoot her. Baxter paid for the second day in cash and decided he could do his cyber-search just as well there anyway. He walked down to the same restaurant where he had eaten the night before. His lunch was breaded clams, seasoned fries and another tall microbrew. This time, he opted for a blonde lager. He felt funny ordering it. It sounded like he wanted a blonde logger.

He chose to finish his second beer inside as a gentle mist of rain became a torrential downpour. The rustle of rain on the wooden deck reminded Baxter of the crumpling of wrapping paper on Christmas morning; another unpleasant memory he wished he didn't have. He noticed that the restaurant had a Wi-Fi connection and he wished he had brought his laptop. He looked at the sheets of rain outside and decided that it is was better that he hadn't. Instead, Baxter sat quietly looking out at the ocean. It looked angry, but docile. It seemed to reflect his mood at the moment. He was always angry, but most of the time he felt restrained. Lately, he felt more relaxed; as if he was fine-tuning his vengeance. He was ruining his own career, but somehow he transferred the blame to Emily Troy.

He consumed two more beers before the rain let up enough for him to walk back to his motel. Housekeeping had made up the room in his absence. Somehow, he always felt suspicious of them when they did. Baxter checked over his possessions to make sure they had gone unmolested. When he felt confident that they hadn't been touched, he opened his laptop and established the protocols that allowed him to communicate with Nathan Saunders. The message he sent was simple, to the point and seemingly innocuous. I MISS YOU. It wasn't designed to illicit any action on Nathan's part. All he had to do was open it. Belinda B. had provided him with a passive program that would simply retrace the steps that were necessary to get the message to the recipient. It was so simple; it was likely that Nathan had overlooked it.

Baxter tried watching television. There was nothing on that interested him. HBO was showing its own programming and he didn't know enough about the episodes to get into them. Basic cable provided a bit of information about world events, but that no longer interested Baxter. There were a few sitcoms on at eight that he thought were stupid and crime dramas at nine that seemed to be indistinguishable from one another. He thought he might like them if he ever got the time to get into them, but he had a mission. That was all that mattered.

At ten fourteen, his laptop made a *bloop* sound indicating he had received an email. He anxiously opened the latest message. It read simply IS ANYTHING WRONG? Baxter waited a few minutes before replying. He didn't want to seem too anxious. Finally he typed, NO. SORRY. JUST A WOMAN THING. Then he opened the program and watched a list of text scroll down his screen. He could hardly believe the number of dummy addresses and code repeaters that were in play. The program was finally stopped by a series of firewalls that prevented him from knowing the exact address where Nathan was hiding. It did, however, reveal the town: Tierra Del Mar. That was less than ninety minutes away. Baxter powered down his computer, packed everything he wouldn't need right away and prepared for an early departure in the morning. He was a bit excited and thought he would have trouble going to sleep, but he had a bit of residual fatigue from his exhaustive trip west. He went out like a proverbial light.

Agent Baxter was on the road before dawn. He had a few preparations to make before establishing contact with his targets. First would be to find lodging. He found a fairly modern inn that was not far from the beach. Check-in was not until three, but it was off-season and there were several rooms available. The clerk slyly indicated that for a slight *surcharge* he could give Baxter the room early. Agent Baxter agreed. He was given a keycard and directed to the elevator. The room was nice enough, but a little stuffy. It must have been a while since it had been rented. The third floor balcony looked out over the ocean, but a line of houses prevented him from being able to observe beachcombers and other tourists. It satisfied him for the time being. He would have to do some exploring to determine the exact location of Emily Troy and company.

Baxter busied himself unpacking and settling in. There was a small café, little more than a coffee shop really, not far from the inn. The walk to the café was part wooden boardwalk and part sandy paths lined with sea grass. Baxter wore leather sandals, kakis, a white short-sleeved cotton shirt and a baseball cap. His tinted glasses were just for effect. He wore contacts that changed his eye color and corrected his vision to better than 20-20. He had let his facial hair grow out over the past couple of weeks and had the beginnings of a respectable beard. This disguise was designed to match his backstory as a mystery writer.

The sun was just peaking over a ridge when Baxter reached the coffee shop. He ordered a bagel with cream cheese and a vente mocha with a double espresso. It was like dark hot chocolate on steroids. He felt a jolt of energy permeate his system and he felt suddenly motivated to explore the beach. Instead, he walked along the boardwalk and window-shopped at the few stores that he found there. Most of them didn't open until nine, but one was already open and had something in the window that interested him. Baxter went in and looked around at the selection of shells, glass balls and dried starfish. Finally he asked the price of the item in the window. The price that was quoted to him didn't really seem that high, but he haggled anyway to avoid looking suspicious. He didn't want to seem too anxious. He was only able to get the owner to come down seven dollars, but he would have paid twice the asking price if necessary. Both he and the owner were happy with the deal when he left the store. Baxter headed back to his room at the inn to modify his purchase.

By noon, the sun was shining and the beach became populated. Days without rain were less frequent this time of year and people took advantage when they could; even if they had to play hooky from work. The beach was still less busy than most beaches one would find to the south in California. Baxter walked slowly but steadily along the beach avoiding the occasional blanket, cooler and beach umbrella. He carried his modified purchase in his left hand; a metal detector. He fit right in. Others on the beach who were also looking for hidden treasure gave him dirty looks as though he was invading their territory. There was no way he could let them know that his detector had been modified with long distance listening equipment. He could have been right on top of a chest of pirate gold and his detector wouldn't have gone off. Baxter was listening for conversations that would lead him to the Troy family. He avoided wearing the special dark glasses since the family knew what they looked like. If there had been time, he would have had Grandy make him a set in a different style frame. But he decided to make do with what he had.

His first day as well as his second day yielded nothing but conversations involving the weather, sunblock, diets, boyfriends and the occasional marital indiscretion. On the third day, Baxter picked up only three key words, but they were enough to convince him that he was headed in the right direction. The words were ALMA, DOCTOR and AGENTS. They came from the direction of a small dune away from the beach. Baxter had eased over to the dune slowly so as not to attract attention; but whoever said the words was gone when he got there. He wasn't discouraged. He had a starting point for the next day perhaps. Next to the dune were two logs which must have served as benches; also a fire pit was dug out of the sand. The remnants of a small bonfire blackened the bottom. The thought occurred to him to come back at night. It would be easier to remain concealed and his targets might be less likely to be on guard. Baxter went back to his room to await sundown.

The sun sat more rapidly than predicted due to a large bank of dark purple clouds on the horizon. They looked like snow clouds, but probably foretold of rain for the following day. The lack of cloud cover during the day allowed for most of the heat of the atmosphere to escape into the evening sky. A brisk chill settled over the beach as the gentle waves lapped the shore. The moon had already set when Baxter arrived on the beach. He felt comfortable wearing his special dark glasses since he was nearly invisible himself in the darkness. People were dark silhouettes on a dark background.

Fires dotted the beach and a few individuals with faces aglow in the light of them sat wrapped in blankets trying to convince themselves that they were having fun. Baxter made his way to the small dune cautiously, only because he knew that Emily had stolen special dark glasses like his. Through his glasses, the entire beach was bathed in a green glow like something extraterrestrial. People had glowing green eyes when the infrared beams reflected from their retinas. A young couple walking near the surf whispered and giggled softly. They looked around and presumed they were unseen because they couldn't see anyone else. They quickly undressed and ran down the beach naked for about twenty yards before the cold got too much to take. The two realized that streaking was a bad idea and tried to dress just as quickly. Unfortunately, the girl had dropped her shirt and was unable to find it in the near pitch darkness. Baxter could see where she dropped it, but wasn't about to tell her. The boy with her finally got a clue and gave his shirt to her. He was lucky that he could not see the expression on her face because he had taken so long to offer.

Baxter got to the dune and a few individuals were there. He couldn't get close enough to make a positive identification of any of them. He flipped the controls on the earpiece to various settings, trying to find one where only one person was visible. He had no success and was about to give up when he saw one of the men speaking in sign language. He seemed to be speaking to a girl wrapped in a blanket. Baxter was sure it wasn't a coincidence. He moved in a little closer, so as not to be noticed but close enough to see without the special dark glasses. There was no one around the fire that he could recognize. He only had an old picture of Nathan and it had become apparent that Alma Troy had changed her appearance. Emily was, of course, invisible. They would have been difficult to identify in broad daylight. In the darkness, it was nearly impossible. He was freezing and was about to give up when he heard a muffled, but familiar voice. Charles Troy joined them from the darkness.

Charles leaned down and kissed the girl wrapped in the blanket on the head. Then he sat down next to the woman who must have been Alma Troy. Doctor Cornell joined them next and Baxter was beside himself; but he was also confused. *Who is the girl?* he thought. *Do they have relatives out here we didn't know about?* His head was swimming, refusing to let him accept the obvious. The realization that Emily was now visible angered him more than ever. It meant that the researchers were right; that her invisibility wasn't viable. His career was in shambles for nothing and it was all because of her. It would have been easy for him to take out his pistol and erase her from existence. With his special suppressor, they would not even know where the shot came from. In the darkness, he could disappear without a trace…just as SHE had. He felt the butt of the gun under his shirt. Baxter's hand tightened around the grip and his thumb prepared to pull back the hammer. He was determined to do it. He would kill her and let the rest of them suffer her loss. Emily stood up, presenting him with a clear target. He pulled the pistol from his holster and aimed the precision sight at a spot just behind her ear. Baxter controlled his breathing and squeezed the trigger ever so slightly. Emily lost the grip of her blanket and it dropped to the sand. Nathan bent down to pick it up. In the firelight, Baxter could see that she was pregnant…at least six months. His hand began to shake and his finger, numb with cold, inadvertently pulled the trigger.

CHAPTER 19: TRAJECTORY

Life is a paradox. It is so fragile and so resilient at the same time. A single action can radically alter its course forever. There are points in time where all opposites meet in conflict. Love battles Hate. Hope battles Despair. Destiny battles Chance. Life battles Death. The victor in each of those conflicts determines the course, or in some cases the termination, of lives.

Emily Troy felt something sting her on the back of her neck. At the same moment, Nathan noticed a flash of light in the darkness. As far as they knew, the two events were unrelated. Emily touched the place on her neck which was now burning. She looked at the streak of dark red on her fingers. Nathan noticed her actions and examined her neck. A thin crimson line ran across her porcelain skin just below her hairline. The line ran parallel to the ground and looked like it had been made with a scalpel…or a laser. He asked Emily if she was alright in sign language. She responded that she was, but she was puzzled as to what had caused the injury. Her mother noticed the conversation and examined the wound herself. "We need to get something on this," she said. "You don't want that to get infected. What in the world could have caused this?"

They reached a consensus that the injury must have been caused by an ember from the fire. The conjecture was a stretch, but no other explanation seemed to fit the facts. It was too cold for insects and the wound did not look like it was made by one anyway. No one present was anywhere near Emily when the wound occurred and she knew she did not inflict it on herself. The ember theory would have to do for the time being. They were all cold and a little tired. Alma suggested that they retreat to the condo for hot chocolate and perhaps a movie. Everyone eagerly agreed. Emily wrapped her blanket around her shoulders and patted her belly. Nathan folded his arms around her and kissed her lightly on the cheek. She recoiled slightly, hurting his feelings. She signed that his whiskers scratched a bit and it had surprised her. He smiled and signed that he would shave as soon as they got back.

* * * * * * * *

Agent Baxter was horrified. In his deluded mind, killing Emily Troy was a just thing to do. Killing her unborn baby was not. He didn't consider himself a monster. If pressed, he would have sworn that he could see the bullet leave the end of the suppressor in slow motion. In his mind, he could trace its path as it headed straight for her. As her blanket slipped revealing her pregnancy, his hand shook ever so slightly; altering the trajectory of the projectile. Baxter imagined he could see the bullet trace a thin line of red across the back of Emily's neck, sever a thread of her flaxen hair and bury itself into the sandy bank behind her. He did actually see the bullet bury itself in the sand bank. A small avalanche of sand covered the impact point, erasing all evidence of its existence. Baxter slid around the side of the small dune and backed away into the deeper darkness.

His hands were still shaking several minutes later as he trailed the family back to the beach house where they were staying. Baxter kept clearing his mind of disturbing images.

He imagined the 22 magnum projectile splintering and each of the secondary projectiles splitting off on their own twisted paths. Baxter had been so focused on revenge that he had not considered the outcome. He could see a splinter of lead penetrating the amniotic sac and finding its way to the unborn child inside. The agent used his hand to physically brush away the images in his mind. He kept reminding himself that, although it was close, it didn't happen. Baxter decided that he wasn't a sociopath after all; just driven. Driven by what, he didn't know.

The family (which now included Doctor Cornell) walked a short distance to a tall beach residence that was divided into two condos. It had Yankee blue shake siding and a window that faced the ocean. The window was actually two windows connected at an angle which formed a triangular window seat. Agent Baxter could only tell that a window seat was there from the throw pillows that leaned against the glass. A porch light between the entrance and the garage door emitted a welcoming glow. As the family passed beneath it, Emily's hair shimmered like iridescent gossamer. For a second, Baxter thought he could see through her. Charles Troy was the last one in; he looked out into the darkness before closing the door behind him. Shadows moved on the wall next to the window and the outline of Emily could be seen staring out in the direction of the dark horizon. Agent Baxter made a mental note of the condo's location and headed back to his room at the inn. He was freezing and he needed to collect his equipment.

The walk was much farther than he had estimated. It seemed somehow longer in the dark. When he finally arrived, the night clerk barely looked up. Baxter went up to his room and fumbled with the keycard. He was certain that it had been demagnetized somehow, but the green access light came on after his fourth try. Once inside, he noticed how cold the room was. Either he had been foolish enough to leave the air conditioning on, or housekeeping had turned the thermostat down. Either way, Baxter muttered a curse as he flipped the knob from COOL to HEAT. He quickly undressed, turned on the shower and adjusted the water temperature. He was careful to test it several times. He was so cold; it would have been easy to scald his skin before he realized it. As he stepped into the shower, a chill swept over him. It seemed inconsistent with the warm spray of water and the steam that now formed a thin cloud layer near the ceiling. The orange glow of the recessed heat-lamp looked like the sun on an alien planet. Sand washed off Baxter's feet and legs and created small furrows towards the drain. He had not been aware he had picked up that much sand and wondered if it would clog the pipes.

After a quarter of an hour the hot water was still abundant, but Baxter thought he had been in the shower long enough. The heat-lamp timer clicked off just as he stepped onto the bathmat and he smiled at his impeccable timing. He suspected that the room was warmer by now and was a little surprised by how well the heater had worked. He adjusted the thermostat to a more comfortable level. Then he looked out the sliding glass door at the black ocean. Seeing his own reflection in the glass, Baxter realized he was still naked except for the towel around his shoulders. He was pretty sure that no one could see him through the glass, but he felt vulnerable anyway. In lieu of pajamas, he opted for sweat pants and a t-shirt. He sat down on the edge of the bed and used the remote to flip through the channels of the evening's programming. There was the usual lineup of sitcoms and crime dramas, as well as movies; and HBO of course. Baxter stopped on a channel that was showing a commercial about a steakhouse and he couldn't remember if he had eaten dinner. He was hungry anyway, so he made his way down to the vending machines. The only thing that seemed the least bit substantial to him was a package of cheese and crackers. He also procured a bottle of citrus tea and returned to his room. This time, the keycard worked the first time.

The movie was back on when he opened the door. It was *Sleepless in Seattle* and it was about half over. Agent Baxter hated romantic comedies and he hated *Sleepless in Seattle*. To him, it told a story of a relationship that was going to fail over time. He always overthought things and he always saw the glass as being half empty. The other channels didn't have any programs that interested him so he let the movie play. He ate his meager dinner and sipped his tea. Then he readied his equipment. Getting the right angle for the laser listening device was going to be tricky. Not only did the laser need to align with the receiver, it had to be concealed in some way. He thought for a few moments before coming up with a solution. The solution meant that he would have to be up before dawn again. Baxter intended to mount the laser on or beside one of several decorative streetlamps that lined a boardwalk near the condo. The location also provided him with an area that could mostly conceal the receiver; an area under the boardwalk where the sand had eroded away. It would be tricky to get the exact alignment and he would probably have to dig more sand out around the area. He also needed a folding beach chair and lap desk for his laptop. His cover as a writer would allow him to sit at one location all day without raising suspicion.

Agent Baxter stowed all of the equipment in a black canvas bag, arranged a wakeup call for four-thirty a.m., finished his tea and prepared for bed. *Sleepless in Seattle* was about over and he let it play through the credits. It wasn't because he had changed his mind about the movie. It was because he liked the song *Jimmy Durante* was singing. For some reason, it reminded him of air travel...and he loved air travel. It made him feel important. After the next movie began, he turned the television off, turned out the light and attempted to drift off to sleep. After a few moments Baxter got up, cursed the citrus tea and went to the bathroom. He came back to bed feeling relieved. He tossed and turned for about half an hour as he realized he should not have had so much caffeine that late. He decided that if he was not asleep in the next ten minutes, he would get up for a while. The next thing he heard was his four-thirty wake up call. Baxter didn't feel like he had slept at all, but the clock told him otherwise.

* * * * * * * *

Nathan stood at the large window and looked out at the ocean. He wasn't usually up at dawn, but something was troubling him. It wasn't just that Emily was not beside him when he awoke. Something else was gnawing at his brain that he could not come to terms with. The flash in the darkness and the mysterious wound on Emily's neck had him troubled. He felt they were connected somehow, but he couldn't figure out how. Emily had taken frequent walks on the beach when they first arrived, but not so many when she became visible. She had told Nathan that she felt more vulnerable now that people could see her. It wasn't that she was complaining; she was just trying to adjust. Nathan understood and had let her know that he would be there for her if she needed to "talk". The entire extended family was doing a lot of adjusting. Emily was visible and that was something that had not been the case since she was little; and she could talk in her own voice. That was something that had NEVER been the case.

Emily still walked on the beach sometimes. Lately she had done it more often. She seemed to be contemplating her pregnancy. All mothers-to-be worried about the child that they were bringing into the world. They all hoped it would be healthy and grow up happy. Emily's concerns were compounded by her own unique biology. She had wondered what percentage of it her child would possess, if any. She never spoke of her concerns to her parents. They had been through so much and had sacrificed everything for her already. She talked a few times to Doctor Cornell about it, but he couldn't offer much in the way of counseling. Her case was just too unusual to make predictions. So she talked to Nathan; both in sign language and verbally. Emily liked sign language better because it was easier not to get emotional when she spoke. She spoke verbally when he was asleep. She knew he couldn't hear her. She just needed to sound things out for herself sometimes.

Nathan was concerned and was about to go out and look for her. The rest of the house was asleep and he considered waking them, so he could let them know where he was. Communication is very important when hiding from the government. He was about to head upstairs when Emily appeared beside him. *What's wrong?* she signed.

Where were you? She could see the concern in his face.

I couldn't sleep, she signed. *I set the sleep timer on the TV and watched a movie; one of my favorites. I must have fallen asleep before it was over because I don't remember seeing the ending.*

I meant where were you this morning? he signed. *You weren't on the couch when I came down.*

Yes I was, she signed. *I just got up and saw you standing by the window.* Nathan looked at her with an unusual expression. He had never looked at her with a feeling of distrust. He trusted her unquestionably. Perhaps it was his state of mind from the night before or that the truth didn't seem to fit the facts, but his mind was swimming with confusion. Finally he signed, *Is it possible you were invisible?*

It's possible, she signed. *...but you could always see me when no one else could.*

I know, he signed. *That is what has me confused. Do you think it is possible that you could become invisible again and even I wouldn't be able to see you?*

I don't know, she signed. *I wouldn't think so. I think maybe we need to talk to Doctor David.* Nathan started for the stairs. Emily took his arm gently. *When he gets up, sweetheart. We can be patient.*

You can, he signed. *I am not sure about me.*

Doctor Cornell came down the stairs fifteen minutes later. It didn't seem that long to Emily, but it was an eternity in *Nathan years*. He urged Emily to tell the doctor about their concerns, but she chose to let him get his morning coffee first.

"What is up with you two?" he asked after his first sip. "I can tell something is going on."

"Nathan came down this morning and couldn't see me on the couch," said Emily in her whisper of a voice. "We were wondering if I am…relapsing. I guess that is what you would call it." Doctor Cornell took another sip while he composed an answer in his head.

"I suppose that is possible," he said finally. "…but I don't think it is likely."

"Why not?" she asked.

"I have studied you for a long time, Emily," he replied. "As best I can tell, your invisibility was the result of a recessive gene that dates back to a time we know very little about. What I suspect is that it was a defense mechanism which some primates possessed. It was what allowed intellectual primates to evolve alongside the fittest. That is why we have such diversity of physical builds around the planet.

"When the roaming hunters/gatherers began to farm, they formed communities. Thus, civilization was born. There was little need for camouflage because people began to govern themselves. The invisibility wasn't necessary anymore. I have no doubt that there are others like you out there. The reason we don't know about them is because of the very nature of the condition. It probably works at varying degrees with those who possess the gene. Some probably just have trouble getting noticed at a bar or in a restaurant. Others are like you were; probably invisible all the time. We really have no way of researching it. It's not like they are going to come forward to be studied. We have seen firsthand what happens when they do…and I am sorry about that, by the way. It was my research that led the government to you. I was careless and I shouldn't have been."

"You were just trying to help, Doctor David," said Emily. "We wanted your help. You were just doing what you thought was best."

"Still," he said. "I wish I had done some things differently."

"Welcome to the human race, Doc," said Charles Troy, coming down the stairs. "What are we talking about?"

"Nathan couldn't see Emily on the couch this morning," Doctor Cornell answered. "That is unusual on several levels."

"What do you think has happened?" asked Alma, joining the group and the conversation.

"Without an entire medical complex at my disposal, I can only speculate," replied the doctor. "…but I suspect her DNA has been altered by the baby. Recessive genes are coming into play that we never knew were possible. Hypothetically, a mother in the wild with the ability to blend in with her environment would do so involuntarily as she slept to protect herself and her young. Because the baby is a new variable in this equation, even Nathan wouldn't be able to see her. The evidence seems to bear out that hypothesis."

"So why didn't we notice it before?" asked Emily.

"Because it happens when you are asleep I suspect," said Doctor Cornell. "Usually, you are away from others or the lights are off. It is also possible that this is a new development in your body chemistry as you get closer to delivering."

"Great," said Emily. "As if childbirth wasn't going to be difficult enough…"

"There may be a plus side," he replied. "It may be possible for you to control it when you are awake. You could conceivable turn your invisibility on and off at will with practice."

"That would be a neat trick," responded Emily. "I am just not sure how I would do it."

"You have us to help you," he said. "We can start observing you when you sleep. We can also work with hypnosis. I haven't hypnotized anyone in a while, but I think I remember what to do. Maybe we can implant a trigger word in your subconscious that will allow you to turn your invisibility on and off like a switch."

Emily conveyed the parts of the conversation Nathan had missed to him in sign language. He smiled as he thought about the possibilities. He had done about as much as he could do to set up new lives for them all. He was going to need more resources to finalize things. His smile faded as he thought about his mother.

I haven't heard from my mom in a while, he signed to Emily. *I am worried about her. I sent her a couple of encrypted messages, but she hasn't responded.*

She is probably fine, signed Emily, trying to look positive. *She knows that the more contact she has with you, the more danger we are in.*

I know, signed Nathan. *I am just worried. Even the last message I got didn't seem like her. It was different somehow. I haven't even told her that she is going to be a grandmother yet.* Emily touched his face softly. Alma stiffened a little. She wasn't ready for the prospect of being a grandmother herself. Emily still seemed like a little girl to her. She suspected that it was because she had missed so much of Emily's childhood. Her mood became brighter when she considered that she might not miss it with the baby.

She secretly hoped it was a girl, but she knew she would be happy with either.

"Who wants breakfast?" she asked, changing the climate of the room.

* * * * * * * *

Agent Baxter had a lot of information to work with. He didn't even know if he had his listening device calibrated properly until Doctor Cornell began to speak. Then he realized that it worked remarkably well. He thought about sending Grandy a bonus and then decided against it. He didn't want to be too generous. Grandy would expect it all the time if he did. *Better to keep him humble*, he thought. Then he chuckled to himself. He knew Grandy was anything but humble.

He opened the screen on his laptop that allowed him to use the Wi-Fi to passively monitor movement in the condo. Baxter had to fine-tune the settings because he was also getting readings from the couple who lived in the adjoining condo. He found that on this particular morning, they were enjoying a bit of romance on the cooking island in their kitchen. Baxter didn't need that kind of distraction. There was nothing he really needed to know about the Troy family for the time being. He just wanted to make sure the surveillance system worked. And it worked well. The audio went in and out like the couple in the next condo. He smiled again and then got serious. It was also difficult to track conversations when parts of them were done in sign language. It was almost as if they were taunting Baxter. He had become familiar with sign language after being assigned to the case. He could understand quite a bit and carry on a modest conversation. But he was nowhere near as proficient as the Troys, or Doctor Cornell for that matter. Unfortunately, he needed line-of-sight to know what they were saying. Baxter had a sophisticated video surveillance camera set up with the laser, but it only allowed him to monitor what could be seen through the window. He would need to place cameras inside the condo to get a complete view of the inside. To do that, he would need everyone to leave or he would have to experiment with something. He decided that a combination of the two might be the best course of action. The weather was milder today and the evening was supposed to be pleasant. Baxter listened for a while longer, but there was little more that he could learn right now. He felt a little twinge of remorse when Nathan talked about his mother. Sue Saunders would have liked to have known that she was going to have a grandchild. But that wasn't possible now and it was his fault.

Baxter shook off any feelings of regret he had and resumed his role of a cold, duty-driven agent. He felt that maybe the agency had given up too easily when it came to the research done on Emily Troy. Knowing they could study the baby and the effect the pregnancy was having on Emily might cause them to reopen the case and reinstate him as lead agent. It was a longshot, but there was a chance. If not, he had resigned himself to disappearing along with the Troys. He chuckled again at the private joke he had just made as he packed up his equipment and headed back to his room at the inn. He collected the surveillance cameras that he would need and waited until the afternoon. Baxter took a nap in the meantime because his sleep the night before had seemed brief and troubled. He awoke around four-thirty. *Ironic,* he thought.

The Troys and Company headed for their spot at the beach as Baxter had suspected. They resumed their places behind the small dune and roasted chicken shish-kabobs over the fire. The men drank beer and Alma drank chardonnay. Emily drank orange juice...or a virgin screwdriver as she called it. Afterwards, they sat quietly and watched the sun peek in and out of a cloudbank as it dropped to the horizon. Agent Baxter waited until he was sure they had settled in before making his move. He casually walked to the beach house. When he was sure no one was around, he took a syringe out of a case and double checked its contents. It looked similar to the one Emily Troy had turned on him in the fifth-wheel some time ago. He removed the cap guarding the needle, took a deep breath and injected it into his bloodstream. He waited ten full minutes for it to take effect before realizing he would not be able to tell. According to the studies he had read, Emily Troy could see herself when no one else could. His only way to test if the experimental compound he had just injected into his system was working would be to try to get someone to look at him.

Agent Baxter knew he had to hurry. He didn't know how long the compound would last and it was unpredictable at best. He noticed a gossamer shimmer on the back of his hand and he smiled. That was a good sign. The couple that lived in the next condo came walking up the boardwalk, headed for their home. Baxter stood ten feet in front of them and jumped up and down waving his arms like a mad man. The couple stopped and looked. Baxter froze since he was sure he now looked like an idiot.

"What do you suppose caused that?" asked the woman.

"I don't know," replied the man. "Old wood, erosion, the surf, earthquake. I don't really care. I am just anxious to get you back to the house."

"I hope you are this enthusiastic AFTER we get married," she said.

"I will be if you are," he responded. They hurried their pace to the condo, almost running over Agent Baxter. He was confident that they hadn't seen him, so he went to the Troys' home to pick the lock of the front door. He inserted the torsion wrench in the slot and began to work the tumbles with the rake pick. Baxter had worked for about two minutes with no success when it dawned on him to check the knob. He felt like an idiot when he found that the door was not locked. It seemed unusual to him that the Troys, who were always so cautious, would leave the door unlocked. He locked it behind him and looked around for suitable locations to plant his surveillance devices. He had just placed a fake book on a high bookshelf when he heard a toilet flush somewhere in the condo. He turned and locked in place. Nathan Saunders was staring directly at him.

CHAPTER 20: INTRUDER

Nathan looked at the shimmer of light in front of the bookcase. He thought for a moment that it may simply be a prismatic reflection through the window. It then occurred to him that Emily might have come back to the condo. *Emily*, he signed before realizing he could not see her response. He moved in the direction of the shimmer, but the door opened before he got to the bookshelf. The rest of the family, including Emily, was returning from the beach because of a pop-up shower. Nathan looked back at the bookcase, but the shimmer was gone. Gone too was the sunlight that had been shining through the window. Threatening clouds replaced the clear skies and large raindrops spattered against the glass.

Nathan shrugged, feeling foolish and decided that the shimmer had just been a trick of the light. He smiled when he saw Emily come through the door, holding a blanket over her head. For a moment, she rested it on top of her head and around her shoulders. The glow and innocence of her face reminded Nathan of a renaissance painting by Raphael or Bellini. She smiled when she saw Nathan and threw back the blanket. Her golden hair shimmered in spite of the sun's absence. They embraced and Nathan's hand traveled, almost involuntarily, to Emily's stomach so he could feel the baby move. It didn't, but he wasn't disappointed. It was as if the baby felt safe and secure in his presence and he was fine with that.

The family shook off the rain and settled into various parts of the house. No one noticed the front door open and close as Agent Baxter made a hasty retreat. He did not get all the surveillance equipment planted that he wanted, but he would make do with what he had. The rain was coming down heavier as he left and he was soaked by the time he got back to the inn. The invisibility reagent wore off in the elevator. Baxter saw a brief shimmering flash reflected in the polished brass doors and knew somehow that he was visible again. He got back to his room and was unpleasantly surprised to find that housekeeping had once again adjusted the thermostat to a temperature that would be suitable for storing meat. He flipped the dial to heat and turned the thermostat all the way up in defiance; an action he would regret around three in the morning. Baxter quickly got out of his wet clothes and took a hot shower. He decided that he should purchase a bathrobe on his next visit to the store. He dried quickly and put on clean clothes, noticing that he was going to have to do laundry soon.

The signal from the spy camera hidden in the Troy's bookshelf was too weak to transmit to the inn. Baxter had a contingency plan in place that might solve some other problems as well. One of the condos in the beach house next to the Troys was closed up for the season. If the power was still on, he thought he could use that as a base of operations...and do his laundry. Another early morning was going to be involved, so he arranged his customary 4:30 a.m. wake-up call and went to bed. After an hour of tossing and turning, he decided he was hungry and made another reluctant visit to the vending machine. As he stood peering at the meager selection of snack items, the delicious aroma of tomato sauce and melted cheese assaulted his nostrils. He followed the scent to the front desk where he found the night clerk about to get lost in a medium hand-tossed deluxe pizza with extra cheese. He had to fight back his own drool as he asked who had delivered it.

"The bistro down the beach," the clerk said. "They even deliver for free. I really don't think they are interested in making money. There isn't that much business volume and their prices are so reasonable. They use real ingredients too; nothing processed." He handed Baxter a flyer from a rack on the desk. It had the complete menu and prices, along with a coupon at the bottom for two dollars off. Baxter thanked him and went back to his room to place an order if possible. It was rather late. The phone rang for a long time and he was about to give up hope when there was an answer. Baxter thought it sounded like a party was going on in the background. He asked if they were still delivering. The person on the other end seemed almost offended at the suggestion that they were not. He took Baxter's order and it arrived at his door forty-five minutes later. Baxter did not find out until later that the person delivering the pizza was also one of the owners of the bistro. He and his life-partner Carter bought it while it was in foreclosure. Carter had recently inherited a substantial trust and the two were set for life. The restaurant was their passion and a handy tax write-off. The pizza delivery guy and part-owner's name was Winston. Agent Baxter never questioned if it was his first or last name and Winston didn't offer.

The pizza was better than any pizza Baxter had ever tasted. He ate more than he had planned, but managed to stash the rest in the mini-fridge before he was tempted to eat it all. With a full stomach, fatigue took over and he fell asleep without turning off the light or the television. Troubling dreams invaded his sleep. Images of his criticizing mother morphed into images of his criticizing superiors. They seemed twice their normal size in his dream and he felt as though he was pinned to the ground by an unseen force.

Looking to the left, he could see his father. He was sitting in the corner as if he was in a *timeout*. When Baxter first looked at him, he was wearing his usual slacks and cardigan sweater. The next time he looked, his father was wearing what looked like a toddler's sailor suit from the early twentieth century. His mother/supervisor combo dissolved and Baxter was sitting at an antique school desk with school-aged children in the rows of desks around him. They all seemed oblivious to him, but the stern school teacher was looking right at him. The teacher was a very tall bony man with round wire-rimmed spectacles and a hairline that had receded well into near oblivion. He was wearing a frock coat, a ruffled shirt, white stockings to his knees and had buckles on his shoes. He looked as though he had just come from signing the Declaration of Independence. He cleared his throat and demanded, "Master Baxter! Come up and work this problem out on the blackboard!" The students who had seemed to ignore his presence were now all looking at him, as if they were all part of a tribunal. It was then that he realized he was sitting at the desk dressed only in his underwear. And the underwear he was wearing was not just any underwear; they were *My Little Pony* underwear. He had a thousand reasons not to want to leave the modest security of the rustic desk, but the gaze of the headmaster felt like it was burning into his forehead. He looked past the headmaster to the problem on the board. It was complicated and intricate. There were so many numbers, equations and symbols that he did not know where to begin.

"Any time now, Master Baxter," said the headmaster. "Surely, you can work out a simple problem like this?" Agent Baxter looked over at his father in the corner, who was now wearing a dunce cap like in cartoons. His father morphed into his own image and Baxter realized he was always going to be a failure if he did not get up and try to solve the equation. He tried to force himself to stand, but discovered someone had put glue on the seat of his chair. He felt the fabric of the underwear rip as he tried to get up. He held his position half-sitting and half-standing as the classroom erupted into cruel laughter. Baxter felt his face turn crimson and his temples throbbed as his blood pressure rose. He didn't know if he could take much more, but his unconscious mind had pity on him. The school bell rang and all the children ran out to recess. The headmaster still stood at the front of the classroom looking at him as the bell rang incessantly. "Well?" he asked as he smacked an oversized wooden ruler on his palm. "Aren't you going to answer?" He smacked the ruler harder and harder. The bell continued to ring in long bursts. The silence between the peals was deafening. The smacking sound of wood hitting flesh got louder and synced with the bell. The noises began to hurt like skin scraping on a rough sidewalk. Baxter closed his eyes tightly in the dream. Then he forced them open and he was back in his room at the inn. However, the annoying bell was still present. His 4:30 wake-up call was persistent. He reached over and answered it. It was automated, so all he had to do was lift the handset off the cradle.

Baxter's bed and clothes were soaked with sweat. His head hurt and he had a bad taste in his mouth. While the pizza was excellent, the combination of spices and grease were not the best things to ingest before going to bed. He felt the dream meant something, however. Usually, a dream with so many symbols in it suggested something significant. He began to analyze it as he showered. Baxter came to the conclusion that the headmaster represented the agency and that the problem on the blackboard was about Emily Troy. The children were his fellow agents who he just knew were ridiculing him when he wasn't around. He wasn't sure what his father in the corner meant...or the *My Little Pony* underwear. He felt that maybe those were questions for an actual therapist…or not. Baxter was determined to find out what the symbols meant and to formulate a solution.

An hour later, he was crouched under the eave that sheltered the front door of the condo near the Troys. He deftly picked the lock and waited to hear an alarm. When no alarm was heard, he checked inside to make sure there was no silent alarm. Had there been one, he was prepared to disable it; but it wasn't necessary. Baxter suspected the condo was heavily insured and was used just for vacations. There were no indications of family keepsakes or mementos; no family albums or even pictures. The condo looked as if it had been decorated strictly for a brochure. The house was dark. All of the storm shutters were secured and only the smallest amount of light came in through a small beveled-glass window in the door. Baxter flipped the light switch and was disappointed to find that it didn't work. He tried another switch just to be sure it wasn't a blown light bulb. It wasn't. He brought his items into the condo anyway. He didn't want his bag sitting in full view of the public. He sat down on the fashionable sofa to consider his next move. Without a power source, the batteries in his equipment would only last a few hours at best. He could try to syphon energy by reconnecting it at the meter, but that might cause an investigation. Baxter would only do that as a last resort. The beach house was nearly identical to the one that the Troys occupied and also contained two condos. He thought that he might pirate energy from the other condo in his building, but it too was unoccupied. He was about to give up and make other arrangements when an idea occurred to him. Baxter felt like an idiot that he had not checked it first. He went down to the small ground-level garage, opened the panel box and flipped on the house's main circuit breaker. The sudden burst of light from the light bulb in the ceiling seemed blinding. He flipped the light switch off and went around the rest of the condo extinguishing lights. He was afraid that if any of them could be seen from the outside, they would shine like beacons and let people know that the condo was not empty.

Agent Baxter settled into the condo as if he owned it. The first thing he did was start a load of laundry. He was careful to disconnect the dryer vent and run the duct into the hallway. That way, no one would notice the heated air coming out of it from the outside. While the first load was in the washer, he went about setting up his receivers and other surveillance equipment. Then he sat down on the floor next to the fashionable gas fireplace and booted up his laptop. The only clothing items that he had even close to being clean were the dress shirt, boxer shorts and black dress socks he was wearing; and they were destined for the laundry next. The light from the screen of the laptop and the flickering blaze from the fireplace illuminated the room in a soft, but eerie glow. Baxter didn't know it, but he looked like an evil super-villain bent on world domination…while wearing boxer shorts. The laptop's large screen divided into quadrants, displaying various views of the nearby condo. The upper left quadrant rendered the passive Wi-Fi surveillance images in a three-dimensional wireframe display. Individuals were depicted as ghostly silhouettes against a black background. Only one member of the family was up and about so early. The individual sat on the window seat looking out at the ocean. Baxter checked the camera feed in the lower right-hand quadrant. It was from a camera mounted on the same antique streetlamp as his laser listening device. He could barely make out the image of Emily Troy, lost in her own thoughts. Baxter labeled the silhouette as E. Troy. Then he fine-tuned the remainder of his screens and graphs while he waited for other family members to rise.

Agent Baxter went to check the progress of the washing machine. He felt vulnerable and a bit unprofessional doing surveillance in his underwear. When he returned to his laptop, he detected a low, but rapidly swelling growl that he could not identify. It sounded like a cross between a werewolf and a zombie. Creepy unnatural light in the room made his imagination run wild. The hair on the back of his neck stood up and he suddenly felt deathly cold. He reached for his pistol for security. He couldn't believe how cold it seemed against the palm of his hand. A chill went through him that caused him to involuntarily shrug his shoulders. Baxter's eyes flitted from screen to screen trying to identify the source of the unearthly growl. The growl became sporadic coughs intermixed with sounds of someone clearing their throat. All of the sounds coalesced into a horrible death rattle that subtly died away. The image of Emily rose from the window seat, walked to the kitchen and poured a freshly-brewed cup of coffee.

Agent Baxter was glad that no one was there to see him panic because of a coffee maker. It angered him that he had been shaken so easily, but it also made him admire Lyn Grandy's attention to detail. He adjusted the listening device slightly to filter ambient noises and continued to listen and observe. There was nothing really happening at the Troy's and Baxter (relieved that the Zombie Apocalypse had not come and caught him in his underwear) began to drift off. In his half-sleep, he imagined Emily walking through the fog on the beach. She wore a chiffon gown and a white hooded cloak. He could see that she was barefoot, but she left no prints as she walked. The fog swirled around her as if enveloping her in a protective field. She cradled her belly in her hands and looked to be on the verge of delivering. Suddenly, she looked directly at Agent Baxter with a glare so sharp that it seemed to burn through him. He caught his breath as he started and returned to reality. Whether it was Emily's accusing stare or the sudden silence of the house that caused him to become alert, Agent Baxter crouched on one knee with his pistol held in the ready position. The palpable silence seemed so loud that he wondered how the cries of the seagulls outside were able to penetrate it. He began to perspire and could detect a shimmer of light on the walls of the living room. He looked around furtively and realized that the silence of the house was due to the washing machine having completed its cycle. He stood, silently praising himself for his quick response to an imagined threat, then went to move his clothes to the dryer and start his second load.

Agent Baxter stood naked in front of the open closet in an upstairs bedroom. Empty hangers hung from the bar in a way that seemed somehow grotesque to him. Apparently, the regular occupants of the condo didn't leave any of their clothes behind. He looked in the bathroom to see if he could find a towel or something. The bathroom linen closet was almost as empty as the bedroom closet. He looked at himself in the mirror and chuckled. He was standing in the bathroom naked, holding an automatic pistol with a noise suppressor. He felt pretty foolish. As Baxter was about to leave the room, he noticed a flash of cloth through the crack of the door. He closed the bathroom door and found a robe hanging on a hook. It was a woman's robe, probably left by accident. It was pink; it was made of satin…and it fit Agent Baxter perfectly. He chalked it up to the lady of the house being husky and not to his own subcompact frame. He didn't feel any less foolish, but at least he felt less vulnerable.

Baxter heard voices as he made his way downstairs. He flattened himself against the wall and cautiously proceeded. They sounded as though they were in the house and he wondered if the tenants had come home to roost. He couldn't afford to be caught in the house, especially wearing a pink dressing gown. He had taken precautions to cover his tracks thoroughly. No one knew where he was or who he was, for that matter. If it became necessary to do a bit of *wet work*, then so be it. The residents of the condo would just be collateral damage. Baxter knew that was a possibility when he started his self-assigned mission. He took a deep breath, threw himself down the stairs in a neatly-executed flip, landed in a crouched position facing the living room and delivered two slugs right into the back of a man's head. A startled woman stood next to the man with a terrified look. Agent Baxter fired two more shots. The slugs struck her between the eyes so closely that they connected into an "eight". Blood splattered on the wall behind her from the golf ball-sized exit wounds in the back of her head. Everything seemed frozen in time as Agent Baxter heard the jingle of the spent casings bouncing on the tile floor under his feet.

CHAPTER 21: CHANGES

The birth of a child and the death of another human being have one thing in common. They both change the life of the person causing them irrevocably. Agent Baxter stood transfixed, staring at the face of the woman whose life he had just ended. The whole scene seemed to be in slow motion, but more than that. It was as if he was watching it as it was illuminated by a strobe light. A thin blue tendril of smoke rose from the barrel of his revolver. His mind tried to make sense of the scene and attach a name to the face of the life he had just permanently altered. It looked familiar in the dim light, but he couldn't make it out for sure. At first, Baxter thought it was Emily Troy. He hadn't actually seen her a lot, considering that she had been invisible most of her life. He began to realize that it must be her mother, Alma. In the light from the fire and the computer screen, they looked very much alike.

Many questions filled his head simultaneously, as if he was the subject of a press conference. *How did they get in? What were they doing here? What are you going to do now? Do you think anyone knows they are here?* The strobe flashes became more intense and seemed like camera flashes. He imagined a crowd of reporters taking his picture and then saw a front page headline with his picture below. He was wearing a pink satin dressing gown in it. The light from the strobe turned to alternating red and blue. Agent Baxter heard pounding on the door behind him and demands from local law enforcement that he open the door. *How did they get here so quickly?* The questions in his head continued. All the while, the image of Alma Troy remained frozen with an expression of terror etched on her face. Her expression turned to one of condemnation and he thought he saw her raise her arm to point an accusing finger at him. A sudden chill went through him as he began to realize the consequences for what he had just done. Accident or not, he would not escape judgment for his actions.

The flicker of the strobe started to steadily diminish in intensity until only the light from the laptop and the glow of the fire remained. As the light faded, so did the image of the woman Agent Baxter had determined was Alma Troy. The blood splatters on the wall behind her began to evaporate like summer rain on a hot sidewalk, leaving only two perfect bullet holes in the paneling. The pounding at the door stopped and he realized it had been the pounding of his heartbeat in his own temples. Baxter crossed the room to where the bodies should have been. Nothing was there. He examined the wall and found all of the bullet holes, including the one that had dispatched the unidentified male. The bullet had lodged in the wall after penetrating a painting of a lighthouse. It had created a hole about the size of a dime to the left of the lighthouse in the picture, just above the horizon. The defacing looked somehow natural; as if the sun was being eclipsed.

Agent Baxter's knees suddenly became weak. He felt nauseous and resisted the urge to find the nearest waste receptacle. Instead, he sat on an ottoman in front of his computer screen. The voices he had heard were coming from the surveillance equipment inside the Troy's beach house. Baxter made a mental note to commend Grandy on the quality of his work. The entire family was up now, but the conversation was little more than cursory morning greetings and routine exchanges. One glowing silhouette was very close to the one of Emily. Baxter labeled it "Nathan". He confirmed his inference by checking the external camera. Sure enough, Nathan was sitting behind Emily at the window. He had his arms around her in such a way as to cradle her belly in his hands. He was also looking out at the sea as well; no doubt wondering what the future had in store.

Agent Baxter's hands were shaking. Cold sweat formed on his forehead and he wiped it off with his hand. An iridescent shimmer flashed across his palm and he wondered just what effect the invisibility agent was having on him. Much of the report on the compound had already been redacted by the time he got to read it. He was able to infer some of the side-effects and the length of others by piecing together key words in the report. Obviously, hallucinations were a major side-effect. So were heightened senses and paranoia. He began to think that maybe H. G. Wells knew what he was talking about…perhaps from personal experience. Baxter tried to think clearly and focus on his mission. Then it dawned on him that he had no clear objective. He had been determined to rid the world of Emily Troy and her family. Taking her back to the research facility alive would not only be problematic; it would most likely not be very well received. He considered giving up, but his mother's almost maniacal belittling laugh filled his ears. He turned around just in time to see her image melt into the wood paneling. Whether it was fear, paranoia or outright anger, Agent Baxter determined at that point to abduct Emily Troy and decide her fate afterwards. He leaned in to look closely at the screen. Emily was still looking out the window at the sea. Her passive expression became a scowl. She turned her head and appeared to be looking directly at the camera. Baxter saw her eyes open wider, a nearly imperceptible shimmer enveloped her face and she was gone. He leaned in to make sure his monitors were functioning properly. As he touched one of the keys on his keyboard, a loud buzzer went off. Agent Baxter fell back on the ottoman and landed on the floor with his posterior exposed in a most undignified manner. He cursed as he straightened his pink satin dressing gown.

The dryer had announced that his clothes were ready. Agent Baxter didn't know if the buzzer on it was unbelievably loud or if he just thought so because of his heightened senses. He was in such a hurry to get dressed that he burned his abdomen and parts south on the still-hot zipper of his pants. He didn't care. He just wanted to get out of that pink satin dressing gown. He took his underwear from the washer and placed them in the dryer. For the time being, he would be going *commando.*

It was not going to be easy to get Emily Troy separated from her family. They seemed to be with her everywhere; like a security team or an entourage. Still, she had to do some things by herself. Going to the bathroom or taking a shower still seemed to be unaccompanied activities most of the time. Occasionally Baxter saw that Nathan and Emily showered together, but that was rare since her family was almost always present. The agent determined to wait until the fewest number of people were around before taking action. He would take out anyone left behind Emily if he had to. All he had to do was to wait for the right moment. He wasn't sure how long that would take, so he made himself at home in the vacant condo. The rest of the day was relatively uneventful. Baxter busied himself with taking inventory of what meager stock there was in the house. There was little in the way of toiletries and nothing at all to eat in the kitchen. It seemed that it was going to be necessary to secure provisions for the stakeout. He might have to be there a long time.

Making sure that he wasn't seen exiting the house, Agent Baxter walked casually down the beach to the row of buildings that served as a town. A convenience mart with a wooden general store façade was the only place he was going to be able to get groceries without returning to his car. He didn't mind. He didn't need a lot for the time being and he really didn't want the trouble of walking all the way back to the inn; even though he knew he would have to eventually. Baxter walked through the mart and filled his arms with things he thought he might need. He looked around for a basket or something to put the items in. He couldn't find one. Most people don't do a majority of their grocery shopping in a convenience store. He adjusted the items in his arms and lost the small can of over-priced coffee. There was a metallic clatter when the can hit the floor and something like a drumroll as it rolled down the small narrow aisle. The clerk looked up from his magazine. Baxter looked back and shrugged sheepishly. Even though he was prepared to kill if necessary, he felt awkward and embarrassed. The clerk had a curious expression for a moment, but then went back to reading. Baxter retrieved the can of coffee and positioned it more securely in his arms. Balancing a ridiculous number of items, he went to the counter and waited for the clerk to move his magazine so he could set them down. The clerk didn't. He just kept reading, oblivious to the world around him. Baxter wondered what the article could have been about that kept him so absorbed. He read the upside down headline of the article: MIGRATION PATTERNS OF BLACK-TAILED DEER. *Really?* thought Baxter. *This is what has him so engrossed?* He stood for a long time waiting to be noticed. Finally, he took a moment to center himself and said, "Excuse me." The clerk nearly fell off of his stool.

"Where did you come from?" the young man said incredulously. "I didn't even see you come in!"

"You looked right at me while I was in the aisle," replied Baxter.

"I did?" he said. "Wow…I must be tired. This article isn't even that good. Will that be all?"

"I think so," said Baxter. "For the time being anyway…" The clerk rang up the sale, which amounted to a weekly grocery total for a family of four. Baxter begrudgingly handed over cash so as not to leave a paper trail. The clerk bagged his items in the only bags he had available. Each was only large enough to hold one or maybe two items at most. Baxter took each of the bags and placed them over each wrist alternately until he looked like a balloon salesman with half-deflated wares. Heading back to the condo, he was sure he was going to be noticed because of the cumbersome sacks he carried. He wasn't. Half of the time, he appeared as no more than a shimmer of light. The other half, he was nothing more than a shadow. Baxter enhanced his stealth when he reached the condo, even though it wasn't necessary. No one was around; and if they had been, they couldn't have seen him. Once inside he shook off the chill, emptied a can of concentrated soup into a bowl and mixed in only half the recommended amount of water. He liked his soup thick. He placed it in the microwave to heat up. The air soon filled with the aroma of beef with barley. It reminded Baxter of soup his grandmother had prepared for him. She had passed away when he was nine, but he still missed her. He felt a tear roll down his face and quickly wiped it away. *What is wrong with me?* he thought. *Damn those chemicals!*

Agent Baxter sat next to the fire and ate his soup. It tasted better than any soup he had ever tasted in his life. It wasn't because the soup was fresh or perfectly heated. It wasn't even a name brand. Baxter knew it was because of his enhanced senses. He thought that there was finally a positive side to the chemicals for a change. Even the bread that he had with his soup was excellent, in spite of being near its expiration date. He sat and looked at the fire and wondered whose energy bill he was running up. He glanced at the screen of his laptop from time to time. The movement of the household was relatively normal. He wasn't interested in bathroom schedules or eating habits; although Alma pushed vitamin-rich menu items on the expecting Emily. The evening's entertainment consisted of television sitcoms since a steady rain had moved in from the west. The family's planned bonfire and cookout had to be cancelled. Baxter thought about abducting Emily later while the family slept, but that would mean too much collateral damage and too many questions by authorities.

Instead, he watched the screen and listened to a comedy about awkward research scientists. Baxter had never had much time for TV, so he wasn't sure what it was. Mostly, he watched the fire and listened to the rain pelt the window. He could hear the angry surf against the shore and the waves dashing against the rocks. It all seemed to fit his mood perfectly. He was angry, yet calm. He could be violent, yet focused. He wasn't sure of his direction, but he was resolved. Maybe tomorrow, he could obtain his quarry. He would then decide what to do with her.

Baxter wished the fire was from actual wood and not gas. He liked the crackle of a fire. He thought about finding a video of a fire on the internet, but passed. It still wouldn't be the same. His soup was gone and his bowl was in the sink. Only one family member of the Troy household was still up. Charles Troy sat in front of the TV watching an old movie. Baxter knew that it was *Strangers on a Train*; mainly because an announcer said, "Now back to *Strangers on a Train*."

"Daddy?" Emily seemed to appear out of nowhere. "Are you awake?"

"Just resting my eyes sweetie," said Charles. "What's wrong?"

"I just have a bad feeling," she said in her soft, angelic voice. "It's different than usual. I have had a lot of emotional rollercoaster rides for the past couple of months. But this just seems different; like something terrible is about to happen."

"I remember those rollercoaster rides," said Charles. "I never had them myself, but your mother had a Season Pass when she was pregnant with you. You have to admit, your system has a lot going on all the time. I am surprised you haven't been coming to talk to me every day. You are amazing in so many ways." Emily sat on the arm of the chair and laid her head on top of his. He hugged her in his most reassuring way and patted her back three times to silently say, "It's all right."

A scowl crossed Agent Baxter's face once more. His childhood home life seemed more like a Theme Park in Hell. It wasn't because his parents had been particularly abusive. It was because he had been very sensitive as a child. He got picked on in school and felt that his home should have been a sanctuary. Instead, his mother had been as cruel as the bullies on the playground, so he had no safe refuge. He resented the Troy family for their close-knit affection for one another. He resented the relationship between Nathan and Emily. They seemed meant for each other; like two puzzle pieces that could not possibly fit anywhere else but together. If Fate had been so careful to place the two of them together, what had happened in his case? Why hadn't he found someone? Why had he been miserable his entire life? Agent Baxter began to feel feverish. He was about to adjust the flame in the fireplace when a chill went through him and he left it as it was.

"You will be fine," said Charles softly. There wasn't a trace of doubt in his voice. In spite of all they had been through, he really did believe what he said. Baxter remembered reading an article about self-esteem and self-destructive behavior. It had said that much of how an individual feels about themselves is formed very early in childhood. It made the basic *everybody-knows-that* statement that encouragement and positive affirmations of a child lead to a productive well-adjusted adult. That part was not surprising. What surprised Agent Baxter was the other half of the article. It had stated that if a child is told that he or she is *bad* at an early age, it can affect him or her for their entire life. The article went on to say that the child takes the rebuke to heart and believes they are bad and undeserving of happiness. An emotional downward spiral begins and continues until adulthood. The study showed that subjects either sought out bad relationships or sabotaged potentially good relationships. Baxter hadn't thought much of the article at the time. Now, it made total sense to him. His brow furrowed as he remembered nearly every time his mother had told him that he was worthless and a disappointment.

"I have to be honest," said Emily. "I do not feel reassured. Don't get me wrong, Daddy. You are great and I am so thankful that you are here for me. I guess my blood chemistry is way out of whack."

"Did you eat anything?" asked Charles. "You know you need to eat. You have a baby to think of."

"Is that your solution for everything? Food?"

"Well...not everything," replied Charles. "We could watch *Dr. Phil*."

"Goodnight Daddy," said Emily in a soft sarcastic tone. "Don't stay up too late."

"You sound like your mother," said Charles. "Goodnight sweetheart."

Emily's silhouette disappeared and reappeared in an upstairs bedroom. Baxter thought there might be something wrong with the equipment and ran a diagnostic. Charles Troy sat motionless in front of the TV. After a few moments, Baxter became aware of a soft intermittent buzzing. He checked his system again, only to discover that it was coming from Charles. He had fallen asleep and was softly snoring. After about twenty minutes, he made a choking sound that seemed to wake him up. He rose from his chair and turned off the TV and the lights. He fumbled through the darkness to find the stairs and made his way to his own bedroom. As Agent Baxter tracked him from multiple angles and vantage points, he marveled at how effectively a blind Charles Troy made his way in the dark.

With the house dark and still, Agent Baxter decided it was time for him to get some rest as well. It was easy for him to drift off in front of the fire. His feverishness and chills had subsided and he felt almost euphoric. The darkness in his mind melted into an idyllic scene in a shopping mall of all places. Baxter had always felt giddy at shopping malls. He thought that having many stores and attractions under one roof seemed like the future. When he was little, he thought the whole world would be like a shopping mall and he would never have to go outside. The climate would always be controlled and everything in the stores would be free. His mental image of a shopping mall was also his mental image of Heaven. Baxter didn't set his standards too high.

The utopian paradise in his mind began to dismantle. The disruption was subtle at first…only a general feeling of dread. Then, there was a vibration under his feet. The vibration turned to impact tremors. Something large and imposing was headed his way. People began to move toward the exits in a concerned, but orderly manner. Baxter stood in the center of the mall near a cellphone kiosk. Sunlight coming in through a skylight became obscured by inky storm clouds. Color drained from everything, creating a sepia *mallscape*. The recessed mall lighting began to extinguish in the distance. There was the echoing sound of circuit breakers being tripped as the darkness advanced closer to him. Finally, he was standing alone in a single harsh spotlight as if he was on trial. A shadowy figure approached. The figure was larger than life, at least twice his size. A bony, oversized hand reached out of the darkness and pointed an accusatory finger at him. The flesh began to scorch in the light and floated away in black particles like burning plastic. The smell stung Baxter's nose and he wiped the floating particles from before his eyes.

"Where have you been?" demanded the shadow. "I have been looking for you everywhere!" A hideous version of his mother's face loomed into the light. It was grotesquely misshapen and twice its normal size. The flesh dissolved in the light as had the flesh on the hand. The eye sockets of the now-exposed skull contained huge, bloodshot, floating eyeballs. The brow of the skull caved in toward the center to create a disapproving glare. The bared pointed teeth still managed to form a frown and a pale fleshy tongue could be seen struggling behind the gaps in the teeth.

"You are cursed!" said the dreadful shadow image of his mother. "You will never amount to anything! You will never be allowed to be happy…and you will never, EVER…be loved!"

"Why are you being like this?" Baxter pleaded. His voice was that of a six year-old. "What did I do that was so wrong?"

"You were born!" shouted his mother. "Wasn't that enough? You were a disappointment from the beginning. Do you think I wanted a *boy*?" Baxter's own brow furrowed. He had taken all he intended to. His mother had belittled him his entire life; in front of his few friends, in front of his relatives and even in front of his class. He had had enough. From somewhere, he produced two stainless steel Desert Eagles. Baxter pointed them directly at the image of his mother. He noticed that his hands were also the hands of a six year-old. Somewhere in his psyche, he thought that might be significant. His mother opened her gruesome cage of a mouth to release the disgusting monster tongue inside. Before it could begin its onslaught of demeaning and abusive attacks, Baxter began to fire the weapons in his hands. At first, he alternated. Then he graduated to firing both guns simultaneously. Bone and tooth fragments stung his face and he could feel blood trickling down from the wounds. The fifty-caliber slugs penetrated the enormous tongue that had taken on a life of its own. Gray ooze dripped from it and burned into the tile like acid when it hit the floor. Baxter was sure he should have emptied both clips, but he kept firing and the guns kept delivering. Blue smoke and the smell of cordite filled his nose and his lighted circle. He began to choke on it and the giant tongue seemed to be regenerating. It turned into a snake-like form and wrapped around his neck. He couldn't breathe, but he kept firing. The light above was blinding him, but was beginning to fade. Darkness enveloped him and he continued to choke. The smoke smelled like…

Gas! The room was dark and Agent Baxter smelled the strong aroma of gas. In his fitful dream, he had closed his laptop and somehow extinguished the flame in the fireplace.

He quickly turned the gas valve to the off-position and opened the front door without his usual caution in order to air out the house. It must have been just before dawn because a dull light filled the room as the gas exited into the fresh air. Agent Baxter took the pink dressing gown from the back of a chair and waved it like a bullfighter's cape to usher the gas out of the condo and into the light fog that had rolled in. As his eyes adjusted, he began to see what must have transpired in the night. A throw pillow had been kicked up against the decorative fireplace screen, which had been subsequently knocked over extinguishing the flame. Had it caught fire, it would probably have been safer. The picture above the fireplace (another lighthouse) was marred with fourteen bullet holes in a relatively tight pattern. The sound of the gunshots would probably have caused him to wake up had it not been for the state-of-the-art suppressor.

When he was sure there was no residual gas in the condo, he closed the door and set about righting the room. He moved his surveillance station to the dining table so he wouldn't be tempted to fall asleep in front of it. Baxter wondered what all the symbolism in his dream meant, but then he decided he really didn't want to know. Instead, he blamed it all on the unusual compound he had injected into his system.

The screen of his laptop showed that the family was up and about already. The tone of the conversation indicated that today would be a shopping day for supplies. An extended family of five needed to make frequent trips to the store. Now that Emily was pregnant, it was an extended family of six. Emily stated that she was feeling tired and really didn't feel like going.

"Can we go tomorrow?" she asked.

"Sweetie..." said Alma. "We can handle this. You don't have to go."

"But I want to do my part," she said.

"We will be fine," replied Alma. "If there is one thing I know how to do, it's shop. Besides, I have these two strong, able-bodied men to do the grunt work."

"You mean three," said Emily, indicating Nathan.

"I mean two," said Alma. "You don't think we are leaving you here by yourself, do you?"

"I don't need anyone to watch over me," she said sheepishly, trying not to sound too anxious about the prospect of being alone with Nathan.

"I insist," said Alma. "You need your rest. We have my grandchild to think of. No more discussion. The subject is closed." Emily hugged her mom and Agent Baxter winced. His opportunity had arrived, but Nathan would be a complication.

Charles and Alma Troy drove away in the SUV with Doctor Cornell. Emily waved from the door until they were out of sight. Then she locked the door and began to sign to Nathan. Baxter could only guess what the conversation was about, but they quickly ascended the stairs and headed to the upstairs master bath. He heard the shower start and could see the two silhouettes apparently getting undressed. Baxter knew that they would be at their most vulnerable for the next few minutes. He selected the items he knew that he would need and a couple more things, just in case. The fog had thickened to a point where stealth was not entirely necessary. Baxter picked the lock to the front door and closed it quietly behind him. He silently ascended the stairs and headed toward the sound of the running shower. Standing next to the door, he heard sounds that could have been back-washing or lovemaking. He wasn't sure. Either way, it continued for about ten minutes. After that, he detected noises that were probably the result of kisses. Then, he barely ducked back out of sight as Nathan exited the shower while Emily remained behind. Baxter slid into the Troy's bedroom just as a naked Nathan came around the corner from the bathroom. He was toweling himself off and was headed for Emily's bedroom. Baxter took a deep breath, aimed his weapon to a point on Nathan's head and squeezed the trigger. A red spot appeared behind Nathan's right ear and he went immediately down.

Baxter shook off any regret he might have had. He had a job to do and this was no time to get emotional. Standing at the door of the bathroom, he watched Emily continue to shower. From the back, he could not see the protrusion of her belly. That was going to make his job easier. He watched her for a moment; marveling at her physical perfection. Any guilt he felt was overwhelmed by a sudden pang of vindictiveness seasoned with a generous helping of lust. He admired her body for as long as he dared before raising his weapon and aiming at her. His hands were not shaking and he was resolved to carry out his self-imposed mission. Emily leaned over to turn off the water. Baxter's heart went into his throat as he squeezed the trigger.

CHAPTER 22: VENGEANCE

Alma Troy had an uneasy feeling in the pit of her stomach. She didn't like leaving Emily. She had lost her before and her heart sank at the thought of ever losing her again. She was fine with leaving her alone with Nathan. After all, Emily was already pregnant. It wasn't like there was any other mischief they could get into.

Mischief. Alma thought that was a funny word to use to describe bringing a new life into the world...and a remarkable life at that. The tests that Doctor Cornell had been able to do while they were on the run had suggested that Emily's invisibility was hard-coded into her DNA. The gene that had been recessive might become dominant in Emily's child. When Emily became visible after she was pregnant, the doctor hypothesized that the combined DNA of Emily and Nathan in the baby had altered Emily's body chemistry. Only time would tell if the effect would be permanent, or if she would revert back to permanent invisibility after giving birth. A sudden chill went through Alma and she had a strong urge to tell Charles to turn the car around. But she resisted the urge and they drove on.

The store was enormous and had nearly everything a person could want or need. It was designed along the same premise as a Costco or Sam's Club. A family could buy a side of beef and a freezer to keep it in within just a few aisles of each other. On their first trip there, the entire group had obtained complete wardrobes, grooming supplies in bulk and bought their dental care. Even though it was ninety minutes from where they were staying, they only needed to make the trip once a month because of volume purchasing. Nathan had even been able to buy the latest in computer software and hardware there.

Alma hurried down the aisles collecting items she was sure that they needed, completely ignoring the shopping list. This caused her to actually take more time going back to get the items she had missed.

"There is no need to be in this much of a hurry," said Charles. "The kids will be fine."

"You don't know that!" Alma snapped. Charles looked at her with surprise and concern. "What's wrong?" he asked compassionately.

"I don't know," answered Alma. "Just a feeling that I can't shake. Can we go soon?"

"I guess we could schedule another trip," said Charles. "As long as we get the essentials today. Doctor David is in the pharmacy section. He is getting prenatal vitamins and a few other items he needs for his research. As soon as he joins up with us, we will go."

In spite of all the time they had been on the road together, no one in the family felt familiar enough with Doctor Cornell to just call him Dave. Even though he had insisted, they still felt he deserved to be addressed as Doctor. It was a matter of respect. He fished through a selection of prenatal vitamins, analgesics, topical ointments and other basic first aid supplies. He waited until his fake identity was called and he went to the window to collect several prescriptions he had written for himself and the family. Among them were several antibiotics, heart medications and, of all things, hormone replacements for both sexes. No one in the extended family needed them. Doctor Cornell got them to use as a form of reagent when testing Emily's and Nathan's blood. He worked as though he still had a Nobel Prize in mind even though he knew that would never happen. He had grown so close to the family that he would do nothing to jeopardize their lives or freedom. He casually walked toward the checkout where he found Charles and Alma waiting for him impatiently.

"What's wrong?" he asked. "You don't have everything on the list. Do you really want to come back so soon?"

"There is something wrong," said Alma. "I feel it."

"Are you sure you aren't just feeling a little separation anxiety?" asked the Doctor. He tried not to sound patronizing, but didn't do a very good job.

"I know what I feel," replied Alma tersely. "We need to go!" Doctor Cornell knew better than to argue with a mother when it came to her child. He helped load the items onto the belt. They had to wait for an excruciating period of time while the person ahead of them tried to use a fistful of expired coupons. The person also had an expired membership card which had to be renewed before they could proceed. All the while, Alma was getting more and more anxious; to a point that Charles thought she looked as though she was vibrating with impatience. He touched her wrist to calm her down. It felt cold to the touch and he decided he would just let her work through it herself.

After what seemed like three hours (it was actually fourteen minutes), they were headed back to their SUV to return home. Alma was sure that Charles was driving slowly on purpose, in spite of the fact that he was actually driving eight miles per hour over the speed limit. He was about to state that they had forgotten one of the main items on their list, but decided not to because of *the look*. Instead he drove steadily home; all the while a knot was growing in his stomach. Even he thought he was driving too slowly and had to constantly reassure himself that he was not by looking at the speedometer. He even flicked it a couple of times to make sure that it was working properly. When he did, Alma looked straight ahead, but he could see a slight smugness in her expression through his peripheral vision. The last half hour was like traveling through molasses. Charles didn't remember so many stop signs on the way to the store, but now there seemed to be one every twenty feet. The silence in the vehicle grew as the temperature seemed to drop. When they finally pulled into the driveway of the condo, the heart of everyone in the SUV froze. The front door was cracked open about four inches.

Alma was the first one out of the car and she headed straight for the door. Charles was afraid of what might be waiting inside and he tried to get out quickly enough to stop her. In doing so, he forgot to unfasten his safety belt and came to a sudden stop. By the time he had freed himself, Doctor Cornell had reached the door and Alma was already inside. Charles heard a scream that turned his blood to ice. The distance from the drive to the entryway seemed to pass by as a series of photographs which faded into one another. He passed Dr. Cornell on the stairs and didn't remember hitting a single step. At the top of the stairs, Alma was on her knees next to Nathan's naked body. She was sobbing uncontrollably. Nathan was stiff and cold to the touch. Doctor Cornell finally reached the others and knelt down to take Nathan's pulse. His rapidly beating heart sank when he didn't find one.

Charles began to search the house for Emily. He searched every room frantically, calling out her name as he did. Tears began to form in the corners of his eyes and he wiped them away. He knew he had to be strong for Alma. When he didn't find her in the house, he went through every room again; sweeping every inch with his hands just in case she had somehow become invisible again. He was about to give up all hope when Doctor Cornell called from the upstairs hallway.

"Charles! Come up here! I need help!" His cry was desperate. Charles raced up the stairs to find Alma cradling Nathan in her arms while Doctor Cornell continued to check for a pulse.

"I got one, Charles," he said with a worried smile. "It's weak and it is very slow, but I got a pulse! Help me get him to a bed. We need to get this boy warmed up." The two men lifted Nathan up and carried him to the closest bedroom. Alma pulled down the covers on the bed and retrieved a comforter from the closet. Doctor Cornell left the room to get his medical bag and to prepare a treatment. When he returned, he gave Nathan an injection and placed a heating pad on his chest. After a few moments, his pulse became stronger and more regular. Alma held his hand for reassurance and to share a little bit of her body heat.

"I found this," said Doctor Cornell in a solemn tone. "It was in his neck, behind his ear." He held out a small tranquilizer dart. The red tassel-like stabilizer was the color of blood. "For the dart to be this small, the drug must have been very powerful. It's a wonder Nathan is alive at all. His symptoms are that of hypothermia. We will need to treat him as if that is what he has."

"Who could have done this?" asked Alma. "...and where is Emily?"

"I suspect the government is still behind it," said Doctor Cornell.

"But what could they possibly want with her now?" asked Charles. "She isn't even invisible anymore. I thought we were rid of them."

"I don't think we can begin to understand their motives or how they think," the Doctor responded. "Maybe Nathan can shed some light on what happened if he comes to...I mean WHEN he comes to."

"So we just have to sit here and wait?" cried Alma. "They win? The bastards have my little girl! I am not going to just sit around and do nothing!"

"Honey...there is nothing we can do," said Charles. "If there was, don't you think I would be out doing it? She's my little girl too...and she is carrying our grandchild."

"Oh, God! I didn't think about...Oh, God! Do you think they want the baby?" Alma began to shake and had to let go of Nathan's hand. Charles knelt beside her and held both her hands in his.

"This is not over," he said softly. "We didn't go through everything we have been through just to lose it all now. We are going to find her...and the baby." Alma sniffed heavily and wiped away her tears. In a half laugh she said, "You talk like the baby had been born already."

"It might as well be," replied Charles. "That is how I feel about it. I don't even know the gender, but I love it already."

"It's no wonder I love you as much as I do," said Alma. She began to sob softly.

"I think we might need to let Nathan rest for a while," said Doctor Cornell. "We should do something productive in the meantime, like bringing in the supplies from the car." Charles and Alma silently agreed. Alma looked back at Nathan as she left the room. It was as if the secret of Emily's whereabouts were locked inside him and no one had the key.

It didn't take long to get everything from the car to the house since they had cut their trip to the store short. Charles made the last trip to the SUV to make sure they hadn't left anything behind. On his way back to the house, he stopped in the driveway and looked around. The early fog had thinned to more of a veil that thickened as he looked out to sea. A foghorn would have seemed appropriate, but all he heard was the cry of seagulls and waves lapping the beach softly. He tried to think clearly and believe what he had told Alma. He knew there was something he had missed. There was a solution to this mystery. He just needed to keep emotions out of it. There would be plenty of time for emotions when the mystery was solved.

Doctor Cornell was sitting on the window seat looking at the tranquilizer dart when Charles came back into the house.

"This is pretty high-tech stuff," the doctor said, examining the dart. "There is a tracking chip in here. I guess this is a multi-purpose dart. You couldn't pick one of these up at Radio Shack. The government is definitely behind this."

"I need to talk to you," said Charles. "...but not here." The volume of his words barely qualified as a whisper. It was more like he was mouthing the words. Doctor Cornell got his meaning and stood up. Charles told Alma that they needed to check something and then whispered directly in her ear. "Stay close to Nathan. We shouldn't talk here."

The two men met in the driveway and Doctor Cornell was about to speak. Charles casually put his finger to his lips and then closed it into a fist to cover a fake cough. Doctor Cornell got the meaning and kept quiet while the two men got into the SUV. They remained silent as they drove a little way up the coast to a seaside restaurant. If they were being observed by some government agency, their actions would have looked suspicious. It would seem like the last thing they would do in their situation would be to go somewhere for lunch. But nothing was normal.

It was a little early for the lunch crowd, if one could ever call it a crowd. There was always room in the little bistro/microbrewery. Charles and Doctor Cornell had their choice of tables. They chose a quiet one in the corner instead of one of the booths that lined a wall. That way, they could sit close and keep their conversation down without looking any more suspicious than they already did. They ordered tall dark lagers and split an order of chicken fingers since neither man really felt like eating.

"They knew we were gone," whispered Charles softly. "They must have been monitoring us."

"I don't know, Charles," said Doctor Cornell. "I go over the house regularly to check for *bugs*. So does Nathan. He uses those glasses to check for infrared and the like. We have found nothing."

"I don't know how they did it," said Charles. "I just know they are; and if they are, they must be close."

"Well…Nathan is the wizard when it comes to the electronic stuff. I am just a simple country doctor."

"Doctor, yes…simple, by no means," replied Charles. "I think we need to check outside the house. I have heard of some pretty techy stuff that can be done from the outside. Some of it has been disputed as internet hoaxes, but some might be real. We should proceed with the assumption that it is all possible."

"Charles...this is hard to say...but, you know Emily..."

"I know," said Charles. "...but I have to hope for the best. Alma is barely holding on as it is. She thought all of this kind of thing was behind us. I can't even entertain doubt right now."

"I guess you're right," said Doctor Cornell. "I suppose negative ideas wouldn't help anything anyway. So is that all you wanted? We couldn't have said this stuff in the driveway?"

"Actually...no," replied Charles. "I think I spotted something...outside of the house. I didn't want to tip them off."

"What did you see?" Doctor Cornell leaned in closer.

"I think I spotted that outside surveillance equipment, but I'm not sure," said Charles. "We will need Nathan to verify it and he will have to be careful not to be noticed doing it."

"We are assuming that Nathan is going to survive," said Doctor Cornell coldly. "I cannot make that promise."

"If he doesn't, we will need another strategy," said Charles. "...but for right now, that is the plan we are going with."

"We should get back then," said Doctor Cornell. "I have a patient to look after." Charles motioned to the waitress for the check and a *to-go* box. They finished their beers and headed back to the car. The fog seemed to be lifting as the day wore on and a small patch of blue gave the promise of a potentially sunny afternoon. As they drove back, they looked at each seaside house suspiciously. Charles didn't want to think that Emily could already be in another undisclosed government research facility…or worse. He tried to keep positive. When they arrived back at the condo, Charles motioned to the antique-looking streetlamp subtly by only averting his eyes for a second. Doctor Cornell got the gesture and looked around the beach casually so he could inspect the device out of the corner of his eye. It was almost unnoticeable. The device blended in with the lamp and looked as though it might have been an electric eye that turned the light on at dusk; except that there was also one of the devices on the side of the post. Doctor Cornell nodded and the two men went inside.

Alma was upstairs when they returned, sitting on the edge of Nathan's bed. Color had returned to his face, which was a positive sign.

"He stirred a few times while you were gone," she said. "He also made a couple of grunting noises. I think he might be dehydrated."

"It's possible," said Doctor Cornell. "Who knows what that drug had in it?"

"I hope they didn't use it on Emily," said Alma. Her throat tightened a bit before she could complete her thought. "I hate to think what it would do to the baby." Charles hadn't thought of that. A frown darkened his face and he had to shake off a feeling of dread. Alma wiped her moist eyes and held Nathan's hand again. She looked at his face only to see that he was looking quizzically back at her. After a moment, he took his hand from hers; bringing his other hand from beneath the comforter he signed, *What happened? What is going on?*

You were knocked unconscious, signed Alma. *Don't you remember anything?*

Where is Emily? Nathan's eyes widened with fear.

We are trying to find her, signed Alma. *You need to rest.*

I want to help, signed Nathan. *Why am I naked?*

We don't know, signed Alma blushing. *We probably don't want to.*

"Ask him what he remembers," said Doctor Cornell.

I can still read lips, signed Nathan. *I don't remember much. Emily was in the shower and I was going to…change clothes.* Alma knew that Nathan was about to sign that he was going to get into bed. She was thankful that he changed it.

Emily was in the shower? she signed. "Charles…Emily was in the shower!" Charles left the room for a moment and returned quickly. "The shower curtain is gone! What does that mean?"

"It means someone wrapped her in it when they took her from the house," answered Doctor Cornell before thinking of the implications.

"It means she's alive," said Alma hopefully. "If they had killed her, they wouldn't need to take her with them." They all seemed to breathe a collective sigh of relief at the revelation. It didn't mean there was nothing to worry about, but it was at least one less thing.

Nathan asked for some water and Alma also brought him some soup. He started to recover from the tranquilizer quicker than Doctor Cornell had suspected he would. "Those new designer drugs," he said. "There is no telling what the government has that they are not telling us about."

"They have Emily," said Charles. An angry look crossed Nathan's face and he got out of bed before remembering that he was naked. He fell back and threw the comforter across his lap. Alma pretended not to notice even though she did.

I should get you some clothes, she signed as she left the room blushing. She continued to blush as she came back, realizing that she was already in Nathan's room. *Maybe you should find something yourself,* she signed and left the room again.

Nathan dressed and after a few minutes, he joined the family in the living room. Charles had written out his suspicions about the surveillance equipment for Alma and she covertly conveyed the information to Nathan. He nodded and went straight to his laptop. He checked for programs running in the background and found none. He swept the room for anything out of the ordinary and found nothing. Then he remembered a website he visited once that had an article about a passive Wi-Fi surveillance technology. It was still in the experimental stage, but a few hackers had managed to use it successfully. *This is the most likely way they are doing it,* he signed once he had done his sweep. *If we disconnect the Wi-Fi that should effectively blind them.*

We don't want to do that, signed Alma. *We want them to think we are lost and clueless.* She quietly conveyed her conversation to the others and they agreed. Nathan donned the special dark glasses and looked at the light post out the window. He was careful to stay out of the line of sight with the equipment mounted on it. Flipping through the settings on the side, he found two that revealed surprising images. One was an infrared setting that showed an array of glowing lights on the streetlamp. Another setting that Nathan was not familiar with showed the beams from passive lasers that were being used to pick up sounds inside the house. Through the lenses of the glasses, the beams crisscrossed like telephone lines. Nathan got very excited and took Alma's hand. He led her to a point in the upstairs hallway where they could not be seen. He relayed his findings to her and asked her to let Charles and Doctor Cornell know what he would need. Alma was very excited when she came back downstairs. She gathered the two men together in a corner of the kitchen and spoke to them in the lowest of whispers.

"Nathan says the cameras and equipment on the post are still operational. He says it doesn't look like it can transmit very far. He can trace its signal if one of you can get some special electronic items for him. The problem is the closest place to get them is three hours away."

"I can leave right away," whispered Doctor Cornell.

"I think you should stay here," said Charles. "Nathan may not be as well as he lets on. Your medical skills might be needed. I will go. I will get back as soon as I can."

"Okay," said the doctor. "...but be careful. Who knows what these people are capable of?"

"I know all too well what they are capable of," Charles responded. "That is why I am going to hurry."

"Charles..." said Alma. "Be careful. If I lost you....well, just be careful."

"I am always careful," said Charles. "Take care of our future son-in-law. He has an important job to do."

"I will," said Alma. "He is like my own kid now. We may be all he has."

Charles had forgotten that Nathan's parents hadn't contacted him in a long time. He tried to console himself by thinking that they were just keeping a low profile for Nathan's sake. In reality, he knew what the government people were capable of. Charles shook all of the negative thoughts from his head. He was going to be alone with himself for the next six hours. He didn't need to have those kinds of conversations going on in the car. He kissed Alma, shook Doctor Cornell's hand and patted Nathan on the back. Charles held his shoulder for a moment and looked at him thoughtfully. Nathan knew what he was doing. He reached over and patted him on the shoulder as well. Charles backed the SUV out of the driveway and headed north along the coastal highway. He played the radio very loud to drown out the voices that kept trying to intrude on his calm. This was going to be a long drive.

CHAPTER 23: TARGET ACQUIRED

Nathan lay dead or dying on the plush carpet. Blood gushed from the gaping wound in his head and pooled beneath his face. He was wet and naked. His skin was the pale blue and yellow color of a cadaver. The stark contrast of the bright red blood against the pallid skin made Emily nauseous. If she could have opened her mouth, she might have vomited. Somehow, she managed to control her stomach muscles by breathing deeply through her nose. The image of Nathan dissolved into darkness. Emily wasn't sure she was conscious. She tried to touch her eyes, but her hands wouldn't move. Pain in her wrists let her know that she was restrained. She tried to force her eyes to adjust to the light, but it was no use. For the time being, she was blind.

Agent Baxter had been busy. Through a series of dummy internet IPs, he had managed to contact a low-ranking official of the agency. The official, Embry Turner, was the closest thing to a friend that Baxter had. They were not much more than work acquaintances that went out for a drink once in a while. He wasn't sure how much he could trust Turner, but he was willing to take the chance. He was surprised when Assistant to the Deputy Director Turner returned his email message so quickly. It had only taken three hours. That is the same as ten minutes for a government bureaucrat. Turner was a good agent, but not a strictly *by-the-book* kind of guy. He knew when to turn a blind eye to shady activities and when to step in; at least Baxter hoped so. In his email, Baxter had informed Turner that he had reacquired Emily Troy and needed assistance with her extraction. Turner's return message asked for his location and the condition of the target. He didn't seem particularly concerned about Baxter's absence or the fact that he had pursued the Troy family without an official sanction. Agent Baxter thought it might be a sign that his superiors admired his initiative.

Assistant to the Deputy Director Turner informed Agent Baxter that it would be at least twelve hours before a team could be mobilized in the area. Assigning a group to extract Emily Troy would be a delicate matter, considering the unique nature of her abilities. Agent Baxter informed Turner that her condition had changed in several ways. He wrote him that she was no longer invisible, that she could speak...and that she was pregnant. After a long pause, a message lit up his screen: STAND BY FOR FURTHER INSTRUCTIONS. That was the last message Agent Baxter would receive for the next few hours. When another message finally did come in, it was a request for a detailed report of Agent Baxter's pursuit and subsequent acquisition of his target. Agent Baxter had a detailed file prepared already. He had been documenting his activities since the first day he left the agency. It had been his intention to edit a few of the details which involved his unacceptable security breaches, but in his haste he hit the send button before removing them. He suspected he might be subjected to disciplinary action when he returned, but he had obtained his objective and that was the most important thing.

It had been Agent Baxter's intention to kill Emily Troy and her family. Emily's pregnancy had stayed his hand during his assassination attempt. He was plagued by headaches after that...struggling with what action to take. The headaches subsided after he became committed to her abduction. Soon, she would be spirited away and the family would never find her again. He would make sure of that.

Now he just needed to keep them at bay for the next twelve hours or so. Baxter didn't think that would be a problem. They had no way of knowing he had her secured in a condo just a short distance from their own.

He looked at his watch and decided it was about time to check on Emily. The dose he had shot her with was not as potent as the one he had given Nathan Saunders. He didn't want to kill her. He really didn't care about the boy. Baxter opened the door to the master bedroom and flipped on the light. Emily was already awake and her eyes squinted tightly in the sudden flood of illumination. The bed on which she lay was stripped of bedding and her arms were secured to the headboard by a series of reinforced pull-ties. Her ankles were bound with another pull-tie. The pink satin dressing gown had been carelessly tossed over her naked body, not completely preserving her modesty. Baxter adjusted it in an attempt to convey that her abduction was not about sex. Emily tried to protest her abduction, but the duct tape across her mouth prevented it. Baxter sat on the edge of the bed and looked into her light blue eyes that were shooting daggers back at him.

"I would like to talk," he said after a moment. "This can be a one-way conversation or you can keep your voice down when I remove the tape. It is up to you." Emily was not quite sure how to respond. Finally, she rolled her eyes and shrugged. Baxter, realizing his foolishness, took that as a "yes".

"Fast or slow?" he asked. Emily gave him a quizzical look and he yanked the tape off fast anyway. "Sorry. I couldn't resist." Emily clenched her teeth until the stinging went away. She didn't want to have the tape replaced, so she spoke in a quiet, but stern voice.

"You bastard," she began. "What have you done with Nathan?"

"I knocked him out," said Baxter. "…the same as you."

"Why are you doing this?" she pleaded. "Why can't you leave my family alone? And while we're at it, why am I naked?"

"I will answer your last question first," replied Baxter. "You were in the shower. I wasn't going to take time to dress you. Secondly, I am doing this because it is my duty. You have a gift that the government needs and you have no right keeping it from them. I think that answers both of your other questions."

"Did any of you even think about asking?" she responded. "Did it ever occur to you that I might have been willing to cooperate without being held prisoner?"

"That has not been our experience," he said. "…and sometimes the necessary experimentation goes beyond what a person is prepared to endure willingly. There is also the security issue. Abduction is the preferred protocol in these cases."

"What about my rights?"

"When it comes to National Security," said Baxter. "…the rights of the individual are forfeited."

"Did you read that in a manual or something?" asked Emily sarcastically.

"As a matter of fact," said Baxter. Then he realized she was mocking him and stopped. "Now we can handle this in a couple of ways. You can behave and a few nice men will be here to collect you in a few hours or…no, that's it. You will probably just need to lay here in the dark with tape over your mouth."

"Well, before you do that, can I put some clothes on?" she asked. "Don't you think having a naked pregnant woman bound to the bed is going to make a bad impression on your fellow agents?"

"It will all be in my report," replied Baxter. "They will understand."

"Well then, unless you also want to explain the mess they are going to have to clean up, you might want to let me go to the bathroom." Emily's calm demeanor was a little unnerving to Agent Baxter. However, he knew she was right. They don't usually have to deal with bodily functions in spy novels and movies. He wanted this to appear perfectly professional.

"That can be arranged," he said finally. "…but if you try anything, I will put one in your back."

"Where would I go?" she asked. "I don't even know where I am."

"Good point," he said. Baxter pulled out a tactical knife and cut the reinforced pull-ties on her wrists. Then, watching her carefully for sudden moves, he slid the blade between her ankles and cut the other tie. Emily rubbed her wrists to regain her circulation and then sat up on the edge of the bed with the gown held close to her chest.

"Are you going to turn around so I can put this on?" she asked.

"That wasn't part of the deal," he responded. "I am not letting you out of my sight."

"You sir, are a pervert!" Emily stood up, tossed the pink satin dressing gown over her shoulder and walked to the door. Looking back over her shoulder she asked, "Are you going to show me where the bathroom is or do you want me to just explore this place?" Agent Baxter was taken off guard by Emily's sudden casual attitude about nudity. He walked to the door and pointed down the hall with the barrel of his pistol. She strode down the hall with the gown draped over one arm like a waiter in a French restaurant. Once in the bathroom, she tried to shut the door but Agent Baxter stopped it with his foot.

"Really?" she asked. "You aren't even going to let me have this little bit of privacy?"

"Sorry," he answered. "I can't take any chances." Emily sighed in disgust and said "perv" under her breath. The next few minutes were awkward for both of them. Baxter wasn't used to people performing bodily functions in his presence; especially women. He considered making casual conversation, but that also seemed less than professional. So he abandoned any attempt and tried to occupy his thoughts elsewhere. He backed away from the edge of the door, but continued to watch Emily though the bathroom mirror. For a moment, she seemed to be straining. Then he saw a golden shimmer reflect on her skin briefly. Agent Baxter thought that apparently she still had a little of her ability left.

"Whoa!" said Emily. "That was a big one!"

"I am not even sure I want to know what you are talking about," he said, involuntarily holding his nose.

"The baby kicked," she replied. "I have never felt a kick that strong. Why? What did you think I meant?"

"It doesn't matter," said Baxter. "Get your business finished and let's go."

"Everything's done but the paperwork," she said. "...just like with your job." In spite of her attitude, which he could not help but see as justified, he liked Emily. Baxter knew that she would probably be more than willing to kill him if she got the chance, but there was just something about her. He couldn't explain it. She stood up, prepared to flush the toilet and said, "Do you want to check this first...you know, for your report?"

"Funny," he said. "I have a lot of duct tape." Emily flushed the toilet and put on the pink satin dressing gown. She felt she had made her point with gratuitous nudity for the time being.

"Do you suppose I could get the belt to this?" she asked.

"Sorry," Baxter said. He wasn't.

"Look," said Emily. "Do you really need to tie me to that bed? I'm not going to run away and I am sure I will get really uncomfortable just lying there. Couldn't you tie me to a chair or something? You could still watch me."

"I suppose," Baxter responded. He was beginning to enjoy Emily's company. It began to bother him. He was no longer sure he would be able to kill her if necessary. He could, however, tranquilize her if need be.

Agent Baxter needed only four pull-ties to bind her to a dining room chair. He used one for each wrist, binding her to the supports in the back. He then used one for each ankle, binding them to the legs of the chair. The satin gown kept falling open revealing her breasts, so he retrieved the belt from the bedroom. He closed her robe and tied the belt securely.

"Are you sure you don't want to just leave it open?" Emily asked. "You probably don't get cable here."

"You are getting closer and closer to that duct tape," answered Baxter. He went to his laptop and turned it so the screen was away from Emily's view. Then he removed his automatic weapon from its holster and replaced it with the tranquilizer gun that he had used on Emily and Nathan earlier. He was sure he no longer wanted to kill her. But he didn't know why.

Agent Baxter turned the volume down on the surveillance equipment so Emily could not hear the conversation from her family's condo. Looking at the images from the passive Wi-Fi signal, he could see that only three individuals remained in the condo. He wasn't sure how he felt when he saw that the image labeled NATHAN SAUNDERS was up and walking around. He was sure that he didn't care; but somewhere inside him, he did. Charles Troy appeared to be missing. Baxter concluded that he was out in a hopeless attempt to find Emily. The others paced nervously and took turns staring out the window. At one point, Alma Troy suggested that they all eat something. Doctor Cornell accepted the suggestion, but Nathan apparently declined. It was hard for Baxter to tell, since sign language was hard to read in the passive surveillance.

"So how long have you been watching my family?" asked Emily in a disapproving tone. "I suppose you have watched everything we have done?" The statement was more of a condemnation than a question.

"I have only observed in a professional manner," replied Baxter, trying not to sound defensive. "You brought this all on yourself. You could simply have cooperated."

"But then we wouldn't have all of this wonderful bonding time," she said. "See what I did there?" She smiled and Baxter had a hard time not finding her adorable. Her tiny voice matched her tiny frame and it was hard to see her as anything but fragile. When sarcasm or reprimands came out of her mouth, they seemed out of place and disarming.

"It will all be over soon," said Baxter. "If you are lucky, I may not have to kill anyone else."

"Else?" asked Emily. "Who have you killed so far?" She began to worry about Nathan's parents...mostly his mother.

"I really don't want to talk about it," said Baxter. "Talking about it dulls my edge."

"You are a bastard!" shouted Emily.

"It's cute when you swear," said Baxter. "I am sure it doesn't have the impact you want it to." That infuriated Emily even more, but she wasn't going to give him the satisfaction of laughing at her. She took a few deep breaths before continuing.

"Are Nathan's parents alive?" she asked directly.

"I am not giving you any information," replied Baxter. "It might compromise my mission. You have made my job difficult enough. Don't ask me again." Emily was sure she had her answer.

"Then what about my baby?" she asked finally. "Is he or she going to be a prisoner too?"

"That is not my department," said Baxter. "My job is Target Acquisition. Someone else will be responsible for Detainments."

"Do you people even have souls?" Emily asked. Her eyes welled up with tears. "How can you all be so heartless?"

"We do our job for the greater good," said Baxter, trying not to sound sympathetic. "Your ability has the potential to save lives."

"You just keep telling yourself that," Emily responded angrily. The tears ran down her face and she tried to move her hand to wipe them away. The restraints didn't budge and she was left with her face glistening in the dim lighting of the room. A shimmer washed across her face, which Agent Baxter found curious. He ignored her comments and went back to his laptop. In between checking the surveillance, he added entries to his report. It kept him busy. He was afraid to go to sleep again because of the hallucinogenic nature of his dreams. He wondered how long it would be before the effects of the drugs he had injected wore off.

For the next two hours Emily was silent. Agent Baxter couldn't tell if she was brooding or just bored. Either way, he enjoyed the silence. He began noticing a shimmering light out of the corner of his eye. When he turned to look at it directly, it would disappear. At first, he thought she was moving away from him…into the dimmer light. But the picture on the wall behind her served as a reference point. She wasn't moving. Baxter thought it was possible that the light from his laptop screen was fading and he adjusted it accordingly. Emily would clear her throat periodically and he finally asked her if she wanted some water. She declined and he went back to his work.

Emily had been experimenting for two hours as well as a few weeks. It was fortunate that she had kept her experiments a secret since they were being watched. She had been trying to get Agent Baxter's attention by clearing her throat. She wanted to gauge his reaction; to see if he could see her. The experiments had been easy with her mother. Alma could tell when she disappeared, or at least to what degree. Nathan could see her no matter what, so he was of no use with her tests. In the same way, Emily could always see herself; so she needed help. Her invisibility was easier to control when she was with family. Now that she sat across from someone who could kill her, she wasn't sure she could do it.

She also spent her time surveying her surroundings; picking up bits of information and the locations of items around the room. After she had collected all of the useful Intel she could, Emily feigned fatigue and pretended to nod off a few times. When her act proved to have no effect, she finally spoke up.

"Can I go to bed now?" she asked. "I am really tired and I have lost most of the circulation in my limbs." Agent Baxter looked up from his screen. He appeared to be agitated and was irritable. It bothered him that Charles Troy had not returned.

"I suppose you will also want to go to the bathroom again?"

"If it's not too much trouble," Emily responded. "I don't want to inconvenience YOU." Her sarcastic rebuke was not lost on him. Baxter cut the ties roughly to release her and she was certain that he had nicked her ankle. But an examination of it showed no injury. She turned away from him when she stood up and for a second, he thought he lost sight of her.

"Don't do that again," he said.

"Do what?" Emily responded innocently. Agent Baxter thought his hallucinations might be flaring up so he decided to drop it. He didn't want to show any chinks in his armor. He led Emily upstairs by gripping her arm tightly. She was sure that he was leaving bruises, but she didn't complain. He shoved her into the bathroom roughly and said, "Make it quick!"

"It will take as long as it takes," Emily said defiantly. "...and it might get a little unpleasant in here. You may want to close the door."

"You must think I'm an idiot," replied Baxter.

"That...has nothing to do with it," said Emily. "I am just warning you that with the baby and everything, you might not be prepared for what you are going to hear...or smell." Baxter grimaced. He hated this game. Finally, he pulled the bathroom door shut with the final admonition, "No tricks!"

Emily began to produce some of the most ungodly noises that Baxter had ever heard; and he had lived in a frat house in college. He held his nose even though the door was closed; just in case the odor might waft up from underneath. He didn't think a girl her size could produce the volume that she was producing. He was grateful she had turned the faucet on in order to mask some of the noise. Then she started a steady stream of urination that seemed to go on for several minutes. Baxter could not imagine how big her bladder must be.

Emily was a master at making fake bodily function noises. As a child, she spent a lot of time cupping her palm in her armpit to produce faux flatulence. Her parents found it extra amusing because it was one of the only audible ways she could communicate with them that was not electronic. She was even able to execute a double blast using both hands simultaneously. In addition, she used the glass next to the sink to collect water that fed her fake urine stream. The whole point was to get Agent Baxter off guard so she could put her plan into motion. It was a risky plan that depended on her being able to control her invisibility. Emily took a deep breath and centered herself. She imagined herself doing a test with her mother. A feeling that was something between a warm tingle and a chill went through her and she felt it was time. She flushed the toilet, turned off the faucet and said, "You can come in now." Agent Baxter made sure to assert his authority as he opened the door.

"I can come in any time I plea..." Baxter felt something grip his throat and pull him back. He lost his balance and fell backwards into the hallway. His head hit the wall so hard that he left an indentation in the drywall. A rush of wind blew past him as he pulled the belt of the pink satin dressing gown from his neck. He reached for his weapon, but realized his special dark glasses were still downstairs. He struggled to his feet and was halfway down the stairs when he saw the front door close behind the invisible Emily Troy. Baxter had to make a choice; follow right away or find his special dark glasses and risk losing her trail. He chose the former and headed out the front door. Something crunched under his feet on the porch. It was a broken pair of special dark glasses Emily had somehow stolen. She had already broken them and they were useless to him now. Baxter slowed down and thought for a moment. The sand was still wet from the rain and Emily was leaving footprints. He followed her trail down the beach as far as he could. It was night and a heavier fog had rolled in. The decorative streetlamps allowed him to find clues of Emily's whereabouts, but he kept losing her in the dark spaces between the lights.

Emily didn't know which way to go. The fog was disorienting and she wasn't sure where to head anyway. She could tell that the ocean was on her left and she thought the lamps looked familiar. She really didn't think she would get as far as she did; she had no plan from that point on. Her bare feet were freezing and the pink satin dressing gown, which she now held closed with her hands, did not provide much warmth. She was desperate and thought she knew which way the road was. Emily headed up a narrow wooden walkway to a light at the edge of the road. Her mind was in a near-panicked state and she began to grasp at straws. Suddenly, she could see headlights in the thick fog. She decided to flag down the motorist even though her instincts told her that only serial killers traveled deserted highways at night. Emily stood under the light and waved her arms frantically. Her robe came open, but she didn't care. She thought that if it would help the driver decide to stop, all the better. The car came closer and closer, but wasn't appearing to slow down. Emily couldn't imagine why the driver couldn't see her. Then it dawned on her that she was still invisible. She closed her eyes and concentrated. Behind her, a cough erupted in the darkness. She felt a sharp pain above her right kidney and the light from the streetlamp seemed to dim. The darkness and fog closed in around her and she slumped to the ground. Agent Baxter remained in the darkness until the car passed. Emily became only slightly visible under the light. Baxter suspected it was part of the latent self-preservation aspect of her invisibility. He smiled as he picked her up and carried her back to the condo. He had recognized the vehicle driving by in the fog late at night. It was the SUV that belonged to Charles Troy.

CHAPTER 24: COUNTER ESPIONAGE

The fog seemed almost supernatural in nature. It had remained present for the last two hours of Charles Troy's trip. It seemed to be the same fog that had blanketed the coast earlier in the day when he left for his journey. He had driven out of it when he was two hours up the coast. Now, two hours from home, he was back into the thick clouds of it. The fog was misleading in that it did not seem to diminish visibility that much. However, a couple of near-misses with the indigenous deer population convinced Charles Troy otherwise. He slowed to a much more cautious speed and became keenly alert. After a few minutes, his fingers began to hurt and he realized how hard he had been gripping the steering wheel.

The fog seemed more like darkness of a different hue. It made the surroundings dreamlike and caused Charles to imagine things along the side of the road. He imagined hitchhikers carrying oversized packs and women in white wondering aimlessly along the highway. Every ghost story and urban legend came to mind. He had a nearly uncontrollable urge to check his backseat for an escaped lunatic. Yet Charles remained strong. He dared not take his eyes off the road for even a second. He played the radio, but there wasn't much on except Country music and religious programming. He was not a big fan of either. There were no CDs in the car, so he began to talk to the (hopefully) imaginary lunatic in his backseat.

"So what shall I call you?" he began. Charles hoped he wouldn't get an audible answer. He breathed a slight sigh of relief when he didn't. Yet he didn't want to offend his passenger, imaginary or not. He tried out several names in his head; not daring to speak any of them aloud. *Norman? No…too clichéd. Michael? Jason? Freddy? No! Absolutely not. He was nervous enough as it was. Ed? Maybe… Ed could work.* He couldn't think of any killers named Ed. Charles was about to say the name out loud when the last name came to mind…*Ed Gein.* He was the model for *Norman Bates* and the basis for *The Texas Chainsaw Massacre*. Charles finally settled on *Henderson*. The name didn't sound like anyone connected with a crime that he could remember. *Yeah, Henderson,* he thought.

"So Mister Henderson," he began. "How long have you been out?" After a long awkward pause, Charles realized that he probably shouldn't ask many questions in his conversation. Besides, lunatics usually don't like to be interrogated.

"This is some kind of weather I guess," Charles continued. "The worst fog I have seen in a while. Guess you are lucky not to have to be out on a night like this. It must make victims hard to track. I am glad I don't have your job. I don't have the patience for it. Also, the hours; you must never have time for yourself. That is dedication to your craft, my friend." A growl came from somewhere in the back and Charles Troy gripped the wheel tighter and froze. He had to force himself to release his stranglehold on the wheel and get back on the road. The tires on the right side of the SUV had run over the *rumble strips* that were there to alert drivers when they were leaving the road. He pulled the vehicle back to the center of the lane and then pulled over the *rumble strips* again just to make sure that was what he had heard. The sound satisfied him that it was, but he decided not to talk to

Henderson for a while. He gave Country music another chance and found he liked it better than the creepy silence coming from the backseat.

Charles Troy's headlights cut through the fog and disappeared into a mass of gauze. Occasionally, a clear space of about fifty yards would appear in front of him and he would think that he was finally coming out of the fog. Then he would drive into the next fog bank and it seemed as though a sheet had been thrown across his windshield. It was nerve-racking. He couldn't use his cruise control, as he was constantly slowing down and then speeding up. His back was hurting from keeping his muscles tensed. It felt like a reprieve from the governor when he finally saw a sign that let him know he was only a few miles from home. Light from streetlamps along the road seemed to appear out of nowhere. They looked like orbs of light floating in a fabric of dreams. The lights were a bit mesmerizing and Charles drifted over the *rumble strips* again.

"Whoa! Sorry about that Mr. Henderson," he said with nervous humor. "…didn't mean to wake you." Charles was almost certain he heard a grunt from the backseat. The fog was thinner as he approached the condo. While he was able to relax a bit, he still thought he was seeing things. For the briefest of seconds, he believed he saw a ghost girl trying to flag him down. She faded away just as a dream fades and he drove on, rubbing his eyes one at a time. Charles pulled into the driveway of the condo, killed the engine and sat for a moment to decompress. His back ached and his hands hurt. Rubbing his dry eyes had seemed to do more damage than good. They itched and his lids were sore. He got out of the SUV, went to the rear and cautiously opened the back. He didn't want Mr. Henderson jumping out at him after getting this far. In the back, there was nothing but the box of items which Nathan had requested. Charles balanced the box on one arm and closed the hatch as quietly as possible so as not to draw attention to himself. He was afraid that he was being watched and did not want to raise any suspicions about what they were doing.

Alma ran to meet him at the door. She looked as though she had just driven several hours in the fog.

"Did you find any sign of her?" she asked, reciting their pre-arranged script. Her execution was perfect and it startled Charles for a moment. He believed for a second that she actually thought he had been looking for Emily. If Alma had not been a librarian, she could probably have had a successful career as an actress.

"No sign," he answered. "I am so sorry. I checked everywhere I could think of. Then the fog got so bad, I had to pull over and try to wait it out." Charles was no slouch when it came to acting either. He hoped Emily's captor would buy his story of why he had been gone so long. Otherwise, it wouldn't be plausible.

"What have you got there?" asked Alma, continuing to play her part.

"I managed to pick up a few items from the store that we missed this morning," said Charles. His explanation diverted from their script, but was better than what they had planned. Alma smiled at the improvisation and her eyes registered approval.

"You must be tired," she said. "Let's get you inside." They closed the front door behind them and Charles placed the box on the cooking island. Then, they ignored it for a while to keep from drawing attention to it. They didn't know how closely they were being watched, but they weren't taking any chances. Alma signed to Nathan that he should make some pretense of going to the kitchen for something; a drink or a bite to eat. Then he could remove items from the box as he passed. Nathan nodded that he understood and waited until the couple sat down before acting. Nathan was not quite the actor that the Troy's were. He walked stiffly and deliberately to the kitchen. He faked a stretch and a yawn before opening the refrigerator and peering inside. Charles hoped they were not being watched too closely or their plan would be blown. Everything was a crapshoot by this time, however. They had no way of knowing how often they were being watched, or if they even were. *They* had Emily and there really didn't seem to be a reason for any further surveillance. Still, the indicators on the lamppost suggested otherwise.

Charles and Alma sat together holding one another's hands. It was part of the role they were playing, but they were also in some serious need of comforting. Alma looked over at Nathan and felt so sorry for him. He was so alone. Emily was the only anchor left in his life. He tried not to show it, but Alma could tell that he was hurting. He sat motionless with his back to the window. Even though the blinds were drawn, Nathan didn't trust the equipment outside. He carefully assembled the electronics that Charles had obtained for him. After completing each component, he would wait a reasonable period of time before going and retrieving another; each time, looking in the refrigerator or getting a glass of water. Periodically, he would look through the blinds with the special dark glasses to make sure the equipment was still working. When all of the components were finally assembled, he needed to go outside. Nathan took the equipment with him that he had constructed. It was a small receiver/transmitter dish about the size of a coffee cup. A swivel clamp allowed him to attach it to a drainpipe bracket without too much trouble. Once that was done, Charles fed him a length of thin cable through a side window. He only opened it about half an inch and snaked it through the crack with one hand. Then he paced nervously for a few minutes before sitting back down with Alma. It was all part of the act.

Nathan played his part like a professional. He felt more comfortable in this role and moved more naturally. He sat down hard in the chair as if he was disgusted and put his head in his hands. Alma rose to comfort him and placed her hands on his shoulders. He touched her hand with his fingers and nodded. She returned to Charles' side. Nathan took a breath, opened his laptop and attached a line from the components he had assembled. A scramble of letters and symbols flashed across the screen too fast to read. Nathan responded to them as if it was an alien language he understood. Slide bars appeared on the screen, along with gauges and numbers. He made a few adjustments and frowned. He tried several other combinations with no results. Nathan was getting frustrated. Even though his laptop was equipped to convert voices into text, no one appeared to be talking. He couldn't be sure he was even on the right frequency. He had hoped he might be able to pick up some kind of video feed, but so far there was nothing. He smacked his forehead hard and Alma got up to see if she could help. She stood at an angle from the window and signed, *Is there anything I can do?* Nathan nodded subtly and handed her a pair of ear buds. He thought that it was possible his text conversion wouldn't work if the voices were too quiet. It was times like these that he felt disabled. Alma sat at the end of the sofa so the line from the ear buds would reach. Charles got up, went to the bathroom and then sat next to her to keep suspicions down. Nathan patiently tried different pattern combinations on the slides. Alma could see the screen at an angle and marveled that he was able to understand everything going on in his cyberworld. She remembered how intelligent Emily was and swelled with pride when she thought of the potential of her unborn grandchild. The thought of the two of them out in the world all alone and defenseless made her sad. Her heart migrated to her throat and the tears in her eyes made it difficult to see. Alma was losing hope. She wiped her eyes and got lost in a daydream.

In her dream, Emily was a beautiful child standing next to the field of wheat. Her eyes were bluer than the sky and her hair was the color of the sun. The wind was blowing through her hair and her summer dress. She didn't look happy; she looked alone. Alma had always felt guilty for that. In her own way, Emily had always been alone. Being born silent and then becoming unseen meant that she always had to seek out others to be noticed. Nathan had been a blessing in that he could see her when no one else could. Alma was so pleased that she had found someone. The Emily in her dream turned to Alma and held out her arms. As she did, she seemed to get farther away. Alma tried to run to her but felt as though her feet were frozen to the ground. Emily's mouth opened as though she was trying to speak, but all she could manage was a muffled cough. Then she choked a little on her own saliva and coughed again.

Alma sat upright in her seat. *She coughed!* Alma signed with definite purpose. *I heard her cough!* Nathan made a few adjustments to increase the gain. Then he looked at Alma for confirmation. After a moment, her face brightened. *I think I can hear her breathing*, she signed. *Nathan! You are a genius!* Nathan blushed softly and continued to work. Once he was sure that he had the right place, he began to zero in on her exact location. After a few moments, his expression turned as dark as storm clouds over the ocean. He bared his teeth as he signed with purpose of his own, *She's next door! She's been right next door the whole time!* His first instinct was go charging over there to rescue her. Charles lowered his hand, palm down to suggest that he calm down before acting. They needed a plan. They were dealing with the government and the government had guns. He signed to Nathan that they needed to gather as much Intel as possible before making a move. Nathan reluctantly agreed and sat back, making more adjustments to his gauges. Since he knew he was in the right place, he was able to engage his closed-captioning voice translator. Now he just needed to wait for someone to say something to make sure it was working.

****

Emily coughed again. The tranquilizer made her throat dry. She kept choking on what little saliva she was producing as it was. She awoke once again strapped to the chair. Her head had fallen back, closing off her windpipe and causing her to choke. She had been unceremoniously bound with no regards to her modesty. Her robe hung open and her feet were tied so tightly that she couldn't feel them. Emily looked around the room. She thought she was alone. After a moment, she could see Baxter. He stood next to the door looking out the window. She didn't know why she hadn't seen him the first time she looked. He seemed nervous. Emily did not know that he had seen her father a short time ago. It was a close call; Baxter didn't like close calls. After a little while, he seemed confident that the family was not mounting an assault. He saw that Emily was awake and walked over to her. She glared at him with contempt. He drew back and slapped her across the face so hard that it tipped her chair up on two legs. The chair came down hard, jolting her. Emily looked at Baxter with shock.

"That is twice you have bested me!" he shouted. "Do you think you are smart? Do you think you're funny? Do I amuse you in some way? It will be the last time! Do you understand?" Emily just continued to stare at him. The look of contempt was gone. It was replaced with one of panic.

Baxter had not resorted to violence against her before. What he was actually capable of became glaringly apparent.

"Now I'm going to ask some questions," he said. "...and you are going to answer them. Is that understood? I SAID, IS THAT UNDERSTOOD!?!" Emily shrank back, almost toppling her chair over backwards. She nodded slightly; her pale blue eyes wide with fear.

"Fine. I see that we understand each other," he said in a controlled manner. "You seem to have evolved a little since we first met." He tried not to sound like a Bond villain. "You developed a control over that power of yours. I want to know how you do it."

"I just did it," she said softly. "I thought about it and I did it. Why is it so important that you know? Are you putting it in your report as how I got away...?" Baxter slapped her again before she could finish her sentence. That brought her glare back.

"It doesn't concern you why I need to know!" he shouted. "All you need to be concerned with is if I am going to keep you alive long enough to turn you over to my bosses!" Emily relaxed a little. She knew an empty threat when she heard one. If he was going to kill her, he would have just killed her. Still, she didn't like getting slapped. She thought she might as well cooperate. *Pick your battles,* her mom always said. Emily made expressions with her face; opening her mouth wide and then squinting her eyes. She was trying to sooth the muscles in her throbbing cheek since she could not use her hands. Finally, she looked at Agent Baxter sincerely and spoke in a way she would speak to any respected authority figure.

"I'm not sure I know what to tell you," she began. "Becoming invisible is not an exact science. I have to force myself to a balance point between peace and fear…maybe anger. It is kind of like walking on a tightrope. There has to be a positive emotion on one side and a negative emotion on the other. It gets easier the more I do it. It works best when I am defensive; probably because it was a defense mechanism. I don't think it would work if I was being aggressive."

"You seem to know quite a bit about it," replied Baxter. "How come none of that came out in the report when we were testing you?"

"Uh...probably because I didn't know how to do it then." It took almost all of Emily's willpower not to follow the statement with, "Duh!" Baxter also resisted the urge to slap her again. He caught the implied "Duh!" She continued more respectfully.

"The doctor had theories which we worked out," she said. "He has been studying my case for years. He knows quite a bit. Still, he wasn't able to isolate the total cause. He says it is because my invisibility is due to more than one aspect of my metabolism. Some of it is chemical; some of it is light reflection of my cells. He even has a theory that there might be a subsonic sound I emit that causes part of it. He said maybe that was why when I turned visible, I could talk for the first time. Then again, maybe it is just a miracle."

"So how did you practice?" Baxter asked with an almost compassionate tone in his voice. He appreciated her candor and closed her robe as a gesture of respect.

"I practiced with my mom," Emily answered, responding to the treatment. "I couldn't practice with Nathan because he could always see me. I knew I could do it because there would be times that my mom couldn't see me when I was standing right there. The first few times, I just thought it was her eyesight; but after enough times, I thought it might be possible to use this ability."

"What about hallucinations?" asked Baxter.

"What do you mean?" asked Emily. "Like dreams and stuff? I have some very vivid dreams; too vivid if you ask me. I see people I care about die. But nothing while I am awake, if that's what you are asking. Why?"

"We have something in common," replied Baxter. "They managed to isolate a compound from your DNA at the lab. I injected it into my system. I became invisible like you…for a while. However, I have had a few hallucinations and some pretty bad dreams. Still, I think those will go away in time. I think I just need practice."

"You turn invisible?" asked Emily. "Seriously?" She had more skepticism than surprise in her voice.

"That's right," he said, almost defensively. "I have even been in your condo. That boy of yours looked right at me and couldn't see me." That statement puzzled Emily. She wondered why Nathan couldn't see Baxter if he was invisible…perhaps because of her DNA.

"So, while we wait for my associates," he said. "…we are going to practice and you are going to tell me if it is working."

"Associates?"

"Yes," said Baxter. "They will be here in a few hours…and I want to have this thing down by then. Think of what kind of agent I will be with this ability. It is tempting to dispose of your entire family and keep my ability a secret."

"You know it only seems to work passively, right?" asked Emily. "I am not sure how effective you could be as an agent if you become visible every time you shoot somebody."

"You let me worry about that," said Baxter. "Besides, I might need another injection of your DNA. Hmmm…that would sound dirty if taken out of context. Okay, let's begin."

For the next two hours, Baxter tried to center himself between positive memories and anger. Nothing seemed to work. He started to think that Emily was lying to him; either about how she did it or about being able to see him. He thought it was possible that she couldn't see him and she just wasn't telling him. But her eyes followed him, so Baxter concluded that he needed to work harder. It was extra difficult for him because he did not have much in the way of positive memories. There were not too many "happy places" he could go to in his head. Yet there seemed to be an overabundance of negative places.

He thought back to college. Life was a little better then. Personal achievements were recorded in the form of grades and that seemed tangible to him. There was also a girl. There's always a girl. She broke his heart later, but she was gentle about it. She cared about him, but she couldn't be with him. She recognized the baggage he came with and was sure she wasn't strong enough to cope with it. Baxter loved her and despised her at the same time. He imagined her in front of him and was balanced between the two emotions. Her face blended with that of Emily. The soft compassionate but sad countenance of his college sweetheart melted away into the surprised expression of Emily Troy. Emily had never seen someone become invisible before. She was always on the other side of the invisibility. It was fascinating to her and a little frightening. An iridescent shimmer washed across

Agent Baxter as he began to fade from view. He felt a sense of power and accomplishment as he saw Emily's expression change. He knew he had conquered it and better yet, he knew he could control it. Willing himself invisible was easier than he had thought it was going to be. He moved to the right and reappeared. Emily jerked her head to look at him. She wondered if she appeared as suddenly when she became visible. Agent Baxter disappeared again and moved to her left. Again, she seemed completely taken off guard by where he reappeared. He disappeared once more and stood directly in front of her. Then he backed up and watched Emily search for him in vain. He smiled smugly at his newfound skill and thought that the dreams and hallucinations were a small price to pay. Baxter reappeared once more near the door. He was delighted to see that he had amused Emily with his act. A huge smile crossed her face. Then a bright light appeared to engulf him before darkness closed in around him. Charles Troy stood behind him with a tire iron gripped tightly in his hand. "Nobody slaps my little girl, you son of a bitch!"

CHAPTER 25: TURNOVER

Framed in the doorway, surrounded by a halo of fog-diffused light, Charles Troy looked like a fusion of maniacal killer and gladiator. All Emily saw was her daddy...the superhero. Beads of sweat had formed on his brow and he was breathing heavily. It took all his energy and will power to keep from beating Agent Baxter to a bloody pulp. After a few calming breaths, Charles turned his attention to Emily. Nathan had already pushed past him and was working to loosen her bonds. Alma Troy and Doctor Cornell arrived a few seconds later. They had been told to hold back just in case the situation turned ugly. The doctor knelt next to Baxter and felt his pulse. He worried that Charles had killed him in his rage.

The family had taken turns listening through the ear buds to the conversation between Emily and Agent Baxter. After Nathan had identified the source of the transmission and subsequently, Emily's location, they devised a plan for her rescue. It all was about to go awry however, when Charles was listening to the surveillance and heard Baxter strike Emily. Her father rushed out of the house and went straight to the SUV. From the back of the vehicle, he obtained a tire iron and it took all three of the others to keep Charles from rushing over to the house. It was fortunate that Baxter was occupied with Emily and missed the commotion. Otherwise, he might have been prepared when they were finally moved to action. Charles knew he would need to move quickly. Neither he nor anyone else in the household had any skill with picking locks. He knew he would make a lot of noise jimmying the deadbolt with the tire iron and that he would have only a fraction of a second to act. It caught him off guard that Agent Baxter had not reacted to his breaking in. Charles considered it a fortunate turn of events and immediately rendered his enemy inert.

Emily rubbed her arms and ankles, trying to get her blood to circulate in them once again. They began to tingle and the deep lines where the bonds had been began to hurt. Alma rubbed the injuries and kept kissing her daughter on the head. Emily hugged her mother and stroked Nathan's face. Then she stood and embraced her father so hard that he lost his breath for a second. He hid that fact from her though. He didn't want anything to distract from the moment.

"This guy must have a hard head," said Doctor Cornell. "He is going to have a 'goose egg' for a while, but I think he will be okay. We should keep watch on him just in case."

"I really don't care if he dies," said Charles, still in Emily's embrace.

"Well...maybe you should," said Doctor Cornell. "Being pursued by a government shadow agency is a lot different from an All-Points Bulletin issued by law enforcement. Everyone would be looking for us then."

"So what is your recommendation, Doctor?"

"I suggest we get him out of here," the Doctor replied. "We can keep watch over him at the condo. We should take everything else too; all of his equipment and every trace that he was here. You heard him tell Emily that his people were on the way."

"Okay," said Charles reluctantly. "You are probably right."

Doctor Cornell and Charles Troy carried Agent Baxter back to their condo. They bound him to a chair using the same type of ties he had used on Emily. Nathan, Emily and Alma followed carrying some of the equipment and weapons Baxter had at the other house. Nathan went back with the empty box that had held the surveillance equipment he had assembled. He collected the rest of the items in the condo, swept the house a final time to make sure they hadn't left anything and returned to find the others gathered around Agent Baxter. He had regained consciousness and pulled at his restraints when he tried to rub his aching head. It was apparent from his expression that he knew the tables had been turned on him and idle threats of retribution or incarceration were pointless. He adopted a resigned posture and waited for someone else to say something. Finally, Charles spoke up. His tone was one of curiosity; not anger.

"I really don't know how you didn't hear me come up behind you," he said. "Aren't you people trained for this kind of stuff?"

"I think I can answer that, Daddy," said Emily. "He told me he had been having hallucinations and bad dreams. I think becoming invisible messes with his senses. He is not used to it, so he doesn't know what is real and what isn't. I have that sometimes myself, you know." Doctor Cornell had an entire file dedicated to Emily's dreams. The way she described them was so vivid that he thought she might suffer a psychotic break in the future if her condition wasn't kept in check. The incidents became less frequent as she got older however, so he thought she would simply grow out of them.

Doctor Cornell took Agent Baxter's pulse and blood pressure. Then he examined the lump on his head. Alma got a plastic bag, put some ice in it and wrapped it in a dishtowel to form a compress for his head. The agent thanked her in what seemed like a sincere way when she placed it against the lump. Alma couldn't tell why, but she felt sympathy for him.

"He seems to be doing okay," said Doctor Cornell. "We should still keep watch on him for a few hours."

"That's okay," said Charles. "I really don't want to let him out of my sight anyway."

"I hate to be the one to address the elephant in the room," said Doctor Cornell. "...but we have kidnapped a government agent. We need a plan."

"I'm thinking 'accidental drowning'," Charles responded. "The sharks would cover our tracks."

"I think we should just disappear again," said Emily. Then she realized how it sounded like a pun coming from her. Agent Baxter continued to smile peacefully.

"Are you sure he's alright?" asked Alma. "He doesn't look right."

"He could be going into shock," replied the doctor. He checked for the usual signs and seemed satisfied that he was not. "He might be hallucinating again."

"Well, we can't take him anywhere for medical treatment," said Charles. "So if he gets bad, we are going with my plan."

"I think he will be okay," said Alma. Her tone was both compassionate and worried. Her sympathy puzzled Charles, but he let it go.

"What about the government agents on the way?" asked Emily. "What can we do about them?"

"It may sound like an immature solution," said Doctor Cornell. "…but I suggest we turn out the lights and pretend no one is home."

Nathan had busied himself inventorying Agent Baxter's weapons and equipment. He signed, *We have this.* He held up the pistol that fired the tranquilizer darts. He aimed it carelessly at Baxter, pretending it was an accident. Baxter didn't react. Emily saw what Nathan was doing and moved between him and Baxter so he would put the weapon away.

"That may be our only recourse," said Doctor Cornell. "We are not ready for another move. They would catch up with us in no time."

"Maybe we should just turn ourselves in," suggested Alma. "Maybe they would be lenient on us since Emily is going to have a baby."

"What is wrong with you?" responded Charles emphatically. "These people are monsters!" He cupped his hand to the side of his mouth so Nathan could not read his lips. "…and they killed Nathan's parents just to find us. What do you think they will do to us?"

It was obvious that Alma was conflicted. Charles could not understand Alma's mood. This man had abducted her daughter. *Why isn't she being more aggressive toward him?* he thought. Agent Baxter had a suspicion as to why and he planned to use it to his full advantage. He had read the report on how Emily seemed to win over the attendants who were caring for her at the facility. He surmised about the defense mechanism in the body chemistry that instilled loyalty. Baxter knew there had to be more to it than simple charisma. Emily couldn't talk or be seen at the time without special equipment; so body language and flirtation would not have been easy, if even possible. He was sure that whatever the cause, the effect was working for him now; and it was working on the weakest compassionate link. Alma absently stroked his shoulder. The gesture was not lost on Doctor Cornell, but he kept silent about it. Instead, he asked Alma to join him outside. He didn't like leaving Charles alone with Baxter and he quietly whispered to Emily that she should keep an eye on them both. Charles' aggression seemed to be in direct opposition to Alma's compassion and he was sure there was a connection.

Alma Troy seemed slightly less compassionate after she had been outside for a few moments. She assisted Doctor Cornell in removing the surveillance devices from the lamppost near the windows of the condo.

"You really seem to like that government man," he said.

"Not really," she said. "I really don't like him. He kidnapped Emily and he has done a horrible thing to Nathan's parents."

"Do you realize you were comforting him when we were inside?"

"Really?" she responded. "I guess he just seemed so helpless. I am not sure what I was thinking. Oh, my god! Did Charles see?"

"I don't think he saw much," said the doctor. "He seems pretty fueled with rage. We probably need to get the agent away from us or get away from him as soon as possible."

"You are right," said Alma. "What are we going to do?"

"Don't worry," replied Doctor Cornell. "I will get Nathan working on some new identities for us. Then we will need to head in another direction…again. I am thinking maybe Colorado or New Mexico this time."

"What about the baby? I don't want the little thing to be born on the run."

"It can't be helped," he said. "There never was a way that this scenario was going to play out simply. We just need to make it the best way we can."

"I know," said Alma sadly. "I just thought that the Universe would cut us a break sometime. We deserve one, don't we?"

"I'm sure it will," replied Doctor Cornell. "I just think that our break is on backorder. It will get here eventually."

"I sure hope so," said Alma. "We'd better get back in. There is no telling what Charles might do. He seems so angry."

Doctor Cornell was certain that their respective attitudes towards Agent Baxter were partially because of something akin to pheromone emissions. The Doctor had read a research study that showed how women were attracted to certain male pheromones, while the same pheromones made men aggressive. He suspected that was the case here.

Normally, Alma was rational and kind. Charles was easygoing and slow to anger. When they returned to the condo, Charles was sitting in a dining room chair that he had placed in front of Agent Baxter. Charles glared at him with seething rage. Agent Baxter looked back at him with casual indifference. Emily stood next to them like a referee, preparing to intervene if necessary. Doctor Cornell spoke quietly to her and then asked Charles to join him outside. Nathan poured over Baxter's laptop, collecting as much information as possible. He motioned to Alma and began signing to her.

There is an email here that says other agents will be here in about two hours. Nathan was nervously excited. He had been excluded from many of the conversations and didn't know if there was a plan of action. *What are we planning to do?* Alma signed back, *I think we are planning another move. We should start packing, I suspect.* Nathan frowned and nodded in agreement. Then he nodded in Baxter's direction with a shrug meaning *What about him?* Alma just shrugged back.

Charles felt calmer almost immediately once he was outside. Doctor Cornell filled him in on the plans to escape to another state. Charles didn't like being on the run either. But he knew it was necessary and he would do anything to protect his family. In his calm state of mind, he looked directly at Doctor Cornell with a deadly seriousness in his eyes. "You know we have to deal with him, don't you? He is never going to stop looking for us; not now."

"I know," said Doctor Cornell. He had resigned himself to the inevitable. "I just didn't want to say anything in front of the others. Hippocratic Oath and all."

"Do you have any ideas?" asked Charles.

"Actually, I do," Doctor Cornell replied. "There is a small section of beach behind the rocks that is only accessible during low tide. I am thinking that if we take Baxter there and inject him with his own tranquilizer, the incoming tide will do the rest for us. It will look like an accidental drowning and the rocks will mask the injury on his head. Who knows…the sharks may eliminate the rest of the evidence."

"The sharks in this area are not that big," said Charles.

"I didn't say the plan was perfect," answered Doctor Cornell. "This is my first time."

"Well, we'd better get moving," said Charles. "The tide is starting to come in and it will be daylight soon. Better to get this done while it is still dark."

"Maybe we did finally catch that break," said Doctor Cornell.

"What?" asked Charles.

"Never mind," he said. "I will tell you later. How much do we tell the others?"

"I think they need to know everything," said Charles. "First, we will need to tell Nathan about his parents. He still doesn't know. It might make him more agreeable to our task."

"I will tell Alma and Emily," said the doctor. "As a physician, I am trained in giving bad news."

The two men returned to the condo looking like jurors returning to a courtroom. Before they delivered their verdict, Charles stretched a length of duct tape across Baxter's mouth. He didn't want him pleading with anyone and making them have second thoughts. Doctor Cornell took Emily and Alma aside and used his considerable bedside manner to explain the necessity of their decision. It surprised him that they were more agreeable that he had expected. Nathan was another story.

Charles signed to Nathan that they had decided to let nature do away with Agent Baxter. Nathan, with an attitude that did not surprise him, protested. He always had an admirable moral compass. Charles told him of the fate of his parents and Nathan thought he might be lying just to convince him that killing Baxter was the right thing to do. Charles looked him in the eyes and Nathan could see the truth. *Do I have to be a part of it?* Somehow, he managed to communicate his resignation in the question. *No,* signed Charles. *We will do what needs to be done. You will need to stay with Emily.* Nathan nodded. Charles thought he saw tears. *Would you take the ladies upstairs? Please?* Charles touched him on the arm after he asked. Nathan nodded and motioned for Emily and Alma to go with him. Doctor Cornell went through Agent Baxter's things and brought out a case containing syringes. They were conveniently marked as tranquilizers. Doctor Cornell suspected it was to keep them from getting mixed up with the invisibility agent.

Everyone had been shocked when they learned that Agent Baxter had injected himself with a compound made from the samples the facility had taken from Emily. They were more shocked to find out that the compound had worked. Not only had it worked, but apparently it was replicating itself in Baxter's system to a point where, with practice, he could turn invisible at will. In his experiments with invisibility, he discovered that he did not need to be at peace or in a defensive mode to become invisible. His modest experiments revealed that he could be aggressive and remain unseen. That meant that his ability exceeded Emily's. It also meant that he could be the greatest *intelligence asset* the agency had ever seen…or not seen. His mind reeled at the possibilities.

Charles and Doctor Cornell were stuck with the problem of getting him to the section of beach without bindings. Marks indicating that he had been restrained would make it obvious that his death was not an accident. Yet, they didn't want to drag his unconscious body down the beach. They compromised with trash bags. Charles put five plastic garbage bags inside each other and cut a hole in the top for Baxter's head. The Doctor got a sheet from the bedroom and secured it around the trunk of Baxter's body. He then cut the restraints through the plastic bags and removed the binding ties. Doctor Cornell hoped that there would be enough time between them walking to the spot on the beach and the tide coming in for the marks to go away.

They really didn't have a lot of time. The two hours that Nathan had stated was just an estimate. The other agents could be arriving anytime. It might already be too late, but they couldn't dwell on that. Charles got Baxter to his feet and ushered him out the door. He held the knot of the sheet tightly in his grip. Doctor Cornell followed with the hypodermic. The sun began to rise as they neared the alcove. An execution at sunrise seemed almost fitting somehow. The incoming tide washed across their feet and the water was unbelievably cold. Baxter offered no resistance and seemed to resign himself to the fact that this was the last sunrise he would ever see. Doctor Cornell began to feel regret and went over other possible solutions in his mind. He frantically searched for some way out of their situation, but couldn't find one. Charles Troy was resolved to end it. His rage was back and the image of Baxter striking Emily was strong in his mind. He pushed Baxter on down the beach hard enough that he almost stumbled.

As Agent Baxter stumbled, he swung around...wrenching the sheet from Charles' hand. Then Baxter head-butted him so hard that both men saw strobe lights. Doctor Cornell tried to ready the tranquilizer, but Baxter kicked him in the groin and he dropped to his knees. The hypodermic needle slipped from Doctor Cornell's hand. The incoming tide washed over it and it was buried in the sand; lost forever.

Agent Baxter began to dissolve as he ran back up the beach. He changed directions several times and crossed over his own footprints to confuse the two men. He then reached the wooden walkway and was sure that he was safe. Baxter struggled to release himself from his plastic bag cocoon and was almost free when he felt a sharp pain in his chest. Looking down, he saw the red-feathered end of a tranquilizer dart sticking out of his chest. A bright light flashed in front of him followed by enveloping darkness.

CHAPTER 26: PENANCE

Agent Kellum lifted his special dark glasses and then lowered them again. He shook his head and smiled at the effect. One moment, the glowing image of Agent Baxter was there; the next it wasn't. He lowered his rifle as Charles and Doctor Cornell came running toward the wooden walkway. Charles tripped over Agent Baxter's invisible, unconscious body and tumbled forward. Doctor Cornell almost followed him, but managed to stop just in time. Agent Kellum held his rifle in a nonthreatening, yet available way indicating he could use it if necessary.

"Gentlemen, would you come with me please?" he asked with an inflection which made it clear that it wasn't a request. "…and would you mind terribly bringing Agent Baxter along? We are a little shorthanded at the moment." The two men felt around to find Agent Baxter's arms and then hoisted him up. The scene was a bit comedic with two men looking as though they were pretending to help a drunken buddy get home. They all headed back to the condo and Charles felt a pang of impending dread. He wasn't sure what he would find in the condo, but wasn't surprised by the two additional agents waiting inside. They were not holding weapons and the rest of the family seemed to be sitting quietly around the dining table. Doctor Cornell and Charles deposited Agent Baxter on the sofa and then joined the others.

"We have a lot to talk about," said Agent Kellum. "There are a number of laws that have been violated here and a number of secrets that need to remain secret. The question is how we are going to effectively handle this situation."

"Probably the same way you handled Nathan's parents I suppose," said Emily cynically. "Isn't that how you people handle all your problems?"

"When it becomes necessary in the interest of national security," responded Agent Kellum. "We prefer detention if possible. Termination is only a last resort."

"By whose standard? Who decides who lives and dies?" Emily was fuming. She was tired of all the espionage and the invasions of privacy.

"Someone far above my pay grade, I assure you," replied Agent Kellum. His demeanor was disarming and hard to read. It was difficult to tell if he was being malevolent or sympathetic. He was a tall man of about fifty. He could have been younger, but time and his job had done a number on his face. Deep crevasses lined his face which looked a little like a satellite photo of Mars' surface. When he smiled, it seemed as though part of it might chip off. His teeth indicated that he was probably due for a cleaning and the follicles of his eyebrows looked like they were having a riot.

Agent Baxter began to materialize on the sofa. The two men had not been aware that they had been carrying him backwards; they had deposited him face down in what they had thought would have been a sitting position. The sight of him provided a bit of comic relief to the tension in the room.

"Ah...I see our friend has rejoined us," said Kellum. "...in body if not in spirit."

"He's the one you should be taking into custody," said Alma angrily. "You have no idea what he has put us through."

"Actually, we have detailed reports," said Kellum. "...and he is being taken into custody. We don't just shoot our own field operatives for the fun of it...well, not every time." He grinned and Emily thought for sure that a chunk fell off of his face. She was mistaken.

"This is an awkward conversation," Kellum said, becoming serious. "We came here with the expressed purpose of target acquisition. That being done, we are charged with the duty of damage control."

"So we are the collateral damage," Charles responded. It was obvious to see that his blood pressure was rising.

"I am afraid you misunderstand," said Agent Kellum. "Negotiation and public relations has never been my strong suit. Agent Cantrell, would you mind explaining from this point on?"

"I'm glad you found your voice Emily," said the agent who stood behind her. All Emily had noticed when they stormed the condo were the special dark glasses and the black suits. "Michael?" she uttered.

"You know him?" asked Alma astonished.

"He was at the facility," replied Emily. "He helped me..." She shot a look at Agent Kellum. "...cope with my abduction."

"Yeah...about that," Agent Cantrell lowered his eyes. "We really should not have been holding you. I was new to the agency and didn't know what I was there for. I thought everything was legitimate. You see…even shadow agencies have shadow agencies. Sometimes they do jobs that the government doesn't want to do or take credit for. Occasionally, they go off the rails and somebody has to step in."

"That is where we come in," said Agent Kellum. "We have to do damage control when someone becomes a loose cannon. That is what happened here. The facility where you were detained has been closed down. It was a low-level security risk anyway. That was why it was so easy for you to escape. Had this been a legitimate operation, you would still be detained and this conversation would not be taking place."

"So what does all this mean?" asked Alma. "What happens now?"

"Now, we try to set things right as much as possible," said Agent Johnston, joining the conversation.

"Maxwell?" said Emily. "You also got a promotion?"

"You know him too?" asked Charles. "Really? What is going on?" It was obvious from Nathan's look that he was getting a little jealous. That was unusual for him. Emily reassured him by placing her delicate hand on his hand that was involuntarily forming a fist. He relaxed and Agent Maxwell Johnston continued.

"The agency thought it best to keep the security circle tight on this case," he explained. "The less people who knew about you and your case, the better. After our security clearance was increased, we were promoted from within. We finally got a break when Baxter started filing reports. We came here as quickly as we could before any more damage was done." A chill went through Charles and Doctor Cornell simultaneously as the two men realized how close they had come to murdering a government agent.

"So what do you mean, 'set things right'?" asked Alma.

"If you are all willing to cooperate, your government is willing to forget any of this ever happened," answered Agent Kellum. "It shouldn't be too hard since your government is not aware of most of it anyway. You can return to your lives in Iowa, with one provision."

"And what is that?" asked Charles skeptically.

"You must sign a non-disclosure agreement and submit to a passive amount of surveillance to make sure you live up to it," explained Agent Kellum.

"So you are saying that we will pretend that none of this ever happened and you will just monitor us for the rest of our lives to make sure we do. Am I getting that right?" Charles' blood pressure was not getting better.

"That is pretty much it in a nutshell," replied Kellum. "The alternative is a secret research facility in, ironically, Colorado. I think you were headed there if my Intel is correct." Charles breathed out a heavy sigh and his blood pressure leveled off.

"So I take your silence to mean that we have an agreement?" asked Kellum, holding out his hand. Doctor Cornell intercepted it and shook it vigorously. "Oh, by the way Doctor…you are going to have to cease all research into Ms. Troy's condition. You might just need to give up that dream of a Nobel Prize." Doctor Cornell frowned and released Kellum's hand. He nodded with angry submissiveness. Doctor David comforted himself that he would at least be able to return to private practice. He had given up on the idea that practicing again would ever be possible.

"We will be providing back stories for you to explain your absences," said Michael. "We have also brought all your expenses up to date. That was the least we could do."

"What about Nathan?" asked Emily. "How is he supposed to explain the loss of his parents?"

"Who told you that his parents are dead?" asked Michael. "Was it this bastard?" He indicated Baxter, who was starting to stir.

"We didn't get word from them. We just assumed," replied Emily. Michael moved over next to Nathan, looked him sincerely in the eye and signed, *Your parents are alive and well. They do not know anything of your situation. He* (pointing to Baxter) *shot them up with another experimental drug that causes amnesia. It erased about two weeks of memories. They didn't contact you because your back story was that you were in Europe traveling for a college class. You will have to explain the baby yourself however. Congratulations by the way.* Nathan's eyes were wide with disbelief. He wasn't sure how to react. *Thanks*, he signed and shrugged. Michael detected the distrust in his manner, as well as a hint of jealousy. He moved to a place where his hands were unable to be observed by anyone but Nathan. *You don't have to worry*, he signed. *Emily is not my type…if you know what I mean. Don't ask.* Nathan smiled and signed, *Don't tell.*

"So here we are," said Agent Kellum. "I cannot stress how important your cooperation is. We will work with you as long as you work with us. From time to time, someone may come to you for biological samples. They won't demand them, but it will be better if you don't refuse. That is how this operation should have been handled in the first place. Your government is not the monster the media portrays it to be. If it was, you would never have heard about sexual indiscretions of Secret Service agents. They would have just made the problem go away."

"Are we in agreement then?" asked Maxwell. "Can we work together?" Charles took on the mantle of the family patriarch and said, "I think, speaking for my family…and my extended family…" Alma held her breath. Charles' moods had been unpredictable of late. "…that we accept your proposal. What do you want us to do?" Everyone let go of the collective breath they had been holding…even Agent Kellum. He did not want the responsibility of dealing with the alternative solution of the problem. He had been given free rein in handling the situation. One scenario would be to gain the trust of the family and then make them disappear. He had not yet dismissed that as an option. He would have to see how things played out.

"I suppose the next step would be to pack," said Michael. "You're going home." Emily stood, smiled and embraced him. She whispered *thank you* in his ear and it gave him a chill. He winked at Nathan who lifted his hand in a weak wave. Nathan didn't know if Michael had been putting him on or if he was flirting. He never would.

The family packed their belongings while the agents secured Baxter in bindings that were a bit more state-of-the-art than plastic bags. He was placed in the back of a windowless black van. His ankles were secured by shackles that were bolted to the floorboard. No one had bothered to remove the duct tape from his mouth, so his protests went unheeded. Baxter had regained consciousness on the way to the van and had no idea of what was going on. He turned invisible several times and realized that it afforded him no special powers. To the contrary, the chemistry in his system seemed to spark unwarranted animosity, so he sat quietly. *Pick your battles,* he remembered hearing somewhere.

Agent Johnston returned to the condo and cornered Emily in the kitchen.

"I wanted to thank you privately for not saying anything about us helping you to escape," he said. "That would not look good on our records."

"You helped me so much," she replied. "I couldn't betray you like that." She smiled and said, "You aren't going to use the *flashy thing* on me, are you?"

"I get it…Will Smith…I get that a lot, especially now," Maxwell said.

"You mean because of the black suit?" Emily asked.

"…and the dark glasses," he responded. "Anyway, I just wanted to thank you and congratulate you." He placed his hand on her belly in a way that seemed a little too familiar. Maxwell had seen her naked when few people could see her at all. He felt closer to her than he probably should have. Emily eased his mind by placing her hand on his. She felt a bond with him too.

"Will I be able to let you know when the baby is born?" she asked.

"We will know," Maxwell said smiling. "We will be around." The words both comforted Emily and worried her. She was glad she had allies in the agency, but she had apprehensions about what kind of experiments they might want to do on the baby. A wave of resolve washed over her. The image of a mother bear protecting her cub came to mind.

Emily had a power and she had escaped them once. She could do it again if necessary.

Nathan finished packing most of his belongings and returned to the living room to collect his equipment. He was surprised to see that all of the surveillance equipment had been taken, along with everything they had brought from Agent Baxter's condo. They had even taken his personal laptop. Nathan turned to see Emily and Agent Johnston in the kitchen and released a fury of signing. Emily was sure that Nathan was experiencing jealousy again, but was surprised and a little disappointed that his tirade was about his laptop and electronics. Agent Johnston was not as skilled in sign language as Agent Cantrell and was not sure what the problem was. Emily picked up on his confusion and explained why Nathan was angry. Maxwell responded by shrugging and looking nervous. Nathan threw his hands up and went back to his room to bring down what was left of his belongings.

The extended family was surprised at how quickly they were able to pack and how little they had actually accumulated over the months. They packed everything into the SUV and assembled in front of the condo for a final conference with Agent Kellum.

"We will collect the fake ID's when you arrive in Iowa. Until then, feel free to use them for travel expenses. Then all records of them will be erased." There was an air of finality in his voice. It was disconcerting. "When you arrive, you will be reintroduced back into your former lifestyles."

"Like tigers being reintroduced into the wild?" asked Doctor Cornell.

"Something like that," said Agent Kellum, not sure if Cornell was being sarcastic or not. "We will monitor you on your trip. Make sure you do not deviate from the course laid out by your navigation system."

"We don't have a navigation system," said Charles.

"You do now," Kellum responded. "...courtesy of your United States government." He smiled and Charles felt like he had just signed up to live in a goldfish bowl. Still, it seemed like a small price to pay for safety. It was kind of like going into the Witness Relocation Program; except they were relocating back to where they started. There would be adjustments, but there had been adjustments before and they had handled them. The extended family boarded the SUV and Emily waved goodbye to her two government connections. Nathan looked askance at her as she did. *What really went on in Ohio?* he signed. *Nothing you need to worry about*, she responded. Then she spent the next hour relating the story to him again to smooth his ruffled ego.

Alma reached over and took Charles' hand even though he was driving. "I can't believe we're going home," she said.

"I won't believe it until I see it," he replied. "These people have a history of going back on their word. Just keep alert." Alma realized that Charles was not going to share in her excitement until he felt safe. She turned to Emily and asked, "Have the two of you thought about what you are going to do when we get back?"

"Well," said Emily. "We are not sure. There is so much to process. So much has gone on and so many things have changed in the last twenty-four hours. Maybe we need to get settled in before we make any plans."

"That is very mature of you," said Alma. "...and you're right. We don't even know how Nathan's parents are going to react to your...condition." Nathan tensed a little. He knew his mother would be fine with it and he was glad to know that she was still alive. His step-father was another story. Nathan had felt a little relieved when he was told that he was dead. He felt guilty about feeling relieved though. He no longer felt alone now. The Troy's had become his family and he felt that they would support him when the time came.

In spite of his apprehension, Charles Troy felt as though a weight had been lifted from his shoulders. He had endured so much and had gone through such hell when Emily was missing. He had always harbored a deep fear of losing her. It was difficult enough to feel like he could protect her when she was only silent. When invisibility became an issue, it nearly drove him insane. Charles couldn't put a bell around her neck or a flashing light on her head to let him know where she was. He even crossed the line into insanity when she was abducted. His worst fear had come to fruition and he had no idea how to handle it. He had played out all the scenarios a thousand times and never developed a failsafe plan of action. The thought occurred to Charles that, even though the government would be watching their every move, his family was safer knowing they were there. Before, they had been alone in the world; keeping a secret and fearing discovery. Emily was visible now. She could talk. There were no more secrets to keep. Maybe the worst part was over. Charles smiled a relaxed smile for the first time in a long, long while.

The trip back to Cedar Pike, Iowa took longer than expected. They made frequent stops due to fatigue. The events of the past few days had worn everyone out. They stayed overnight in comfortable hotel chains for a change. They no longer felt the need to stay off the beaten track to avoid detection. They ate in nice restaurants instead of roadside diners and "greasy spoons", although the food was not nearly as good. They crossed the Wyoming border into

Nebraska and it was as if the state line marked the boundary of how far the Old West was allowed to intrude east. The terrain seemed to instantly go from sand and rock to farmland and trees. The fields had been harvested, but looked nothing like the prairies they had been looking at for the past few hundred miles. Emily was actually able to enjoy the scenery this time. She marveled at the Grand Tetons majestically mirrored in Jackson Lake. She wished they had time to go through Yellowstone National Park, but they felt they needed to get home and were told not to veer from the navigator's directions. Charles had promised that they would come back after the baby was born.

When they crossed into the state of Iowa, Agent Kellum met them at the border. Two other agents who were unknown to them were with him. Charles began to worry that his relaxed attitude had been premature. The navigator indicated that they should pull over in an eerie display of sentience. The agent waved at them like they were his family. Charles and the others were on their guard.

"This is where we part company," Agent Kellum said. "...for a while at least. We need you to remove your items from the SUV and put them into these two vehicles." The two vehicles were identical to the ones that had been owned by the Troy family and Doctor Cornell. "It will fit the back stories better if you arrive in the vehicles that people remember you driving. Best not to raise any unnecessary questions, don't you think?" The family knew that the question was rhetorical, so they proceeded to take their bags out of the SUV and put them into the other vehicles.

"Doctor," Kellum said. "It would be best if you did not arrive in town at the same time as the Troys, so we have arranged accommodations for you for the next couple of days. Is that alright with you?" Doctor Cornell didn't trust any of it. He felt like the situation was something dreamed up to dispatch him or abduct him so they could make him perform experiments. His reason rose up to quell his panic. *If they had wanted to kill you, they would have done it already*, it said. *They had a lot of opportunities between here and Oregon.* The doctor smiled a weak smile and nodded. He moved his bags into the car that had been secured for him.

"You know, Emily still needs me as her doctor," he said, involuntarily pleading his case.

"We know," replied Kellum. "We know. Your patient is very important to us. She will need the best of care and as her attending physician, you are best suited for the job; so you can relax." Emily hugged him and kissed him on the cheek.

"You take care," she said. "We will see you soon."

"I wish you didn't make that sound so final," the Doctor said nervously. "I will be okay." He wasn't sure. Charles and Nathan shook his hand and Alma embraced him in a way that let him know just how much she appreciated his caring for her daughter. "The holidays are coming up," she said. "You will be having Christmas with us. I am not taking *no* for an answer."

"Wouldn't miss it," he said. "Go on. I will be fine." After an awkward moment of no one wanting to leave first, Charles took the initiative and got behind the wheel of the Chevy Equinox that had been provided for them. It was a slightly newer model than his old one and was equipped with an in-dash navigation system that his did not have; a *gift* from Uncle Sam no doubt. The family joined him sans Doctor Cornell and they all had the same sick feeling that they would never see him again.

The family stayed silent for the last leg of the trip. The whole ordeal weighed heavily upon them and there were too many unanswered questions they were not sure they wanted answered. Nathan would have to inform his parents of some of the events that had transpired; i.e., that he was going to be a father and they were going to be grandparents. Charles could see that play out in his mind. *Mom...Dad...My girlfriend can turn invisible and we were chased by a government agent. We almost killed him and now we are in a kind of Witness Protection program...oh, yeah...Emily is pregnant.* He laughed at the thought of their reaction. *She's pregnant!?!?* Yes...THAT was what they would take from all that. He began to laugh hysterically. He must have really been tired.

They pulled into the long gravel drive of their farm and it felt as though it had been a decade since they had been there. After a few minutes, it was as if they had never left. They brought their bags into the house and Nathan stood awkwardly in the entryway...not quite sure what to do. Alma noticed his discomfort and signed, *Take your bags up to Emily's room. We will deal with everything else later.* Nathan glanced over at Charles who smiled slightly, nodded and then motioned to the stairs with his head. Emily smiled and hugged her dad.

Tomorrow, they would notify Nathan's parents that he was back from "Europe". The Troys would invite them over so they could tell the Saunders the big news. It would be an awkward conversation, but they all had a lot of experience with awkward conversations. Charles looked around the house for the surveillance equipment that he knew was there. He wondered just how thorough and invasive the equipment was. George Orwell came to mind and he wondered if there was any spot in the house where he could not be seen. He would feel better if he saw the doctor again….WHEN he saw the doctor again. It was the first of December. He hadn't noticed that Thanksgiving had come and gone. Holidays had not been high on their list of priorities. Charles looked out the screen door at the cloud bank that was forming on the horizon. He heard the rumble of distant thunder and wondered how intense the storm might be. He remembered back to the first night they discovered Emily's invisibility. There had been a terrible storm that night too. Charles felt as though a circle had been completed and he closed the front door.

CHAPTER 27: RECOMPENSE

The wind through the open windows of the old farmhouse blew the sheers across the darkened hallway. They looked like specters beckoning an unsuspecting victim to his eternal doom. The thick dark atmosphere was illuminated intermittently by lightning flashes. In spite of the brightness of the flashes, the thunder only seemed to rumble in the distance.

Joseph Oliver Baxter, intelligence asset for an unnamed government shadow agency, stood silently at the end of the hall. He held his 22 magnum Automag with customized suppressor in his hand. He donned his special dark glasses and adjusted them to night vision. The flashes of lightning blinded him, so he switched the setting to infrared. Creeping down the hallway, the sheers wafted across Baxter's shoulders trying to get him to play. He brushed them away roughly and continued his quest. At the end of the hallway was the bedroom of Emily Troy. Agent Baxter knew this from the recon he had done in the house and the reports he had read. He found himself standing next to her door before he knew it. He opened it slowly and it creaked on unoiled hinges.

A loud thunderclap outside seemed to announce his intrusion into the room and he froze in place. No one seemed to stir, so Baxter proceeded. There were two red glowing silhouettes on the bed indicating Emily was not alone. Wearing the infrared glasses, he was unable to tell which one was Emily Troy. It didn't matter. Nathan Saunders was next on his list. He would make it quick and efficient. He leveled the weapon directly at the forehead of one of the images. The suppressor coughed twice and a spatter of rapidly cooling heat signatures on the pillow and sheets indicated that he had hit his target. The other silhouette stirred and softly said, "Nathan?" Agent Baxter pointed the barrel at Emily, held his breath and squeezed the trigger twice in rapid succession. A glowing pool of blood formed around her head. It seemed to be increasing in temperature instead of diminishing. Baxter thought it might be because of her odd metabolism or because so much blood had been produced by the gunshots. Perhaps he had hit an artery and it was feeding the pool with fresh blood. But to him, it didn't matter. He had finally accomplished his mission. He had rid himself of the quarry that had eluded and shamed him. He would eliminate her parents subsequently and move on to his next assignment.

Baxter removed the special dark glasses and surveyed the fruits of his labor. Two human-sized lumps under a handmade quilt glistened with their own blood in the meager light. He smiled in an evil way and turned to finish the job. A huge motionless shape stood in the doorway. It was silent and imposing. Lightning flashed behind it, outlining its menacing form. The hair seemed to be in tangles and the arms were outstretched threateningly. Another lightning flash illuminated the room and Baxter saw the form was that of Alma Troy, fuming with rage. He leveled his pistol at her and fired repeatedly into the trunk of her body. He emptied the clip and she still stood. He dropped the gun to his side and seemed to shrink in her presence. She seemed to grow in stature and she changed as she did. Alma Troy began to morph into the hideous incarnation of…his mother. She had followed him from the shopping mall. She pointed a bony decaying finger at him and shouted "Idiot! Can't you do anything right?" She pointed behind him. Baxter turned to find Emily Troy and Nathan Saunders laughing at him and pointing. They morphed into children on the playground, but they were still pointing and laughing. He looked down and he was also a child. He was standing in the middle of the playground in his underwear; his soiled underwear. Baxter began to scream and pulled his hair. The 22 magnum Automag was still in his hand. He placed it to his temple and pulled the trigger. The clip was empty. He threw the weapon at the two children and they melted into a thick fog. The fog darkened and began to envelop Agent Baxter. It wasn't fog; it was smoke. Thick black smoke filled his lungs and he began to choke. He coughed, wheezed and tried his best to catch his breath. The blackness began to turn to white as he lost consciousness. He seemed to finally feel at peace as the bright light closed in around him.

****

Doctor Karon Stuart flicked the drip indicator on the IV running into Joseph Baxter. She had injected a sedative into the line and it rapidly coursed through his system. He had been stripped of his agent status for the time being, pending further observation. He was strapped to a bed in an observation room. The room was located in a secret government facility in Colorado. Thanks to him independently acting as a test subject, Baxter would be the focus of invisibility studies for the foreseeable future.

"He's psychotic you know," said Doctor Spencer. "We have had to sedate him every night since he's been here."

"I know," replied Doctor Stuart. "I thought we might be able to stabilize him with drugs, but I think we may have to resort to surgery."

"Do you mean a lobotomy?" asked Doctor Spencer.

"I am thinking about slight alterations...and bio-electronic implants," she said smiling.

"You know those haven't been approved, right?" he said.

"Official sanctioning is kind of a gray area," she said. "If he doesn't leave the lab, no one has to know."

"Shouldn't we ask Baxter if he wants to submit to treatment?" asked Doctor Spencer. Both of the doctors stood in silence with serious expressions on their faces. The expressions suddenly twisted into gales of laughter. Tears streamed down Doctor Stuart's face as she tried to catch her breath. Finally, she was able to form words.

"You said that with such a straight face," she shrieked in a shrill falsetto.

"I know," Doctor Spencer responded. "My face was beginning to hurt." After a few moments, their laughter died down and they got serious.

"We will begin doing preliminary tests this week along with the other tests we are doing on his invisibility," Doctor Stuart said, still wiping tears from her eyes.

"We will have to keep separate records," said Doctor Spencer. "Three sets."

"Why three?" asked Doctor Stuart.

"One for the invisibility study," he said. "One for the bio-electronic implants and one for the reactions of the two together."

"I think you are overthinking, but you may be right," she said. "It can't hurt anyway."

"What do you think he dreams about when he has these fits?" asked Doctor Spencer. He was almost talking to himself.

"Who knows," said Doctor Stuart. "He has a lot of demons. I heard a rumor that he killed his own mother. But it was just a rumor. He does have a lot of baggage no matter what the case."

"Well, he won't when we get done with him," Doctor Spencer responded. "...or, he might end up needing a baggage handler."

"The White Zone is for loading and unloading only," said Doctor Stuart. *"There is no stopping in the White Zone."* They began to laugh again and left the room. Joseph Oliver Baxter lay peacefully strapped to the hospital bed in the secret government research facility in Colorado.

****

Nathan Saunders had a life changing experience. He had been willing to give up everything to be with Emily Troy. He could see her when no one else could; both physically and emotionally. The bond between them couldn't be broken even though it was tested to its limits. Emily empathized with Nathan's silent isolation in ways no one else on the planet could. She knew what it was like to be alone and different. They were a perfect match in more ways than either of them knew.

Researchers appeared from time to time to gather samples and perform tests. The tests were done with respect and were not deliberately intrusive. Emily was surprised when they also wanted to run tests on Nathan. The loyalty effect she had had on Michael Cantrell and Maxwell Johnston also worked on the researchers. They told her the test results when they were not supposed to. They were powerless to resist her for some reason, but they kept that out of their reports. The researchers told her that when she and Nathan created a child together, their DNA fused because Emily shared DNA and body chemistry with the baby. It was that fusion which caused her to become visible after she entered her second trimester. It confirmed Doctor Cornell's hypothesis. The researchers studied Nathan's DNA to see if the effect could be replicated in the lab. To date, it had not. Nathan and Emily really were made for each other.

Nathan went home to his parents expecting to be severely reprimanded or disowned. His mother was overjoyed to see him again and overcome with emotion. Somewhere in her unconscious mind, Sue Saunders knew of the government intrigue and his run from the authorities, but mental blocks prevented her from remembering. She just knew she was happy to have him home. His younger brother Jimmy did not share her enthusiasm. He loved his older brother, but he had his eye on Nathan's bedroom. Jimmy thought he might inherit it if Nathan stayed away. The older brother signed to him not to worry. He had news to tell them soon. David Saunders was the real surprise. Nathan had expected him to be furious or at the very least, indifferent. Instead, he embraced him in a way that he never had before. Nathan was even sure he saw a tear in the corner of David's eye. Sometimes, it does not take much to change a person's attitude. Sometimes, a single act of kindness or adversity can make an irrevocable impact on a person's life. Sometimes, it can be a chemically-induced mental block. David Saunders had all of those. He could not explain why, but he loved Nathan as his own. Nathan wondered if, in some bizarre way, Emily's DNA had joined with his somehow. If so, no one ever revealed it.

Nathan told his parents about his relationship with Emily at dinner one night at the Troy's farm. It was about a week before Christmas. Emily remained invisible until he could introduce her at the right time. Her swollen belly would have tipped them off right away and he wanted to break it to them gently.

Mom? Dad? I have to tell you something, he signed. *I do not want you to freak out.*

What is it Nathan? You are worrying me, Sue signed.

I am going to marry Emily, he signed. It seemed to be easier to blurt out difficult news in sign language. Stammering was eliminated. Sue and David sat stunned for a moment. Finally, David spoke up and said, "What Emily? Their Emily? She's invisible. How can you marry someone who is invisible? Won't that mean letting someone else in on the secret?"

"Whoa, wait," said Jimmy. "What are you guys talking about?" Emily's existence as well as her condition had been kept from him over the years. He was a talkative boy and they were certain he would not be able to keep their secret while he was at school. David grimaced because he had been careful for so long and had just revealed the secret in the heat of the moment.

"Who's invisible? Are you guys messing with me?" Jimmy grinned widely, sure that he was being *punked*.

"There is a little more to it than just that," said Sue, ignoring Jimmy's confusion.

There is a lot more to it than that, signed Nathan, reading her lips. *We are getting married, but not until after the baby is born.*

"Baby?!!" exclaimed Sue. She knocked her fork off the table and it clattered onto the dining room floor.

"Are you telling us she's pregnant?" asked David. His demeanor was unusually calm.

More than that, signed Nathan. *You are going to need the whole truth.* He motioned to Emily who had been standing there the whole time. She shook her head. She was not sure she was going to get the desired acceptance from Nathan's family. He leaned over and kissed her on the cheek. Sue thought it was sweet. Emily finally relented and slowly materialized. She had learned to control the rate of invisibility even though she didn't know why that would ever be necessary. Sue beamed at her soon-to-be daughter-in-law. David and Jimmy looked stunned. Jimmy spoke up first.

"No way! Seriously, NO WAY!" He seemed unable to say anything else. He still had more verbal capacity than David, who seemed lost for any words at all. Finally, he stood up and walked over to Emily. He held out his hand weakly to shake hers. He was not sure he was going to be able to stand for very long. His mind was questioning what he was seeing…not seeing. Emily took his hand gently. David swallowed hard. His throat was so dry, he felt like he had just swallowed broken glass. He had never imagined how beautiful she was. In an uncharacteristic display of affection, he embraced her. He felt the bump of her belly pressing against him as she returned his embrace. At that moment, his heart melted. Whether it was Emily's chemistry or the emotion of the moment, their bond was set.

Jimmy started chattering like a squirrel on Ritalin. "Can you teach me to do that? Can you? Please? That would be so cool. The stuff I could do in school. The stuff I could get away with. Do you have any other super powers? Can you fly? Are you able to read minds? Ooooo... Can you walk through....?"

"Jimmy!!!" shouted Sue. "Settle!" Emily and David released each other and she turned to Jimmy.

"I'm sorry Jimmy," she said softly. "This is about it. I was born this way I guess. I can't teach anybody to do it. Until a while ago, I couldn't even talk. Talking feels like a super power to me. You seem to do that pretty well." Jimmy smiled, but he was a little disappointed by what Emily had said.

"You should be grateful for what you can do," she continued. "Nathan would love to be able to hear. You can do that; he can't. Everybody has something they can do that no one else can. They need to concentrate on those gifts and use them for good. That's what makes them superheroes. Not flashy powers." At that moment, a wave of iridescent color flashed across her face. It seemed to emphasize and negate her point at the same time. Jimmy was mesmerized at the display. Realizing what had happened, Emily leaned in and whispered, "If I figure out how to teach it, you will be my first student. Deal?"

"Deal!" he said, shaking her hand so hard that it caught her off guard. She was just glad he didn't spit in his palm first. Jimmy went back to his seat to contemplate the possibilities.

"So, do you two have a date set?" asked David, finally finding his voice.

"We don't have a date, but we have a place," replied Emily.

"Where?" asked Sue and Alma simultaneously.

"It's a surprise for now," said Emily. "...but it will be terribly romantic."

We think the baby will be born in April or May, signed Nathan. *So we were thinking a June wedding. Old fashioned.*

"It sounds perfect," said Sue. "I just wish you would let us know where, so we could make plans."

"We will let you know in time," said Emily. "Let's get this childbirth thing out of the way first."

"Good idea," agreed Alma. She turned to the Saunders and said, "...and speaking of that, we have to fill you in on a few more things."

"What else could there possibly be?" asked David.

"Well...how do I put this delicately? You will get a visit from a government agent soon," Alma said. "They will have you sign a nondisclosure agreement and they will put surveillance equipment in your house to make sure you live up to it."

David bolted upright in his chair. He had never been a fan of government intrusion into a person's life. He was doubly riled because of what was hidden behind the mental blocks in his brain.

"What if I say no?" demanded David. "This is America. I am a free citizen."

"You have the right to refuse," said Charles calmly. "However, if you do, our only alternative is to enter a government relocation program to keep Emily safe. Nathan will probably come with us and you will never see him again."

"Are you threatening me, Charles?" David's nostrils were flaring. Emily moved to his side and placed her delicate hand on his shoulder. His rage instantly left him. "It's not a threat Mr. Saunders," said Emily. "It's just the way things are. It's for our safety…all of us." His shoulders slumped as he felt the influence of Emily's body chemistry. At that moment, he could deny her nothing and had no idea why.

"I guess you're right," David conceded. "Who am I going to tell anyway? No one would believe any of this. I do have a condition though."

"What's that?" asked Charles. Turning around in his seat, David looked at Emily and said, "*Mister Saunders* was my grandfather. If we're going to be family, you need to call me David."

"I was planning on calling you *dad*," she said. "…if that is alright with you."

"Your father won't object?" he asked.

"I'm *daddy*," said Charles smiling. "I am fine with you being *dad*."

"I've never had a daughter," said David. "This is going to be new for me."

"It's going to be fun for me," said Sue excitedly. "Oh, my…we can go shopping! For girl stuff for a change." Emily had never actually been *shopping* per se. Most of her life she shopped online…and more recently, just took what she needed.

"You are going to need an entire maternity wardrobe," said Sue. "…because those sweats are just not going to get it. You will thank me soon. When that belly starts pushing the limits of an expanding waistband, believe me; you will thank me."

"I think we can change the subject now," said Charles, feeling uncomfortable about where the conversation was heading. "We haven't even eaten yet." The events of the evening had dominated their attention and they completely forgot that dinner was about to be served. Emily sat near the corner between her father and soon-to-be father-in-law. Nathan sat, likewise, between his mother and soon-to-be mother-in-law. The main course was a succulent dish of lamb cutlets and roasted red potatoes seasoned with rosemary and cracked pepper. The dish was complemented with steamed green beans delicately flavored with sea salt and a dash of fresh lemon. Lemon berry tarts were served for dessert.

Everyone adjourned to the living room after dinner to talk over a few other matters of concern. They were matters every family would discuss when a wedding was in the works; not just a family that was under the watchful eye of the government because one of them had the gift of invisibility.

"Has anybody given any thought as to how Nathan and Emily are going to support themselves?" asked David, acting as the Devil's Advocate.

"Nathan has a job," said Alma. "He told me I could tell you. I think he is a little shy about bragging on himself. The government offered him a job and he took it. They were so impressed by the way he eluded them and created new identities for all of us, they asked him to come and work for them. They want him to do the same thing for their field agents. You are looking at the government's newest Intelligence Asset." Sue was speechless. David looked at Nathan differently than he ever had. The look was one of pride and respect. Nathan didn't know how to take it. He had never seen that look from his step-father before. David stood, walked over to Nathan and shook his hand with both hands and said, "I'm proud of you son." Nathan's eyes misted up. He hoped David did not see that as a sign of weakness. David put his hand on Nathan's shoulder and Nathan could see that his eyes were misting too.

"Does that mean that Nathan gets to be a spy?" asked Jimmy excitedly. "Will he get a gun and cool gadgets?" *Nothing like that*, signed Nathan after he wiped his eyes. *I will be working with computers mostly.*

"So like a cyber-spy," said Jimmy. "That's cool. Mom, can I have another tart?" Jimmy had the normal attention span of a boy his age. His mother nodded even though the last thing he seemed to need was more sugar. However, this was a special occasion. Her family was together and cohesive for the first time that she could remember. They had a wedding to plan and a baby to prepare for; even if not in that order.

Charles and Alma couldn't be happier. Nathan was the son they had never had. They were comforted in the fact that Nathan would be able to work from home most of the time and Emily would be safe. Charles had struggled with the fact that they would be moving into a place of their own. He was glad Emily would be in good hands and, for once, glad that the government would be keeping a watchful eye on her too.

Charles and David cleared the dishes from the table and proceeded to prewash before loading the dishwasher. Alma and Sue sat with Emily, offering suggestions about the wedding. Emily smiled and told them that she had something special planned for the wedding and honeymoon; and that it was a secret. She said they could plan the reception though. Both of them seemed disappointed, but Emily assured them that they would be a part of the wedding and would love what she had in mind. Not knowing drove them crazy, so they turned their attention to the baby.

"We have to know if it is a boy or a girl," said Sue. "…so we can know what to buy for the little thing."

"We want to be surprised," said Emily. "We just want it to be healthy and happy, like other parents." A bolt of energy went through her. *Parents,* she thought. After everything that had happened in her life, parenthood should have seemed commonplace. But she had considerations that other couples did not have to face. Her DNA was special; when combined with Nathan's, there was no telling what the final result was going to be. She told Alma and Sue that she would like to get some air. Emily went out on the large porch and sat on the porch swing. The weather was brisk and Nathan joined her with a handmade quilt he took from the back of the couch. He wrapped it around her shoulders as he sat next to her. The full moon was just barely hidden by the roof of the porch and the light it cast on the surroundings was so bright, it looked artificial. Emily felt safe in Nathan's embrace. It had been a long time since she had felt really safe. She heard Nathan say, "You are safe with me. You will always be safe with me." Her eyes widened and she stared at him. He signed, *What? What is wrong?*

Did you just speak to me? she signed. He shook his head. Then she looked him in the eye and thought, *Did you just speak to me?* Nathan put his hands to his ears and smacked them to make sure he was not hearing things. He thought, *How did you do that?* Emily heard it as if he had spoken it. His voice was incredibly sweet. He thought the same of hers, even though he had nothing to compare it to.

So this is the new superpower? she thought. *Reading minds?*

Maybe it is just us, thought Nathan. *It would have come in handy if you had developed it sooner.*

I know, right? thought Emily. Nathan was delighted with the inflection in her words.

We will need to try this on the others, she thought. *I am not sure I want to know what they are thinking all the time.*

I am not sure I want you knowing what I am thinking all the time, thought Nathan. *Do you think there is a mute button somewhere?* He grinned and Emily thought, *This is going to be great.* They sat out on the porch silently…in their minds too. They shared images of the first time they met. The sun was shining and a warm breeze blew across the amber wheat field. Emily wasn't sure if it was a memory or a fantasy. Neither of them cared. It was a pleasant memory and it seemed to warm them. They stood up and Nathan wrapped the quilt around the two of them. They embraced and kissed. No words, spoken or unspoken, were needed for the moment.

CHAPTER 28: WITNESS PROTECTION

The birth of Emily Troy's baby had to be carefully orchestrated. Doctor David Cornell was in attendance because he had been her attending physician her entire life and was fully aware of the potential complications with the birth. A team of specialized government Intelligence Assets was on hand to assist. Emily felt as though she was the main attraction in a sideshow as she lay on the delivery table with her feet suspended in stainless steel stirrups. The members of the delivery team were all wearing special dark glasses except Doctor Cornell. He had a pair hanging from his pocket just in case he needed them. The five person team consisted of three females and two males. The males stood discretely at an angle to maintain at least a modicum of Emily's modesty. Once the contractions got stronger, she could not have cared less who was in the room or what they could see. She had at first opted for a water birth, but could not get a solid grip to be able to safely deliver the baby. Instead, she was poised in a half-sitting position on the delivery table.

Nathan stood beside her, holding her hand. She dug her nails into the back of his hand with each contraction. He actually found the pain a pleasant alternative to the hand cramps he had been experiencing while rubbing her lower back for the past three hours. He and Emily had found her *mute switch* so he could safely think about how much he wanted the whole thing to be over without making her feel bad. They also discovered that the ability to read minds was something only the two of them shared. They really were meant for each other. Nathan looked at the monitor and saw another contraction on the rise. He could tell it was going to be a big one and braced himself for it. Emily dug her nails into his hand so hard, he was sure she had drawn blood. She hadn't, but the marks would not go away for some time. Nathan considered them a badge of honor.

Emily worried between contractions. She didn't know why, but something seemed wrong. It could have been the worried look on Doctor Cornell's face or the fact that government agents were watching over the birth. She was one of the few people in the world that had to worry about additional complications during childbirth. Given the nature of the child's DNA, there was no telling what effect it might have or what kind of problems may arise. Another large contraction drove all negative thoughts from her mind. She knew she needed to devote all of her attention to the situation at hand.

"Okay Emily," said Doctor Cornell in a calm and compassionate way. "...I think that is about the last one you get for free. On the next one, I want you to push really hard. Do you think you can do that?"

"Do I have a choice?" Emily asked sarcastically.

"We have a little problem here," the Doctor said, trying to not sound overly ominous. "The baby is turned the wrong way. It is going to be born breech. We might be in for a rough ride."

"I like the way you say, *we*," she said. Emily was trying to keep the mood light. There was no point in making everybody worry.

"I will help as much as I can," said the Doctor. "...but most of this will be up to you. Are you ready?"

"I guess I have to be," replied Emily. *Are you ready sweetie?* she mentally projected to Nathan.

Just a second, he thought. He adjusted her hand so that her nails would press into a fresh patch of flesh on the back of his hand. She smiled just as the last contraction hit. Emily bared her teeth and pushed as hard as she could. Nathan felt her nails dig deeper into his hand than before. He was sure there would be blood this time. In his mind, he heard Doctor Cornell say, "We have a leg!" Nathan's eyes widened. He wasn't sure how he heard what was said. He looked down and could see a small purple leg extending from Emily's birth canal. He could hear the monitor and Emily's heavy breathing. It was all going on in his head, but it was almost as clear as if he was actually hearing it. The sounds were only slightly muffled.

"Are you ready for another push?" asked Doctor Cornell.

"Stop asking me as if I have a choice!" exclaimed Emily. Nathan heard the words as if they were in an echo chamber. He realized that Emily's mind was transmitting the sounds she was hearing to him through telepathy. He became oblivious to the pain Emily's nails were causing in his hand; even when they finally did draw blood. Another push and the baby was halfway out. "You have a little girl," said the Doctor. "Now we just need to see who she looks like." Doctor Cornell knew the worst part was over. Nathan looked into Emily's eyes and they thought simultaneously, *We have a girl.* The final push seemed a little anticlimactic as far as pain went. It seemed the worst part was over and the baby entered the world with a "plop" that Nathan heard. Emily panted for a couple of moments, but stopped to listen for the baby's first noises. Everyone quit breathing and the only sound that could be heard was the beeping of the monitor and the ticking of the large clock on the wall. Doctor Cornell aspirated the baby's mouth and she coughed slightly. Then she took in a deep breath and let out a wail that could be heard down the hall. Everyone felt allowed to breathe once more and they all smiled in a silent celebration…even the stoic agents standing outside the door.

Nathan heard his daughter cry and he began to cry as well. Emily was already crying when Doctor Cornell looked at Nathan and asked, "Would you like to cut the umbilical cord?" He handed Nathan a large pair of surgical scissors, unaware that Nathan had heard his question in his head. His hands were shaking as he took the scissors. Doctor Cornell said, "You are going to do fine." Nathan cut the cord and thought it felt like cutting through a garden hose. The cord was much tougher than it looked…and disgusting. The doctor placed the baby in Emily's arms.

"Congratulations Mom," he said with tears in his own eyes. "She is healthy, happy…and as far as I can tell, normal. She might be hungry if you would like to feed her." Emily's modesty was gone for good and she breastfed her baby, not caring who was watching.

"Have you thought about a name?" asked one of the female agents in attendance, whose eyes were also moist.

"We were thinking Emma if it was a girl," said Emily. "Nathaniel if it had been a boy."

"Sounds perfect," replied the agent, whose name was Julie.

"Emily…Emma seems to have caused a little damage coming into the world and I am going to have to do some repairs," said Doctor Cornell. "Do you think her daddy would mind holding her while I do some work?" Nathan's knees got weak and Emily suggested that he sit down first. He had forgotten most of his motor skills for the moment. He sat down hard in a chair and the attendant handed Emma wrapped in a yellow hospital blanket to him. Nathan's hands were shaking until he felt her tiny form in them. Her helpless shape gave him strength and he became suddenly confident. He held her close and looked into her beautiful face. He touched her pink lips with his finger and she opened her eyes. Their gaze locked as he stared into the bluest eyes he had ever seen. They were the color of the sky on a cloudless summer day. Emma looked into his as if he was the only man in the world. For a while he would be. Her small hand gripped his finger and in doing so, held his heart in the palm of her tiny hand. At that moment, he was willing to die for her. More so, he was willing to live for her. Emily smiled as she watched the two of them bond. Life was perfect at that moment. Maybe all of the adventures were over and they could just live their lives as normal people. Nathan looked into the face of his beautiful daughter and he was sure that she smiled at him. A shimmer of iridescent light flashed across her face and he knew their adventures were just beginning.

****

June proved to be a perfect month for the wedding. Since the birth of Emma, the grandmothers had been taking turns doting on her and helping with whatever wedding arrangements that Emily would let them. She kept most of it a secret with the exception of fittings for tuxedos and shopping for dresses. Emily did not have any friends to stand up with her, but she had bonded with Julie, the attendant at Emma's birth. She had also made contact with Angela, the EEG tech who had been kind to her when she was confined to the facility in Ohio. She knew she was going to have to cultivate a few more friends as Emma got older.

Nathan had his brother Jimmy stand up as his best man and invited Michael Cantrell to balance out the numbers. Maxwell Johnston was invited to oversee security. That pleased him more than simply being an usher.

As the big day approached, Emily had a dinner for the future wedding party and presented them all with plane tickets and hotel accommodations.

"Seattle?" asked Charles. "You want to get married in Seattle?"

"Honey…I don't understand," said Alma. "There are so many romantic destinations where you could get married. Why Seattle?"

"It means something special to both of us," she said hugging Nathan. "*Sleepless in Seattle* is our favorite movie. It was playing the night we…it's our favorite movie."

"Okay…I understand that," said Charles, trying to ignore the near Freudian slip. "Where in Seattle?"

"The Space Needle of course!" exclaimed Emily. "Where else?

"Seriously?" said David. "You can do that?"

"You'll see," said Emily.

The wedding invitations went out to a large number of family members and friends of the Troys and the Saunders. Nathan had a few friends and Emily had none to speak of. Alma and Charles had a few friends and several relatives. The Saunders had many more and they were glad to participate in Nathan's wedding. Everyone seemed to consider him disabled. None of them could possibly know that he had more abilities than any of them.

The guests were most amazed that travel arrangements and accommodations had all been paid for. They wondered where the money came from. David Saunders wondered too. Charles Troy suspected that Nathan had used a little computer magic; but in reality, the money had come from the budget of a government shadow agency and had been labeled as a classified covert operation. The staff of the SkyCity restaurant was temporarily replaced with Intelligence Assets with the exception of the chef. He was a master chef with impressive credentials and was bound by a nondisclosure agreement, even though the wedding was not completely unusual. The agreement was a precaution in case Emily became overcome by emotion and revealed her ability to everyone present.

The time of the wedding came and everyone wondered why it was being held at night. Eight-thirty seemed a bit unusual to people from Iowa. Four-thirty would have been more proper.

The time came and Nathan looked splendid in his black tuxedo. He felt like a secret agent and had the ID to go with it. A number of Intelligence Assets guarded the exits and wore special dark glasses as a precaution. The guests sat in white folding chairs; white bows with pink accents were tied to the chairs next to the aisle. Pink flower petals littered the white runner leading to the altar. Both mothers lit candles for the couple while David Saunders held his granddaughter. She was dressed in a little white dress that was similar to the bride's gown. No one knew that until the music began to play and they all stood to see the most radiant bride in history. Her countenance seemed to be glowing and they wondered how the couple had managed that effect. Charles Troy escorted his little girl down the aisle and presented her to Nathan. He had grown to love Nathan like his own son and had no problem handing over responsibility for Emily...as long as they stayed close to home.

The minister began with the prepared ceremony and reminded the crowd that Holy Matrimony was a sacred institution and was not to be taken lightly. Women in the audience began to weep openly and more than one of the men "got something in their eye". When the time came for the vows, the guests were a bit curious as to how it would be handled. No sign language interpreter was in attendance. Emily began.

"Nathan...You are my love, my life and my perfect soul mate. There is no other person on the planet who could do for me what you do. There is no other person on the planet who would have done for me what you did. You saw me when no one else could; in more ways than I can say. I will love you forever and I look forward to sharing the rest of my life with you." A wave of crying washed over the crowd and for a moment, David thought Emma would join in the chorus of tears. Nathan held Emily's hands and the guests waited for him to begin speaking his vows in sign language. Instead, he shocked the crowd when he began to speak.

"Emily..." he said softly. "You are my life and I would lay it down for you. You were an angel when I first saw you and you are an angel still. You heard me when no one else could; in more ways than I can say. I will love you forever and look forward to spending the rest of my life with you."

The crowd collectively gasped. No one, not even the government agents, expected Nathan to speak on his own. The minister, not knowing anything was unusual, continued.

"Do you have the rings?" he asked ceremoniously. The best man and the maid of honor placed the rings on a white satin pillow. The glowing couple placed the rings on each other's fingers and exchanged the traditional vows. The minister concluded the ceremony with the closing line, "I now pronounce you husband and wife…you may kiss the bride." As they kissed, fireworks began to erupt behind them over Puget Sound exactly on cue; arranged by Agent Kellum as a wedding gift. The flashes for the bursts of colors masked Emily's emotional shimmer and momentary invisibility. The only one curious was the minister and he was also bound by a nondisclosure agreement.

The couple kissed for such a long time, it became uncomfortable to their relatives. They finally turned to face their guests and the room erupted in applause that rivaled the noise of the fireworks over the Sound. The couple actually ran down the runner to the reception area, causing rose petals to be thrown into the air and softly drift back down. Standing in the reception line, Nathan braced himself for the barrage of questions that he knew would all be the same. He decided to be proactive and took a glass from a table and hit it with a fork a few times.

"Can I have everyone's attention?" Nathan began. "I know you have a lot of questions about my ability to speak. Let me just say; I could tell you, but then I would have to have you all killed. Believe me. I know people." He smiled and everyone thought he was joking. Looking around at the security which seemed to be at every exit, no one wanted to take the chance and simply wished the couple happiness and the best of luck.

The reception was as perfect as the wedding. The couple was toasted many times. Emily had to toast with ginger ale since she was breastfeeding Emma. Nathan got a little tipsy, but nothing he couldn't handle. There was the traditional dance for the bride and groom and then the dance with the father of the bride. In the end, everybody danced with just about everybody. Most of the guests would fly home in the morning. Emily and Nathan would remain for a week...with a security entourage.

The couple went out on the observation deck to be alone. They looked out over Puget Sound at the full moon that reflected on the water. They held each other and said nothing...even in their minds. They were completely content. Their parents gave them a few minutes of alone time, but finally had to have some answers. Both sets of parents joined the couple, trying not to look like an inquisition. Before they could speak, Nathan spoke up.

"I know what you are going to ask," he said. "We wanted it to be a surprise. No one knew but us. However, I suspect I will have to file a report when I get back to work. When Emma was born, I began to hear through Emily's ears. We can communicate telepathically. As long as she is in the room, I can hear what she hears. I hear in stereo when the baby is present, so I think it works with her too." Emily picked up the explanation from there.

"We thought it would be a nice surprise," she said, "...if Nathan could say his own vows. Since he can hear through me, I have been working with him to help him develop his speaking ability. It was rough at first, since he had never made any sounds; but he is a quick study."

The two couples were dumbfounded. In a twist of irony, they were the ones who couldn't speak. Finally, they settled for communicating the old fashioned way. They all took turns embracing the couple. Emma protested her lack of attention and Emily promptly took her. "I suspect she is hungry, poor thing. I will be back in a little bit." The two grandmothers followed Emily back in. The three men stayed on the observation deck for a bit, pondering the future. None of them knew that the couple would get to use the name *Nathaniel* the following year or that the child would possess a power none of them dreamed of. They looked out at the moon as it prepared to dip below the horizon. The grandfathers shook Nathan's hand, patted him on the back and went back inside to visit the open bar. Nathan stayed a while longer. He looked out at the open panorama before him and down to the streets below. Standing next to the curb looking up was a lone figure. He was dressed as the other Intelligence Assets. He was also wearing special dark glasses. He stood for a moment and then seemed to dissolve like exhaust from a tailpipe. Nathan figured he was just one more security detail assigned to protect them. After all, there was no way he could be Agent Baxter.

Made in the USA
Lexington, KY
16 February 2018

IMPERCEPTIBLE

Emily Troy holds the key to tactical invisibility and the government wants it. Born with a genetic mutation that renders her unseen, she must escape the clutches of rogue government agents, but the only person who can help her is a thousand miles away. Her struggle is magnified by an additional element; she has never been able to speak since birth. She must seek out Nathan, a deaf boy who inexplicably is the only one who can see her. Together, they must find her family and elude the shadow agents by using her most valuable asset… her wits.

Alan D. Henson, author of Demons Within, is a writer, artist and a dreamer of dreams. "What if…" is his mantra as he delves into areas of the psyche, special abilities and alternative universes. His writing style is engaging and thought-provoking. His characters are memorable and three-dimensional (sometimes more than three). Two near-death experiences gave him a glimpse of "the other side" and he endeavors to convey the sensation of the experiences in his writing. His crisp storylines keep you on the edge of your seat and anxious for the next chapter.

Cover designed by Alan D. Henson

Cover Model: Madelyn Easter